I0633717

Taste of Memory

Book One of *Tales of Tasimu*

By

Celu Amberstone

This is a work of fiction. Similarities to real people, places, or events are entirely coincidental.

TASTE OF MEMORY

First edition. February 29, 2024.

Copyright © 2024 Celu Amberstone.

ISBN: 978-1990581175

Written by Celu Amberstone.

Note to the Reader

This book was originally published in a slightly shorter version in 2011 by Kegedance Press under the title *The Dreamer's legacy*. That book is now out of print. Taste of Memory was my original title for this work. I have also included in this edition parts of the original story left out of the Kegedance edition.

Taste of Memory is a work of fiction. I hope you'll read and enjoy it as such. Though I've drawn material in the abstract from places I've lived and from my own mixed race background, any resemblance to people, places, cultures, Indigenous or other languages in our world is purely coincidental.

Dedication

This book is dedicated to all the refugees and displaced indigenous peoples around the world. It is also dedicated to my children and grandchildren. Not being a woman of material wealth, my writing is my legacy to both them, and all the children who are our cherished future. Also in dedication, I offer my eternal gratitude for the traditional teachings of my grandparents, aunties, and the other Elders I've met over the years who have taken the time to teach me. The wisdom and strength of my Elders has always been, and will continue to be, an inspiration in my life.

Acknowledgements

I would like to thank for their support, my four sons, my daughter, my father, my brother and sister, and my friends when I needed them. Paula and Lila, your friendship and help with proof reading, cover design, and other editing was greatly appreciated.

Daniel, your edits and suggestions were beyond price for the first edition of this book.

I would also like to thank the folks at Kegedonce Press for their dedication, hard work, their vision, and their fearless determination to encourage Aboriginal writers of all types.

A Tribal History of Long Ago, Rushton Archives: First interview with subject 297

THE EXPLORERS FROM *the empire who came north named all the tribes they found tazacatik. And somewhere along the way they shortened it to "zaunk" when they wanted to ridicule us and make us feel small. I'm not sure what either word meant to them, but we called ourselves, the Qwani'yaTsa'adi. Loosely translated, it means "Fish People" in today's common tongue. We caught whitefish mostly. Summer and winter, smoked or baked—even sometimes raw, we ate a lot of fish. Our traditional home was on the southern shores of Big Ice Lake, not far from where it flows into the Socanna River.*

Like the land that has tasted our blood and shared our memories, we can endure almost anything. A quiet people and shy around strangers, we stand back and observe before we speak. Some outsiders mistake our reticence for stupidity, but they are the foolish ones. In currents of jade green, indigo and black, our thoughts run deep. In our dreams we swim Big Ice Lake's hidden currents with Dalo the loon, Qwa'osi the otter and Co'yeh the lake seal, to bring back the magic found in the caves of the Great Aseutl, Kunai.

Our healers and wise ones found their power in natural things such as winds, rocks, ice, and the whistling fires of the Spirit-Lights. The land doesn't belong to us; we belong to the land. It holds our Qwakaiva, our ancestor's bones and our tribal memories. My daughter Qwachula's mentor with the long Chamuqwani nose and kind eyes gave me a quizzical look when I first said this to him, then he thought about it some more and nodded his head in agreement.

I promised my daughter to recount the story of my youth, but the world has changed so much. Why should these children who have grown up in such a different way believe me? They will think my memories lies, or worse yet, the demented ramblings of a senile old man.

But I suppose I must tell them. What does it matter that most will think them just the fancies of my imagination? The ones with Qwakaiva, the ones in whom the Blood runs true, they will be empowered and keep the ceremonies alive that bind the world together.

Chapter One

"You're not welcome here. Go!"

I froze with one foot upon the trading post steps. Mother had sent me for more tea, but I'd no wish to enter if the trader was angry. Jombonni had repeatedly warned his son Kutima and me not to raid the candy barrel, but did we listen?

No.

I peered through the open door into the store's dim interior. *Maybe I should find a cousin to get the tea... Dog fart! Only a coward would run and hide*, I told myself. *If he knows about the candy, go in and confess.*

But Jombonni wasn't talking to me—the trader hadn't even seen me. He faced two broad-shouldered men wearing wide brimmed hats and dirty canvas trousers. I breathed a sigh of relief and stepped onto the porch. My relatives would want to know this juicy tidbit of gossip.

The strangers had their backs turned, intent on the thin, pale-skinned man in the white apron behind the counter, shaking his fist. I crept up to the door. Who were they? Probably miners from the new settlement. These rude newcomers were always swaggering about, leering at our young women, and poking their noses into our snug homes when they thought only children and old people were about. They weren't welcome in our village.

Unfortunately, the only store in the area was at our end of the lake, so we had to put up with their visits for supplies.

"What's a matter, Trader Man? We got dust enough to pay your price," one of the surly pair growled.

"I don't care how much gold you have. You and your brother started a fight after I sold you liquor last time," Jombonni said. "I told you then, you were nothing but trouble and not to come back to my post. Now get out."

Oh, Kunai, the Jomas brothers!

Dread knotted itself in my gut. Where were Uncle Tli and his friends? If they saw these particular men, there *was* going to be a fight—like last time. Miners. I hated them. I wished there were no yellow rocks in our streams. I wished they would go away and leave us alone.

"The mud-grubber deserved what we gave him," the other brother protested. "The crazy zaunk started it."

Jombonni slammed his hand down upon the counter top. "I said get out and I meant it. I'm not selling you anything."

The second man to speak put a hand on the long bladed knife holstered at his hip. "You Zaunk-Loving Bastard, I'm gonna—"

Jombonni's pale face turned a bright pink. As if reaching for something, one of his hands dropped beneath the counter. "Do what; kill me like you did Tall Walker?"

"I don't know what you're talking about. Is one of your lazy, good-for-nothing zaunks missing?" the first miner laughed. "Such a shame, ain't it?"

Not long before, Tall Walker made the mistake of arguing with these same brothers at the post. The traders broke up the dispute before weapons could be drawn, but later when the fisherman went missing, even Jombonni, who tried not to take sides, thought the disappearance suspicious.

Some people suspected the Jomas brothers might be to blame, while others insisted that the miners had nothing to do with it. The greedy Aseutl living at the bottom of the lake had merely chosen a new victim. Uncle Tli and his friends scoffed at such a notion and threatened revenge on the brothers when next they saw them.

Jombonni's flushed turned a deeper shade of crimson, and his mouth hardened into a determined line. "Get yourselves gone—now."

A boy's frightened face materialized from behind a barrel then it disappeared back into the storeroom. A moment later two of the post's burly workmen appeared in the warehouse doorway, walking in to flank their boss.

The other miner saw them and placed a hand on his brother's arm. "Let's go."

The tangle of unease in my stomach tightened. This was very bad. I didn't want my uncle to be hurt—or be killed, too.

I hastily scanned the surrounding buildings and dock area, but the sun had risen above the eastern peaks, fanning out in a ribbon of silver across the green water. Several fishermen joked with each other by their canoes farther along the beach. Their faces were lost in shadow and I couldn't recognize them. Fearing the worst, I raised my hand to shade my eyes and squinted harder.

Oh, Uncle, please stay away.

Then without warning the light reflecting off the water intensified. The knot in my gut tightened. I stifled a cry and closed my eyes.

Too late...

As hard-edged and piercing as glass, the brightness was trapped inside my head. There was no escaping the Spirit-Sending devouring me. Suddenly powerless and terrified, I clung to the doorframe, determined not to draw the attention of the foreigners inside the post.

Ensnared within a whirling storm of disjointed images, I saw scavenging dogs, wannigua demons, and dead men and women lying in the snow. A village was in flames, people screaming. What village? I wanted to see, but the mists thickened.

"Let's go. The zaunk-lover will sing a different song when the steamboat gets here," one of the miners said, his voice echoing through the tumult of the foretelling.

"Things are gonna change around here. Just wait and see, Trader-Man, when the steamboat comes."

When the steamboat comes—comes ... The miner's words reverberated in my head. I trembled. The paddle-wheeler was coming, true enough. But unlike other visits, this year its bounty of trade goods was an illusion. Hidden among its many boxes and barrels was an unspeakable evil. Change was coming, certain and terrible.

<<No. It's not true.>> in the mind-speech of the Spirit-World I begged the Otter, our village's guardian, <<Qwa'osi, say it isn't so!>>

Smothered by smoke and blackness, I heard a mechanical roaring and the thunder of fast water over boulders in a narrow channel. My body convulsed. I choked on the stench of hot iron and fish slime. Suddenly I was drowning in foaming water, dark currents sucking me down into the abyss. Panicked I struggled to get away, but only discordant laughter mocked my efforts.

<<Qwa'osi, save me!>>

Determined to swim out of the chaos, I focused my Qwakaiva, my Spirit-Power, as Grandfather had taught me. With great effort I banished the sounds and images of the foretelling and replace myself amid the harmony of the physical world.

Still dizzy and weak, I perceived a strange chill in the summer air. The world before my eyes now revealed a new jagged clarity. The glowing spirit fires around living things had a bluish-grey tinge that warned of some unspeakable sorrow.

Change.... What did the miner's threat truly mean? I loved my friends, family and our mountain home. I didn't want our lives to change—ever.

I was vaguely aware that the men inside the store had stopped talking. The enraged brothers were heading for the doorway, where I stood shivering and gulping for air. I needed to get away, before the torrent of red anger and black fear engulfed me, but at that moment my body felt too sluggish to move.

As the taller of the two yellow-haired brothers came out onto the porch, he backhanded me with a blow that sent me sprawling. "Out of the way, brat." Without looking back, the miners stomped off the porch heading toward the dock.

I'd always given the miners the healthy respect I might a vicious sled dog, staying out of their way when I noticed them lounging round the post. But at that moment I wished I already had the knife Uncle Tli had promised me next time the steamboat arrived.

If I had my gift-knife—I'd show them...

I picked myself up off the porch's weathered floorboards and wiped my mouth, leaving a trail of scarlet down my forearm. My face throbbed. Stumbling away from the post, I headed down the beach in the opposite direction to the miners. Once out of sight, I crouched and splashed cold water over my aching face.

"Tas? Are you all right? Kutima told me to come find you."

Still dripping, I turned. My brother-cousin Samiqwas stood on the shingle. When he saw my face, his brown eyes widened. "What happened?"

I waded out of the water and started walking down the beach, not wanting to talk to anyone—not even my best friend. "It's nothing."

Samiqwas fell into step beside me, frowning. "Did Matoqwa do that? If he did, I'll—"

"No. I haven't even seen Matoqwa today. Just forget it. I don't want to talk about it." He snorted, calling me a bad name in the traders' language. I balled my fists and rounded on him. "Take that back, Dog Fart."

Impatient for an answer, he hopped out of reach of my swing. "Some angry miners were getting into their canoe a while ago. Did they try to steal you? Did they want to make you their slave?"

Samiqwas had reason to be worried; it had happened before. "No."

Samiqwas was a square-built boy with his mother's round face, and his father's large hands and feet. He was proud of the length of his twig and how far he could piss. Being a year older, over the past winter he had shot up in height, making the difference in our ages more apparent.

Glancing towards the trading post, I swatted at a mosquito and watched the glowing disk of the sun illuminate the blue ice of the glacier across the lake. The dark silhouette of the brothers' canoe made its way up the eastern shore. Still furious and hurting, I focused my anger on the disappearing canoe.

<<Kunai, I seek vengeance. Open your enormous jaws and swallow them—boat and all.>>

In the shadowy depths of the lake I sensed a being of immense power stir, roused from its dreams by my summons. Cold yellow eyes opened and contemplated me. Appalled, I shrank from that enigmatic gaze. Icy dread flowed through my veins, chilling me to the bone.

I must have cried out, for suddenly strong hands grasped my shoulders, breaking the contact, plunging my Spirit back into my physical self. I took a ragged breath and opened my eyes. Samiqwas was holding me. "Tas? What's wrong?"

My tongue frozen to the roof of my mouth, I shook my head, unable to speak. Everywhere I turned, evil omens assailed me. I pushed myself away from him. He was only trying to help, but right then his touch burned like stinging nettles brushed against my skin.

When I remained silent and started walking, he spun me around to face him. "Tas, answer me. What's wrong?"

Before I could guard my tongue, I blurted, "The steamboat hasn't cracked on the rocks like the traders fear. It's coming—soon."

He beamed. "Haya! That's wonderful news."

Taking a petty delight in shattering his excitement, I growled, "No, it isn't! I wish the steamboat would go away—drown." *Before the shadow onboard it covers us all.*

In those early days as the ice cleared, the old paddle-wheeler chugged north each year up the Socanna River from Fort Protection to our home on Big Ice Lake. The boat's arrival, and the trading that followed, was the most important event of our year. During the summer, children spent every spare moment on the lakeshore, hoping to be the first to sight the steamboat. There was a bag of hard candy waiting at the post as a prize for the lucky one who brought the news.

But the steamboat was late that year. The snow-melt from the spring run-off had passed through the river's channel and still there was no sign of it. The traders were worried that the boat had been wrecked in one of the rapids down river. They feared it wouldn't show up at all, to restock the post for the coming winter. My adult relatives all shared the traders' concern.

Samiqwas stared at me as if moose antlers had just sprouted from my skull. Then, trying to be reasonable, he said, "Tas, Everyone will suffer next winter without those trade-goods. Why would you say such a terrible thing? You aren't making any sense."

"I know," I grumbled. "Stop pestering me." I took several deep breaths as Grandfather had taught me, trying to dispel my emotions and bring back clarity.

"Well? Is the paddle-wheeler coming or not?" Samiqwas pressed.

Fighting back nausea, I mentally kicked myself. Why hadn't I kept my big mouth shut? Kunai's sudden interest in me, a village in flames—how could I tell him what I'd seen? My brother-cousin's spirit was like a hunter's blade, bright silver and sharp edged; he wouldn't understand. Even I didn't understand.

When it suited him, Samiqwas boasted to our friends of my ability to connect with the Unseen Ones in the Spirit-World. But swimming in the twilight realms was beyond him.

"Yes. It's coming," I said, my voice taking on a longsuffering tone.

Walking a few paces closer to the water, he held his hand to his eyes and looked out across the lake. "I don't see anything."

"So? I said the boat was coming, didn't I? It will be here by tomorrow—maybe later today, but—"

He made a rude noise, sparking my anger anew. Was he deliberately trying to bait me? Still glaring at his back, I hurled a stone into the water with more force than necessary.

Would that mean miner have hit Samiqwas if he'd found him standing in the doorway of the store?

I hurled another stone. Probably.

Another stone, but maybe Samiqwas would have fought back—maybe stabbed that evil man with his father's knife.

His knife...

"Uncle Tli is going to buy me a bright steel knife of my own this year, you know?"

"So?" Samiqwas picked up a flat stone from the shingle and skipped it effortlessly over the water. The stone hopped three times before it sank. A smile curving his lips, he patted the knife resting in its worn leather sheath at his hip. "I already have a steel knife. Uncle Tli can buy me a fox trap if he wants to give me a present."

To have a knife made of iron, not one made of bone or chipped stone meant that a boy was recognized by the hunters of our village as nearly a man-grown.

I had no such knife, and still slept in my mother's furs....

Samiqwas and I were like brothers; I loved him with all my heart. But his drawing my attention to his father's gift and his new status, only fuelled my annoyance with him.

"Yes, you have a knife. But it's just an old one your father didn't want any more. Mine will be new."

Out of the corner of my eye I saw his mouth tighten, but I pretended not to notice. I picked up a rock and arched it out over the lake, trying to imitate his throw.

The rock sank, much to my disgust. It was so humiliating. Boys half my age could skip rocks better than I could. I dared not look around for fear he would be laughing at me. My still aching cheek hurt all the more for the flush I was sure darkened it.

Too short for my own liking, my face oval not round, my hair wavy not straight, my eyes a deep violet rather than a warm dark brown, I hated all the differences that set me apart from my relatives.

Swallowing down the lump clogging my throat, I kept my eyes focused on the water. I tossed my next stone—with similar results. Then I threw another, deliberately casting wide, so that the rock hit his leg instead of the water. He whirled round to face me with fist raised. I thought he was going to hit me, but whatever he saw in my face made him change his mind. He lowered his hand.

Stifling a grin, he stepped up beside me. "You're holding them wrong—look." He scooped up a handful of stones and patiently showed me the proper way to hold them.

Choosing to ignore my childishness, his generosity shamed me all the more. I knew he was being kind, trying to make peace between us, so I did as he suggested. I let go of my anger and my fear for the future. I let my bad feelings sink into the lake with the stones.

When Samiqwas saw I understood how to skip them, he became bored. Looking around for something else to occupy his energy, he spied his father and his father's brother down by their moored fishing canoe. Waving a farewell, he headed in their direction.

"Hey! Where are you going."

He turned round to face me, still walking backward. "Why, to tell them what you said, of course. Maybe they'll want to take the canoe out to look for the paddle-wheeler. If they do, I'm going."

I flung my handful of stones into the water, not bothering to watch where they fell. "Wait for me," I shouted. "I'm the one who told *you*. The bag of candy is *my* prize."

He laughed. "Careful, Tas, or your belly will grow as big as old Grandma Bear's. Don't worry. I'll share the prize when we get back."

Chapter Two

When I raced up to the canoe, panting like a dog, Samiqwas waved, stifling a grin as they paddled out into the lake. There *was* room in the canoe; they could have waited, but there was no point in my asking. His father Ko wouldn't have taken me.

I was in my fourth summer the last time Ko let me ride in his canoe. On that day Ko decided to take Samiqwas and me fishing. We had been excited about getting away from our mothers. Fishing, we were going fishing, just like we were men.

Unfortunately, neither fishing nor child-minding was what Ko had in mind. Out of sight of the village, he anchored the canoe and threw out a baited line for us to tend. Then he pulled out a half-full bottle of waskyja and proceeded to ignore us.

I recall that it was warm that day, the winds fitful, gusting strong, then dying away to nothing in a few more heartbeats.

Not knowing the proper songs to lure fish to our bait, the hook remained disappointingly empty. After a while Samiqwas and I grew bored. And being bored we began to play a foolish game, involving leaning far over the side of the canoe.

Then, the wind gusted up without warning, tipping me head-first over the side into the icy water. The cold sucked the air from my lungs before I could cry out. Helpless, I sank down into the green water like a stone. Without being aware of doing so, I must have called to the Spirits in the lake, using my Qwakaiva.

As I struggled, I was dimly aware of unseen scaly bodies, brushing against my flailing limbs. They tangled their sharp claws in my snarling hair and pulled me upward. Rubbery lips kissed my cheek, whispering into my mind words I couldn't understand—frightening me all the more.

I'd almost drowned before Ko got me back in the canoe, choking and crying. I'd been as terrified by the Spirit-World's first touch as I was by nearly dying.

When we returned home Ko received such a scolding from his wife and my grandmother that he swore never to take me in his canoe again. And no matter how much I grew—or how I begged, he never changed his mind.

When the canoe was only a dark spot on the lake I turned away. My heart was still troubled by my recent vision, but in the way of boys, I set future worries aside, inflamed by the current injustice.

I was the one who had seen the steamboat first—it wasn't fair that Samiqwas would be awarded the prize. I kicked a twig off the dock in frustration. I was having a terrible day!

I considered telling Jombonni, before they got back, Then I decided against it. The southerners didn't believe in things like Spirit-Sendings. Jombonni had to see something with his eyes to believe it. He would only laugh at me if I went there now.

But Uncle Tli would believe me. Now that the miners were gone—and it was safe—maybe uncle would even take me out on the lake to see the steamboat, too.

If I could find him....

Glancing round I saw his canoe by the big fir—but no uncle. Leaping off the dock I raced back to the village to find him.

My older-uncle, Da'wabin, had married into a village down the Socanna River. I rarely saw him, but Uncle Tli, Mother's younger brother, lived with his wife's family in our village. When I arrived out of breath at his wife's lodge, I learned to my dismay that he was already on the lake, fishing with his wife's brother Chugai. That, of course, was why his canoe was still on the beach.

Sensing my distress, Shilshigua smiled and offered me some freshly baked bannock. I shook my head and left the lodge, trying not to be rude in spite of my disappointment. Tears of frustration were pooling in the corners of my eyes. I hadn't wanted her to see; I was nearly a man, wasn't I?

Suddenly, I'd had enough. Why was I always the one staying home with the women? It was time to confront my mother and find out about my father.

In the early days, before the traders came to the arctic to exchange their goods for our fish and furs, we lived in small family groups spread out upon the land. By the time of my birth, however, most families had made for themselves warm earthen lodges on the slope above Big Ice Lake, near where it flows into the Socanna River. It was only the hunters that spent much time on their family's trap lines in the bush.

According to the custom of my people, I lived with my mother, my mother's parents, and my Aunt Tuulah, her husband Ko and their three children, of whom Samiqwas was one. I marched into our earthen lodge and planted myself in front of Mother with arms folded across my chest.

Sunlight streamed down the open smoke hole, illuminating the interior of our home with a golden hue. The embers of the morning's cook fire sent up lazy tendrils of blue smoke to mingle with the sunlight.

Mother was sitting on our sleeping platform, stitching a pair of winter boots to sell to the trader. She was a slim woman with luminous dark eyes. When she thought no one was watching, her mouth often curved downward in a wistful expression. Grandmother was also in the lodge, sitting on her own bed, her thick body bent over her sewing.

Taking in a deep breath, I demanded to know why I didn't have a father of my own, to give me knives for presents and take me in his canoe. I was furious with this unknown stranger who'd sired me, then left. And I was also angry with Mother, because maybe she'd done something to anger him and make him leave me.

Mother glanced up, frowning at my rudeness. Her eyes widened when she saw my bruised face and bloodied lip, but she resumed her sewing without comment. When I remained glaring at her, silently demanding an answer, she sighed and finally said, "Always running here and there, chasing seeds and berries. Little Rock Squirrel, be patient. You may meet him someday."

"There is more to the world than this tiny village, Grandson." Like a fox crouched over a mouse den, grandmother had such an expectant expression that it diverted my attention away from Mother's evasions.

"Perhaps your father, when he comes again, will take you home with him and teach you. Would you like that, Little Rock Squirrel?"

I gaped at her. "Take me away? Leave all my relatives?" That idea was a sobering thought, and one I hadn't considered. "But why would I have to go away for my father to instruct me in hunting and fishing, Grandmother? Ko lives with us. Why can't my father?"

"Hunting and fishing, eh?" She shook her head and chuckled. "No, I'm not talking about that; any man in the village can instruct you in such skills. But your father's Qwakaiva is *different*. And so for that reason, his teachings, his gifts, are—special."

"Are you speaking of a Qwakaihi's power? But I don't need a father to learn about the Spirit-World. Grandfather's teaching me about that." Though not with much success, I reluctantly had to admit. Like Fire and Earth, or Water and Wind, our Qwakaiva didn't exactly oppose one another, but neither were our powers compatible.

I didn't want to leave my family and friends. I didn't want to go away with a stranger—even if he could teach me how to use and control my Spirit-Gift. The thought appalled me. In fact, after the morning's disturbing revelation, I wished more than ever that I had no Qwakaiva at all.

Oblivious to my growing distress, Mother scowled. "You sang a different song when you learned I was pregnant," she said to grandmother.

"Perhaps. And now that these brutish miners are trying to steal our land, I have reconsidered my earlier rashness."

Mother snorted and jabbed her needle into the soft leather hard enough to prick her own finger. "Don't fill the child's head with such foolish notions. Tasimu can't do anything about the miners. Nor can he go with his father. It isn't possible."

"Of course he can go with him. You don't truly believe that do you, my girl? Your own father went with him for a time, so why not the boy? He is his son. Surely the blood—"

Her normally soft voice nearly a shout, Mother said, "Stop! I won't listen." Pushing her sewing off her lap with an impatient gesture, Mother walked to the wooden grub boxes by the wall and began rummaging around in the nearest one.

Grandmother remained unruffled. The fine steel needle she was using to sew a pair of mitts went into the wolverine skin without a break in its rhythm.

"Surely you miss your handsome Star Swimmer under your furs?"

Mother let out a startled sob, and I saw tears in her eyes before she turned away. "My son is all I need. Why do you torment me with cruel words."

I heard no more after that. Not finding what she was looking for in the box, Mother realized at the same moment how closely I was listening, and vented her frustration upon me.

"Tasimu, where is the tea I sent you for at the trading post?"

Tea. With everything else that had happened that morning I'd completely forgotten about my errand to fetch more tea. I hung my head, staring at the smooth stones by the hearth. "I'm sorry. I forgot."

Mother slammed down the wooden lid on the box and straightened. "Well, go right now and get it. Ask Kutima or his mother to find you some if Jombonni says they don't have any till the paddle-wheeler arrives." She made a shooing motion with her hands. "Go on, quickly now. Your grandmother will be thirsty soon."

The tea was only an excuse to get rid of me, but I did as she wanted. She wasn't going to tell me anything more about my father with Grandmother sitting there, I was certain of that. I might as well get the tea and be done with it.

As I shuffled down the trail their words kept turning round and round in my head. At least I now knew my father's name, Star Swimmer. But knowing his name still didn't explain why he never came to see us. Had my parents quarrelled and parted with harsh words?

Maybe, maybe not. That answer didn't <u>feel</u> right. No, there had to be some other reason.

Perhaps he was a Chamuqwani trader who lived far, far away. That would explain a lot if true. I studied my arm tanned a rich brown by the summer sun. Kutima's father was the head of the Chamuqwani traders at the post. His skin was quite pale in comparison to mine. Since I was as brown as the rest of my relatives, my father was probably not a Chamuqwani.

And hadn't Grandmother hinted that he possessed powerful Qwakaiva? No Chamuqwani I'd ever heard of had that kind of power. But what <u>could</u> the mystery surrounding him be?

I was determined to ask Mother more questions, but by the time I returned both women were gone, frustrating my resolve.

I put the packet of tea in the grub box and wandered outside, unsure what to do next. Then three of my small girl-cousins saw me. They cried out, wanting me to come be their sled doggie and pull them on an old grass mat. That was the last thing I wanted to do, so I hid behind Aunty Qwatsitsa's woodpile until they gave up looking.

Fearing they might find me again if I stayed to search for Mother, I left the village by the back route and took the path to Hot Springs Creek.

Pouncing like a hungry lynx, the echoes of my vision leapt to torment me as soon as I entered the trees. I swayed as the smell of smoke seared my throat and I heard again the ghostly sounds of people wailing.

Go away with my father—a stranger? As I fought the panic once more, the thought of leaving with him seemed preferable to the future I feared might await us if what I'd seen was true. Never before in my life had I yearned so much for that unknown man's love and strong arms about my shoulders. In my secret heart, I begged him to protect me from the terrors of unwanted revelations.

At that moment, I hated my Gift. I didn't want to be different, plagued with such frightening Qwakaiva, a power I could neither understand nor control.

But I had no father. And neither Mother, nor other relatives ever spoke of him. My grandfather, however, was a man used to unravelling mysteries. I decided my only option was to look for Grandfather. And, I had a good idea where I might find him at that time of day.

When I stepped out of the willows, he was sitting on a log by the creek. He was wearing the blue and red woollen shirt Aunt Tuulah had made for him, buckskin leggings and high-topped soft leather boots with greased rawhide soles to make them waterproof. In spite of his years, his square body had a hunter's power. He must have just finished his bath, because his grey hair was loose, hanging down his back in long ropy strands.

Not wishing to disturb his contemplation until he was ready to acknowledge me, I sat down quietly on the other end of the log and waited for him to finish smoking his pipe.

Tucked among the folds of glacier-capped mountains, Big Ice Lake was long, narrow and very deep. That day, its water had turned indigo in the afternoon light. High up among the eastern peaks grey clouds were gathering.

In such a long narrow valley a storm could blow out of nowhere, churning the water from a placid green to a milky froth in moments. I couldn't see the paddle-wheeler or any of our fishing canoes from where I sat. Maybe the fisherman had seen the clouds, too, and headed to shore. Our fishermen were always alert to the slightest change in the weather. But in spite of all their precautions, someone was occasionally lost to the Aseutl in the bottom of the lake.

Had Kunai truly killed and eaten Tall Walker? Or had it been the miners who had killed him, then sank his canoe and fed his body to the creatures living in the depths? I shivered, not sure if I wanted to know any more truths that day.

As if divining the essence of my thoughts, Grandfather startled me by speaking. "The Aseutl is a capricious beast. Sometimes he will gift a seeker with power—if they please him. At other times, when he's tired of fish, and hungers for the taste of red meat, Kunai will claim a human for his meal, feasting on both the unfortunate's flesh and Qwakaiva."

Feeling another chill run down my backbone, I asked, "Was the Great Aseutl's touch what I felt when I fell out of Ko's boat?"

Grandfather sucked on his pipe, considering the question. "I cannot say. When you are older perhaps the Spirits will speak to you of that time. Then, you will know who is your soul's companion, the one from whom you receive your Qwakaiva."

Recalling mysterious golden eyes, I blurted, "But what if I don't like the one? What if it is Kunai?"

"Kunai?" Grandfather laughed, but his mirth seemed forced. "Do you believe he favours you? What a strange notion." His tone of voice was teasing, but the smile he gave me was more like a grimace than a friendly grin.

Then, at my horrified look he stroked my tangled hair. "Now, now, Little Rock Squirrel, don't be afraid. I was only teasing you. We have Qwa'osi, the Otter Warrior to befriend us in the Spirit-Realm, remember? Qwa'osi is a sly one you know, you wear his token. Kunai cannot hurt you."

He lifted the otter claw strung on a leather thong that always hung around my neck, showing it to me. "See, the Otter favours you. I have spoken to him on your behalf. You are safe as long as you wear his token."

Unlike other times when the shadowy beings swimming at the edge of my consciousness threatened to come too near, that day, Grandfather's reassurances didn't comfort me.

"I hate my Qwakaiva," I cried. "Tell Qwa'osi to take it back."

The vehemence of my tone must have startled him. He was silent for a time, then his expression smoothed and he shook his head. "I cannot do that, Grandson."

"Why not? You are a man of Power."

"That ability is beyond my skill."

"And what of my father? Can he do such a thing?"

"Your father." As motionless as a lynx observing prey, he scrutinized my face. I suspected he was studying me with his Spirit-Sight, but I didn't care. I desperately needed answers.

"Who has been talking to you about your father?" His tone was gentle, but I sensed the iron resolve hidden beneath its softness.

With my own Spirit-Sight, I could see red spikes in his spirit fire. He was angry. But with me—or someone else?

"No one has been talking to me. That's the problem," I grumbled. "Samiqwas has a father—it isn't fair."

Seemingly relieved by my answer, he chuckled. "Not fair, eh? Perhaps not, but I doubt if your father will be back anytime soon—and that's for the best—believe me." He patted my shoulder, but his heart wasn't in the gesture. "So you will just have to make do with only me and your uncle."

For the best? I swallowed down the lump of sadness, suddenly choking me. How could he be so cruel? His smug assurance of my father's abandonment left me feeling hollow inside.

It also irritated me, so I cried, "Grandmother doesn't think it would be for the best. She wants my father to come here to make the miners go away and leave us alone."

"Oh she does, does she?"

"Yes. She also wants him to teach me special things. But I don't want to go away—I hate my Qwakaiva. I don't want to see terrible things. I just want the Spirit-Power to leave me alone!" My bravado failed me and I choked on a sob." Please, Grandfather, take it away."

Finally realizing how upset I was, he put an arm around me and squeezed me close. "I'm sorry, Grandson. I can't take away what the Unseen Ones have gifted. Qwakaiva is given to someone for a purpose. It is to be used for the good of the People, never selfishly. I doubt if even your father could change the pattern of your fate."

I sniffed and wiped my nose on my sleeve. "Then will you tell me about him? I'm not a baby now. I want to know."

Alas, Grandfather's answers weren't any more enlightening than those of my female relatives. Sly as the Otter whose power he borrowed for his healings, it was only later I realized how he'd tricked me. As I pestered him with questions, he diverted me, by taking me to find tree fungus we could later carve.

And in doing so, I also was distracted from warning him about the coming disaster I'd witnessed in my vision.

Chapter Three

When Grandfather and I returned from Hot Springs Creek, Mother told me to stay and help Grandmother while she took some fish soup to our ailing Aunty Qwatsitsa. I didn't mind at first; I was looking forward to spending more time with Grandfather. To my disgust, however, he left soon after he ate. Not wanting me to sit idle, Grandmother told me to chop more wood and stack it in the mudroom.

In our small, isolated community, there were about two hundred people—most of whom I was related to in some way or other. Below our village of earth lodges, closer to the shoreline, the traders had built a pier and some square wooden buildings. The biggest one was a combination store and warehouse. The other smaller cabins were living quarters for the traders, their families and servants. And the last, a building set apart, was a temple to their god where a sour old priest lived.

Many of the Chamuqwani called our homes dirty and "primitive," because they were made of earth and poles. I didn't care what they said; our lodges were warmer in winter than their cabins by the icy lake. An A-frame structure tacked on to the front of the lodge's door kept out most of the drafts from the living area. These "mudrooms," as we called them, were also handy places to store firewood, outdoor equipment, and food.

It seemed like I'd been stacking firewood against the wall forever, when I heard the paddle-wheeler's high-pitched whistle blow. Dropping the kindling I'd just started to arrange in its basket, I poked my head outside.

Samiqwas waved as he raced past our house, shouting the news. "The steamboat is here. Everyone come—quick!"

Several relatives pushed back hide door flaps to listen then disappeared inside to get ready. From beyond the blanket that led into our living quarters, Grandmother grumbled, "What was that boy yelling about?"

Warm air and the smells of wood smoke and fried mushrooms brushed against my face as I pulled open the blanket. "Samiqwas says the steamboat is here, Ami."

Grandmother and my youngest cousin Seicu were the only ones in our lodge at that moment. While Grandmother cleaned up after a recent meal, Seicu sat on her mother's bed, dressing her woodenheaded doll in its new fur parka. Grandmother was unimpressed by my news. She grunted and continued sweeping.

My heart sank in disappointment. Did she really expect me to continue with the chores she'd assigned me now? I could hardly stand still; I was so anxious. In the distance Samiqwas continued to shout as he ran up the hill to where some of the men were chopping down dead trees.

Turning away from Grandmother's broad back, I saw Seicu staring at me wide-eyed. As if she had read my mind, she announced, "I want to go see, Ami."

Seicu was the family's youngest. Everyone but Grandmother spoiled her, because she'd been a sickly baby. Though she'd grown stronger in the last two years, the habit hadn't waned. Many people still worried that she wouldn't remain among us long.

Unlike my brooding water affinity, Seicu's Qwakaiva was fire-bright and passionate. She could be giggling and happy one moment, then angrily stamping her feet or crying the next.

When Grandmother ignored her, Seicu's eyes grew moist with tears. The Elder hated when she cried to get her way. If Seicu tried that ploy now, we might be stuck here until Mother or Aunt Tuulah returned to rescue us. That wouldn't happen any time soon, because they probably were at the dock already. In the crowd they wouldn't notice our absence.

I could hear many people talking in excited voices as they hurried down the path. Hoping to ward off trouble, I said, "I'm done with the wood, Ami. If you don't need me, I will take her to the dock, so she can see the steamboat."

Grandmother glanced once more at the girl on the bed, giving me a sour look. She knew what I was up to. Then she relented. "All right, you both can go."

Doll in hand, Seicu hopped down from the bed platform. She climbed the low earthen steps and took my hand. I let the blanket fall, and we hurried outside to join the people heading for the dock.

That year along with the boat's usual cargo came a large number of soldiers and miners. I saw them leaning over the railing of the paddle-wheeler as it pulled alongside the pier. Trailing behind the boat was a string of flatboats and rafts, burdened with additional newcomers and mounds of supplies.

More miners, more trouble. I shivered and led Seicu deeper into the crowd of my excited relatives.

Though I would never admit it—even to Samiqwas—I secretly admired the Emperor's soldiers. The tall, grim-faced men in their grey uniforms, watching everyone with cool detachment, were so fierce-looking and warrior-like.

But there was nothing admirable about the other Chamuqwani aboard the boat. In broad-brimmed hats and patched and dirty trousers, they pointed at us and joked to one another in their loud foreign voices. The bilious yellow of contempt given off by their spirit fire splashed over me in a sour deluge. I gagged and took a step backwards, nearly stepping on someone's toes.

What was wrong with those people? How could they have such strong opinions about us? They didn't even know us. A few of our young men also eyed the strangers warily. I hoped there wouldn't be any trouble to spoil the coming festivities.

The sun had slipped behind the mountains by the time the paddle-wheeler was moored securely to the pier. The grey clouds I'd seen earlier, hovering over the eastern peaks were gone. No rain, and the long summer twilight would offer plenty of light for unloading.

Eyes alight with speculation, the adults in my village were as excited as the children. Everyone hung around the dock and the store, getting in the way. They discussed what they hoped the trader had ordered for them, and what they would buy first with their credits.

Each year it was amazing to see how many canvas-wrapped bundles, wooden barrels, big trunks, and other supplies the Chamuqwani could fit on their steamboat. We examined anything left unattended, jumping out of the way of the cursing workmen, only to resume our explorations unrepentant when they returned to other duties. In the boxes and trunks there were mysteries to discover and dream of owning someday. Tomorrow there would be so many wonders to stare at on the restocked store shelves. I knew I would hardly sleep that night.

Thinking about all those marvels reminded me of the candy prize that rightfully belonged to me. Lifting Seicu to my shoulders, I said, "Can you see your brother?"

She squirmed about, slapping her doll into my face, then answered, "No."

I spat fur out of my mouth and urged, "Keep looking. If you find him; he will give us candy."

She wiggled some more, slapped me with her doll a few times then pointed. "I see him; I see him! He has candy. Yey!"

Grabbing her swinging feet, I stopped to peer through the press of bodies, wishing, not for the first time, that I was taller. "Where is he, Little One, I can't see him?"

She tipped her head forward so she was looking at me upside down, her eyes bright with excitement. "Where?"

She pointed more insistently towards the far end of the dock, away from the unloading. "Over there, Silly Cousin."

When I still hesitated, unable to see over the backs of two Chamuqwani carrying a heavy chest, she whacked me on the arm with her doll. "Oh, you are too short, Little Rock Squirrel. I will show you."

Before I could take another step, Seicu grabbed one of my ears as if it were the lead on a dog sled harness, and twisted my head in the direction she wanted me to travel.

"Ouch! Stop that." I pried her fingers off my ear and rubbed it. "That hurt—and don't call me that baby-name."

Seicu giggled. "All right, baby." Then she grabbed my hair instead, swinging her feet. "Ah'hup, Doggy." I growled as she pulled on my braid, and that got her giggling even louder. I started moving before she could inflict more damage.

As the activity around us thinned, I spotted my cousin. He was sitting with his legs dangling over the dock, surrounded by a group of his admirers. Seicu let out an ear-piercing squeal as we approached, and he looked our way.

When he saw us, he took the red and white candy stick from his mouth and grinned. My eyes flicked to the nearly empty bag in his hand.

"Don't worry, Little Rock Squirrel, I saved you some."

I scowled at his use of my baby-name in front of our friends. I hated when he called me that. He knew it and did it just to tease me, too. The others laughed, of course, which made me even more annoyed.

Seicu held out her hands to her brother, nearly falling off me in her eagerness. Samiqwas made a grab for her, giving her a kiss as he lifted her from my back and set her on her feet. I rolled my shoulders to ease the ache and stared across the lake, taking a moment to let go of my pique. Seicu was growing; sometimes it seemed like everyone was growing but me.

When I turned back to them, Seicu clutched her doll in one hand and held a long, striped candy stick in the other. She looked up at her brother with adoring eyes.

My Qwakaiva had given us this windfall—not Samiqwas. A part of my soul wanted to be recognized for that fact. The other part of me was appalled by such a thought. What did it matter who gained the prize; it was the sharing that was most important. I knew that, and yet I still longed for people to think well of me—as they did my cousin. I wasn't a show-off or selfish. I just wished he had waited to share out the candy until I arrived.

When Samiqwas saw how upset I was, he put a reassuring arm around my shoulder. As he gave me my candy stick, he sang my praises to the others. "It's true. My brother-cousin saw the paddle-wheeler with his Gift, so I could tell the trader the news and claim the prise for all of us to share. He will be a great Qwakaihi someday, a Treasure of the People."

Treasure of the People, eh? There was still a glint in his eye that let me know that a trace of his earlier joking still lingered, but I could also sense the truth in his words. Samiqwas was proud of me. I was content, and so chose to ignore Cohasi's snicker and Matoqwa's snort.

I stayed talking to our friends for a time, but when they began daring each other to take a canoe out on the lake to explore the miners' rafts, I reluctantly took Seicu and left.

As I neared the store the bell on board the steamboat clanged three times, and then a man in a red coat blew a long horn that sounded like a mountain goat bleating. Everyone on the peer stopped what they were doing and stared.

As the sound faded, the line of soldiers standing at the end of the gangway straightened. A pale big bellied man with no hair on the top of his head paused to stare at the activity on shore then started down. He was dressed in black jacket and trousers. On his jacket a blue lightning bolt was stitched across the image of a bear rearing up with jaws open wide.

Two men in similar clothing, wearing the same picture on their jackets followed him. The shorter one carried a leather trunk on his shoulder, the other, a man so tall and thin he seemed no more than skin and bones, walked just behind the fat man holding a large red umbrella over his head.

"There's no sun or rain in the sky," someone nearby murmured, "So why does he need to shelter his head at this time of day?"

"Crazy foreigners! A good coating of seal fat mixed with mint and tsami root to keep away the bugs would be a far better covering than that silly stick covered with cloth—pretty colour though it is," a woman said.

As the strangers neared the end of the gangway, the soldiers thumped fists to their chest in an honouring gesture. The man under the umbrella nodded his acknowledgement, and then stepped forward to greet Jombonni.

Seicu giggled, distracting me. "Man got funny hat."

"It isn't a hat it's an umbrella."

"How you know?"

"Kutima showed me a picture in one of his father's books," I said impatiently. "Hush now I want to watch what they do next."

The chief trader shook hands with the man under the umbrella. Then he led his visitors to a nearby cabin. They all went inside and closed the door spoiling my view.

"I want big umbrella like funny fat man," Seicu announced.

"Sure. Ask uncle Tli or your father to get you one—tomorrow." Still puzzling over who these new arrivals might be, I paid her little notice.

"Little Rock Squirrel?"

"Hmm?"

Screwing up her face as if about to cry she tugged on my hand to get my attention. "Want umbella now, Little Rock Squirrel. Want now!"

I bent down to quiet her. "No. and if you cry I'll take you home to Grandmother. You want to go home?"

"N-no," she sniffed.

"Then don't cry," I warned.

Glancing around for a way to distract her, I happened to catch sight of Samiqwas's older sister, Esuli, standing with one of her admirers. Deciding I'd done enough babysitting for a while, I whispered to Seicu, "Let's go see Esuli. She might have a treat for you, too."

My bossy older sister-cousin had recently returned to our home from her shillsham ceremony. Upon the arrival of her first moon-blood she spent three moons alone in the mountains, praying and preparing herself for womanhood. Fending for herself hadn't done her any harm. Her lean brown body was strong, her black hair long and thick, her clear-skinned face, bright and smiling. She had many suitors.

Seicu held out her hands and shouted her sister's name.

Hurrying over, I handed her to her sister with a straight face. Tsali, the young hunter she'd been talking with, gave me a knife-edged look. Trying not to laugh and spoil my joke, I climbed the porch steps to the trading post and flopped onto one of the long benches set against the wall. This quiet spot would be a great place to watch everything.

My mind was spinning in circles. I could hardly believe it. The boat was here at last. Nothing bad had happened—surely I had misunderstood the sending. I set aside my misgivings and focused my mind on what was truly important to me. Uncle Tli had promised that this year he would buy me a bright, steel knife of my own. I'd helped him skin out the catch last winter; he'd said I'd earned it.

In those early days, our lineage was claimed through the mother. A child's uncles on his mother's side of the family took on the roles that most fathers do among the Chamuqwani.

Unfortunately for me, Tli was often too busy with a new wife, her relatives, and his wife's first baby, to give me more than his passing attention. In all fairness, I suppose he was doing the best he could. With his older brother married into a family down the Socanna River, he must have felt like he was sinking in water over his head with so many responsibilities.

I knew that, but I still resented his neglect. I was jealous to the point of tears at times, for Samiqwas's good fortune in having a father's attention. Not that Ko himself was any prize, if I believed the gossip I overheard when people thought I was elsewhere.

Still, he had given my cousin a knife and did take him hunting on occasion. Well, soon I would have my own knife. Maybe this coming winter I could go on one of the really long hunting expeditions with Tli.

What would my new knife look like? There were so many kinds to choose from. I couldn't make up my mind which I wanted. Would I get a fine long butchering knife, its wide, silver blade slightly curved at the tip?

Or maybe I should ask for one of the new tube knives, the ones with their many small blades that folded up into their bone handle. They were very useful, each blade having a different purpose. And I couldn't forget the many styles of knives, so handy when scaling and preparing fish for the drying racks. Which would Uncle Tli choose for me—or would he let me choose for myself?

Lost in my own thoughts I jumped when I felt something hard being slipped into my hand. I looked down at the small square of folded brown paper, felt the hard round lumps inside it, and looked up open-mouthed. My friend Kutima gave me a shy smile.

I slid my hand a little closer to my side so no one could see the packet. On other occasions, Kutima had been punished for taking candy from the store's big wooden barrels to give to his friends. It was an old scandal among us that his father beat him. And though I did like candy, I didn't want to be the cause of him receiving another harsh punishment.

Kutima's mixed parentage gave his skin a pale golden colour. And because his father made him stay in to work on his lessons most of the time, his body was softer than was common among the hard-working boys of our village. He was aware of his unique appearance, and his status as a trader's son. He could be bossy round the post, but the differences between us also made him shy when he was allowed to do things with the children in the village.

Samiqwas and most of the other boys didn't like him much. They teased him about his plumpness, but I think they were afraid of him, too. He was learning his father's magics. He could write in the post's big black ledger, and read the priest's blue god-book.

The stolen candy and other small treats were perhaps Kutima's way of trying to gain our favor. I'm ashamed to say, we all took advantage of his generous gifts when he offered them. I was no different than the rest in that regard, but I genuinely liked Kutima—and not just because he gave me treats. I would often hang around the store to help him with his chores, if I wasn't needed elsewhere.

"What's this for," I murmured.

Kutima blinked his watery brown eyes and shrugged. "For you. Your cousin claimed the prize from my father, but I know it was you who saw the boat first."

How had he known that? Samiqwas wouldn't have spoken so freely of my Qwakaiva to one living at the post. No, Kutima must have known in some other way. Our mothers were friends; perhaps he had overheard the talk about me.

My Gift was no real secret. I'd heard some of my relatives boasting of how the Spirits favored me—in spite of the old priest's condemnation of our ways.Fortunately for me, Kutima was also quite secretive about the things he knew. I had no fear he would tell the priest to get me in trouble.

He was supposed to be one of the Chamuqwani god's "Chosen," and not believe in what his father called our "superstitions." But in a host of little ways he let me know, like at that moment, he respected the old ways and my Qwakaiva.

Well, his homage was noted, some of the precious stash would find its way into the lake as an offering to the Spirits, with a prayer for his good health. I could do that much for him.

"Thank you. Want some?"

He shook his head. "I have to get back before I'm missed."

"Wait, who was the fat man with the umbrella and the ice bear on his coat that your father met at the dock?

Kutima glanced up nervously at the ice bear and lightning bolt sign hanging over the trading post door. "He's some official from the trading company headquarters down south. The rich lords and the Father Emperor sent him north to check on how father is running the post."

Things are gonna change when the steamboat comes....

Feeling the cold hand of warning at the back of my neck, I blurted without thinking, "Are the bossmans angry with your father? Are they going to send him away?"

Kutima's eyes widened, then he shook his head vigorously. "No. I have to get back inside now. I have a lot of work to do."

"Can I help?"

Kutima paused as if considering, then shook his head. "They won't want any Za—anyone from the village inside right now. Only those who can read can help with the sorting." He hurried towards the open door. "Thanks for offering, Tas. See you later."

Zaunk? Had that been what he'd been about to say? Mud Grubbers, Slime Eaters, and Zaunk, those were what the southerners called us when they wanted to hurt us, or make someone angry.Hard,ugly words and so bitter a taste upon the tongue.

Chapter Four

Much to my disgust, the trading post's usual routine was disrupted that year, because of so many quarrelsome newcomers camped by the lakeshore. These rude and dirty men demanded to be allowed to trade their yellow rocks for supplies, as soon as the post's shelves were stocked the following morning.

They said it was their right to be served first, because they were Chamuqwani and better than any zaunk.

Several fights broke out between our young men and miners.

I'd been afraid for Uncle Tli, but fortunately for him, and my peace of mind, his wife and mother-in-law kept him busy at home during the worst of the trouble. He hadn't been one of the ones the soldiers singled out for a whipping, which to a man's shame, was their usual form of enforcing their laws.

When the temple bell finally rang at midday, we knew all was ready for the village to have our turn at the trading. There was a ritual about the event that had to be performed in its proper order, however. The children all knew better than to rush to the store.

First of all, everyone had to gather at the Chamuqwani God's temple, with the priest leading us in prayer. I hated the ugly square building, because it always stank of sour sweat. As large as the post warehouse, the stone gather-hall was cold even in summer. It was also bare of furnishings save for the crude statue of the Mighty Djoven, holding a lightning bolt on a dais at the back of the room. Two thick wax candles placed on either side of the altar were lit for the occasion. At the statue's feet, a brazier wafted the thick smoke of resinous incense into the air.

It was a torture for everyone to stand silently waiting, but to my relief, on that particular trading day the priest took pity on us and made his prayers short. Maybe he was as curious as we were ourselves about the goods that would now be on display at the post.

As we filed from the temple, chief trader Jombonni, dressed in white shirt, black jacket and trousers, and fine broad-brimmed black hat, led the procession of traders and villagers to the store, to settle their accounts.

Everyone in the village as well had dressed up in their best clothes for the occasion. The men wore fine woollen shirts of red and blue trade-cloth, leather loin aprons, caribou skin leggings, and high-topped rawhide-soled boots. Each man's long black hair was tied back in a thick club wrapped in leather strips.

The women wore their best blanket shawls with ermine trim and brightly coloured yarn fringes. Their long tunic-style dresses were made from the same trade-cloth as the men's shirts—only much longer. High-topped boots trimmed with strips of beaver fur and died porcupine quills adorned their feet.

Their long black hair was greased and plaited with bright coloured ribbons. The thick, shiny braids bound together hung down their backs. Framing their faces were masses of long shell and glass bead streamers, dangling to their shoulders from woven headbands.

I raced Samiqwas to the post, and for the first time that season I beat him. I was very proud of myself. Maybe I was growing after all.

Then, my happy mood soured. The fat official who'd arrived with the steamboat was sitting on a carved chair in the yard waiting to view the trading. Behind him his tall servant held the bright red umbrella above him.

Accompanying him were several grim-faced dark-skinned soldiers. They spoke to no one, not even Jombonni. The menace they represented wasn't lost on anyone. They carried their thunder-weapons for all to see.

"I hope the fat man brought those soldiers here to protect us," an Elder said. "If the miners should start more trouble—"

"Protect us? Not likely," someone in the crowd scoffed.

I glanced toward the tents that had sprung up overnight along the shoreline. *Protect the miners, maybe.*

Turning away from the soldiers, I grasped the otter claw around my neck and prayed, "Qwa'osi, keep us safe from all these bad men."

Where was Uncle Tli? Anxiously I searched for him among the approaching villagers. Uncle had powerful hands and the lean body of a hunting fox. He also had a temper that could ignite in a moment when he felt injustice threatened the Qwani'ya people of our village.

When I found him he was glaring at the fat official and the soldiers. Then, he leaned forward and muttered something to Matoqwa's older brother, Qwati, who laughed. I was too far away, but Shilshigua must have heard, because she frowned and hugged the baby that she carried in the side-sling upon her hip.

Hoping to distract him, I hurried over. "Uncle, can I help you carry your trade goods?" My face must have betrayed my fear, because he laughed and tousled my hair.

"Don't look so worried, Nephew. Let's go trade for the knife I promised you." Motioning me to precede him, we climbed the porch steps.

The trading post always smelled good to me, a mixture of wood smoke, exotic spices, sweet candy, and salt-fish. The room where the trading took place was a rectangle, divided down the middle by a long wooden counter about waist high on a man.

In one corner in front of the counter, an iron wood stove squatted, its grey hide caked with old grease and soot. A few benches had been placed around it, and on cold winter days some of the men gathered to talk with the traders and drink hot sweet tea laced with waskyja. But on that clear summer day the stove sat cold and abandoned. Only a few elders sat there to await their turns at the trading.

There were shelves nearly to the ceiling, stocked with all kinds of wonderful items on the traders' side of the counter. Further back, beyond the front shelves, extra goods were stored in the back warehouse. Jombonni and his men stood behind the counter and the people lined up in front. When it was a person's turn, he or she would point to the things wanted on the shelves, and one of the traders would look in the post's black ledger book to see if they had enough credits to pay for the desired item.

The chief trader's real name wasn't Jombonni, but Jombonni was the closest pronunciation we could make to the odd sounding foreign word that was his true name. He was a tall thin man with a sandy moustache and a funny little bald spot in the middle of his thinning brown hair. He was friendly, with a booming laugh. He'd lived among us for years, spoke our language well, and took an interest in the gossip of the clans. He drove a hard bargain, but no one complained over much that he cheated them.

When the paddle-wheeler came in summer, and on the equinox holidays sacred to, Mighty Djoven, The Thunderer, he would hand out a piece of bright coloured ribbon to each of the women, and a free mug of the Chamuqwani's fiery liquor waskyja to each man. The children received long sticks of striped candy.

Once inside the trading post I dared not say anything to Uncle Tli. I knew better than to distract him, but each time he'd look around, I'd be at his elbow. Anxiety gnawing at my gut, I took note of the mounting pile of bright yarns, trade cloth, traps, and food stuffs piling up at his feet. I hoped he wouldn't run out of credit before he got around to bargaining for my knife.

At last he ended my torture and pointed to the display of knives on the wall. Jombonni let out one of his booming laughs and gave me a knowing wink. Then, he took down several knives for my uncle's inspection. Face expressionless Tli waited as Jombonni told him the price for each one as he set them on the counter.

"That one is five fox pelts. And that one—it's a fine blade, yes? That one is nine. And that one, a true wonder, that one would cost three wolf pelts."

Nine pelts; I liked that one. I glanced up at Uncle, hoping he could see the pleading in my eyes.

Tli shook his head sadly. "Knives are too much. My wife wants more oat-mush—for the baby—too much."

Jombonni nodded. "Food for a baby is important, but your nephew is a fine young hunter. With a good knife he could be a lot of help to you this winter. Then you could buy more food and pretty things for your family."

"Maybe, but he helps already, a good boy."

"I agree, but stone tools break so easily. With a good steel knife he could help even more than he does now."

"Mmm." Tli pointed to the knife I liked. "Three fox and one beaver."

Jombonni shook his head and my heart sank. "I can't do it—the Father Emperor's man is here. He would be angry with me for giving away his master's goods. Eight Fox pelts."

"Too much. Four beaver pelts."

Jombonni held up another knife, that one smaller than the one I now wanted more than anything in the world. "I can let you have this one. Six beaver."

Tli studied the knife with slow deliberate movements, taking it from its sheath, testing its sharpness. Behind me impatient relatives anxious for their turn grumbled. My stomach clenched; I, too, wished he'd hurry, but I was also afraid of the outcome. What if he thought all the knives were too much and wouldn't trade for any of them?

"That one is no good for a hunter. It is only a toy, a baby's knife."

A baby's knife? Samiqwas and the other boys will laugh their heads off if he doesn't buy me something. I will be shamed—an outcast—forever!

They bargained for a while longer, at last settling on a knife with a blade about the length of my hand, having a slight curve to its tip. It had a ridged bone handle that would fit my grip well when I pulled it from its sheath. Uncle agreed on a price of seven fox pelts; I was stunned. It wasn't the one I'd wanted, or the most expensive or grand of the knives on display, but it was a sturdy serviceable tool that would help me in my work over the coming year. And, as I examined it more closely, I realized that it was a far better knife than the one I would have chosen.

I was so proud of that knife. As soon as Uncle Tli handed it to me, I ran outside and removed the blade from its leather sheath to stare at the silver metal in the sunlight. Samiqwas had been generous about letting me share the use of his knife, so when he came over to see my prize, I willingly handed it over.

He drew out the blade and nodded his approval. "Let's go down to the shore and find some driftwood to test its sharpness," Samiqwas suggested.

Smiling, I agreed and we hurried down to the lakeshore.

ABSORBED IN OUR OWN concerns, we'd been paying no attention to the activity at the trading post, until shouts and a woman's high-pitched scream alerted us to trouble. I slipped my knife back into its sheath and looked around. We'd drifted farther along the shore than I'd realized, and now a stand of willow and birch blocked the view. "What's going on?"

Samiqwas shrugged. "We better go see."

Fear goading us, we raced up the beach.

As we neared the post a Chamuqwani shouted, "Dirty zaunk—kill the bastard!" And in response, one of my Qwani'ya relatives cried, "Greedy, ignorant foreigners, go back to your own lands and leave us alone!"

Samiqwas sprinted ahead and I soon lost sight of him among the jostling crowd. No matter how I tried to squeeze through the press and follow, a kick and a punch aimed at my head was all I got for my effort. Wiping blood from my nose I backed out of the crush. Spotting Aunt Tuulah and Mother standing together on the trading post porch, I headed in their direction. Aunt Tuulah clutched Seicu close to her side pushing the sobbing little girls face into her dress. Mother stood wide-eyed, a hand to her mouth, staring at something going on amidst the milling people in the yard.

Hoping to see better from there, I leapt up the steps and joined the women. Tugging on her arm, I shouted over the noise "Amima, what's happening?"

"Some Qwani'ya men are fighting with miners."

"Where's Uncle Tli?"

Mother opened her mouth, but Aunt Tuulah spoke before she could get the words out. "Where have you been? Weren't you supposed to be helping him?"

Trade goods! A twinge of guilt tugged at my heart. I'd been so excited about my knife that all other obligations flew out of my mind. "Yes, Aunt Tuulah, I was. I—I forgot."

"You forgot, eh? Do you think your uncle will be happy when he hears your excuse?"

"No, Aunty. But where is he? I can help him now."

"The last time I saw my brother, Tli was accompanying Shilshigua and her mother back to the village."

Mother shook her head. "He's not there. He came back—with Mother."

Tuulah's eyes widened. "Mother's inside the store drinking tea. Where did he go after that?"

"I don't know. I wasn't paying attention." She stood on her toes peering into the haze of dust surrounding the brawling men. "Sister, can you see him? Is he there?"

"I don't see him—oh, I can't tell."

I strained my eyes, but couldn't find my uncle. In the midst of the shouting people, a man with yellow hair appeared for a moment, then disappeared once again. He seemed somehow familiar, but I couldn't place the recollection. With their wide brimmed hats and the hair growing all over their faces, it was hard to tell one miner from another. "What happened, Amima? How did the fighting start?"

"The trouble began when the Jomash brothers and their friends pushed their way into the store and demanded to be served."

The Jomash brothers—now I recognized the yellow-haired one.

Things gonna change when the steamboat comes

"Rude, dirty miners," Grandmother said as she joined us. "They demanded that Jombonni trade with them first, because they were better men than any of us." She snorted. "Without our help most of the miners—including those troublemaking brothers, would have died last winter. And how do they repay us? By destroying fish traps, and stealing our food and invading clan-owned territories in search of pretty yellow rocks. Rocks! Those men have no sense."

I closed my ears to her complaints; I'd heard it all before. Something else far more disturbing had caught my eye. Face purple with outrage, the fat man was gesticulating to a group of soldiers. Off to one side his turned-over chair and smashed red umbrella lay abandoned.

While I watched, more soldiers hurried up from the peer. Bellowing "Give way!" and using their thunder weapons like clubs, they waded into the crowd, bloodying anyone too slow to get out of their path.

The fight was over within moments after that. Miners and villagers alike backed away, and I got my first clear view of the combatants. On one side Chugai, Ko's brother Gagayii, Uncle Tli and Matoqwa's older sister's husband from downriver were struggling amidst several soldiers. Not far from them, the Jomash brothers and three of their friends were being guarded by a similar group of grey-clad men. Though loosely confined, they continued to inflame our young men by shouting curses and nasty names, which the soldiers did little to stop.

Over the elders and Jombonni's protests, the soldier's headman and the Father Emperor's official halted the trading for the day. "I'm sorry, friends," Jombonni said. "These men are concerned for everyone's safety. He feels everyone needs time to set aside their bad feelings, before we can resume the trading again."

Grandmother muttered under her breath, "That fat man is more concerned for his *own* safety than ours."

"When will we be able to come back?" an Elder asked.

Jombonni turned back to the men for more talk in their language. "They will meet together tonight. They'll decide and let us know tomorrow." He held out his hands palms up. "I'm sorry, but I'm sure all will be well in the morning."

Muttering, the people started to drift away, then realizing that the soldiers had no plans to let our young men go home without being punished for their part in the disturbance, they came back to see.

When he understood the penalty the soldiers intended, Jombonni protested loudly on our behalf. "A whipping for the men of the village is unjust and too harsh! The Jomash brothers are troublemakers. I've banned them from the post before for fighting."

"Go back inside now and tend to your business," the soldier in charge said. "These zaunks need to be taught a lesson. Fighting with the Emperor's miners won't be tolerated—especially in times of war."

Jombonni folded his arms across his chest and glared. "If these men must face a whipping, then so should the miners involved."

"The miners will be dealt with in due time," the officer said.

"But—"

The trading company's official smirked. "If you can't be counted on to obey orders without insolence, then you'll be replaced."

Jombonni's bravado deflated like a fish bladder poked with a stick. Without another word, he brushed past the women and went back inside.

The Jomash brothers and the rest of the miners involved in the trouble were sent back to their encampment with nothing more than a stern warning. Uncle Tli and the other men from the village were bound to the porch rail, stripped of their shirts and flogged with a long whip until their backs were bloody.

Chapter Five

With the trading unexpectedly over for the day, the village defiantly went ahead with plans for a celebration. In preparation for this annual event, several fires were built on a grassy bluff overlooking the lakeshore out of sight of the Chamuqwani buildings.

Two days before some hunters had killed a moose, a special treat at that time of year. When I arrived with Mother, the old women were roasting the meat on iron spits hung over the flames. As the meat browned, they cut off the cooked chunks, then returned the rest to the fires to cook some more.

Placing the roasted meat in flat reed baskets, younger women carried the trays to a plank table where mounds of flat griddle cakes and bowls of fresh berries dusted with white store-bought sugar awaited the hungry people. Countless kettles of strong black tea, as sweet as birch syrup and nearly as thick, completed the feast.

After we ate, five of our best singers took their hoop drums from sealskin cases, and stepped to the fire to warm them. When the stretched hides sounded just right, the men formed a line at one side of the central fire and began singing. Old men and women recognizing the song joined in, their high-pitched voices echoing across the lake in the twilight.

When the younger men and women began dancing, Samiqwas and I watched the snaking lines for a time. Soon enough though, we became bored and joined some of our friends down by the lake. Most of the children who were old enough to leave their mothers were doing the same.

It was a still night, the lavender sky above streaked with coral, the outlines of the grey peaks softened by an evening mist, collecting far out on the lake. I could hear the drumbeats echoing off the nearby hillsides, before the sound was flung wide across the deep green water. The smells of wood smoke, roasting meat, and rotting lake weeds mingled on the air.

I hurried as usual after Samiqwas. In a long flat area near the water's edge, we joined some boys lining up for foot races. Further down the shore I could see another group engaged in a stone-throwing contest.

Most of the boys in the group we'd joined were older than I was. I'd no intention of joining their game and looking foolish. Samiqwas, however, feared nothing and stepped up alongside Slylum for the next race.

He didn't win, but he ran well, ten times better than I could have done. Tigali shouted ko'heyin praise of Samiqwas's attempt. My cousin beamed and lined up again.

I watched for a time, shouting ko'hey whenever anyone made a particularly good effort, but I was cold and bored just standing around watching. I wanted to do something to warm up and show my own skills. Waving to Samiqwas, I wandered further along the beach. Walking on logs and leaping over clumps of grass, I headed for the stone-throwing group.

I took in several deep breaths as the Qwakaiva of Earth and Water enveloped me. I lifted my face and sang a prayer song, just for the joy of it. High above the eastern peaks, pale ribbons of phosphorescent green light snaked in shimmering spirals across the violet sky. I shivered, wondering if I had inadvertently called them. This was the first time I'd seen the Spirit-Lights since the summer sun had paled the night sky. Summer was waning, but it was still too bright at night for them to be more than a ghost of their winter greatness.

Continuing down the beach, I blew into the hollow made by my clasped hands to call them closer. Then I sang a song to the lights as I picked up stones. I held them between my palms and felt a tingling power awake deep in the heart of each one before I put it in the pouch at my waist.

My hands grew warm; the stones would do my bidding. The evening felt charged with power. I laughed, feeling suddenly as carefree as willow blossoms blown on the wind. I leaped into the air and did a few dance steps in time to the distant drum as I joined this new group of boys.

Most of the stone throwers were my age or slightly younger. They greeted me warmly with teasing calls. All but Matoqwa, the oldest among them, who scowled and turned his back on me. I stuck out my tongue at his back, returning the insult.

When someone laughed, he mumbled something fierce under his breath and began throwing stones with a vicious intensity. His brother Cohasi shouted a praise call as one of his stones jumped four times before sinking. Then other boys began to throw, trying to match his feat, and the tension dissipated.

The heat from the stones' Qwakaiva nearly burning a hole in my pouch, I joined the shouting line. My hands moved as if the will of the Spirit-Lights guided them. I tossed stone after stone into the water. Three, four, five times they jumped. Again and again, my throws were impeccable, my Qwakaiva unbeatable. My arm, my whole body flowed gracefully with each movement. I gave no thought to the other boys, ensnared in the power twisting and crackling through the world that I'd given a focus.

My mind spun with a storm of images—warm sandy beaches, and golden stones shimmering at the bottom of green pools—white fish leaping high, their silver scales bright in the sun, jump, jump, jump, splash.

I didn't notice the other boys had stopped throwing until harsh laughter smashed through my shell of concentration. When I dropped my arm and glanced around, they were all staring at me. Cohasi made the sign against evil when he thought I wasn't looking. My stomach heaved; I couldn't breathe, couldn't think.

I stared dumbly at Matoqwa too shocked to speak. He curled his lip and spat on the ground. "Siyatli Boy, are those scales I see at the nape of your neck? Or maybe there's a lake seal's brindle fur under your hair, eh? Why don't you crawl back into the lake with the rest of your slimy kin?"

Matoqwa might have said more hateful things, but Samiqwas, who'd come up unnoticed, decided at that moment to smack him on the side of the jaw. Matoqwa staggered, then, roaring with outrage, he charged his adversary. Grim-faced, my cousin met his charge with another bone-jarring punch. They fell to the ground, rolling over and over, each one trying to gain the upper hand.

Trembling, I stood watching, unable to think or move. A part of me wanted to race down the beach and keep on going. But the part of me loyal to my brother-cousin wouldn't leave him to face his enemy alone, in case Cohasi decided to join the fight.

I needn't have worried; the dispute didn't last long. Tigali and a few of the older boys heard our shouting and came over to break it up. Prying the combatants apart, the older boys asked no questions, they merely dragged both fighters to the lake and pushed them into the icy water. Amidst howls of laughter, Samiqwas and Matoqwa came up spluttering and dragged themselves ashore dripping.

Samiqwas grinned and slapped his opponent on the back. Matoqwa wasn't as ready to forgive and forget, but under the watchful eyes of the older boys, he reluctantly let the matter drop.

When I was certain that Samiqwas would be all right, I fled. Soon after, a bedraggled Samiqwas trudged along in my wake. Behind us, the rock skipping contest resumed.

The Spirit-Lights still gyrated in the violet sky. A low humming like the sound of angry insects whirled around inside my head. On the lake the mists were creeping ever closer to shore. The world about me felt brittle and as dangerous as a broken waskyja bottle smashed on the rocks. I shivered as if it had been me who had been dunked.

I kicked a stick out of my path and said without looking at him, "Aunt Tuulah is going to be mad when she sees your best shirt." He just shrugged.

I'd been moving aimlessly, only wanting to distance myself from the others. We'd nearly reached the place where Hot Springs Creek emptied into the lake before I was paying attention to my surroundings again.

An old spruce blown down in a winter gale lay sprawled along the creek bank. Its roots arched into the air, while its crown tip fanned out into the water. Sprinting ahead of me, Samiqwas began breaking off dry branches and laying them in a pile near the arching roots.

"Have you got your make-fire kit with you? Mine's wet."

I stared at him stupidly for a long moment. My mind still mulling over Matoqwa's words, I had a hard time making the connection. I finally nodded and reached for the hardened clay vessel covered with leather, tucked into my belt. I crouched and placed a wad of dried moss on the sand, then struck the stone to the metal. When the red spark jumped into its fluffy nest, I blew on the smouldering ember until the whole mass burst into flames. Samiqwas added a handful of spruce needles and twigs. We broke off larger branches and kept adding them until we had a comfortable blaze going.

Taking off his wet clothes, Samiqwas draped them over the arching tree roots to dry. Going to the creek, he washed the blood from his bleeding nose. When he came back, he lay down by our fire with a big sigh, like a tired sled dog. I crouched on the other side of the fire, feeding it more twigs, and watched him. He closed his eyes. A trickle of blood still leaked from one nostril. "You'll have a nice bruise around your eye. He must have punched you good."

Samiqwas chuckled. Without opening his eyes, he said, "Wait till you see Matoqwa's face."

My eyes travelled over the smooth brown contours of his body. Strong arms and legs, firm buttocks, black mane tumbling loose from its lacing, to flow down his back in an inky cascade, he was beautiful. I saw the golden eyes of his Spirit-Guardian, the Wolf, staring at me with a wary attention from the halo of smoke cast off by the fire.

I'd never seen my cousin in quite that way before. The roaring was suddenly back in my head again. I took in a ragged breath, the night sliding out of focus around me. I looked away, concentrating my attention instead on the writhing patterns of gold and crimson within the flames. What was happening to me—to the world around me? Had I unwittingly awakened some sleeping evil with my foolish desire to win a stone-throwing contest?

What had Matoqwa really meant by his insult? Did everyone know some dark secret about me? Was I a Siyatli, one of the half-human creatures sired by a magical being living at the bottom of the lake? And why now was my cousin, my brother, my best friend so silent? Why wouldn't he even look at me?

I tossed the stick I'd been playing with into the flames with an angry gesture. Fire hissed a complaint, tiny red sparks shooting into the air with a snapping sound. Samiqwas opened his eyes and looked at me.

"What did Matoqwa mean?"

"I don't know what you're talking about. I didn't hear him."

"You didn't hear him." I jabbed Fire hard with another stick, and sparks shot up once again. "If you didn't *hear* what he said to me, why did you punch him in the face to stop him from saying more, hmm?"

Samiqwas sat up, picked up a twig, and began pulling its grey-green moss off, tossing it into the flames. "I didn't hear what he said, truly." I gave him a disgusted look. "And I hit him because, because I wanted to—that's all—I just wanted to."

"Tell me—please."

Ignoring my plea, he jumped to his feet to check his drying clothes. Finding them still wet, he scowled, then leapt atop the log and began walking up and down its length with arms outstretched for balance. "There's nothing to tell."

Siyatli, is there a lake seal's brindle fur under your black hair? Why don't you crawl back into the lake with the rest of your slimy kin?

No, no, I'm no lake seal man's child—no enemy! Qwa'osi, tell me it isn't so!

I watched him for a time then my anger flared once more. Why was he lying?? He'd never done that before. Picking up the nearest object I found by my hand, I threw it.

Samiqwas had reached the end of the log and was coming back towards me. The pinecone hit him square in the middle of his chest with a hard thunk. The log rocked, Samiqwas teetered, lost his balance, and then landed hard on his backside in the grass. He gaped, picked himself up and walked back to the fire rubbing his chest.

"Why did you do that?"

I glared at him, but refused to answer.

"I don't really know what Matoqwa was talking about," he finally said. As I reached for another pinecone, he held up a hand. "No, wait. I don't know much—but I'll tell you the little I *do* know. I don't think Matoqwa really believes you're a Siyatli. He was making it up, because he was angry that you were beating him at the stones."

"Maybe, but there has to be more to the story. Tell me."

He let out a long-suffering sigh, and busied himself with adding more twigs to the fire. At last he said, "I only overheard my mother and one of her friends joking about your mother having a lake seal man for a suitor when she was young. That's all I heard, because they saw me and stopped talking. That's all I know—I swear it!"

Waves of ice pounded through my veins. My chest tight, I could hardly breathe. *Spirit Stealer, fish thief, was I truly kin to one of Co'yeh's hated warriors?* No, impossible!

"Your mother never talks about him, does she?"

"No. Does yours?"

"No, but she may know. When your mother was so—ill—she may have confided in her sister. Amima might tell you if you ask her."

I'd already thought of that, but never found her alone to ask. "Maybe.... But why would anyone think my father one of Co'yeh's kin? What if one of those creatures heard that kind of joking and sent bad luck to us for a punishment?"

Samiqwas shrugged and reached for his shirt. "It is crazy talk, true, but everybody likes to gossip about a mystery. And your mother's lover is a big mystery—even you have to admit that. So people talk. So what? Matoqwa is a dog fart. What he says means nothing—just forget about it."

Samiqwas was fully dressed by the time he finished talking. His clothes were dry but dirty. Crouching by the dying blaze he shovelled handfuls of sand onto the fire to put it out. "I'm getting hungry; let's go back to the dance and see if there's any food."

I stood, pondering his words, but made no move to leave. "Why wouldn't people think my father was a Chamuqwani trader or—a tribal refugee from the south? Plenty of those men come through our village. Mother could have taken a fancy to one of them."

My voice trailed off as Samiqwas began shaking his head. "There are times—like back there." He pointed with his lips up the beach. "Sometimes—" He took a deep breath and tried again. "You're different, you know. Your Qwakaiva—it's special—like Grandfather's—and that kind of power can make some people uneasy."

The queasy feeling was back in my gut. "But—"

"I know. Just forget about it."

But I couldn't just let it go. I wanted—no, needed—to know who my father was. It was important to me.

Chapter Six

A s we climbed the slope, Mother and Aunt Tuulah were standing near the cliff edge. "You boys get Seicu. We need to go home, now."

"Go home?" We looked at one another. Samiqwas shrugged. No one had ever called us to come home from the summer celebration, but the tone of their voices, and the spiky grey light outlining their bodies, stopped me from arguing.

"Something's wrong," I murmured.

"I'll get Seicu. She was sitting in a patch of crowberries near the base of the trail." Samiqwas said. "You go on. I'll be right behind you."

Slylum and two of his cousins were coming down, eating meat and griddle cakes. They gave me odd looks as we passed.

Siyatli. The new story of my strangeness was bound to be all over the village by morning.

Samiqwas and I hadn't been paying attention to the adults' celebration, but as we approached the top of the bluff, my eyes almost popped from my head. A large group of miners and off-duty soldiers were standing to one side of the fire. They were passing large jugs of waskyja among themselves and joking about the People and the dancing. A few of the boldest of our young women stood nearby, giggling and whispering behind their hands.

As I watched, one dark-skinned soldier, with curly hair like a mountain sheep, smiled and held out the jug in their direction. None of the girls had taken the men up on their offer—yet—but they were considering it. Jombonni and the clan elders sitting by the fire had also noticed the strangers' advances and weren't happy. To make things worse, those of our young men who weren't dancing were passing around their own jug of waskyja and glaring at everyone.

The night air crackled with the sharp scent of danger and the sour stench of fear. I couldn't understand why no one as yet had asked the Chamuqwani to leave, but I hoped someone would soon.

Her mouth and cheeks stained purple with berry juice, Seicu complained, "Not sleepy. Want pick berries." From Aunt Tuulah's hip she held out her hands to Mother. "Aunty, please take me berries."

As we trudged up the trail to the village and away from the celebration, the little girl's maddening whine filled my head to bursting. Finally, my aunt had had enough. "Noisy Gull, be quiet or the Ogre Woman of the Mountain will hear you. She will put you in her basket, take you home, and eat you."

"Tuulah!" Mother gasped

Seicu cringed, buried her face in Aunty's shoulder and started crying. Samiqwas gave his mother a reproachful look, picked up his sister and put her on his back. He bounced her up and down snorting like a buck deer, making her laugh. Pushing past the glaring women he trotted towards the village. Seicu's delighted laughter floated back through the trees, growing fainter as he put more distance between us.

I would have liked to follow him, but I'd been lagging behind, not wanting to go home any more than Seicu. Now both Aunt Tuulah and Mother angrily faced each other on the path ahead, blocking off my escape. I considered disobeying and going back to the celebration, then decided not to risk being caught. I would be missed at home and get into trouble for it.

"You shouldn't have lashed out that way," Mother scolded. "The child already has too many nightmares as it is."

Tuulah sighed. "I know. Father will scold me for frightening her, too. He told me that ghosts in the lake are calling to my sweet girl, wanting her to join them. He says it wouldn't take much for her spirit to give up its body and follow them."

Mother's tone softened and she took Tuulah's hand. "Don't worry about her so much. She's recovered fully from the coughing sickness. She's fine now—everyone says so. It's you I worry about more than my niece."

"Me? Whatever for?"

I crouched low as Mother turned her head and pointed with her lips back toward the dance. Tuulah made no comment. Quickening her pace, her walking stick punched deep holes into the damp moss.

"Where is Esuuli? Should I go back and look for her?" Mother asked, changing the subject.

"She's all right," Aunt Tuulah said without looking back. "I saw her go off with that Tsali boy in his canoe, just after the Chamuqwani came. That boy is smart. He won't let anything happen to her. Don't worry about them. I've already talked to Shell about a possible wedding in the spring."

Mother seemed startled—as was I. Well, well, my bossy big cousin getting married? Did Samiqwas know? I could hardly wait to tell him the news. I remembered seeing Tsali and Esuuli together outside the store; I should have guessed. Things were definitely going to change around our home.

I wondered idly what it would be like having the shy Tsali for a new relation. I didn't know him all that well. He was a good hunter and fisherman—everyone knew that—but he was so quiet. How had he found the courage to approach my cousin?

"Will you go back after Seicu is settled?" Mother asked. "Ko was with his brother by the food table."

"I saw him too. But he was drinking, not eating."

"The old people are still there—nothing will happen." Mother's tone had been soft and reassuring, but the muddy swirls of worry in her Spirit-Fire gave the lie to her words.

Tuulah let out a mirthless laugh, not believing her either. "Gagayii had another bottle under his vest. He'll share with his brother—as always. Mother will leave when the singing dies down and the drinking increases. And our father can't do anything. He isn't of Ko's lineage."

"Maybe Father can talk to Ko's uncle, and he can talk to Ko."

Tuulah gave her sister a withering look. "And, maybe Ko's uncle will be too drunk by that time to listen as well—then what?"

"I didn't know he was drinking again."

The women were stopped in the trail once more, facing one another. I eased off the path and crouched down behind a blueberry bush. They would be furious if they discovered me.

After staring for a while in silence, Tuulah stepped around Mother and announced, "I'll be back later."

Mother's face assumed an exasperated expression. She often had that look, because there were a lot of stubborn people in our family—including her. "If you don't like what your husband is doing, Sister, put his things outside our door and be done with him."

Tuulah made a disgusted sound in her throat and started walking. "With all those soldiers and miners barging into our dance, who knows what might happen. Now that the children are safe, I have to take care of Amima."

"I repeat, if you aren't happy because of his drinking then return his things to his mother's lodge and be done with him."

"I can't."

"Why not, because of the children?"

"Yes. No. It isn't only that."

"What then? Tell me??"

"Forget about it."

"I want to help. What?"

Tuulah shook her head and started walking. "Off in your dreams most of the time, you don't understand anything, do you?"

"What do you mean by that? Come back here and talk to me." Mother shouted at her retreating back.

"Never mind—there's no point—tell my daughter I'm sorry. I didn't mean to scare her."

Mother made a disgusted sound deep in her throat and started walking back to the village. I trailed as silent as a hunting lynx in her wake. By the time we reached home more families had left the dance and joined us. Near our lodge I caught up to her and put my hand in hers. She must have guessed that I'd overheard, but she only gave me one of her sad smiles and ruffled my hair as we stepped into the lodge.

Later, when all was quiet, I lay on our sleeping platform and watched the patterns made by the grey smoke drifting up through the smoke hole. The drums still pounded, but mingled among its beats were shouts and the occasional peal of high-pitched laughter. Someone's tied-up sled dog howled, then other dogs joined in the song.

The night sounds made me feel incredibly sad, and I didn't know why. This was my home. I wanted my life always to be so beautiful. I had no name to give my unease, but it wasn't just the dance tonight that troubled me. Like black currents in the lake that warned of an unseen predator, my troubled thoughts had reminded me of yesterday's Spirit-Sending.

I mustn't forget again. I would warn Grandfather in the morning. Surely with all his power, he could stop evil. He was a great Qwakaihi. He would know what to do.

"Amima?"

Something in my tone of voice made her put down her sewing. Coming over, she pulled back the furs and crawled in beside me. Making herself comfortable, she took me in her arms. "What is it, my boy?"

Inhaling the scent of poplar resin and bear fat that always clung to her hair, I shamelessly snuggled closer to her warmth. "Why are the old people always complaining about how bad things are since the traders came? I wouldn't have my new knife and you wouldn't have a copper cooking pot or a sharp silver needle if they weren't here."

She laughed softly and brushed hair off my forehead. "That's true, but other gifts aren't so welcome as cooking pots and knives."

"You're talking about waskyja and Ko's drinking, aren't you?"

She continued to stroke my hair as if it soothed her. "Yes, the Chamuqwani drink is very bad. And some people like Ko have a problem knowing when to stop."

"Then why don't the elders tell Jombonni to stop trading it to us."

I couldn't see her face clearly in the dim light, but there was no mistaking the frustration in her voice, when she said, "Maybe because some of them like to drink waskyja now and then too. But the problem is more complicated than just the waskyja."

I thought about that as I listened to the night sounds outside, then I said, "I've heard Grandfather telling Uncle Tli that he's worried about the land. He thinks too many animals are being killed to pay for items we get from the post. He thinks the Ancestors and the Spirits might become angry with us if we don't stop."

"Hmm. Your grandfather is a wise man."

"Samiqwas said Uncle Tli tried to warn the traders, but they only laughed at him. Do you think Grandfather is right, Amima? Will the fish in the lake and the animals abandon us to starve?"

"I think you need to go to sleep now. Qwa'osi will protect us, my son." Mother kissed me, then rose and went back to her sewing.

Chapter Seven

After the old people came home and went to bed, Mother gave up on Aunt Tuulah returning before Ko finished his drinking. She banked the fire and crawled under the sleeping furs beside me. Her soothing warmth eased my heart, and finally I slept.

In my dream, a pack of unknown dogs chased a small herd of caribou far out onto the lake ice. Exhausted and unable to go any further, the caribou formed a protective circle around their young and faced the yammering pack with antlers lowered.

The dogs were massive creatures with shaggy yellow coats and glowing red eyes. In twos and threes they leapt in to snap at the caribous' thin legs, then darted back to avoid their lethal antler thrusts. The ice was stained red with blood, the buck and his strongest does failing as I watched.

I could hear the pack's triumphant howling ringing in my head, when suddenly the ice split wide. The hungry dogs and the wounded caribou forgot about each other, scrambling desperately to avoid the black water. Kunai raised his great head out of the lake. Green-gold eyes with vertically slit pupils contemplated the struggling beasts. Then he turned his cold, unblinking stare in my direction.

Fear clutching at my heart, I forced myself awake and never learned what happened to the caribou or the dogs. I'd taken my new knife to bed with me, tucking it under my pillow—in case of trouble. Such a puny talisman was no protection against the Great Kunai, but it's hard, physical presence near to hand had been a comfort nonetheless.

Mother and Aunty were already up and making the morning meal. A big pot of fish stew bubbled on the iron grating set over the fire. The most delicious smell wafted throughout the lodge. Mother saw me watching her, smiled, and motioned me over to the hearth. Still muzzy-headed from sleep, I stumbled from the bed platform and headed for the privy.

Outside, the summer fog blanketed the village in damp woolly folds. When I returned home, a tendril of its mass followed me. It slithered inside on its belly like a hungry weasel, before I could get the inner door flap closed. I felt its clammy touch on my neck as I took my place by the fire, and pulled my wool blanket tighter about my shoulders.

Blinking a stray wisp of smoke from my eyes, I cradled the warm stew Mother handed me, grateful for its heat. The steaming broth contained big chunks of white fish, wild onions, lake lettuce, crowberries, and oat-mush to thicken the broth. Trying to banish the uncomfortable feeling that cold green eyes were still watching me, I raised the spoon to my mouth.

Aunt Tuulah was cooking griddle cakes and spreading the golden slices with lake seal fat and honey. There was also hot black tea for those who wished it.

Mother served the old people still sitting on their bed platform, then went to sit beside Seicu with her own bowl. Ko sat alone across the fire from Samiqwas and me, drinking a steaming cup of tea. There was a large purple bruise on his cheek. He stank of waskyja and looked red-eyed and haggard. The smoke from the fire kept blowing in his direction, making him cough.

Offering him no food, Aunt Tuulah ignored him, her mouth a thin line, her movements sharp and angry as she moulded the soft dough into flat cakes and slapped them with extra vigour onto the hot soapstone griddle.

Everyone looked a little pale and worn out that morning. Seicu was fretful. She'd had a bad night as Mother predicted, crying out more than once in her dreams. Seicu's nightmares had increased after the miners began digging further up the lake. She claimed she could hear the Earth Spirits crying in pain.

I'd barely finished my first bowl of stew and was contemplating the next piece of griddle bread my aunt had just flipped, when the temple bell unexpectedly began ringing.

"Now what?" Grandmother grumbled. "Who is making all that noise? Some young men still celebrating, no doubt."

"That old priest jealously guards his bell. I doubt if he would let anyone from the village close enough to touch it. There must be a good reason for him waking us so early," Grandfather said.

The adults glanced at one another warily. Finally Mother ventured, "Maybe there's some kind of trouble." Aunt Tuulah snorted and busied herself with her cooking.

While we were still discussing whether to go to the temple or finish our meal, we heard a crier coming round with news. "Come out," he shouted. "Come down to the temple, everyone, immediately! Trader Jombonni has important news for us. Come, come now!"

"Important news, bah," Grandmother said. "What could possibly be so important that Jombonni must rouse us from our warm hearth on such a dismal morning? The man has no sense at all."

Tuulah shot Ko a withering look as if somehow this unexpected summons was *his* fault. He returned her stare for a time, then dropped his eyes and sipped his tea.

"I think it isn't the trader who commands this but the soldiers or the Emperor's man who came on the steamboat," Grandfather said quietly.

I glanced up from the griddle cake I'd snatched from the pile, and saw the frightened look in Mother's eyes before she turned away to grab her shawl.

"Whoever has called for us to assemble, we'll know more if we go down to hear what they have to say," Grandfather continued. He reached out a hand to help Grandmother to her feet. She scowled, ignoring his hand.

"I'm staying right here. I'm no slave to come at this foreigner's bidding." Seicu whimpered and crawled up on the bed beside her. For once the old woman didn't rebuke her for whining. Instead she put an arm around the child and pulled her close. "You can tell me what he wants later."

The fog had retreated from the slopes around the village, but clouds still obscured the glacier, the grey water of the lake rough as tree bark. My blanket whipping behind me like a sail, I started running, hoping to warm myself with the exercise. Samiqwas sprinted to catch up.

We arrived panting at the temple, but even so we weren't the first. Some people were already there. But wary as a wolverine scenting the buried trap, they clustered in small groups outside the open door, talking in low voices, reluctant to enter. Ignoring the adults, I peeked inside. Some of the elders sat cross-legged near the altar.

Jombonni's son Kutima was also in there, crouching by the wall, talking to his elderly aunt. Unsure what to do next, I glanced back outside.

Grandfather was engrossed in conversation with our headman Tsanqwati. Mother and Aunt Tuulah had been waylaid by a cousin and were involved in an animated discussion of Esuuli's marriage prospects. Samiqwas looked in their direction and rolled his eyes, then motioned with his chin to a group of our friends bounding down the footpath.

I shook my head and stepped inside, heading in Kutima's direction. I didn't like abandoning my breakfast on such a dismal morning, but since I was here, I was determined to satisfy my curiosity. And if I waited for my family to stop talking, I might be forced to stand in the back, where I would see almost nothing.

"What's going on?" I whispered as Samiqwas and I squatted beside Kutima. He glanced at me, but didn't give me his usual smile.

"Nothing—yet."

I made a rude noise and his mouth twitched. I waited. Finally he said, "My mother's been crying and my father's very angry."

But surely his parents' quarrelling was no reason to summon the whole village? Before I could think of a suitable insult, he dropped a bees' nest of news in my lap.

"There are more soldiers camped by the Socanna River. They're coming here, I think."

"More soldiers than were on the paddle-wheeler?" Samiqwas asked.

Kutima shrugged. "Maybe, or maybe they just got off the boat before it got to the post."

"Why would they do that?" I asked.

Kutima shook his head, but wouldn't look at me. He kept his eyes focused on the floor between his knees.

Samiqwas and I exchanged anxious glances over his bowed head. The presence of more soldiers didn't sound good. "Kutima, are there many more soldiers, and why didn't they come openly into the village? Do you know?"

At the sound of his name, he jerked his head up. Receiving no response, I repeated my question. At last, he said, "I don't know. I didn't see them, but I heard the fat man talking to my father last night."

"Maybe they're here to make all those crazy miners go home," Samiqwas suggested.

Recalling my dream, I shook my head. "No, I don't think so."

"Well then, maybe the war that Jombonni and the priest speak of is coming closer. Maybe the soldiers are here to protect us."

"Protect the miners, you mean," Kutima muttered barely above a whisper.

"What?"

Kutima made a noncommittal noise. Then, the priest, dressed in his ceremonial blue robe, came out of his little room behind the dais, stepped to the altar, and there was no more time for questions. Someone shouted, and the people outside filed in.

When everyone was settled, the priest tossed incense into the brazier. Turning to face the god he raised his hands and intoned a long monotonous prayer. During the incantation Trader Jombonni and two other Chamuqwani entered, walked down the centre aisle, and waited with the people in the front row for the priest to finish.

Jombonni had on his black wool coat and trousers, just as if it were a holiday. His white shirt must have been buttoned too tightly around his neck, however, because his face was a deep pink.

Carrying a scroll in one hand, the stout Father Emperor's official with sagging jowls was dressed in a similar black coat and white shirt.

On Jombonni's other side, a Chamuqwani soldier—and a high ranking one if the gold and black trim on his jacket was any indication—waited. This man's skin was so dark a brown that it looked almost black against his smoke grey uniform. Under his thick leather helmet, I could see wisps of his black hair as tightly curled as mountain sheep wool.

Jombonni was speaking to his companions in a low-voiced murmur, but they ignored him. I glanced at Kutima—hoping he would enlighten me, but the look on his face silenced my question before the words left my lips.

Then I forgot about Kutima, because the priest had finished his prayer. Throwing up his hands in defeat, Jombonni followed the others to the platform and turned to address his waiting audience. The Spirit-Fire surrounding his head pulsed with pent-up rage, and his voice roughened with emotion as he began to speak.

"These men have asked me to translate the Father Emperor's words to you. These aren't my words that I'll speak. I want you to know that, my friends. I only do what these men require."

Jombonni nodded to the man wearing the ice bear's badge. The trading company's official took a pace forward and unrolled his scroll. He read the words in a loud voice, pausing now and then for Jombonni to translate. The speech was confusing, but finally he said things that were too terrible to contemplate.

"Your lonely isolation in this harsh wilderness is ended. Thanks to the beneficence of our kind Father Emperor, you will become loyal and productive subjects of the Empire at long last.

"As I'm sure your trader has already explained to you, The Empire is under attack from evil men to the east. We need the gold rock found in your land to help with the war effort. Lord Hiram your trading company's patron is angered by the trouble between your people and his miners.

"So to prevent further unpleasantness that would hinder the mining, you must accept the Father Emperor's judgment. You must all become good servants of the Empire and leave this lake for a new home we are preparing for you elsewhere in our vast land."

A stunned silence fell over the hall as he finished and rolled up his scroll. My chest emptied of breath as blackness swirled at the edges of my vision. What was that crazy fat man talking about? Samiqwas muttered a bad word in the Chamuqwani language and gripped a fist about the handle of his knife. Leave?

My breath felt tight in my chest. Where could we possibly go? The lord's man went on at more length about how this was the best solution for everyone, but I stopped listening. I felt the ghostly slither of icy scales down my backbone and shivered.

Three winters past, the bonded men of this rich Lord Hiram sledded in and built a tent settlement at the mouth of Yellow Stone Creek. My uncle Tli and several other men with dog teams had been paid handsomely to carry in supplies to this new camp. But supplies alone weren't enough to help these foolish southerners survive in our homeland. Cloth tents provide little shelter from the icy winds of a northern winter. Even with our help, food and fuel ran short. Many of the miners died from the slim rations, frostbite, and their own ignorance.

We thought they would leave the next spring, but instead the ones who survived stayed. And more arrived, as soon as the break-up ice cleared the river. All this activity worried many in the village. These intruders no longer seemed so stupid and harmless.

At first, the miners stayed in their camp up the lake, digging and fighting amongst themselves. That area was no family's trapping territory, so we left them to their own squabbles. But of late, some of our fishermen had come upon parties of miners down by our end of the lake, sifting through the waters in clan-owned territory. They'd been run off of course, but often they returned with their thunder-weapons to enforce their claims.

The grumbling increased as the miners claimed more and more tribal land. Some young men threatened to drive all the foreigners from our home, but I hadn't realized anyone took their ridiculous talk seriously.

I was wrong. Evidently the traders or the miners had been worried enough to petition their emperor to remove us.

When the lord's man finished and rolled up the scroll, the people looked at one another. Leave? Impossible. This lake was more than a dead piece of ground to us, something to be used and discarded. How could we abandon a place whose essence was woven into the fabric of our very souls?

After a long wait in which the clan mothers whispered among themselves, a man arose from among them and stepped forward. Tsanqwati was our headman, and carried the sacred bundle of the Peace Keeper. He was the one chosen by the clans to speak for us with outsiders. He was a tall man for my people, who tended to be short and square-built as a rule. He wore his iron-grey hair in two long braids tied with leather thongs. Normally, his angular face wore a gentle expression, but at that moment his beak of a nose and cold eyes reminded me of a bird of prey rather than a kindly uncle.

Rudely turning his back to the fat man, Tsanqwati said, "Trader Jombonni, explain to these arrogant strangers. This land was placed in our care by the Unseen Ones. Who told the Chamuqwani otherwise? Our ancestors' bones lie here. Who is he to say we must leave?"

Jombonni's face turned a deeper shade of red. "You'll have no choice. A treaty has been signed between the Qwani'ya people and the Father Emperor. The soldiers will *make* you leave, and I can't stop them."

Hearing Jombonni's answer, a low muttering like the buzzing of angry insects, began among the young men clustered by the door.

Tsanqwati conferred with the elders again, then addressing the Chamuqwani directly, he tried a different argument. "We have heard the words of the great lord and the Father Emperor in the south, and we thank him for his interest in us. What we don't understand is how our leaving the lake will help him win his war. Who will fish for his soldiers? Who will trap furs to keep his people warm in winter if we go somewhere else? These foreigners, these miners can't do that. They are bad hunters and fishermen."

Jombonni translated Tsanqwati's words for the men and then listened to their reply. When he turned back to us, he had to clear his throat several times before he could get the words out. "They say that the gold is more important than fish and furs."

Tsanqwati stared incredulously at the fat man. Then he turned to the trader to translate. "A man can't feed his hungry children with rocks—no matter how pretty. Nor will these rocks warm his body on cold winter nights, but furs and smoked fish can keep people alive. Jombonni, tell him to set aside the imaginings of a foolish child and behave like a sensible man. Tell these foreigners to forget about yellow rocks."

Jombonni hesitated, but when pressed he rendered a halting translation. "They say that you don't understand the world outside these isolated mountains. With enough gold they can trade for all the fish and furs they need elsewhere."

"And what will happen to our land when all the yellow rocks are gone? Will these strangers just abandon the land wounded and bleeding? Who will care for the ancestors and the animals when we are far away? Who will restore the harmony that they destroy? Their priests? I don't think so."

Jombonni took a deep breath and continued, "They want you to leave this lake and go to a new place further south. The Father Emperor has promised that by signing his treaty everyone will have plenty to eat and lots of new clothing on this 'Tribal Allotted Preserve' they're setting aside especially for you."

Tsanqwati frowned. "What is this 'treaty' that you speak of? I don't know that Chamuqwani word."

Jombonni glanced at the official, then took a deep breath. "They say there's a paper with Chamuqwani writing on it. The writing says that the

Qwani'yaTsa'adi people give the Chamuqwani their northern lands in exchange for new land further south in the Tribal Preserve."

Angry murmurs grew in volume among the villagers. Tsanqwati's face darkened with emotion, he made a cutting gesture with one hand and the people quieted. "What Qwani'ya people signed such a thing—no one from this village."

"I know," Jombonni said, "but they say it doesn't matter. The treaty has been signed and everyone must go."

"Will we be allowed to come home when they have taken all the yellow rocks they want?" Tsanqwati pressed.

"I don't know. But it'll be good for everyone on this Tribal Allotted Preserve, they say. The children will be taught the Chamuqwani magic of how to read and write in books like my black ledger book. They'll grow up to become good citizens of the empire like all the other peoples of this big land. They promise it is a good place, and you'll be happy there."

"Happy?" Our headman's back straightened, suddenly as stiff as an arrow shaft. "How can these strangers know better than we do ourselves what is good for us? This is our home. Our ancestors' bones lie here. We can't go. We wouldn't be happy on another people's territory. Our Qwakaiva is a part of this land. We would sicken and die if we lose our Qwakaiva. No one from this village signed any Chamuqwani paper. We aren't going anywhere." A stubborn thrust to his jaw, Tsanqwati folded his arms across his chest as if the matter was now settled.

Jombonni's expression conveyed pity, but his next words were spears of ice in our hearts. "Oh, my friends, you have no choice," Jombonni said. "The soldiers are here to see that nothing stops the mining. And after the trouble yesterday it has been decided—over my protests—that the only way to have peace, is to make you leave. If you don't go willingly, they will kill you. Please, think of the children and don't do anything rash."

From outside someone shouted a warning and a soldier barked an order. As the young men rushed the door, they were shoved back inside by soldiers with long knives stuck on the ends of their thunder-weapons. Pandemonium suddenly took over the room. A woman screamed when a soldier knocked her husband to the floor. Children cried for their mothers. Men and women climbed over one another in a desperate attempt to reach the outside.

Another man fell, before the crowd blocked my view. Jombonni and the old priest begged the People to stay calm, but no one was listening. The scent of fresh blood stung my nose. Tendrils of black fear writhed through the haze of the incense-laden air.

At the first sign of trouble, Samiqwas grabbed the dazed Kutima, and the three of us backed against the wall behind the altar, trying to keep out of the way.

Now I wished I hadn't been so eager to be so near the front. I longed for the comfort of my family. I could feel Kutima trembling where his shoulder brushed against mine. Samiqwas was trembling, too; but it wasn't the fear scent I smelled on him or saw dancing in his Spirit-Fire. It was rage.

Then to my astonishment, my brother-cousin grabbed Kutima by his shirt, twisted the fabric tight about his neck, and spun him around. "Stinking pile of fish guts! You knew this would happen, didn't you?"

Like his father, Kutima was tall—taller than Samiqwas—but he was soft and no match for my cousin's hard-muscled fury. Wide-eyed Kutima stammered something unintelligible. Samiqwas slammed him backward. His head bumped against the wall, causing him to bite his tongue. "Answer me, Dog Fart. You knew. Admit it."

Blood trickled out of the corner of Kutima's mouth and onto his chin. "Brother-Cousin, what are you doing? What's wrong with you?" I laid my hand on his shoulder, and he spun to face me snarling like a wolf. The hard, yellow eyes of his Guardian glared at me from the Spirit-Fire about his head.

"Wrong? Wake up, Tas. Pull your mind out of your dreams. Can't you see it? He *knew* the soldiers were going to make us leave, and he said nothing. If he had told us, we could have warned—"

Angry now himself, Kutima yanked free and faced us defiantly, eyes blazing with indignation. "Yes, I knew. I admit it. And what would have happened, if I had told you or Tas, hmm? Would things be any different?"

"We could have warned them." I said quietly. "I thought you were my friend."

Kutima brushed a hand across his face, wiping some of the blood onto his sleeve. He swallowed the rest and glared at Samiqwas. My expression must have revealed the depth of my feelings, because his voice softened when he said, "Oh, Tas, I'm sorry. But if I *had* told you what I suspected, would your family have believed you?"

Samiqwas and I looked at each other. The idea of being forced to leave our homeland was so preposterous I could hardly believe it even now. No, they wouldn't have believed it. They would have thought our wild tale no more than a childish game.

"The soldiers are too many and their weapons too strong," Kutima said, pressing his argument. "If your uncle Tli and the others try to fight they'll die. I couldn't tell—I didn't want to be responsible for their deaths—and my father ..." Kutima's voice trailed off as he fought for control.

I let my bad feelings go and tried to think of what I might have done in his situation.

Kutima must have sensed Samiqwas's unrelenting anger, because he said, "I know you don't think much of me; I don't care. My father has arranged for my mother and me to stay with him, but I choose to go with my people. That's why I'm here today, instead of hiding at home."

While our attention was diverted, the soldier standing beside the trading company's official had removed the thunder-weapon from the sheath at his hip. Pointing it towards the ceiling, he fired. There was a bright flash, its roar nearly deafened me and tiny rock chips pelted down among us.

The weapon had the desired effect; everyone stopped what they were doing and fell silent, facing the men at the front of the room once more. When the echoes of the shot died away and all was quiet again, the soldier spoke in a hard voice that made his words all the more terrible for their lack of emotion. Jombonni translated.

"Commander Mu'Dar says you must not fight his men or you'll be killed without mercy. Men, women or children, it doesn't matter to him. You'll die if you don't obey."

When my people greeted his threat with angry words of their own, a ghost of a smile curved his full lips. He lowered his weapon to point directly at one of the clan mothers standing in the front of the crowd. The cold yellow eyes of a spotted cat watched me from the shifting colours of the Spirit-Flame above his head.

The commander wasn't afraid; he wanted to kill and would welcome our resistance. I followed the direction of his pointing weapon, and my eyes widened. How had he known Ina was our most precious lore keeper? Had he only guessed, or had Jombonni betrayed us? If we lost her—my mind couldn't imagine such a disaster.

Unafraid, the wizened old woman never moved. Eyes as hard as obsidian pebbles, she met his stare. People around her froze. Someone shouted for the angry people in the back of the room to be quiet. The priest continued to mumble his prayers. Jombonni made an ineffectual protest of his own, but the soldier never wavered, and the trader fell silent.

"Since you choose to challenge my authority, you'll remain here in this hall until the steamboat is ready to take you south."

When Jombonni finished translating, Tsanqwati stepped forward again, and this time addressed the soldier. "It's true we don't have the weapons to resist you, but what of our family members who aren't here. What will you do with them? And what of our tied-up sled dogs, who will feed them? If we are forced to make this long journey, we will need our warm clothing, bedding, and food. Allow us to return to our homes to collect these things."

By that time, the priest was paying more attention to the proceedings and loudly voiced his opinion of the captain's plan. He wasn't any happier than we were, about having us cooped up in the temple—for who knew how long. From the little I could understand, however, the old windbag wasn't protesting our leaving our home, but only his inconvenience, and the mess we would make.

The soldier ignored his protests as if they were no more than the drone of an annoying insect. Commander Mu'Dar kept his eyes focused forward and gave the headman another of his terrible smiles. "So you can run away into the mountains and make me waste precious time chasing you? I don't think so. You'll remain here. And as for your missing tribesmen, they are being rounded up as we speak. They'll be with you shortly."

Adding the truth to his words, I heard Grandmother's shouts and Seicu's hysterical crying as rough hands thrust them stumbling into the hall. Moments later other indignant people were also shoved into our midst.

Samiqwas pushed himself off the wall, but I clamped a hand on his arm and made him stay.He shot me an angry look, then relaxed. He couldn't possibly make it through the crowd at that moment. Other relatives were closer; they would care for his little sister. He must wait.

When he finished translating those harsh words, Jombonni angrily turned to the soldier. A heated argument broke out between the four men on the platform. When it ended, unshed tears of frustration welled in the corners of the trader's eyes as he turned back to face us.

"This soldier is a hard man. Believe me; he'll do what he promises, so don't anger him. But I have convinced him to let a woman from each family return to your homes to collect supplies for the trip. The soldiers will escort the women in small groups to get your things. Then they'll bring them back here to wait with the rest of the People. The dogs will be cared for. I know they are valuable animals. They'll be useful to the newcomers. You'll be paid for them; don't worry. I'm sorry. That is the best I can do for you."

As soon as he finished, the priest reluctantly spoke a blessing, and the four men started for the door.

Suddenly Jombonni became aware of Kutima. With a curse, he grabbed his son and shook him. "What were you thinking of to come here? I told you it wasn't safe—I told you to stay at home with your mother."

"I wanted to be with my people—"

Jombonni slapped him hard. Blood trickled from Kutima's mouth again. "You stupid whelp! Your people? Who am I then?"

Their low-voiced conversation faded as the trader hurried to catch up with the others, dragging Kutima behind him. Once they were outside, the door was slammed and locked.

Chapter Eight

Without waiting for me, Samiqwas pushed his way through groups of distraught people as soon as the outer door closed. Yelling for him to wait, I trailed the best I could in his wake. Though the gather hall was large enough to hold the entire village on a holiday, at that moment, with so many people milling about, the search for our family made it seem vast.

We found them at last, claiming a space against the back wall. Grandmother sat with Grandfather's arm about her shoulders. She'd resisted the soldiers and they'd beaten her before hauling her to the temple. In spite of the bruises on her face, she managed to look as fierce as a mother bear protecting her cubs.

Aunt Tuulah had forgotten her quarrel with her husband and now huddled in Ko's arms, sobbing quietly. At her mother's feet, Seicu hugged herself, looking small and bewildered. She brightened and held out her arms when she saw her brother. Mother gave me one of her sad smiles when Samiqwas and I sat beside her.

I glanced around me then asked, "Amima, where is Esuuli?" I thought I'd pitched my voice so only Mother would hear, but it was Aunt Tuulah who answered me.

"That Tsali boy better take care of her good or—"

"Hush now," Ko soothed her. "He's a good young hunter. The soldiers won't catch them. Be at peace, my heart."

Grandmother snorted and sat up a little straighter, glaring at him. "How can my daughter be at peace? If they find Esuuli and the young man, they'll be sent away like the rest of us. And if they escape into the mountains, Esuuli will be lost to her clan forever. Carrion eaters!"

She made the hand sign for hexing someone with evil. My eyes flew wide. "Kunai, kill them all!" she muttered.

Grandfather seized her hand and held on to it, before she could conjure any more curses. "Enough, Woman, do you want to bring bad luck upon us as well? This is a dangerous time. Every word and action of ours has power. We must be very careful—very careful, if we want to survive. The Chamuqwani will suffer for their crimes without your meddling. Let it be. Pray instead for the Unseen Ones to protect us."

I'd never seen him so angry before, and it frightened me. My grandmother, too, wasn't used to him chastising her so openly. Her face darkened. She opened her mouth as if to put him in his place, then she must have realized that it wasn't her husband, but the Otter's Qwakaihi, who was speaking to her. Like air seeping from a fish bladder she folded in upon herself, covering her face with her hands trembling.

Grandfather watched her silently for a long moment, his expression stern, then he relented and pulled her into his arms. To offer them some privacy, the rest of us looked away.

Though I thought myself nearing manhood, I suddenly felt as frightened and as helpless as a babe. I wished I could crawl into Mother's lap like Seicu, but my pride wouldn't allow me to go that far. I did, however, move a little closer to my mother and made no objection when she brushed a cool hand across my tangled hair.

"Don't worry about your sister-cousin; she is a woman now," Mother assured me. "She would have brought Tsali as husband to our home soon enough. If he is as brave a hunter as Ko thinks, then they have as good a chance as any of us to survive. Once we're gone, I doubt if the foreigners will look very hard for the runaways. They'll be too busy digging in the dirt to care."

"And it's good that some of our people remain here to comfort the ancestors," Ko added. "They need to know that we haven't willingly abandoned them."

"True words, sister's husband, though sad ones," Mother said.

"Ati," Samiqwas said, "why didn't some of our Qwani'ya men fight the Chamuqwani and keep them as hostages until the soldiers outside agreed to let us go?"

He considered the question for a moment, then said, "We have squabbles, like any large family, and sometimes those disputes are settled in blood, but such things are rare among us. Everything happened so fast, they probably didn't think of it."

"But if our young men—"

"Like an unhappy sled dog, they make a lot of noise, but rarely bite," Aunt Tuulah grumbled.

"Be glad of that, Sister," Mother said. "Violence only makes more trouble. Maybe it's good that surviving the long cold-time takes too much of our Qwakaiva to have any left over for making war."

"Too bad for us, then," I muttered, staring her in the eye. "Is my father a warrior? Maybe you should have taken Grandmother's advice. Maybe he could have stopped them." Her mouth dropped open with shock, as if I'd slapped her.

"Tasimu," Aunt Tuulah cried. "Show some respect. What's a matter with you? Is everyone drunk or crazy today—"

"Are you all right, Mother?" a man's voice said. Startled, we looked up to see Uncle Tli standing over us. A long cut oozed a trail of blood down his cheek, and he held his arm awkwardly, as if it hurt him.

"Tli," Mother gasped, "Were you fighting?"

Uncle Tli waved her question away. "Mother?"

Grandmother rested her hands in her lap and looked up. "The soldiers hit me, but I'll survive. Don't trouble yourself on my account." Then as if seeing him clearly for the first time, her mouth hardened. "Chamuqwani carrion eaters—what did they do to you?"

"It's nothing. I'm fine—"

"You don't look fine," she snapped. "how badly are you injured?"

"Forget about it, Mother. Didn't I say it was nothing?"

For just a moment I saw the hurt in her eyes, then she grimly nodded, accepting his answer.

"Your arm looks painful, Son, let me help you," Grandfather said.

"Maybe later. I need to go—my wife…" and with that he was gone.

"Tli's mother-in-law tries to keep too tight a leash on him," Aunt Tuulah complained as she watched her brother pick his way carefully through the various family groups. "What is the matter with the woman? Tli has responsibilities to his own people as well as her daughter. She'd better have a care, or her daughter will need a new bed mate. Tli will not stand for her bossing forever."

Oh no, he definitely won't want to stay with his wife, I thought to myself. *He will want to come home so more bossy women can tell him what to do.* Out of the corner of my eye, I saw Ko glance at Grandfather and roll his eyes. Grandfather saw the look, but kept his face expressionless.

Once the doors were closed there was little light in the hall—and no food, so we just sat with friends and relatives on the cold floor and waited. To pass the time, I took out the loop of leather cord I always kept in a pouch at my waist and began idly making string figures between my hands.

Seicu saw me and squealed with joy. "Story, story, make pictures tell me story, Little Rock Squirrel."

I made a face. *Am I doomed to be always called that baby name?* With my stomach churning and my mind in turmoil, the last thing I wanted to do was make up stories for her.

Mother saw my look and patted my shoulder reassuringly. "Go ahead." She motioned with her chin to Samiqwas, who looked nearly as bewildered as I felt. "You both can play with her. It will help pass the time."

MY VOICE WAS GROWING hoarse when Grandfather announced, "I'm going to walk around and see if anyone needs my help." He turned to me. "Do you want to come with me?"

Deliverance! I scrambled to my feet. "Oh yes."

A ghost of a smile curved his lips. "Come along then."

As we walked among the people, I glanced at his empty hands, and asked, "Grandfather, without your medicines what can you do to help the injured?"

"Not much," he admitted. "But talk can soothe a frightened Spirit, and my Gift can ease their pain somewhat."

"I wish my own special Gift was healing—like yours," "I muttered. "Seeing terrible visions and hearing ghosts aren't much fun or useful."

"Perhaps Qwa'osi will gift you with that power if you study harder the lessons I give you, eh?"

I nodded, unable to speak, a lump of hurt and frustration choking back my words. I wanted to please him—and I did try—truly I did. Like Fire and Earth or Wind and Water our Qwakaivas didn't exactly oppose one another, but neither were they compatible—or so Grandfather had hinted many times when I failed at a lesson he'd given me.

"I want to help; please will you show me again what I must do?"

"We'll see. You're a good boy."

As we threaded our way among the families, snatches of conversations caught my attention. "Those men running from the soldiers warned us. We should have listened and gone with them deeper into the mountains."

"And what would you feed your children, hmm? There's little game on those high slopes. Those people are probably all dead by now—"

"Pray, brothers. Mighty Djoven will protect us—"

Derisive laughter, "I don't trust any Chamuqwani—even their god—"

"True enough. The Chamuqwani know more about conjuring than they'd like us to believe. That old priest cursed us. He's a malicer."

A malicer? That was a chilling thought.

THE CHAMUQWANI GOD'S temple wasn't large, and with most of the village locked inside, there was no room to stretch out and rest. We just sat with friends and relatives on the cold floor and waited. There was little light in the hall—and no food. Much later, some strips of dry-meat and buckets of water were handed inside. Then the doors were relocked, and we were left to our misery.

There was also no privy. In a gesture of defiance, people began pissing and defecating behind the statue of the Chamuqwani god. This irreverence made those who had accepted the priest's teachings angry. They were afraid of what the god or the soldiers would do to us in reprisal. The sacrilege was a meaningless gesture perhaps, but when I let my piss spray upon the god's robes, it made me feel a little better. He was letting these soldiers take us away. I hated him. He didn't deserve my respect.

During our first day of confinement, more relatives returned home, were captured and thrust inside the temple with us, but not Esuuli and her lover. I prayed they'd seen the danger and crept away into the mountains.

Shilshigua's maternal cousin's two young daughters were also among the missing. Her black hair tangled around her face, her shawl hanging by a loose end from her belt, the distraught woman pounded on the outer door with someone's walking stick, screaming.

"Let me out, let me out! Oh, please, I won't run away. I just want to find my children—please."

Her pleas were collecting the interest of the young men huddled in their own council. Moving as of one mind, they approached the door, adding their own raucous shouts to the din. When Tli headed that way along with Shilshigua's brother Chugai, I touched Grandfather's sleeve, drawing his attention to the group.

Grandfather had stopped to converse with some clan elders and Tsanqwati before heading back to our family. I didn't have to say anything. He could see the jagged spears of red lightning exploding in the young men's Spirit-Fire as well as I could. There was going to be trouble—and Tli would be right in the middle of it again.

Turning back to the headman, Grandfather murmured something that I didn't catch. The next thing I knew the elders were heading towards the door, their expressions grim. Grandfather had forgotten about me. I tagged along in his wake, trying not to draw attention to myself. I focused my mind on images of white hares standing perfectly still in drifts of new snow. I needn't have worried. Grandfather's focus was centred totally upon his son. I could feel the tingle of his Qwakaiva raising the hair at the back of my neck as he gathered power around himself.

The elders had just convinced everyone to sit down without further trouble, when the soldiers opened the door to let in an old man and spoiled their efforts. As soon as the door opened, Shilshigua's cousin saw her chance to look for her children and squeezed through the opening.

Once outside her headlong rush faltered when she tripped on her shawl. Soldiers shouted and a big blond-haired man with a scar on his cheek grabbed her and knocked her backward into the temple with his fist. Chugai hit the soldier, and he tripped over the fallen woman, crashing to the floor.

Uncle Tli shouted and lunged for the door, but Grandfather grabbed him, pulling him back. "Don't be a fool, My Son, this is pointless."

To my astonishment Tli cursed him and continued his struggle. The hair rose on the back of my neck as Grandfather's Spirit-Fire flared bright silver, and Tli suddenly went rigid, his mouth dropping open in surprise. Unable to move, he seemed caught in the mesh of an invisible fishnet.

"Let me go, Father," Tli growled.

"I will. When you calm yourself and once again have reason." Tli glared, but made no more attempts to free himself.

Cursing and lashing out with their weapons, the soldiers retrieved their fallen comrade and banged the door shut on the shouting people. Seeming not to be aware of her bleeding face, the weeping woman hurled herself once more at the heavy door, screaming.

Grandfather let out a long sigh and released Tli from his power. He stepped away rolling his shoulders. Trails of red stained the back of his shirt. "You're bleeding again from the whipping. Let me help you."

Tli turned, scowling. Ashen-faced, Grandfather leaned against the wall and met his stare. Neither spoke for a long moment, but at last Tli dropped his eyes. He looked like he wanted to cry, but instead he snarled, "I don't want—or need—your help. So much power and your only thought is to use it to stop me from going to the aid of my wife's cousin. If you can do so much, why do you let them confine us in this stinking place? Why don't you use your Qwakaiva to help us drive them from our land?"

Grandfather rubbed a hand over his face. His Spirit-Fire shrank to a thin pale line, exhaustion blurring his features. "Though what I did may seem a wondrous thing to you, it isn't. I would need power many times stronger than I possess before I could turn back this evil. All I could manage was to save my son from possible death at the enemy's hands this day."

Tli snorted. "I don't believe you. And don't expect me to be grateful—because I won't thank you. You are a coward—afraid to use your power to help us. You shame me and your ancestors."

Grandfather blinked, as startled as I was by the venom in my uncle's words. Drawing himself up stiffly, Grandfather said, "I'm no coward—and you know that—but now isn't the time to explain further. Your mind is too clouded with emotion to listen. Believe what you like—as is your right."

"I will," Tli said and stalked off to sit with his wife and her family.

When he was gone, I took Grandfather's arm. My presence startled him, then without a word, he allowed me to lead him back to where our family waited. When we arrived he sat down and covered his face with his blanket, leaving me to answer the women's anxious questions.

Time passed—agonizingly slow; I thought I might die of boredom. The fire in the brazier went out. The light coming through the tiny windows near the ceiling faded away into the grey of a long summer twilight.Our first night of confinement had begun. Shilshigua's cousin's hysterical pleading gave way to a monotonous sobbing that hovered at the edge of my awareness. Children cried themselves to sleep. Men and women talked in low voices, slapped at the black flies, or slept leaning against one another. The entire hall stank of feces, stale incense, and fear sweat.

None of the women had been allowed out to collect our possessions. Outside we heard the Chamuqwani celebrating, and feared the worst.

Chapter Nine

I slept a great deal during our confinement, my mind drifting in a trancelike state over which I had little control. As if the waters of the lake were closing over me, I found it hard to struggle against a soul-numbing lethargy. I was drowning in it. The black current of despair tore me away from the emerald green shallows, dragging my Spirit into the icy abyss.

Around me in the blackness unknown creatures brushed their cool scaly bodies against my skin, sucking away my warmth as they passed. I felt unseen eyes upon me, measuring my worth. I shivered, and was afraid. The otter claw amulet was a comforting weight under my shirt, but I feared my soul was too deep for the otter warrior to find me, for like me, Qwa'osi and his rival Co'yeh were air breathers. Only Kunai could help me, but what gift could I offer to melt the Aseutl's cold heart? I didn't know, and so I floated in the abyss and waited ...

Commander Mu'Dar kept his word and allowed a woman from each family to return to her lodge to collect supplies for our journey. But he waited till the second day of our confinement and by then the miners had looted the village, taking whatever suited them.

Eyes moist with unshed tears Mother and Aunt Tuulah stumbled back into the temple with only a few cracked baskets and some ragged bedding. Face dark as a thunderstorm, Grandmother rose to meet them. "Was this all the soldiers would let you bring?"

Aunt Tuulah dropped her bundle and sank to the cold floor beside it. Tired from worry and a sleepless night, new lines of exhaustion etched her round face. "This was all that was *left*, Mother. Those filthy miners took everything else."

Ko briefly inspected her few belongings and swore a soldier's curse. "So much for the honour of the Chamuqwani."

Coming over to hear the news and see our supplies, Aunty Qwatsitsa snorted with disgust and folded her arms across her bony chest. "My daughters tell the same story. And how, I wonder, do they expect us to survive on this journey without proper blankets, warm clothing and food?"

"Maybe they don't," Grandmother said as she looked into one of Mother's baskets. "Maybe they're hoping we'll all die along the way."

Seicu whimpered and crawled into her brother's lap. Samiqwas hugged her close, looking fierce. Then, plastering a smile onto his face, he bounced her on his knee to make her laugh.

I shivered, the cold hand of a foretelling touching the back of my neck. "Surely not, Ami!" I blurted. "Why would anyone do such a terrible thing?"

"I doubt if they want to, Grandson," Grandfather said, giving Grandmother a reproachful look. "The Chamuqwani are just short-sighted, like the beetles crawling among the tree roots. They don't take into account the consequences of their words and actions."

"Until it's too late," the old aunty said.

"Until it's too late," he agreed.

"Well, I'm going to tell Tsanqwati," she announced. "These Chamuqwani need to pay for what they've stolen."

Grandmother rose to her feet. "I'll go with you. The next time the door opens to allow in the returning women, we'll tell them we want to see Jombonni and the lord's man. If they want us to go with them they'll have to make it right."

"How far away is this new Tribal Preserve?" I asked.

Grandfather shook his head and spread his hands as he rose to follow the women. "No one knows."

"Maybe the Chamuqwani themselves don't know," Samiqwas whispered only loud enough for me to hear.

Mother watched the elders go, then she turned to her sister, and asked, "Do you think the soldiers or the trading company's man will make the miners give back what they've stolen?"

"No. But most families still have credit left at the post. Maybe we'll be allowed to buy enough supplies to last us on this journey."

I hoped so. In another two moons—maybe less—winter would touch our northern homeland with its icy breath.

ON THE FOURTH MORNING of our confinement, the soldiers passed in buckets of hot tea, pieces of hard flat bread, and a foul-smelling stew. It was the first hot meal I'd eaten since Mother's good fish soup the morning after the Dance. It tasted like boiled dog turds, but I choked it down anyway.

After the meal, the soldiers' interpreter announced that heavily armed soldiers would separate the young men like Ko and Uncle Tli from their families. He also warned us that if the men resisted, some of the children and the old people would die.

"How could anyone be so cruel?" Aunt Tuulah wondered.

"They are all wannigua demons," Ko snarled as he stood. He glanced at the grim-faced soldiers outside the open doorway, and then back at his youngest daughter, holding tight to her mother's hand.

"You're right for once, daughter's husband," Grandmother said. "Only a monster could do such a thing." Ko gave her a grudging nod. He turned back to the doorway, smoothing out the angry expression on his face. As he walked outside, he held out his hands for the shackles without a protest.

The smell within the temple was unbearable, and I for one was grateful to be going anywhere. When I stumbled outside blinking in the bright light, I took in a big lungful of the cool air to clear my head. Nothing to me had ever smelled so sweet as the damp lake wind on that terrible day.

As Samiqwas emerged from the temple just behind me, he stepped boldly up to one of the soldiers and held his hands out for the chains. The soldier blinked, then burst out laughing. Samiqwas's face darkened, but he stood as straight as a fir tree with his hands outstretched.

No one could deny Samiqwas was big for his age, but he was hardly a man. I dropped my eyes; why was he making a spectacle of himself? Then I happened to glance at the line of our chained men. Pride shown in Ko and my uncle's eyes. Samiqwas looked so fierce, standing there defying the Chamuqwani. His age didn't matter to them. The courage of a hunter and warrior beat strong in my brother-cousin's heart.

Samiqwas. I wish I'd thought to do the same thing.

When it was clear that he had no intention of moving, one of the soldiers slammed the butt of his weapon into my cousin's back. Samiqwas let out a surprised grunt and sprawled in the dirt. I rushed forward to help him up. As I did, I made an obscene gesture the Chamuqwani traders used when they were angry at one another. I received a painful slap that bloodied my nose, which made me feel a bit better.

The dark-skinned soldier might have done me further damage, but Mother, normally such a quiet gentle person, surprised everyone by punching him in return. Almost as astounded by her assault as he had been by Samiqwas's defiance, he stared open-mouthed as she shouted at him in the broken Chamuqwani she'd learned from the trader and his wife.

"Cowards, what kind of man you are to hit child? Your mother be shamed she bear you." Someone shouted a praise call, and the chained men stirred restlessly.

The situation might have progressed to further violence, if an officer hadn't noticed and barked an order that soon put an end to the trouble. I took my place beside Mother. Basking in the admiring looks directed our way, Samiqwas and I grinned at each other behind the adults' backs, wearing our battle scars with pride.

When everyone was lined up outside the temple, they marched us in a long line down the path to where the steamboat waited.

"Slime eating zaunk." Grimy, foul-tongued men in dirty canvas trews, patched tunics, and wide-brimmed hats, the miners stood in small groups, passing round jugs of waskyja and yelling insults.

"Should'a got rid of 'em a'for now, filthy Zaunks," Someone called.

"You got that right, By Mighty Djoven's hairy balls, get a whiff of that smell!" a black bearded man with a greasy vest shouted.

The soldiers cursed us, too. "Hurry along, you lazy zaunkBastards. We don't have all day. Move!" When the officer wasn't looking, some of them prodded us with their weapons to show off for the miners.

I glanced over my shoulder at my grandparents walking silently behind us, pleading for an answer. How could this be happening to us? Grandfather returned my look, but his expression remained impenetrable. He had no answers to give me, and perhaps that frightened me most of all.

Mother walked beside me, carrying a blanket roll of our possessions. She seemed unconcerned by the abuse. But no matter how I tried to ignore them, the men's animosity settled about my shoulders like a water-soaked blanket. "Why do they hate us so much, Amima?"

At her puzzled expression, I repeated my question. She thought about her answer for a few steps, then sighed and shook her head. "I don't know, but don't let it trouble you. They're very unhappy people. We should feel sorry for them and pray for them."

Incredulous, I jerked to a stop and stared up at her. "Pray for them? Feel sorry for them? How can you say that, Amima? After what they are doing to us, they deserve my hatred, my vengeance, not my prayers."

"Keep moving," a soldier snarled, and pointed his weapon at me.

Gently Mother put a hand to my back urging me forward. "If you let their evil fester inside you it'll poison your Spirit. Treat their words like water rolling off a lake seal's oily back. Ignore them."

Ignore them? Fingering the knife concealed by a fold of my shirt, I stole a look at the soldier walking behind us. "I can't do that," I muttered.

Retreating once more into her own thoughts, I doubted if Mother even heard me.

When we arrived at the dock with the onlookers in our wake, the paddle-wheeler's engine was already rumbling. Its lower deck was piled high with cargo for the return trip downriver. Black smoke boiled out of its tall smoke stacks to mingle with the grey mists over the water. Snugged up tight against the boat's bow was a long barge made of rough planks, placed over a sturdy raft of logs. On either side of the raft, long cables were attached that ran back to winches on the lower deck of the steamboat.

I learned later that the cables and winches were there to help turn the unwieldy raft and keep it in the channel. Also to help steer, several crewmen with long sweep oars stood poised on the raft's rim, ready to guide the clumsy float out into the lake once we were loaded on board.

I wondered how the raft had arrived at the trader's dock without notice. Then I remembered the string of miner's flatboats and rafts the paddle-wheeler had been towing this year. During the past four days, while we were confined in the temple, the Chamuqwani must have taken apart those floats and built this larger raft.

"What a stupid sad joke," Samiqwas murmured as he came alongside me. "We're going to be the boats' main cargo this year, not the salted fish and furs."

The raft they forced us aboard was nothing more than a long float with a flimsy, waist-high wooden rail built around its outer edge to keep back some of the wet. Near the centre, a roofed-over cabin with tarpaulin sidewalls had been erected as a makeshift shelter against the weather. In front of it a large wooden box lined with rocks and filled with sand had been placed to hold a fire.

I stared in disbelief at the tarpaulins. The corner of one wall was already flapping sluggishly in the breeze. If the shelter managed to stand up to the next storm, it might protect a few old people and mothers with small children, but anyone else travelling on the raft would be completely exposed to the weather.

Our chained men were placed closest to the paddle-wheeler's lower deck, where the soldiers could keep an eye on them. The rest of us were allowed to spread out as we pleased. When my family was herded onto the raft at weapon-point, we sat upon the damp planking, huddled among our few possessions and watched the remainder of our friends and relatives being driven on board around us.

Like many of the younger children, Seicu was crying when her mother carried her aboard. Grandmother, right behind my aunt, stumbled as she stepped from the gangway to the moored raft. She gave Grandfather an angry look when he steadied her, as if our misfortune was somehow his fault. Then, ignoring him, she stalked off to sit by her daughters.

Before following her, Grandfather turned back to the people on the shore as if searching for someone. "Who are you looking for?"

He gave me a sad smile and put an arm around my shoulder. "I was looking for Jombonni. I wanted to thank him for being generous. The warm blankets and supplies he bought us will help us survive the coming cold."

"Maybe he's too busy inside the trading post selling waskyja to the miners. I certainly see enough of them over there."

He sighed. "Perhaps you're right."

A lump of sadness formed in the back of my throat, nearly choking me. "I'll miss Kutima. He wanted to come, but his father wouldn't let him."

"I didn't know that. He's a brave boy."

Though Kutima, his mother, and the other traders' wives and children weren't among the exiles, many others in their lineages were going with us. Kutima's Aunt Ri and his grandmother looked so bewildered sitting among their belongings. Their tearful prayers to the Chamuqwani's new god hadn't mattered to the soldiers in the end.

When all were loaded, the paddlewheels churned up great frothing mounds of white water, and raft and boat backed away from the dock. The crewmen stationed on the front of the raft took their long oars and pushed us out into the lake. Then the cables and winches turned the raft toward the mouth of the Socanna River.

As I looked back over my shoulder, smoke rose from the village in dark plumes. The icy hand of the Unseen Ones stroked the back of my neck. I shivered as sounds and images from my vision exploded in my mind. What they hadn't stolen from us, the miners were now destroying with fire.

Commander Mu'Dar was standing among his officers on the upper deck also watching the conflagration. Had he ordered the destruction? His dark features gave me no clue. He was a ruthless man—everyone said so. Maybe he had given the orders to do it, while we were still near enough to see the destruction. Then we would know there would be nothing to come back to, should some of us manage to escape.

I tried not to see Uncle Tli and the other men who sat in their chains. Their surrender without a struggle shamed me. I was angry with them for their cowardice, angry at Grandfather's refusal to use his power like Tli wanted, and angry at myself for feeling that way.

Gazing in the same direction, Aunt Tuulah let out a low, mournful cry. There had been no sign of Esuuli and her lover. Nor had Shilshigua's cousin's daughters been found.

Staring at the smoking ruins of my home, I wondered about the fate of my sister-cousin. No one had mentioned the possibility of Tsali dead and Esuuli held as the hidden-away captive of some foul-smelling, hairy miner, but the thought lingered.

And if Esuuli and the other young ones had escaped detection, could they survive the coming winter—alone—without elders to guide them, and the village burned?

Whatever their fate might be, at that moment, I wished I could share it. Even if it meant slavery, I didn't want to leave my home. Tears threatening to spill from my eyes, I turned away from the nearby shoreline. Across the lake the mountain peaks were engulfed in heavy grey clouds. I wondered what we could have possibly done to so anger the Unseen Ones. Why were they even denying us a last vision of our homeland's loveliness to carry with us into exile?

Behind me, I heard Grandfather mutter under his breath, "Oh, Kunai, have you only ice for a heart? Have mercy on us."

Chapter Ten

When the steamboat reached the first settlement after we entered the Socanna River, I lost all hope of our rescue by other Qwani'ya peoples. Samiqwas and I had gone with Aunt Tuulah to sit with Ko and the other chained men, when the stench of rotting fish guts and charred timber assaulted our noses. At almost the same moment, the blackened ruins of the Deer Clan's fish camp came into view.

"Oh, Holy Unseen Ones, what happened here?" Aunt Tuulah breathed. Quickly she turned Seicu's face into her chest, tempting her with her breast to distract the little girl from the gruesome sight.

In truth, there wasn't much to see from the raft. The wolves and other forest dwellers must have seen to the disposal of the dead. Only scattered bones, charred lean-tos and skeletal drying racks remained.

"All the clan members would have been in the camp, cutting and smoking tasty Red Wanderer flesh for the coming winter," Tli said. "Not expecting trouble they would have been easy prey."

"The Deer Clan were our nearest neighbours," Ko said quietly. "My cousin Chugii's boy married into the band two winters ago."

"Is that so? I didn't know that." Aunt Tuulah glanced at him, then returned her horrified stare to the shoreline. "Who would want to hurt them?"

"Chamuqwani. Who else." Tli snapped without looking at her.

"There weren't very many people in that lineage, were there, Appi," Samiqwas said.

"Too few to fight off their enemy, that's for certain," Ko growled.

"But why would someone kill them?"

"Does a rabid animal need a reason to kill?"

No, they didn't. I tasted the horror of their deaths and the Deer Clan's betrayal on the breeze. Turning my back on the river, I stumbled away to sit by Mother and the old people.

"What's going on?" Grandmother asked.

"I'm not sure, the Deer Clan's fish camp has been burned, the people killed maybe."

Mother gasped. "Oh, Amima, what about Da'wabin? Do you think he and his wife's family are dead, too?"

Grandmother's skin paled, then her mouth hardened and she glared at everyone. "Of course not. Your elder brother is fine. Don't say such a terrible thing—don't even think it."

Mother dropped her eyes and murmured barely above a whisper, "You're right. Of course he's fine. It will be good to see him again. I've missed him since his marriage downriver."

The old woman grunted. "I should've never let the clan elders talk me into such a match. But he's fine—I'm certain of it."

She didn't look certain; she looked frightened and exhausted. Suddenly a bell on board the boat rang, the sound echoing off the tree-lined banks. The bell clanged again, and the paddle-wheeler slowed, and then stopped. The long gangway was winched out and a number of soldiers descended to the shore. They briefly examined the site. Then all too soon, they returned. With no further explanation, the gangway was drawn up, and the boat resumed its course down river.

The wailing of the Deer Clan's ghosts trailed in our wake, calling out to me over the *chuff-chuff* of the steamboat. Grandfather put an arm about my shoulder. "What's wrong?"

My eyes blurred with unshed tears. "I hear the ghosts. They're crying. They want me to help, but I don't know what to do."

He sighed and continued to watch the retreating shore till the river mists and the trees blocked the camp from view.

The ghosts' still clamouring in my head, I faced him. "I hate my Gifts. I wish they would leave me alone!"

For just a moment an unreadable expression crossed his face. Then it was gone, replaced by new lines of sadness. "I know it's hard for you, Grandson, but be patient. When you're older you'll know how to help ghosts and other beings that come to you. But for now," he squeezed my shoulder, "there's little we can do but pray for them. The Chamuqwani aren't going to allow us to do the proper ceremony."

"But Ati, how could the soldiers behave as if nothing's wrong? The Deer were our kin; isn't anyone going to tell us what they discovered about who murdered our relatives?"

Grandfather's mouth hardened. He glanced towards the soldiers lounging on the paddle-wheeler's upper deck. "You have a point. We have a right to know what the soldiers learned on shore." Giving me one last pat on the shoulder, he headed to where some of the elders were sitting.

After a brief discussion, they decided Tsanqwati should ask Commander Mu'Dar for an explanation.

The soldiers' translator, Pete by name, was a small man who walked with a limp. He spoke with a heavy accent that marked him as being from one of the downriver villages. His hair was greasy and thin, his skin pale, bespeaking his mixed origins. He wasn't well liked by the soldiers. Even so, he chose to take up accommodations on the lowest deck with the steamboat's crew rather than be seen by the Chamuqwani as a "Zaunk."

Tsanqwati positioned himself near the makeshift gangway that could be lowered onto our raft. He shouted in a loud voice for Pete to come. When the interpreter didn't appear after a time, the soldiers shook their weapons and told him to be quiet. Tsanqwati ignored their threats, refusing to leave until we received an answer. Finally one of the disgusted soldiers went searching for the interpreter.

Stinking of waskyja, Pete arrived at last, red eyed and staggering. "What do you want?" he grumbled.

"The Deer Clan was our relatives. We want to know what the soldiers found when they examined the camp. Who killed them?"

By that time, one of Commander Mu'Dar's officers, a red-haired man with a broken nose, had come down to the lower deck to hear what we wanted. Pete turned to him and repeated the headman's request. The soldier murmured something and shook his head. "The soldiers don't know who killed them. Commander Mu'Dar didn't order it," Pete said.

"These deaths are the most foul of murders," Tsanqwati said. "The souls of the dead cry out for justice. What do they plan to do?"

Pete translated. The officer shrugged. His face an expressionless mask, Pete turned back to us, and said, "Nothing."

The rage flared in Tsanqwati's Spirit-Fire. When he spoke, bitterness coloured his voice. "Nothing? If we are the Father Emperor's children as you claim, then why isn't there any justice for us like the other peoples of his Empire?"

The officer reddened and looked uncomfortable when Pete translated that. Finally he said, "We have no time to investigate further. If we delay our journey longer, winter may catch us still in the mountains. And if that happens, more people will die."

Tsanqwati shouted more questions, but Pete went back to his bottle and the soldiers ignored us. The officer retreated to the gaming room on the upper deck, so he wouldn't have to listen. Someone shouted that the soldiers were all liars and called for vengeance.

I turned back to the river, trying not to listen to my relatives' angry accusations. The forest we sailed by was silent, but in my mind the ghosts whispered of blood and agony. A lump of incredible sadness swelled in my throat.

"Our dead cry out for justice!" a young man shouted.

Then a woman lifted her voice in a high-pitched keen, her lament soon joined by others. The sound tore at my heart, giving voice to the sorrow threatening to drown me. Tears streaming down my cheeks, I raised my voice with the rest of my people.

It wasn't only the death of the Deer Clan we mourned that day; it was our own fate as well. All that had been taken from us, all the uncertainty ahead, the fear, the impotent rage, our pent-up emotions had suddenly been given a focus by those charred ruins on the beach. Maybe we hadn't the courage to grieve for ourselves, but we could mourn for our unfortunate kindred.

When the first cry of the women's lament rang out across the water, the soldiers and crew aboard the steamboat poured out of the cabins and flocked to the rail to stare down at us. As the eerie wail continued, however, the soldiers' expressions hardened. They shook weapons or their fists, demanding that the People stop.

We ignored their threats. Why shouldn't we grieve? What more could they do to us? Let them kill us if they dared. It was a good day to die.

Suddenly a red-faced soldier jumped onto the raft and pointed his weapon at my aunt, screaming at her and the other women to stop. Aunt Tuulah laughed in his face. Coming closer she unlaced her tunic and bared her breasts. Someone sang out the praise cry for her bravery. Then other women began removing their own clothing, taunting the angry soldiers with their nakedness.

A wild gleam shown in the red-faced Chamuqwani's eyes, and I tasted his fear, sour as vinegar. He was desperate, willing to do anything to make the unnerving sounds stop. I lunged forward shouting a warning, but my words were lost in the confusion.

With trembling hands the soldier raised his weapon and sighted down its barrel. Tuulah remained perfectly still, her eyes never leaving his face. Sensing the danger at last, others around her silenced their own cries and moved back. The man didn't seem to notice.

"Troublemaker! You're the one, you cloocha bitch," the soldier snarled. "You made the voices come back. My head—it hurts. Make 'em stop! I'm gonna kill you for it—" He licked his lips. His finger curved about the trigger.

Just as his finger tightened, another soldier shoved the man's arm towards the sky. The weapon exploded with a flash of light and deafening peal of thunder. A tiny cloud of grey smoke discharged in its wake. Before the crazed soldier could react, the other man slammed a meaty black fist into his face. He toppled like an axed sapling to the planks at my aunt's feet.

Tuulah looked down at the prone man as if she wasn't sure how he'd arrived there. Then, taking in a ragged breath she straightened and met the eyes of her rescuer. Like his commander, this man too was one of the dark-skinned Chamuqwani. He was tall and heavily muscled with full lips and the grey-green eyes of a lynx.

By this time, more soldiers had joined their leader on the raft. He barked an order, and two men picked up their dazed comrade, and half carried, half dragged him back on board the steamboat. The trouble removed, the black man's eyes flicked to my aunt's heavy, rounded breasts, and his lips curved into a smile.

Returning his gaze to her face at last, he said in a badly accented version of our language, "Fix your clothes. You'll get cold."

Tuulah's mouth dropped open in surprise. The man showed his teeth once more and repeated his words. Tuulah closed her mouth, her eyes flashing dangerously. When he continued to smile and admire her breasts, she laced up her tunic with a defiant toss of her head. By this time all the women were silent, watching them.

Seeing Pete hovering at his elbow, the officer addressed us in his own language. "I can't allow this display of grief to continue. The noise upsets my men. Such a disturbance won't be tolerated again. You have been warned."

Regaining her composure Tuulah took a step towards him, her eyes still smouldering with anger. "Why are you here, and not among your own kin? Why do you obey these evil men like a whipped sled dog? Have you no mother, no sisters?"

The interpreter stammered, reluctant to translate, but the soldier knew enough of our language to catch the gist of her words anyway. His mouth hardened and he drew himself up to his full height. "I'm a soldier of the Empire. That is all you need to know in order to obey me."

My aunt looked like a small round ptarmigan facing down a wolf, but she held herself with dignity. "I obey no man." Tuulah gave him a withering look and turned her back on him.

An unreadable expression on his face, the soldier stared at her back for a long moment, then he returned to the steamboat with his men. I let out the breath I hadn't realized I was holding and sank down to the planking. I felt drained, but my aunt had made me proud.

Chapter Eleven

D ay followed upon day as we continued to steam down the green Socanna River and its chain of small lakes. We paused only now and then to take on wood to feed the boat's hungry furnaces. There were no more burnt ruins, but we *did* pass other cold and lifeless villages. Samiqwas and I were staring at one such abandoned settlement, when Grandfather came up behind us. Without turning, I asked, "Ati, what village is this; do you know?"

He was silent for a time staring at the shore. At last he said, "I believe it is Broken Shell Mound Village."

Broken Shell Mound. Without pausing to consider my words I blurted out the thought that came into my mind. "Where is Uncle Da'wabin, Ati?"

"I was wondering that myself," Grandfather said.

"Did miners or soldiers kill the people here, too?" Samiqwas asked.

Gazing out across the river, Grandfather took out his pipe and stuck it into his mouth. He told me he was hording the little smoking mixture he had left, but the comforting presence of his pipe helped him think.

"I don't know."

One of the hardest things to get used to while travelling on the raft was the constant clamour of men and machines aboard the steamboat. I never dreamed a mechanical thing could be so noisy. Men shouted, bells rang, the engine rumbled and chuffed, and the big wheels endlessly scooped up water and splashed it down again.

"It's no wonder the Chamuqwani are crazy—they never get a good night's sleep," Grandmother complained over and over. So stiff she could hardly move, she sat in the shelter by a tiny fire with the other old people, telling stories to the young children.

When I observed the soldiers and traders walking about on the upper decks, they seemed like they were having such a good time. How I both envied and hated them. They had warm beds inside the boat to sleep in, tasty hot food to eat, and card games to amuse themselves. My people, on the other hand, huddled in make-shift shelters atop the raft and nearly froze.

The steamboat's lowest deck wasn't very high above the raft. At meal times the small gangway was lowered so the women could board the boat to collect food for their families. The gangway wasn't left in place, but even so, it wasn't hard for an agile boy or girl to climb up to the deck and go exploring when no one was paying attention.

If the soldiers caught us, they would send us back with curses and a few well-placed kicks. The Sooties, the men who fed wood to the fireboxes that made the steam for the engines, were more tolerant.

The Sooties' faces and hands, as well as their clothes, were covered in soot—which is how they got their name. Mate and the officers who lived on the top deck were always yelling at them and making them do lots of hard work. The Sooties didn't like Mate much, but when he wasn't around, they let us come on the boat and help them. We didn't mind chopping or carrying wood for them, because in return they would give us some of their food, or let us dip our cups into the big barrel of strong tea they kept always simmering.

One evening as I dumped my last load of wood into the fire box and wandered over to the tea vat, Matoqwa said to Cohasi, "Someday I'm going to be like Steamboat Master. I'll have a big new paddle-wheeler painted white and red with a brass bell I can ring whenever I want." Cohasi nodded, giving his brother an adoring look.

Dipping his cup into the steaming vat, Samiqwas laughed. "Do you think the Chamuqwani will ever teach us their magic? Maybe if you are a good little zaunk they'll let you be a Sootie."

Matoqwa balled his fists. "Don't be stupid," Tigali snarled. "Mate's coming." Flinging the tea back into the vat, I hurried over the rail with the rest. Secretly I agreed with Samiqwas, but I had the sense not to scoff at Matoqwa's imaginings. It did no one any harm to dream. There was little else to do.

Though it was still summer, the northern sun is rarely hot. And living constantly upon the water, day and night, allowed the cold to seep into every part of my being, no matter what I wore. I tried to hide among our few belongings or among the bales of smelly furs under the second deck, if I was lucky. But the wind always found me. It scored my face with icy talons, and left my hands and feet numb.

Not content to hide away or sleep, my restless brother-cousin was tormented to distraction by our confinement. When barred from the lower deck by an over-vigilant guard detail, he paced the edge of the raft like a caged wolf, snappish and irritable, his pent-up energies having no outlet.

One day he cut a few rusty nails free of the raft's planking and fashioned simple fish hooks for us. That afternoon we spent throwing out our lines and trolling for anything willing to snap at our bait. In the evening, the fish we'd caught for our family was a welcome addition to the oat-mush, hard cakes, and nearly spoiled salt-meat that made up the bulk of our rations.

Our efforts hadn't gone unobserved. From their high aerie in the little house at the very top of the steamboat, both Pilot and Steamboat Master saw the nice fat whitefish we hauled in. The next morning Pete came to tell us that if we gave some of our fish to the man who cooked for the bossmans and the soldiers, the cook would give us extra food in return.

Uncle Tli overheard the interpreter speaking to us. When Pete finished, Tli put a manacled hand on each of our shoulders. His fingers squeezed slightly, letting us know to keep silent and let him do the bargaining.

"Even though they are still young, my nephews are both very good fishermen. They will fish for Cook, but not for more lumpy mush. My family is cold. Most of our fine warm clothing was stolen by Chamuqwani miners. You pay one blanket for three nice fat whitefish, yes?"

"One blanket! That is too, too much."

Cook was called, and then other Chamuqwani joined in the haggling. By that time, other relatives had taken an interest in Tli's trading and came over to add their advice to the discussion. Some other men offered their own nephews' skill in exchange for trade goods, too.

At the first scent of trade, Tli sent us off to our fishing, while he took care of the rest. We were happy to go. A nice fat string of fish would go a long way to aid his bargaining.

As I tossed out my line and sang my Power Songs to the Deep Swimmers, I felt very proud of the responsibility my uncle had entrusted in me. Each fish I caught would help my family.

In my mind's eye, I saw Grandmother's eyes dulled with pain, her proud face pinched with the chill. Mother laid her cold hands in mine, and from the folds of a ragged blanket Seicu looked up at me with moist dark eyes. My heart swelled with deep emotion; I loved them so much.

"*Hai'ya hay*, listen to me, Scaly Swimmers," I sang.

"Come to me. Have pity on me.

"My family is cold. My family is hungry.

"We need the precious gift of your life.

"Come taste my hook. *Hai'ya hay*.

"Feed my Qwani'ya people. *Hai'ya hay*."

I lost track of time, my mind and body immersed in the power my song conjured. My spirit swam through dark-green water, silver-finned creatures all about me. I felt their sleek bodies brush against me. My spirit-body undulated with the current. I rolled onto my back for the sheer joy of it. I needed their help now, but I also promised them that someday, I too would make the Great-Giveaway, my body feeding other life with my death.

AS WE NEARED THE SOUTHERN boundary of Qwani'ya land, the river's channel suddenly narrowed. Rock walls loomed over its shallow, foaming water. Above the chuff-chuff of the engine and the splash of the paddlewheel, the distant roar of the rapids was an ominous sound.

We'd already passed through several short rapids—with little trouble. This stretch, known as Drown Canoe Rapids, however, was the last and worst before the Socanna widened out into Blue Lake.

Even without being able to speak much of their language, I could feel the tension growing among the Chamuqwani as we neared this dangerous rapids. The winter before had been dry with little snow, and that summer the steamboat missed the spring runoff. Unfortunately, there was no other way to reach Blue Lake and the Fort beyond.

Being good fishermen all, the men of my village knew the river's unpredictability and feared for their families. Pilot and Steamboat Master must have had their own misgivings, because at the last moment the boat changed course and headed for a quiet cove on the eastern shore. Once in the sheltered water, the paddle-wheeler slowed, and the crew threw out its boat's heavy anchor to help the boat resist the strong current.

While the light remained good, Mate, Pilot, and two of the Sooties launched a small rowboat and headed for shore. When they landed, the Sooties stayed with the boat while Pilot and Mate walked into the trees. I was sitting near Uncle Tli at the time. I'd brought him some fish that Shilshigua cooked specially for him, hoping to cheer him up. When he'd finished his meal, I accompanied him to the privy hole cut through the logs. I helped hold his chain. He didn't need my help in such quiet water, but it was comforting to be near him. I hoped he felt the same about me.

Tli was changing, his mood settling into a brooding silence that deepened the further we travelled down river. His young wife Shilshigua and their baby seemed to give him little pleasure. He ate the food she gave him and spoke when necessary, but mostly he stared blindly across the water and ignored everyone.

I hated to see him like that. According to custom, Tli was the one who saw to my punishments when I did something out of harmony with the ways of the People. Sometimes it felt like Tli waited until the women in my family's complaints had risen to the height of a small mountain, before he'd draw me to him on the pretext of helping him with his nets—or some other project.

Then, when we were alone he would start in on me, shaming me until I felt as small as a minnow.

Now I almost wished he'd snap at me like he used to—anything would have been better than his dark, brooding silence. I know Grandfather was worried about him, too, but he was powerless to break open Tli's hardening shell. Tli still hadn't forgiven him for not using his Qwakaiva to stop our removal. He turned away whenever Grandfather came near.

He never spoke against his father, but the easy camaraderie between them had dissolved into a stiff formality that made everyone uncomfortable. Their behaviour was all the more puzzling to my female relatives, because no one but me knew why they were behaving like strangers—and I had been asked not to tell.

"I wonder what they're doing." I had asked with little hope of an answer, so I was surprised when Tli spoke.

"They go to check on the water. The river is very low. Maybe the boat can't cross the rapids so late in the year and we'll have to walk."

I felt a flicker of hope awake in my chest. "Will they let us go home if the boat can't pass?"

Tli snorted and gave me a withering look. "We have no home, foolish boy, remember that. No, they will only make us walk to wherever they are taking us."

I glanced back to the shore, feeling my skin heat. I hadn't forgotten the destruction of our village—not really—I just wished things could be different.

Deciding to move away from Tli and his sour mood, I said, "Amima is expecting me to catch another fish for the old people's meal. I have to go."

He smirked, and then waved me away. "Maybe you should ask the Sooties to give you some of their stinking mush, since you seem to have forgotten your duties to your elders, lazy boy."

It wasn't our way to beat a child, but shame can be as powerful a weapon as a birch switch when used effectively. Tli was very skilled at shaming me—with—or without a good reason. I hunched my shoulders and slunk away. He'd seen me fishing with Samiqwas earlier, and knew I'd caught plenty.

Chapter Twelve

The boat with Pilot and Mate came back in the grey twilight, but no one told us until next morning what they'd decided.

When we assembled for the morning ration of hard-cakes and tea the black soldier who spoke our language, told us with the interpreter's help. "Steamboat Master has decided to risk running the rapids, even though the river is low. When we get underway, stay in the middle of the raft and don't walk about or you may fall in. We'll give you extra rope to tie down your belongings."

"If this crossing is going to be as bad as we all fear, then we are in the greatest danger here aboard the raft. Tell Steamboat Master to let us come aboard the boat for the crossing," Tsanqwati begged.

The soldier spoke to Mate standing nearby, then turned back to us. He shook his head. "No, we can't do that. With added people the boat might become too heavy to pass over the rocks. Also, there isn't enough room with the cargo on board for so many people. The boat will need lots of steam. We must go faster than the current if we want to stay off the rocks. The Sooties will be too busy feeding the furnaces to have extra people cluttering up the deck and getting in their way. It's better that you stay where you are."

"Stay where we are?" My aunt stood up, surprising everyone with her boldness. She folded her arms across her chest and glared. "So, a mound of dead furs means more to you Chamuqwani than children's lives? Come down here. Sit among us if you think it will be so safe. Come, brave man, you can sit by me. I will hold your hand, and dry your tears when you cry out with fear."

This dark-skinned soldier was the same man who had saved her from the crazy one. Sometimes when I'd been running errands for Cook, I'd seen him secretly watching her from the upper deck.

Some of our younger men laughed at her jibe, but most of the people on raft and boat stared at them in a stunned silence. The black soldier's face was too dark for me to see if he coloured at her insult, but for just an instant, his eyes flashed, then he controlled himself and gave her a predator's toothy smile. "I would love to come sit beside you, my sweet, but this isn't the time for such pleasantries. Maybe later."

He'd been speaking in our language, which made his banter with a married woman even more humiliating. For what reason I couldn't say, I happened to glance at Ko at that moment. His brother leaned over and said something to him. Ko glowered like a man with a bellyache.

When their leader's remark was translated by Pete for the soldiers, they guffawed loudly and slapped one another on the back. The soldier allowed the mirth to continue a short time longer, then he turned, and the merriment stopped abruptly.

As he was walking away, Tsanqwati called out to him. "Wait. If the worst should happen and the raft breaks apart, we'll have to swim. Our young men can't do that in chains. I have asked you before to release them. Our clan mothers have given you their word. There'll be no trouble; there's nowhere for us to run. Please unchain them so they'll have a chance. We can't survive in this new land without our young hunters to care for us."

All bantering forgotten, everyone remained silent while the soldier considered. At last he spoke to one of his men, who hurried up the stairs to the second deck. "What you've ask for isn't an unreasonable request," he told Tsanqwati. "I've sent a man to ask my Commander. If he also agrees, I'll have my soldiers release your young men."

Giving Tsanqwati one of his predatory smiles, he said, "I'm not sure the sworn words of women can curb rebellious fires in the hearts of young men, but as you say, there's no place for you to run now."

Keeping the men shackled had fuelled a growing resentment among us. Tsanqwati had brought up the matter many times, but always before the answer had been no. The men would have to wait till we reached Fort Protection. This time, however, Commander Mu'Dar saw the wisdom in our request and unchained them.

THE ROAR OF THE RIVER seemed especially loud as the steamboat headed into the main channel. I sat next to Mother. Our family's baskets and bundles were lashed to the raft's planking around us. Aunt Tuulah had taken Seicu and gone to sit with Ko. Samiqwas was somewhere, maybe with Tigali and the older boys, planning something daring no doubt.

My grandparents sat together nearby. Eyes closed, Grandfather sang softly, his hand tapping his thigh in rhythm with his song.

Hai'ya, Qwa'o-o-osi.
Fast Swimmer.
Clever Hunter.
Follow us down these dangerous rapids.
Share with me your Qwakaiva.

Swim beside me, swift and silent, through the frothy green
water.

I trembled, listening to his chant. The roar of the river increased, pounding in my head like a Qwakaihi's drum. The river narrowed, a ribbon of white water tumbling over dark boulders just ahead. Above its rocky walls I could see the trees on either shore, rushing by at an unbelievable speed.

As we entered the white water, the raft rocked from side to side. Then, it pitched high into the air and came down with a shuddering slap. Someone shouted on the deck above. A crewman holding a long oar at the front of the raft dug in his oar and pushed us sideways, avoiding a collision with a large rock. There was a terrible grating sound, the engine strained, and then the boat and raft shot forward.

Grandmother moaned, her skin paling like rawhide. A baby cried. Icy spray splashed onto my cheek. I wanted to call out to the Otter, as Grandfather did, but I couldn't choke the words past my lips. I swayed and placed my hands flat on the planks. I could feel the rocks' sharp teeth not far below the water's cold green surface. Once again, the raft grated against hard stone, bucked, slewing sideways off a boulder.

Suddenly a man cried out. His long oar splintering into kindling, one of the Sooties lost his balance and tumbled into the white foam. Women screamed. The raft hit another foaming wave, reared upward, then came down with a bone-jarring crash. Disaster hovered, so close, so close.

As the raft settled, a Qwani'ya man rushed forward to take the dead man's place with a spare pole. We were deep into the rapids by then, smoke pouring in a heavy black cloud from the boat's two smokestacks. The raft's timbers creaked in protest as the men on board the boat winched the ropes tight on one side, then the other, in answer to Pilot's bells. At the front of the raft the crewmen with long poles pushed us off the boulders whenever a turn was too close.

I feel the power surging within me, Grandfather sang.
I lay my hands on rough wood.
Power glides like an eel below me.
Qwa'osi, float the wood over sharp rock teeth.
Hai'ya 'eh!

I was so frightened. There was water all about me; I was soaked in it—nearly drowning in it, and yet my throat was too dry to swallow. I prayed that Samiqwas was safe—wherever he was.

Unfazed by the chaos erupting about him, Grandfather sat with eyes closed and fingers splayed flat upon the planks, still chanting. I could see his mouth moving, but the sound of the water was a deafening roar in my head. Nothing could penetrate its clamour.

The Chamuqwani manning the steamboat might be skilled at travelling atop such dangerous waters, but skill in the physical world alone might not be enough. The river was angry. Their appetite for fresh human souls whetted by the drowned crewman, I sensed hungry Water Spirits and the ghosts of the drowned, following us down the rapids in the hope of causing more misery.

We were a long way from Big Ice Lake. So far from its source, I wasn't certain that Grandfather's power alone was strong enough to save us. Determined to help him, I reached for my Qwakaiva. My lips moved silently in prayer, but to my horror, no image bloomed in my mind to aid my summoning. This absence frightened me more than the fast water. Was my Qwakaiva, too, diminished by our long travel?

An ironic laugh bubbled up in my throat, nearly choking me. I had begged the Unseen Ones to take away my Gift. What a cruel joke it would be, if at that moment they chose to answer my prayer. Gathering all my strength I prayed again—harder ...

<<Unseen Ones, hear me. Save my family, my people, and I'll make Give Away. I freely offer you my life, my Qwakaiva—whatever you want. Only guide us down these terrible rapids and I'm yours forever!>>

<<Mine?>> a deep voice in my mind rumbled a laugh. <<Forever is a long time. Do you swear it, young one?>>

I had no idea who I had summoned, but we all might be dead in the next moment. <<Yes.>>

<<Then I will send someone to aid you.>>

Relief flooded over me; help was coming. Yes, now I could sense it. Another being approached, though the newcomer remained a shadowy blur to my inner-eye. <<I'm coming. Open yourself to me.>>

<<Open myself—I don't understand!>> I resisted out of instinct the newcomer's first attempts to bond with me.

<<Foolish boy, banish your fear! You prayed for help—accept it.>>

I wanted to, but in the next moment a heavy wave drenched me with icy water, breaking my concentration. I choked, clawing for air. People screamed. Then without warning, pain exploded in my brain, blotting out the world about me, ensnaring me in a net of agony.

<<Pay attention, young one! Focus!>>

<<Who are you?>> I cried.

<<Never mind that—it's not important—open yourself.>>

<<Can you float us over the rapids?>>

The being growled in frustration. <<I can only taste your strong emotion; I can't see through the Veil what's happening to you. Now stop wasting time.>>

<<I don't know what you want me to do.>>

<<Ah, now I understand. Just focus your Qwakaiva on my image and I'll do the rest then.>>

As I concentrated, the being I'd seen only as a blur of light resolved into the luminous violet eyes and brindle fur of a lake seal.

A Lake Seal!

Hysterical laughter threatened again. I was speaking to one of Co'yeh's Hated Kin. Qwa'osi and his warriors were always on guard to protect us, my grandfather assured me. That was why I wore the Otter's charm. My hand fumbled for the otter claw under my tunic.

It was gone!

In the back of my mind a deep voice rumbled a laugh, reminding me that I had asked for help from anyone, hadn't I? I'd sworn an oath. Shouldn't I accept what was offered? I took in a shuddering breath and willed my fears away.

<<That's right, young one, relax, and don't be afraid. I would never hurt you, My Son, believe that.>>

My son. Wonder and dismay tangled in my awareness, then the brindle seal opened his mouth wide and swallowed my spirit whole.

I caught the impression of sharp white teeth, and then my being was sliding into a warm moist blackness. Panicked, I writhed like a hooked fish. <<Stop.>> the voice soothed. <<Be easy and trust. Look through my eyes and we'll swim together.>>

As the voice promised, in the next moment the moist darkness was replaced by other sensations. I now swam the river's icy water, buffeted by the current, my flippers tucked close to my oily fur. Blurred images in black and green sped by. The ghosts of the drowned raised white talons of dripping foam, calling me to join them. Scaly, blue Water Spirits laughed and, feeling playful, slammed me hard against a rock. I pushed myself off the stone and bared my teeth.

Sucking in a great mouthful of the river, I allowed Water to flow into every part of my being. The next boulder they tried to dash me against, I floated easily above it and spun on. Their howls of anger echoed in my mind as the current whisked me away. I barked a laugh.

Catching the current I allowed it to spit me out onto the surface. When my head cleared the water, I looked about me searching for the steamboat. The boat was racing fast, trying to outrun the current. I sped after it, my back flippers whipping the green water to milky foam. But when I came up to the raft, I sensed my enemy, Qwa'osi, nearby. I bared my teeth, ready to fight. Then I realized he was linked to a Qwakaihi; his power harnessed to aid the people on the raft. For once, we were allies. Ignoring him, I focused my superior Qwakaiva.

Calling upon Air and the essence of the Spirit-Lights, I opened my mouth. A stream of violet light flowed out from between my teeth. The Qwakaiva fanned out, sliding under the raft, lifting it a flipper's breadth above the rocks ...

Boat fly.

Raft fly.

Sail high on the surface of the water, my human voice sang.

Flying, flying.

Over the rocks, over the waves.

Flying, flying.

No harm will come to me and my kindred.

No bad Spirit can curse me.

Flying, flying, over the rocks, protected.

Ya hai'ya ho'a aiya."

As the steamboat battled the rapids, my awareness seemed split in two. I was conscious of my body drenched by spray, slumped in my mother's arms, while at the same time I swam the rapids with my father the seal, feeling Qwakaiva coursing through my furry body at every twist of the channel. I lost all track of time.

As the current finally spat us into the calmer waters of the lake, my awareness changed focus once again.

<<It is over, young one, rest now you'll be safe,>> the seal warrior assured me.

As he withdrew, I cried, <<Father don't leave me. I need you. Mother and my people need you. Please—>>

<<I can't stay, my son. Kunai has lent me his Qwakaiva for only a short time. My power in your world is linked to Big Ice Lake. I can't follow you any further. When you return to your village, I'll come visit you. Kunai told me I had a son with the Gift among the humans. I should have come earlier—I didn't believe—but it is time to see to your teaching. Yes, more than time. I'll come when you return home.>>

<<But we aren't going back home. The Chamuqwani—>>

I had no more time to explain. With the last of his strength, the lake seal spewed me from his mouth in a spray of crimson light. His violet eyes still focused upon me, he sank back into the Spirit-World from which I had unknowingly called him.

The magical being had called me his son. So, Matoqwa had been right when he taunted me. Siyatli, *Witch Boy, go back to the bottom of the lake where you belong.* Matoqwa's taunt echoed in my mind. Tears pouring from beneath my closed eyelids, I lay shivering in my mother's lap.

All along, had Grandfather known about my lake seal father, and the deep voice of Kunai in my mind, the one who was to be my Spirit's Companion? All these years, had he been lying to me?

Then through half-closed eyes, I studied my mother's gentle face. Unaware of my scrutiny, she stroked my hair absently. Her face wore the dreamy look she often assumed. Had she felt the seal man's presence in our world? Had he spoken to her without my knowing, before he left? I closed my eyes again. I didn't want to know. At that moment I hated her.

Fish thief, soul stealer, beware of Co'yeh, grandson. But Grandfather must know who had been Mother's lover? Was that why he had given me the otter claw, to protect me?

Otter claw—where?

My hand felt under my shirt for the familiar talisman. It was gone—as I'd known it would be. But how had I lost it? Surely it hadn't fallen off by the tossing of the raft—not tucked safely under my tunic where I always kept it? Had Mother removed it so my father could speak to me? Or had I taken it off myself, during my trance? I had no idea, and was afraid to ask.

Had Grandfather sensed me and Co'yeh's warrior in the rapids? I didn't know that either. And, what would I tell Grandfather if he should ask to see the amulet?

Too many unanswerable questions, banging around in my head, and making it hurt. What I did know, was that the Otter's power protected me no longer. I could feel the loss. My perception of the world had changed—without the Otter's protection it was a more frightening place. But there was also a new clarity to my Qwakaiva that excited me—though it set my teeth on edge.

<<Father, what have you done to me? Why have you abandoned me just as I began to know you?>>

Too heart-sick and exhausted to understand these new revelations, I tumbled into the sweet, oblivion of sleep.

Part Two
Chapter One

At the bottom end of Blue Lake, we came to a Chamuqwani settlement with a number of log houses encircling a stone temple dedicated to the Chamuqwani god. Two stone warehouses and a trading post had also been erected near a long pier.

"What is this place, Grandfather?" Samiqwas asked in a low voice.

"The people living here call it Fort Protection." He pointed with his chin to a massive walled structure I hadn't noticed until then.

The fort itself was a long rectangular enclosure of upright logs built on a small hill above the settlement. On each of the fort's corners a taller, roofed platform had been attached to the walls. Soldiers with thunder-weapons stood on the platforms surveying the water and the portage trail beyond the lake.

"So many people," I murmured. "This place is so much bigger than home."

"Yes. This is where the steamboat spends the winter each year."

The boat's whistle sounded several long blasts as we approached. People on shore paused in their tasks and hurried down to the pier. The soldiers not on duty flocked to the boat's rail, waving and calling to friends and family members on shore.

"Welcome, welcome home!" People shouted as they hurried to the peer. Quite a crowd had gathered by the time the steamboat chugged into the shallows by the dock. The Sooties tossed mooring cables to the onlookers as the paddle-wheeler eased alongside the pier. The raft bumped against the planking with a hard thump. The jolt caught me off balance, and I fell backwards against Grandmother.

"Pay attention," she grumbled.

I straightened and murmured an apology.

"Thought you were gonna winter upriver with the zaunks and hunt for gold," someone shouted to a crewman on board the steamboat.

"Nah, Cap'n couldn't get this pot-boiler ta' run wi'out me."

These strangers laughed and talked among themselves, calling to the men on board, while continuing to point and stare at us. The word "Zaunk" was repeated many times.

There were soldiers and traders among the onlookers, but there were also many women and children. All wore the Chamuqwani style of clothing. The men who weren't in uniform were dressed in canvas trousers and black wool coats or leather vests, the women in dresses with long full sleeves and pleated skirts that hung down to their toes.

Many of the women and children had the golden skin that told of their mixed parentage, but a few of the women had the pale pink faces of the true Chamuqwani. Those women held themselves apart, shading their pale faces with wide-brimmed hats.

"No friends or family are here to welcome *us*," Samiqwas said. "Grandmother, where's Uncle Da'wabin?"

"He lives with his wife's relatives nearby. Doesn't he?" I asked.

Grandmother shook her head. "I don't know where he is, but I'll find out as soon as I can. He should've been here to meet us."

Damp blankets and tangled hair, we were all wearing dirty clothing. I huddled with the rest of my family among our belongings. I wished there was somewhere to hide. No one felt like talking much.

Grandmother placed a gnarled brown hand on my shoulder, steadying me. I looked up startled. "Don't let them frighten you," she murmured without looking down at me. "These people are nothing—chattering gulls, filthy carrion left for the ravens to devour. You're one of the Qwani'yaTsa'adi; be proud of that. Ignore what they say or do." Like an old bear, Grandmother faced the unknown with chin high, boldly staring into the eyes of anyone who dared to gawk at her.

Seicu was crying, a soft monotonous drone against her mother's shoulder. Samiqwas was trying his best to distract her by making funny faces and tickling her feet, but for once, neither he nor Aunt Tuulah was able to calm her. I glanced around looking for Ko. The little girl loved her father; if anyone could settle her I figured he could. "Amima, where's Ko?"

Startled out of her thoughts, Mother glanced about, then pointed with her lips. "He's sitting with his widowed mother and his brother Gagayii's family," she murmured.

Mother hadn't spoken much above a whisper, but Grandmother must have heard her. Or perhaps her patience just chose that moment to snap. "Give that child to me, and go get your husband. He should be here—with us."

Aunt Tuulah blinked in surprise, glanced in Ko's direction, then rose, handing Seicu to her mother. Grandmother settled her in her lap and spoke to her quietly. To my surprise Seicu's noise subsided.

Ko followed Aunt Tuulah back to us, looking irritated, but he sat down beside his wife without complaint. "Appi! Want my Appi." Seicu brightened when she saw him and held out her arms. Ko gave her a smile and settled her on his lap.

When Grandfather returned from speaking with Tsanqwati, Grandmother asked, "Well, what are they going to do with us now?"

Grandfather shook his head. "Our headman knows no more now than what we've been told already. We'll stay at Fort Protection until it's time to journey on to the Tribal Preserve."

Grandmother made a disgusted noise in her throat. "Fort Protection, and who does this fort place protect? Certainly not us."

A new group of soldiers, led by a yellow-haired man with one ear met Commander Mu'Dar on the pier. They exchanged fist to heart salutes and talked for a time, then the yellow-haired man barked a few orders and the unloading began.

"Filthy Zaunks!"

"Hope the soldiers take'em south soon!"

Just like when we were herded on board the steamboat, we passed through a gauntlet of staring and name-calling strangers. The soldiers marched us up the hill, but we passed by the log fort we had seen from the boat. Behind Fort Protection was another stockade, not as high, but just as large. Along its outer walls, armed soldiers paced the walkway.

The soldiers leading our procession shouted a command to one of the guards on the platform by the gate. The door of bound-together poles opened.

"I see no room for us here. Where are we to stay, and for how long?" Aunt Tuulah muttered.

"Where?" Ko said, "I don't think these devils care as long as it's inside there."

The people walking ahead of us baulked at entering the enclosure, stopping just in front of the open gate. A murmured protest grew louder as news of the stockade's conditions passed down the column. A low-voiced conversation ensued between my grandparents, then Grandfather left us and pushed his way through the people to join Tsanqwati and the elders at the head of the column.

Samiqwas motioned with his chin at Grandfather's retreating back. When no one was watching, we slipped past our female relatives to follow in his wake. Peering between the adults, we got our first good look into the stockade's interior.

Numberless gaunt and ragged people stared, as a sickening stench wafted out to greet us. People coughed, and babies cried. The enclosure reminded me far too much of the temple back home that had become our prison. Roused from their misery, most of the captives seemed apathetic, but others were angry, cursing the soldiers and shaking their fists at us.

Oh, Unseen Ones, protect us! What are we going to do now? I swallowed hard, my mouth going dry with fear.

"Ayah," Samiqwas said. "It smells bad in there."

Looking with my spirit-Sight, I could see the sour green cloud of disease hovering above the walls and shuddered. "I can get used to a bad smell," I said. "But there's more to worry about here than a big stink."

Grandfather must have been looking with his Qwakaiva as well, because he said to the headman. "There's sickness here. We must ask the soldiers to let us stay somewhere else."

When Tsanqwati repeated Grandfather's words to the interpreter, the yellow-haired Commander seemed surprised that we knew, then anger flushed his pale features. "Who told you that? It's a lie."

Tsanqwati said nothing only waited, staring him in the eye.

A flush darkening his face, the soldier growled, "The sickness is unimportant, a few children coughing, nothing to worry about."

"Perhaps, but it would be better if we stayed in some other place, so that our own children won't fall ill as well," Tsanqwati said.

"That isn't possible. I don't have enough troops to guard two encampments."

Tsanqwati continued to stare unblinking. The man gripped the butt of his holstered weapon. "… And, besides, you'll be leaving soon for the Tribal Preserve. You'll wait with the others until it's time to go."

"If we give you our word that we won't run away, will you allow us to camp outside this place? Our clan mothers will swear by the sacred bones of our ancestors—and all the Holy Guardians of our land. We'll obey your orders, but please don't force us in there."

The soldier's mouth hardened into a thin line. "Oh you *will* obey no question of that. Swear by whatever you like, it means naught to me."

Refusing to become angry, Tsanqwati said, "Believe us or not, we've sworn it, and we'll cause no trouble, only let us stay outside."

The soldier sighed. "You have to remain within the stockade—for your own protection."

Samiqwas and I glanced at one another. "Our own protection?" he murmured. "Who's going to hurt us, a bear, a mountain cat?"

The hair on the back of my neck rose as a chilling thought came to mind. "Maybe these new settlers like to steal women and children for slaves." Samiqwas's eyes widened. "Or even worse, kill our old people."

I'd heard of such things, whispered by southern tribesmen around the cook fire when they thought all the children were asleep.

Samiqwas might have said more, but the Commander chose that moment to lose his patience. Threatening us with the points of their long knives, his soldiers shoved us inside.

With an ominous thud, the gate closed behind us.

Chapter Two

The stockade was only a large space surrounded by high, upright log walls. Those who had arrived before us made themselves shelters of blankets, bits of canvas, and saplings propped up against the stockade's walls. Those not fortunate enough to claim such a desired space crouched in the centre area under similar flimsy shelters.

"Children, use your sharp eyes," Grandmother murmured. "Do you see Da'wabin among these people? He'll help us if we can find him."

We saw no one that looked familiar, nor did anyone step forward to greet us with happy smiles. *It'd be a sweet blessing to have a relative in this terrible place,* I thought as I scanned the crowded enclosure. "I can't see him, Ami."

"He must be here. Keep looking."

I thought I might grow roots and sprout leaves, we seemed to wait so long, but at last a delegation of men arose and came forward to greet us. To my surprise, a thin, young Chamuqwani man wearing blue robes with a silver lightning bolt hung on a chain around his neck led them.

"That Chamuqwani priest has no business here," Ko snarled.

"You're right," Grandmother said. "Are these people trying to insult us?"

"We're ignorant of their customs, my dear, but I don't think they mean to give offense," Grandfather said.

Each group stared at one another with no one speaking. Finally, going against the custom that an Elder should always speak first, it was the young priest who took the initiative and stepped forward to greet us.

"Welcome, brothers and sisters. I'm Intercessor Raymonel. May Djoven the Mighty One's blessing be upon you." He held up his hand in the blessing gesture I'd seen the old priest at home use on special occasions. "You look weary from your journey. Have you come all the way from Big Ice Lake?"

He spoke in a badly accented but understandable version of our own language, and he called our home by its proper name, rather than calling it Lake Socanna as most foreigners did. I was impressed.

"Yes," Tsanqwati said, "we're the People from Big Ice Lake."

The onlookers including the priest seemed relieved. "Good. You're the last. We've been waiting for you."

"Waiting for us?"

Next to the priest, a man with golden skin and short grey hair like a Chamuqwani explained, "The soldiers put us in this place while they waited for the people from upriver to arrive. They wouldn't let us leave for the new Tribal Preserve until you came."

"We've waited a long time, too," another man with stringy grey hair and a sour face grumbled.

The priest heard his comment, and rebuked him gently, "Now, now, Believer Mathin, I'm sure we'll all be leaving for the new Tribal Preserve soon. Let's help our brothers and sisters get settled so they can rest, before the meal cart comes."

Some of our villagers were lucky; they had relatives by marriage already in the compound. When these people were located, our friends and neighbours went with them. The rest of us were squeezed in among strangers, who at the priest's insistence grudgingly made room for us. Eventually everyone was settled, to no one's satisfaction.

During the initial confusion, Grandmother grabbed me and told me to accompany her while she searched for Uncle Da'wabin. Spying some women she knew from Broken Shell Mound Village, she hurried over to ask them where we might find my uncle and his family.

The first woman she asked shook her head. "I'm sorry. I don't know a man named Da'wabin." The woman turned away, making a big show of scolding a crying child.

Grandmother frowned, refusing to leave, but the woman continued to ignore her. Finally we moved on.

We asked several other people we encountered, but no one would admit to knowing Uncle's whereabouts. Grandmother became angry at last and stepped in front of one old woman with stringy grey braids, demanding an answer. "Kumla, we've known each other since our girlhood. You know my son. You were present at the marriage negotiations. Where is he?"

Kumla placed her hands on her hips and glared. "Yes, I know who your son is. But I also know he isn't in this stockade."

Her tone was so hostile that Grandmother took a step back as if the woman had struck her. She took a deep breath trying for calm, but her voice was still shaky when she asked, "What's happened? Where is he? Has he been injured?"

Kumla dropped her eyes, and muttered, "No—I don't know. He's just gone."

"Gone? But where?"

"He's gone to the Preserve," another woman with a red sore on her face shouted. "We don't want to talk to you. Go!"

"Preserve? When, how long ago? Why didn't he wait for us?"

"Go away! Leave us alone," she screamed and shook her fist.

We left. The women's behaviour was unsettling. "Ami, what's a matter with those women?" I asked when we were out of earshot. "Why wouldn't they tell us about Uncle?"

"I don't know. Shush now. I want to think."

Being some of the latecomers with no relatives, our camp was in the back of the open area—too near the privy for our liking. Samiqwas and I begged some poles from a neighbour and helped Ko set up a small shelter for the old people and Seicu. After that chore was completed, there was nothing to do but sit outside it and glumly watch the activity going on all around us.

"Matoqwa and Slylum are heading for the front gate," Samiqwas whispered. "Let's follow them and have some fun."

I nodded my head ever so slightly and his lips curved in the barest shadow of a grin. When the women of our family seemed occupied with their own concerns, we rose slowly to our feet.

"Where you go?" Seicu cried. "Want go, too."

"Sit down!" Grandmother barked. "You boys aren't going anywhere."

Aunt Tuulah stuck her head out of the blanket shelter and glared. "Grandmother's right. You're staying right here and taking care of your sister—and Tasimu can help you amuse her."

Seicu with eyes moist held out her arms to us. "Want story, story. Get string, Little Rock Squirrel. Tell story 'bout Qwa'osi."

Samiqwas opened his mouth to protest, but just then a crier shouted for the women to come forward with their buckets. Aunt Tuulah thrust her daughter into Samiqwas's arms. "You and Tas play with her while I get food."

The soldiers opened the gate and brought in the evening meal. Mother and Aunt hurried with our cooking pail and water skins to join the line of women forming in front of the cart.

Stepping out of our shelter, Grandmother scowled at the soldier atop the cart, scooping the gluey mess into the containers held out to him.

"If they wanted us to eat their foul mush all the time, they could at least have the decency to cook it right, or let us do it for ourselves," she grumbled.

Grandfather looked up, his eyes alight with mischief. "Perhaps you should suggest that to them, my dear one."

Her scowl deepened as she took a place beside him outside the A-frame. Then she recognized his teasing and smiled. "Maybe I will." He blinked, mouth dropping open. She laughed softly. "Maybe I will."

The stink of the privy made the oat-mush even less appetizing than usual. I ate it anyway, but it lay like a rock in my stomach. I hoped we wouldn't be here long. I hated it here already.

After our meal, an old man wearing a dirty blanket over his ragged trade-cloth shirt approached our tiny shelter. Grandfather, recognizing him as a Qwakaihi of his acquaintance from downriver, greeted him warmly and invited him to sit with us.

A bit flustered with nothing to offer our guest, Mother reached for one of the water skins. The old man waved it aside with a faint smile. "Thank you, but I'm not thirsty. And you'll need to save what you can for your own use. The soldiers only bring food and water when it suits them. Sometimes they miss mealtimes completely, and never bring enough clean water."

Her face reddening, Aunt Tuulah said, "There's always enough if people share."

"How long have you been in this place?" Grandfather asked hastily.

The old man grimaced, then shrugged. "A moon at least, I think. It's easy to lose track."

"Do you have any idea how much longer they plan to keep us confined?" Grandfather asked. "There's sickness in this place."

The old man shrugged. "Who can understand the minds of such people? But I thought you might recognize the taint without being told."

"Do you know the cause of this disease?"

The old man met and held Grandfather's eye. "Yes, I do. The evil is the fault of the priest, his women and his Qwani'ya converts."

He turned his head and pointed with his lips to a group of people clustered around a large canvas tent erected in the favoured position by the gate. The Qwakaihi let out a mirthless laugh at my relatives' startled expressions. "Yes, it's truly their doing. But their evil has been sent back to them, and now even some of their own haughty Converts have come down with the fevers and diarrhoea. One old breed who had the nerve to accuse me of being a malicer to my face has already died."

Until the Elder brought my attention to them, I'd been only vaguely aware of the two women dressed in long green robes with white veils covering their hair and half their faces that accompanied the priest. I had never seen their like in our village, but I had seen pictures of women dressed in a similar fashion in one of Jombonni's holy books.

Kutima had shown me them once, and when I'd asked, he'd called them Mercy Women. I also recalled their goddess, the Virgin of Mercy, was sister to the Thunderer, Djoven the Mighty. If I remembered aright, those dedicated to her took care of the sick.

"But why would the priest conjure a sickness if the fevers would also kill his own followers?" Grandfather asked.

"Perhaps he thought his Qwakaiva was strong enough to protect them—but it wasn't." An expression of triumph crossed the Qwakaihi's face. "He is young, and, in the way of his kind, arrogant and stupid. It was no trouble at all to send the Evil back to its source, when the conjuring was sent against me and my kin."

At that moment, the priest's followers were singing a loud Chamuqwani hymn. No one looked our way, but I felt a shiver run down my back all the same.

The old man may have felt the chill, too. He pulled the blanket tighter around his shoulders, his mouth compressing into a thin line. "As one who keeps faith with our old ways, Man of the Otter, I have come to ask your help in protecting those who still keep our traditions. I also came to warn you about this priest and his followers, because there're impressionable children among your band who might be sickened, or hooked by his lures for new converts."

Grandfather gave him a noncommittal nod, which made the old man scowl. "The kind of sickness that brings death to a person is a terrible enemy—whatever its cause. I will certainly use my power to help our Qwani'yaPeople you can be assured of that, Friend.

"As you already know, I'm no follower of the Chamuqwani god," Grandfather said. "But I confess I've sensed no harm in the young priest. I detected only his concern when he came forward to help us."

"Yes, he's a sly one in that way, all gentle and kind, but under the surface of his lake, he's as corrupted as a seven-day old corpse in summer, and as treacherous as a Talav Quake Monster, lurking in the black waters under the earth."

He fixed Samiqwas and then me with a long penetrating stare, lingering for an extra moment on my face. I felt the cool touch of his power in my mind and shrank away, surprised by his rudeness and a little frightened.

"The priest will seem mild enough at first—to gain your confidence. He'll talk sweetly to your children, give them extra food when he can, but don't trust him. He's a child stealer. If you let him bathe them in his holy smoke, and give them Chamuqwani names, their souls will be lost to this land and our ancestors forever.

"Don't look at me so sceptically, Honoured Clan Mother. I speak the truth. One of the Chamuqwani-appointed headmen, the one named Royston Fishspear, the follower of this priest and his thundering god, was one of those who sold our land to the Chamuqwani.

"It's because of these accursed Converts that all of us are being forced to leave our homes. The traitors signed their treaty paper, sold our land, then the Chamuqwani took them south with their booty, before the rest of us arrived." He folded his arms across his chest and smirked. "The Father Emperor knew they would die if they were still here when I arrived to claim my vengeance. Ah, but the traitors *will* die, nonetheless. They can't hide forever!"

I heard a pounding in my head and felt my vision blur. Was this true? Had some of our Qwani'ya relatives traded away our land for their own gain? Being much closer to the lands and forts of the Empire, there were more Chamuqwani living among the lower villages. How much pressure had those people endured to cause them to forsake their traditions and conform to Chamuqwani ways? Perhaps quite a lot, but that didn't excuse giving away what didn't belong to them—if this story were true.

And it just might be, I thought. I could remember waking up one night and listening to Mother and Aunt Tuulah discussing whether to tell Grandmother the terrible news. Da'wabin and his new relations had been baptized by the Chamuqwani priest.

Grandmother was furious when she learned of it, but I think she almost forgave him in time. All the same he seldom came to visit. He was lost to us and his presence was missed by all of us. Especially Tli, who had had to assume the responsibilities of the oldest son at a very young age.

Knowing of my uncle's conversion, our visitor's accusations about men selling away tribal lands that didn't belong to them slashed at our unprotected hearts like the claws of an angry mountain cat. I shuddered and looked down at my hands; they were trembling. If those of our own blood could betray us, what was going to happen to us in this new land?

After a long silence, Grandfather said, "This news is very troubling to me, honoured man of the clans."

The Qwakaihi laughed, but there was no mirth in the sound. "Troubled? Yes, you should be, since it was your own eldest son that was one of the men who signed and took the Chamuqwani's gifts."

Grandmother stiffened; her look could have frightened even the Great Aseutl Kunai at that moment, but the old Qwakaihi never batted an eye. "My son is an honourable man. He would never trade away his own sisters' inheritance to any Chamuqwani!"

"Oh? Are you sure? How long has it been since you've seen him?

"You said earlier that the people from the lower villages were gone when you arrived," Mother said. "How can you know who did what?"

Showing his teeth, he merely gave her a smile, as predatory as a hungry wolverine. "Ask the priest if you don't believe me. He was here at the time.

Your brother has converted to the new religion, along with the rest of his wife's family."

Staring directly into Grandmother's eyes, he continued, "Your son changed his name; he took the name of one of their holy men. He calls himself Royston Fishspear now, instead of the good Qwani'yaTsa'adi name you gave him at his naming ceremony. He's your son nonetheless. You'll see when we arrive at this new land."

"I don't believe it," Aunt Tuulah muttered. "There's some mistake."

I tasted sour stomach juices in my throat and glanced about our family circle. Not being of our lineage, Ko looked away, refusing to meet my eye. Muddy colours of bitterness swirled in the old Qwakaihi's Spirit-Fire, but I sensed that he wasn't lying.

Go away. We don't want to talk to you! Did everyone in this place know of our shame? That would explain the old women's reluctance to speak of my uncle when Grandmother asked about him.

Her face flushed, my aunt went against custom and interrupted her elders with an angry challenge. "Why should we believe you or this priest? If the priest was here then, why didn't he go with them?"

"Because, rude young woman," the old man snapped, "the priest is throwing out his nets for more converts to ensnare for his god to gobble up. That's why he stayed, not to help us as he claims."

For the first time in my life my grandmother seemed old and vulnerable to me. Tears pooling in her eyes, she covered her face with her blanket. The old Qwakaihi saw her tears, too. And maybe he was shamed, because he dropped his eyes.

Grandfather put an arm around her shoulder. She stiffened, but he persisted, and at last she leaned against him, still hiding her face. With her resting against his shoulder, Grandfather returned his attention to our guest. His voice was cool, as he said, "You've given me much to pray about. It grows late, but I'll speak to our headman and our clan mothers after the morning meal tomorrow, be assured. I'll pass on your warning about the children to those I think should hear of it."

The old man heard the dismissal in Grandfather's voice and rose. Refastening the twig he was using to hold his blanket upon his shoulders, he offered one last tart piece of advice. "Guard your dreams. The Chamuqwani god's converts work their evil while the unprotected sleep."

"Have no fear for me and mine. I'll be vigilant. Against *all* who wish us harm," Grandfather assured him.

After our visitor left, my relatives laid out their blankets, getting ready to sleep. I sat shivering unable to move, the growing evening's cold seeping into the marrow of my bones. Mother called to me; I said something to her in return, but remained where I was. Finally Grandfather came over and sat down beside me.

I leaned into his warmth and he settled his blankets around us. "Old Chumco had many distressing things to say, but don't let them trouble you overmuch. The truth might not be as bad as that one made it appear."

"Who is he, Grandfather? He frightened me."

"He's a powerful Qwakaihi. But in all honesty, you should also be aware that his reputation is 'many layered', though he mostly does good for people. Treat him with respect, but don't go looking for him either. He's been known to use his Qwakaiva to benefit his relatives, or wish others ill who have crossed him."

Horrified, I stared up at him. "He's a malicer?"

Nestled against his chest, I could feel his soft rumble of a laugh as he settled the blanket more comfortably about my shoulders. "I don't know him well enough to say that. I've no proof, and people are often too quick to judge before understanding all the facts. No, let's not accuse him of being a malicer. It would be better just to say, he's a person with flaws and praiseworthy traits like the rest of us."

"But if he's doing bad things—"

"Whether something is good or bad often depends on who's telling the story, eh?"

"Yes, I know but—"

"It's like the stories they tell of Qwa'osi the Otter and Co'yeh the Lake Seal, isn't it?" He chuckled at my expression. "Most people in our band praise the Otter Warrior and curse the Seal, thinking one our protector and the other a thief. But the relationship between the forces of the universe isn't that simple. Otter and Seal are often uneasy rivals for the same school of fish, but they aren't enemies. Each has its own place in the balance of life." He brushed the hair off my forehead. "So intense, you can't puzzle out the mysteries of the world tonight. Go to sleep now and don't be afraid. I'll keep guard over your sleep."

Thinking of fried mushrooms, wild onions and roasting meat, I drifted into sleep to the sound of Aunt Tuulah singing Seicu a lullaby.

Chapter Three

During the grey twilight that passes for a summer night in the Northlands, clouds rolled in from over the mountains, bringing with them an icy downpour. My teeth chattering and thoroughly miserable, I woke later to a cold wind and rain stinging my face.

Tucked between the warm furs of my mother's bed, I'd experienced many storms. Back home such weather was a part of the seasonal balance of the world—nothing to trouble me—nothing to fear.

Home, a place so far away, both in space and time, it seemed like only a dream now, a longing of my sorrowing heart. Pulling my dripping blanket around me, I crawled under the soaked blankets of our A-frame shelter. There I huddled with the rest of my family and waited for the storm to pass. The waiting seemed endless. This time we suffered the rain, but in another moon cycle—or less—similar weather would mean snow. My chest ached from so much shivering, and my hands and feet grew numb.

"I wish someone would make a fire, and let us sit by it," I said to no one in particular.

"Maybe this new land in the south won't be so bad," Samiqwas whispered to me. "It should at least be warm there. Hot sun—all the time—mm, mm warm." I bared my teeth in an attempt at a smile.

Grandfather continued his low chanting. He was using his Qwakaiva, draining himself, trying to help us survive that terrible night. I should help him, call upon the Seal—

No. Foolish boy, hadn't Father told me he couldn't venture so far from Big Ice Lake again? There would be no point in calling; he wouldn't come, but I prayed, with every speck of power I could gather, that the storm would end soon.

The rain stopped as the sky lightened, but the daylight brought no warmth. Boiling clouds still hid the sun. Wind from the northeast knifed through my wet clothing. Emerging from our shelter to walk to the privy, I saw about me a colourless world of dripping shelters, mud, and miserable people. I splashed through puddles, my feet numb, listening to people coughing and small children crying.

The pit dug for the privy was nearly overflowing with water and floating excrement. I gagged as I spouted my own stream of urine into the foul mess. When I finished and looked around, the priest was standing beside me. Though more comfortably housed in his big tent than the rest of us, the storm had made its mark upon him, too. His blue robe was wrinkled and mud stained, his face blurred with fatigue.

He'd been gazing into the flooded privy as well. When he sensed me looking at him, he turned and smiled. Suddenly shy, I dropped my eyes. I couldn't help recalling the old Qwakaihi's warning. I should go back to my family, yet I was unable to move.

"You're one of the new boys, aren't you?"

I nodded.

He looked back at the pit then at me once more. "This is very bad, isn't it?" His priest's power seeming to hold me in place, he kept watching me with those unnerving blue eyes, waiting for an answer.

Yes, it was, but why was he asking for my opinion? I was only a child. I had no power to change this. What did it matter what I thought? In spite of that, he seemed determined to wait for my answer.

Finally, I stammered, "Y-yes. It is."

"The soldiers will have to do something about this before it gets worse. I'll go and speak to them. Does your family need anything?"

Need anything? We needed everything, shelter, dry bedding, warm clothes, something besides oat-mush and rock-hard cakes to eat—the list was endless. "Fire," I heard myself say, before I could sensor my tongue. "Cold, so wet and cold."

As if I'd said something truly amazing, he beamed down at me. I thought he was mocking me, but when I raised my eyes to look at his face, I saw the compassion in the depths of his sky-blue eyes. At the same moment, the force of his Qwakaiva hit me like a spear thrust. I shuddered and dropped my eyes once more to the mud at my feet.

His voice was low and determined when he agreed with me. "Yes, fires to dry out, they are definitely needed on a day like this. Captain Magoss will have to send us wood for fires or there will be more deaths. And we must go soon, or we'll be trapped here with no shelter or supplies adequate for these poor people to survive the coming winter."

This last he had spoken as if to himself, repeating an old argument, perhaps, forgetting I was there. I started to edge away from him, wanting to return to my family, but he caught my movement out of the corner of his eye, and spoke to me again. "You're a smart young man. What's your name?"

My face grew hot. *My name, give my name to a stranger?* "I have to get back to my family," I mumbled.

He seemed puzzled by my refusal, then he nodded. "All right. Forgive my rudeness. I'd forgotten for a moment how sensitive the unconverted are to giving strangers their names. Your parents aren't among the Mighty Djoven's children, are they?"

I looked away, embarrassed and uneasy, yet still I was unable to break away from the intense stare he was giving me. At last I heard him sigh. "Yes, I can see the way of it. Your family still cling to their primitive notions—no matter. Come visit the big tent. We have singing there in the afternoons and evenings. You'd be welcome to join us. We often share hot tea and flat bread, so do come. You'll be welcome. And tell your father that if your family needs anything, he should come talk to me. I'll try to help."

I nodded briefly and hurried away. My father? I put my hand over my mouth to stop the hysteria from coming out in a bout of uncontrollable laughter. What would this Chamuqwani do if he were to actually *meet* my father? Images of that encounter exploded in my skull, making my brain boil. I doubled over, holding my stomach. I wasn't sure if I wanted to laugh or throw up.

I was so intent on keeping my spirit from shattering, I wasn't paying attention, and I bumped hard against someone. Startled, I looked up, choking on an apology. Chumco was glaring down at me. His eyes were fierce black pools, seeking to ensnare my Spirit in their depths. "What did the blue robe say to you? What did he want?"

I blinked—another adult stranger wanting to hear my words. As if he had sucked the voice out of my throat, I heard myself say in a rush, "He said he would speak to the soldiers about the privy—he wanted to know my name—but I didn't tell him. He wanted my father to come talk to him."

Chumco's eyes widened at this last revelation, releasing me from his power. "Your father?" He barked a mirthless laugh. "Yes, it would be most amusing if the young fool was to ever meet your father. Too bad that isn't likely to happen, this far from your home, eh?

"Don't looked so shocked, Boy, of course I know who your father is. I've known since your birth, in spite of your grandfather's pitiful attempts to shield you from me." He rapped his finger hard against my chest. "I see you've discarded that fool otter charm. Come talk to me when you want to learn the Gifts that are your birthright."

He chuckled softly at my startled expression and allowed his hand to trace the line of my jaw, then brushed it across my hair in a suddenly possessive caress. Power sizzled through my skull. I trembled, my breath coming in ragged gasps.

"How do I know these things? Because like you, my Qwakaiva comes from the dark water under the earth where only the Great Aseutl Kunai and his allies can swim."

Images of cold scaly bodies brushing against my flesh choked the breath from my lungs. Unable to speak, I shook my head in denial.

"Why look so frightened? Kunai offers power and great wisdom to the man who isn't afraid to suffer the tests needed to reach his hidden lair and claim them. One of Co'yeh's kin may have sired you, and one of Qwa'osi's Qwakaihi may try to shield you, but only Kunai can bless you. Master of enigma, of light and dark, it's only the ancient Aseutl who knows your Spirit. And only I can teach you the true meaning of your gifts."

He studied my face for a long moment, and then shook his head. "Perhaps you're still too young, but you *will* come to me, or another whom the Great One favours. Yes, you will come someday for our teaching. You cannot deny your nature forever."

Then he turned away from me chuckling to himself. "So the young fool of a priest wants to meet your father—what a laugh."

Siyatli. Once more Matoqwa's taunt echoed in my mind.

I walked the long way back to our camp, trying to warm my blood and stop shivering. But more than the cold now chilled my bones. I wasn't like him—Kunai wasn't my Spirit's Companion. Maybe the Chamuqwani priest wasn't the only fisherman tossing out his net.

<<You are mine. You have sworn it; never forget that. Mine.>>

That deep voice had spoken to me once before, answering my plea for help while we ran the rapids. I had forgotten—had thought...My fingers grasped for, and found only emptiness. The otter claw that once encircled my neck was gone—lost in the rapids. "Qwa'osi, help me."

I wanted to crawl away and hide from this terrible revelation. Foolish Boy, I scolded myself, where could I hide from the Great Aseutl? I had pledged myself to Kunai, and someday he would claim what was owing.

RETURNING TO OUR SHELTER, I completely forgot about my strange encounters with the priest and Chumco. Standing outside, their faces flushed and angry, Aunt Tuulah and her husband faced one another. "... I need you here, not running off somewhere," Tuulah was saying.

I froze, hoping not to draw attention to myself. Grandfather was nowhere to be seen. Samiqwas was gone. Grandmother was lying in the shelter with a blanket over her head. Also inside the shelter, Seicu sat on my mother's lap, her thumb in her mouth, her eyes round.

Ko let out a longsuffering sigh. "I'm not running off *somewhere*. I'm just going to see how my mother is doing this morning. Why is that so unreasonable?"

Aunt Tuulah folded her arms across her chest still glaring. "Your brother Gagayii can see to her. Your place is here with us—"

"My mother is old—Gagayii has his own family—I've no sister to take care of her. Why do you begrudge her the sight of her son?"

"I don't begrudge her the sight of her son," Aunt Tuulah said, her voice rising. "You aren't being fair!"

"Oh? Then what exactly *is* the problem?"

"The problem is that your mother isn't the *real* reason you're going," she snapped. "You're going because you like sitting around with your brother and his friends, gambling and drinking waskyja—"

"Waskyja?" his voice was becoming louder too. In the shelters around ours, people were stopping what they were doing to look our way. "Have your wits melted in the rain?" he spread his arms wide, showing off his ragged and dirty clothing. "Look at me, woman. Where would I, or any of us, get money for waskyja?"

"You got some on the steamboat—"

Ko threw up his hands and gave her a disgusted look. "You're barking at shadows, sled dog. I'm *not* going over there to drink—"

"You'll be gone all day and I might need you—"

"What could you possibly need me for? There's nothing for any of us to do, but sit in the mud and watch the soldiers walking along the outer wall—and you don't need me to help you do that!"

"I'm *not* looking at the soldiers. I care nothing for that black man!"

"Oh? That isn't the way my mother heard it."

Tuulah's face darkened. "I don't care what your mother said. He means nothing to me!"

"Then why is he always watching you whenever he's around, if you aren't encouraging his interest?"

"I've no idea—and I care less."

"Well, *I* care. You're my wife!"

"Then act like my husband."

"Enough. I'm going to visit my mother."

"Go then; I don't need you. Stay with your mother if you want."

Ko made a disgusted noise deep in his throat and moved his hand in a cutting gesture. "Woman, that isn't what I want and you know it. Don't try to put words in my mouth—I won't be gone all day." With that, Ko brushed past me and stalked away. Aunt Tuulah stared after him dabbing at her eyes with a dirty sleeve.

I looked down at my feet, unsure what to do. Samiqwas appeared out of nowhere and touched me on the arm. Seicu perched upon his shoulder. He motioned with his chin. "Come on. Seicu has to pee. Let's go look around." I gladly fell into step beside him.

The wind had blown away the clouds at last, the sun now giving off a little warmth. Light reflected up from the mud puddles, and tendrils of vapour floated above the drying shelters. People were emerging, talking to neighbours and setting out their possessions to dry.

"Seicu isn't going to like the privy. It's a mess," I warned.

"I know. I took her earlier. I used that as an excuse."

We shared a smile to celebrate his cunning. Then, leaving out my talk with Chumco, I told him about my earlier encounter with the priest.

"I wondered what he was saying to you. I saw you both earlier. And what did the old Qwakaihi say to you afterward?"

My brother-cousin was an observant wolf all right. I felt my face heat, and hedged. "He just wanted to know what the priest had said to me."

Chapter Four

After the ground by our shelter dried, I took my damp blanket and curled up in the sun's heat to doze. My belly was full, I was warm and dry, and it was hard to keep my eyes open.

When the sun disappeared below the stockade wall, the afternoon's chill roused me. I woke stiff and sluggish, my mind still fogged with sleep. Over by the priest's big tent a fire blazed. People were laughing and singing hymns to their god.

I drank a bit of water from one of the water bags, then glanced around our camp, looking for Samiqwas. No one was there but Aunt Tuulah. She was sitting by the shelter, stitching up a hole in one of the blankets with a piece of copper wire Ko had broken off something on the steamboat and sharpened into a crude needle. Her mouth was set into a thin angry line as she jabbed at the cloth with unnecessary vigour.

Pulling my blanket about my shoulders, I called, "Aunty, I have to pee; be back later." She waved at me, never looking up from her work.

Breathing a sigh of relief, I went to find Samiqwas, but didn't see him. I wandered about, peering into each campsite I passed, calling greetings to relatives, but couldn't find him. He must have gone off with the older boys. I was annoyed that he hadn't awakened me to go with him.

The singing coming from Intercessor Raymonel's campsite sounded nice; so I decided to go over there instead of looking for him. I was hungry; maybe they had food. But nearing the big tent, an image of the priest's intense blue eyes suddenly popped into my mind, making me shiver.

The way he'd watched me by the privy, had he known that I was Royston Fishspear's nephew? That thought made me almost turn back, but curiosity won out over good sense and I kept walking. I would stay at the back of the gathering, I told myself. He would never even know I was there.

When I arrived people were sitting by the fire on blankets. Intercessor Raymonel, in a clean blue robe, stood with his hands up raised, leading the singing. The silver pendant worn on his chest flashed as he moved, reflecting back the flames like lightning come down from the sky.

On a log near the fire, several people with musical instruments sat and accompanied the singers. A man and a woman had what I first thought were small hoop drums. When they played them, however, they slapped them against their thighs or palms, making the tiny metal disks strung along the rim ring in time with the music.

The older man sitting between them held an even stranger instrument upon his lap. With one hand he stretched a part of it in and out, while using his other hand to press little pegs. The thing gave out a moaning sound along with a high-pitched melody that mimicked the song the people were singing. I had never heard or seen the like, and it fascinated me.

Most of the songs were sung in Chamuqwani, but a few had been translated into our language. Those I found very disconcerting. One moment the songs sang of Mighty Djoven loving and protecting his little children, while in the next moment they sang of the God striking dead any who displeased him.

I moved in among the standing people at the edge of the circle, my attention split between looking for Samiqwas and watching the musicians. I kept my head down each time the priest turned in my direction, hoping he wouldn't notice me.

As I watched and listened, I also saw for the first time up close the priest's green-robed, Mercy Women. They were the women Kutima said were dedicated to the goddess who was Djoven the Mighty One's compassionate sister. The two women tried to keep the lower portion of their faces covered with their white veils, but the cloth often slipped. One was young, her pale face quite pretty, the other was much older, middle-aged, with hard lines around her nose and mouth.

When I arrived, they were standing behind the musicians, helping with the singing. Later as more people gathered, they went inside and came back with large baskets balanced on their hips. The crowd quieted, seeming to know what came next. Everyone bowed their heads and put palms together over their chests.

I knew this gesture as a sign that it was time to pray. The old priest at home had taught us how to do this. Feeling uncomfortable, but not wanting to draw attention to myself, I copied what the others were doing.

The priest raised his hands in a blessing and intoned a long monotonous prayer, punctuated now and then by praise shouts from his followers. When it was over, his women took their baskets and walked among the people, handing out to everyone more of the hard cakes we were given at mealtime.

As the older of the women drew near, I forgot about my hunger. She gave off a foul odour, and I didn't like the muddy colours of her Spirit-Fire. Her eyes were grey; her expression contemptuous when she thought the priest couldn't see her. I would've liked to move away, but I'd waited too long. The people standing behind me were eager for her handout and pressed forward, preventing my escape.

Then, she was right in front of me, impatiently holding out one of the hard brown cakes. Her hand was red and square, with thick fingers with dirt encrusted under and about the nails. It was an ordinary Chamuqwani hand, save for the slimy green film of sickness I saw with my Gift, that was covering her fingers and now the food that she held out to me. My heart leapt into my throat, choking off the air from my lungs.

In badly accented words in my language, she snapped, "Here, Boy, take it." I shook my head and stepped back, stepping on someone's foot. A sharp blow in the back propelled me forward just as she held out the cake again. Her hand hit me in the chest, the hard-cake dropping on the ground between us.

"What matter you? badboy, pick up eat."

I stared down at the hard-cake. It had broken in two when she dropped it. The green slime crawled like a living creature across the corrupted food. Unable to look away, I stared mesmerized. I didn't know if the priest and his women had started the sickness, but the old Qwakaihi was right when he claimed they were now spreading it.

"Pick it up, Boy; are you stupid?"

I shook my head, my breath coming in ragged gasps. I raised my foot to grind the corrupted food into the dirt, but I was too slow. A big-bellied woman standing beside me guessed what I planned and shoved me roughly aside. I staggered, nearly falling with the force of her blow. Her blotchy face contorted with anger, she yelled at me, "What's a matter with you, Foolish Boy. Haven't your relatives taught you how to behave?"

The pregnant woman picked up the cake and proffered it to the Mercy Woman. She gestured for the woman to keep the broken hard-cake. Thanking her, the pregnant woman gave a piece each to a small boy and girl holding on to her skirts.

Horrified at this turn of events, I righted myself and stammered out an explanation. "Please, don't let your young ones eat the cake. It's tainted with sickness."

The people around us murmured, some making the sign against evil. The priest's woman hadn't followed everything I'd said, but she had understood enough to make her face turn red with anger. When someone who could speak the Chamuqwani language better, explained to her, she glared at me. "Sickness? Nonsense."

"You Ignorant Brat, how dare you!" the woman who had pushed me yelled. "This woman is one of the Compassionate Goddess's Mercy Women. She tends the unwell; she doesn't cause illness." She pointed an accusing finger at me. "Maybe it's you who have caused this evil."

I was so startled that I forgot my manners, and rudely blurted, "Me? But my family just got here. How could I be responsible? The illness was here long before we came."

I could almost taste the fear swirling in the air around me. I took a step backward, my eyes scanning for an escape route. Out of the corner of my eye, I saw Intercessor Raymonel heading in our direction. He called to the Mercy Woman. When she and the others turned at the sound of his voice, I ducked under someone's arm and bolted.

Once away from the big tent, I slowed my pace so as not to excite attention. My body trembling, my thoughts in chaos, I didn't want to go back to my family's shelter. *Damn Samiqwas anyway—why isn't he ever around when I need him?* Fear and frustration blurring my vision, I wiped a hand across my eyes. I wouldn't cry—I just needed a quiet place for a moment.

But in such a crowded enclosure, there wasn't anywhere I could go to be alone. I wandered aimlessly for a time, and then I headed for the privy.

The ditch the soldiers and our men had dug earlier had drained off much of the watery mess to somewhere beyond the stockade wall, but the sight facing me was still a loathsome mess.

As I stepped away and walked around the log partition set up for privacy, four boys confronted me. All about my own age, they blocked my path, making me step backwards as they moved in a solid wall towards me.

"Look, Brothers, see what we've found," the tall boy standing in the middle said. He was a pale boy with brown hair cut short to hang just below his ears. His clothes were as dirty and nearly as patched as mine, but they were cut in the Chamuqwani style, made of canvas and wool rather than trade cloth and caribou hide. Two of the others were also golden-skinned, but the fourth boy was as dark as any other child of the People.

"What we have is a stinking demon-worshiper who's just crawled out of the shit-hole," the darker boy said.

I blinked, and bit my lip. Speaking would only goad them further.

One of the others laughed. "Maybe we should send him back where he came from. Maybe teach him to be more respectful when talking to one of the Mercy Women, eh?"

So, they had been at the singing. Their leader gave me a nasty smile. "Maybe you're right, brother. This little brat needs to learn some manners."

Without warning his hand shot out, and he gave me a shove, nearly knocking me off balance into the pit. I flung my arms wide, clawing for balance and at last my foot dug in. I pulled myself up right and glared. "Maybe it's you who should learn manners. You come at me like starving dogs. Four against one, do you fear me so much?"

The dark boy's eyes opened wide. Their leader tried to shove me again, but I was ready this time and stepped sideways, causing him to lose his balance and nearly fall in himself.

I needed to get out of there, before they jumped me all at once. "Why are you doing this?" I moved sideways. The pack followed.

Stalling for time, I took another step and said, "You aren't rabid animals. Why?"

"Because I hate mouthy, shit-eating dog farts from upriver," the leader said and aimed a punch at my face.

I dodged, the blow connecting with my shoulder. "I only spoke the truth. There was sickness on the food. You were there. Couldn't you see it?" One of the other boys hesitated. Then his friend said something to him too low for me to hear, and he moved with the others toward me.

"Come ahead then, Convert Carrion Eaters." I braced myself as best I could. "But if you think I'm going into the shitter alone, think again."

Sensing movement out of the corner of my eye, I risked a glance in that direction. Matoqwa and Cohasi stepped up beside me. I almost fainted, but quickly got my wits about me. Someone else had come up behind and slightly to my right. I dared not take my eyes off the boys in front of me to see who it was, but I prayed it was a friend

Matoqwa made a point of cracking his knuckles loudly. He balled his hands into fists and twisted his broken-nosed face into a hideous grin. "Need a hand, Little Brother? These Convert boys already stink like rotten fish, so if we dump them in the shitter, their relatives won't know the difference." The leader scowled, but the odds were evened up now, and Matoqwa was big for his age.

Blows might still have been exchanged, but just then, two men I didn't know stepped behind the wall to use the privy. "You boys have a problem here?" the older of the two asked. The Convert boys' leader mumbled something, then he and his friends left without looking back.

Breathing a sigh, I turned to see that the third presence behind me was Samiqwas. As the four of us left the privy in the opposite direction, Cohasi muttered, "Stupid Convert brats. Guess us boys from Big Ice Lake better start peeing together from now on."

Matoqwa saw the expression on my face and laughed. "Don't look so confused, Tas. We aren't going to let any dog-farting Convert push you in the shit hole. You're from home; all us boys from Big Ice Lake have to stick together in this place. No, if anyone is going to push you in the shitter, Siyatli, it will be me."

I smiled, showing my teeth. "You can try—anytime."

"Maybe I will." Matoqwa raised his fist and took a step towards me.

"Oh, let him be," Samiqwas grumbled. "I'd have to sleep next to him if you did push him in."

Matoqwa laughed. "See you later, Little Rock Squirrel."

Samiqwas watched them go, then shook his head in disgust. "You never learn do you, Tas? Bear baiting is dangerous."

"Me, bear baiting? Look who's talking."

He grinned. "Matoqwa called to me to follow him just now. What a surprise to find you going to war in the privy."

Chapter Five

Our evening meal concluded I lay down with my head resting on Grandfather's leg. The adults were talking, but I paid them little attention. Too weary to find my bed, I must have dozed off, because some time later a low-voiced argument awakened me.

The women of my family were trying to keep their words from carrying to the neighbouring encampments, but the tone of their voices was plain enough. A disapproving frown curving his mouth, Grandfather was silently watching, but took no part in the discussion. I'd seen that look before. He wanted to say something, but felt it wasn't his place to interfere in what he'd decided was our clan's business.

Qwani'yawomen and my lineage in particular, have always been strong-minded and self-willed people. And though Qwani'ya people in general shared and cooperated for the common good, that didn't mean there wasn't friction between family members, or between the clans.

Where Mother was dreamy and easy-going, Grandmother and her oldest daughter Aunt Tuulah were both quick-tempered, passionate women—easily aroused. At that moment they were united in their ire against Mother. Arms folded across their full bosoms, black eyes smouldering, they were glaring at her.

"... Call him back to us, my girl. Why be so stubborn? He has the power to help us," Grandmother snapped.

Mother shook her head, silent but determined. "No, he doesn't have that kind of power. It wouldn't do any good to call him."

Him? I wished my tired brain would wake up.

"We should've killed those crazy miners—if we had only known—if they had only waited 'til the boy was grown—" Aunt Tuulah broke off, tossing more sticks on the fire. The sparks swarmed upward like angry insects. "Look around you, they're taking us from our homes—do you want your son to die?

132

Do you want us all to die? Your Star Swimmer can save us. With his people's Qwakaiva empowering us, we can kill these foreign monsters—"

"He won't help us kill our enemies." Tears were in Mother's eyes now. She shrank within herself, her Spirit-Fire lying tight against her physical body, its colours dulled. "You don't understand. Even if I *could* summon him, he wouldn't help us in the way you want."

"Even to save you or his son?" Grandmother said. "I find that hard to believe, My Girl."

I didn't. *He never came to see me before.* Suddenly I was drowning in a river of despair so black I could hardly breathe. I knew Mother spoke the truth. We were too far from the source of his power for him to help us. We would be torn away from the waters and mountains of our home. There was nothing any of us could do about it—not even him.

Why, why did it have to be like this? It wasn't fair! My body stiffened as my own anger welled up in a searing blast. I shared their pain, their frustration, their fear. I wanted the Chamuqwani dead or gone too, but Mother was right. They didn't understand about the ways of power, and their attack on her angered me beyond reason.

Grandfather's hand lay heavy on my shoulder, cautioning restraint, but I shook his hand off and sat up. Not being of our lineage, he might feel it wasn't his place to interfere, but those restraints didn't apply to me. "Leave her alone!"

"What do you know about such things, rude boy?" Grandmother said.

Grandfather's hand squeezed tight on my arm, another warning. I took a deep breath before answering. "Ami, you have lived with a man of power for how many years, and still you ask this of my mother? You should know by now. Qwakaiva can't be controlled in such a manner."

"Yes," Grandmother snapped. "I *have* lived with a Qwakaihi for more years than you've been alive. I do know something about how the Spirits work in our world. But your father isn't a Qwakaihi. He can do many things a Qwakaihi cannot—"

"But not what you want—He's bound to Big Ice Lake."

"Be quiet, rude boy," grandmother snapped. "You don't even know who your father is."

"Are you so sure of that?"

Leaning forward, she stared at me with narrowed eyes. "Just what do you think you know? Tell me."

"I-I know my father can't help us," I stammered. My resolve was wilting under the intensity of her regard. Desperately I turned to Grandfather for help. "You saw—in the rapids, didn't you?"

He patted my arm, offering comfort, giving me strength. "I saw," he said quietly. "You're right, my boy."

"What's the child talking about?" Grandmother demanded.

"During our passage down Drown Canoe Rapids, our grandson summoned his father. He combined his Qwakaiva with mine to help us survive. We would have died otherwise."

Grandmother and Tuulah exchanged triumphant glances. "I knew it," Tuulah murmured. "Didn't I tell you?"

Grandmother folded her arms across her chest, looking smug. "Well then, Tasimu—"

He shook his head and continued, "No, he can't. We're too far from Big Ice Lake now. But even if we weren't, the children are right, my dear one. The seal man wouldn't, or couldn't, interfere in our world in such a big way."

"But, why not?" Aunt Tuulah asked. "The magical people in the lake are our relatives, aren't they? Don't they care what happens to us?"

"They do, and then again, they don't. It's complicated. They aren't a part of our world or living in the bottom of the lake as the stories say. That image is only a convenience, something for our human minds to cling to."

"Where do they live then, Ati?" Samiqwas ventured to ask.

Grandfather's eyes met mine. What words could we find in our human language to explain to them? He took in a deep breath. "They live in a place 'outside.' Their home is a place of Spirit, but it also has substance to those dwelling there. They can see past, present, and future. And because of this different perception, they rarely interfere in the Physical World. They fear destroying the balance of the universe in ways that might bring about more harm than good...."

By the time he'd finished his explanation, Samiqwas looked a little glassy-eyed. The others seemed less confused, but thankfully let the subject drop.

But I couldn't.

Following Grandfather to the privy before we retired for the night, I put a hand on his arm to stop him on our way back. Taking a deep breath, I said, "If you knew so much, why didn't you tell me about my father when I asked you before?"

He didn't speak for a long moment, and when he did, I was startled by the bitterness in his voice. "Co'yeh's kind damage whomever they touch—even when they don't mean to. I'd no wish to lose another that I love to the seal man." Pushing past me, he said over his shoulder, "I would have never told you. And one thing for which I'm grateful is that you'll never see him again. Every day we travel south I thank the Unseen Ones for that blessing."

I stared after him, my mouth agape. Father had helped us survive the rapids. We might have died without the seal's help. Who had Grandfather lost to a seal's unpredictability?

The seeds of anger and resentment suddenly grew roots and bloomed in my soul. My grandfather, the man whom I loved and respected above all others, wanted to deny me my birthright. Well, that decision wasn't his to make. I had a right to know my father! I had a right to be taught how to use my gifts, didn't I?

Later, as I lay in the blankets next to Mother, I wasn't able to sleep. Thoughts of what Grandfather had said tumbled and whirled about in my mind. Then, unbidden, the image of Chumco's weathered face appeared before my inner eye.

<<Come to me, young warrior. I will teach you. Would you like that?>>

<<Teach me?>> my heart leapt at the notion. Then Grandfather's warning about the man deflated my excitement. I couldn't be Chumco's student. He w0ould be angry with me.

<<I can't.>>

I tried to push his insistent summons away, but I was only partially successful. Chumco's presence lay atop the skin of my mind, red and swollen, like an insect bite, demanding to be scratched. I toyed with the idea of seeking him out right then, but decided against it.

I would be missed.

Grandfather might guess where I'd gone and come looking for me. For some reason I couldn't explain, I didn't want that to happen. If I did gather my courage and ask Chumco for teachings, I instinctually knew I must keep the knowledge a secret from my family—especially Grandfather.

Sensing my restlessness, Mother finally asked, "What's wrong, Little Rock Squirrel? You should sleep now."

I made a face. "Don't call me that. I'm not a baby any longer. I hate that name."

She drew her hand out from under her blanket and brushed my hair in a soothing gesture. "No, you aren't a baby," then more hesitantly, "I was very proud of you tonight."

I squirmed with delight under her praise, and yet another part of me was angry. I wanted suddenly to hurt her. "And will my father the seal man be proud of me, too? Amima, you should have told me. Why did I have to learn about him first from the taunts of my friends? Why did I have to discover the truth on my own?"

She dropped her hand. "I'm sorry. I didn't know. You should have told me you were being teased."

Her words shamed me, threatening to put out the fire of my anger, but I hardened my resolve, and said, "Would you have told me if I had?"

She was silent for a long time before answering. "I don't know."

Well, at least she was honest. "Do you hate him now—like Grandfather?"

"No. I would leave my family and go with him—to the bottom of the lake—or wherever—if he would come for me. But he won't—not ever."

Trying to keep the note of desperation out of my voice, I said, "Amima, please, tell me now that I know something about him? Why did you lie with one of the seal men?"

"You've been thinking about this for a long time, haven't you?" I nodded. "I wanted to tell you, Tasimu, but I've made promises that I want to keep."

"You promised him you wouldn't tell me about him?"

"In part, yes. It's complicated."

I was indignant—how could she do that? I had a right to know; he was my father. What was she hiding, what was she afraid of? "Complicated? What's so complicated about it?"

"It just is. I'm sorry."

"I don't believe you! You're just like Grandfather, always keeping secrets!"

She let out a long sigh, securing the blankets about us to ward off the night's chill. "I keep my secrets to protect you."

"Protect me from what?"

"From his enemies—and maybe other magical beings of his kindred."

Her answer made little sense, so I focused on the one part I could understand. "And what about *our* enemies? He might not want to help us, but if he had given me his power, showed me how to use mine—maybe I could've done something to help our people when the Chamuqwani came to take us away."

"You were too young—still are—to use such Qwakaiva wisely."

"Is that your decision to make?"

Goaded to anger at last, there was a noticeable chill in her voice, as she said, "It isn't for you to judge me. When the time's right, maybe he'll speak to you in your dreams. Maybe he'll even take you away with him, as mother wants, I don't know."

"But if his power is rooted in Big Ice Lake, as he told me, how will he find me in this new land so far from our home?"

"There's dark water under the earth everywhere."

"What do you mean by that?"

Ignoring me, she pretended to sleep. Still hurt and angry, I turned on my side facing away from her. I closed my eyes, willing myself into the oblivion of sleep. At that moment I hated them all—for their secrets—for their evasions and lies.

IN MY DREAM, CHUMCO held a glowing crystal in one hand, while with the other he beckoned to me. <<Come closer and tell me what's troubling you, little seal.>>

I hesitated, thinking of Grandfather. <<Have no fear. You're under my protection while in the Dream. No one, not even the Otter's Qwakaihi can hear you. Tell me.>>

Power sizzled and crackled in the ether between us. Before I could stop them, words poured out of my mouth. <<Grandfather lied to me and Mother won't tell me about my father. I have a right to know, but they're keeping secrets, treating me like a baby.>>

<<Baby, eh?>> he chuckled and urged the crystal upon me. <<I agree; you do have the right to know about your father. This crystal is one of Kunai's treasures. If you think you have the strength to pay its price and master it, then look into its depths. You may discover the truth you seek.>>

The crystal pulsed with a rainbow of bright colours as it sang, the talisman was so beautiful. Never in my life had I wanted something so much, and yet once more I held back..<<Take it, young warrior.>> Chumco urged, holding it out once more. The singing grew louder and more seductive in my mind

For a moment longer I resisted, and then Grandfather's cruel words echoed in my mind. *I would've never told you. And one thing for which I'm grateful is that you'll never see your father again.*

Heart aching and desperate, I banished all caution and reached for Chumco's gift....

But as my spirit-hands closed about its fiery curves, white-hot pain exploded in my mind. I screamed and looked down at the charred shadows of my hands. I tried to let go, but couldn't. Elbows and then shoulders, I was being sucked into a vortex of agony. *Betrayed!* <<Elder, why have you done this to me? Merciful Unseen Ones, save me!>>

<<My aim is only to teach you, foolish boy. Pay its price and focus. A Lake Seal Man's blood flows in your veins, I know you can do it. I have faith in your Power, you're stronger than you think.>> Chumco shouted as I fell head-first into molten fire.

Chapter Six

*T*hough much of my consciousness remained within the crystal's protection, it had allowed a part of my being to merge with my mother's younger-self when she lived alone during her First Blood Ceremony.

As I slipped into my mother's dream, a vision of a sandy lakeshore unfolded before my inner eye. It was early morning, the sun not over the mountaintops, the grey mist still cloaking the surface of the green water in feathery tendrils of luminescence.

A young woman walked alone upon the shore. Her black hair loose down her back swayed with the movement of her long brown legs. She had a willow basket balanced on one hip and held a heavy digger like a walking stick in her hand. When she turned to look out over the lake, I saw her face and at first thought I was looking at my cousin Esuuli. But as I continued to observe her, I realized that the oval face with its soft dark eyes and full lips was that of my mother as a young woman.

The sensation was eerie: I could see her walking along the beach, and yet at the same time, I could sense her thoughts and feel the vigour of her lithe female body as if it were my own. This was a woman I had never known. Gone was the dreamy vagueness that I'd grown accustomed to in the person I knew as Mother.

She was alone. This was the time of her Shillsham initiation, a three-month period of empowerment and isolation every girl of the clans endured as she passed from child into woman and received her Spirit-Gift. Qwadalah was sixteen, beautiful, and steeped in the power of her woman's magic.

Making her morning rounds, she checked her fish traps, dug wild onion in a sunny meadow, and collected tender lake weed when she returned once more to the lakeshore. As she continued down the beach toward the shelter she had woven for herself out of willow saplings and spruce boughs, an unusual sight slowed her steps.

While the rest of the lakeshore was bathed in bright sunlight, in the spot where an old log snag lay half buried, the morning mists clung thick and heavy. Setting down her basket Qwadalah turned in a circle, scenting the air like a fox. She should take the long way back to her camp, but she was young and confident in her Qwakaiva. She had survived more than one moon here alone, hadn't she?

What was to fear from a fog?

She moved cautiously forward, her heavy digging stick held before her like a club. Then, climbing the half-buried logs of the snag, she stumbled, startled by the body of a seal, lying tangled and bloody among branches and lake weed in the shallow water.

Edging closer, Qwadalah rejoiced in her good fortune, but she would have to be quick about claiming such a prize before a bear or wolf pack discovered her treasure. Wading into the shallow water, she picked up the seal's back flippers and began dragging it onto the beach. It wasn't an easy task; the seal was heavy, but the thought of its rich tasty meat roasting over her fire lent her strength.

When the seal lay on a patch of grass away from the water at last, she flopped down beside it panting. The day was growing hot, and she was sticky with blood and sweat from her exertions. Insects buzzed around her naked shoulders in an annoying cloud.

She was also growing hungry.

If she made a fire right here, the smoke would discourage the bugs, and she could cut off some of the fat meat to roast, before she began the tedious chore of butchering the carcass.

Qwadalah rolled the seal onto its back and drew her knife. Then, she froze with knife upraised. The hand touching the seal's chest felt the pounding of a living heart. Qwadalah gazed into enigmatic eyes the deep violet colour of water in the depths of the lake. Ensnared in their gaze, she heard a voice speak into her mind.

<<Please, pretty human, don't kill me. I am no seal offering myself for your cook fire. Help me and receive my blessing instead.>>

"You look like any old seal to me. How do I know you are one of the magical people from the bottom of the lake?"

He bared his teeth and made a phlegmy bark of laughter. <<I can see that along with beauty, you are a very clever young woman, too. I am afraid, for the moment, you will have to take my word for that. My wounds, I haven't the strength to change form.>>

To her surprise, Qwadalah felt a tingling warmth growing within the secret places between her thighs. She gasped, then struck the seal hard upon the chest. He let out a startled grunt and blinked up at her, his eyes moist with tears of pain. She said, "Don't do that. I've heard the stories. You treat me with respect, or I will leave you on this lakeshore for the wolves to find."

Sobered, he studied her more carefully this time.<<I apologize. Your knife is sharp, I can see—made of Chamuqwani steel, yes? I only thought to please you so that you wouldn't kill and eat me.>>

"I won't kill and eat you—as long as you behave yourself."

<<I will behave, pretty human,>> he said meekly. <<For as long as you wish me to behave—and no longer.>> When she glared at him, he showed his teeth in a knowing smile, but prudently kept silent.

As in the way of dreams, this image faded to be replaced by others. Next I saw Qwadalah sitting in her Shillsham hut feeding fish and lake weed soup to a man lying atop her spruce-bough bed. The seal man's human form was well-muscled and square of frame, his face high cheek-boned, with sensuous lips and a broad forehead. His long brindle hair was braided into a single plait that lay across his chest.

I could see no wound on the body he had assumed. I sensed his weakness, but he was not as helpless as he was pretending to be. He laughed and joked with her, allowing her to feed him. Qwadalah knew he was stronger than he let on, but she played his game in spite of her resolution to keep him at a distance.

It wasn't that the seal man was using his magic to ensnare her heart. No, it was the power welling up from the womb in her own body that was the culprit, working its female magic on both of them.

In the grey summer twilight when they lay side by side on the boughs, never quite touching, she couldn't sleep for thought of him. Yet she resisted her body's desire, and he kept his word and never used his power to force her to couple with him. Instead she quenched her feelings in talk, telling him all about herself and the people in the village down the lake.

He asked questions, many of which she couldn't answer, but he never told her much about himself, or how he had come to be wounded. Lurking in the shadows, beyond the glow of their growing affection, was a fear that the unknown evil might return, before he was truly healed.

"When my enemies found me and nearly killed me, it was the power of your moon-blood magic that lured me here out of the chaos," he told her when pressed. "If it wasn't for you, my Sweet Red Blossom, I would have died, because I was lost in their conjured fog."

Mother believed him, and she was secretly proud, marvelling at the wondrous power of her emerging womanhood. She had given another back his life with her Qwakaiva, and someday, her womb would nurture and bring forth a child into this world with that same power.

But the peace and joy they shared was never meant to last. The summer twilight's chill was in the hut when his sudden movement roused her. Tendrils of an unnatural fog snaked through the evergreen boughs of the walls and roof to fill the air about them. He had closed the door flap and now sat tensely on the side of the bed, staring at the blanket's brown woollen folds.

"What is it?"

At the sound of her voice, he turned. One look at his face told her the answer she dreaded. He smiled to reassure her, but she could see the desperation pooling in the depths of his eyes. The sight tore at her heart. Turning away, he muttered as if to himself, "Damn them, I am not ready. I needed only a little more time—"

"I will go out and scare them off."

"No." He pulled her roughly down beside him. "It's too dangerous."

"But we can't just hide and do nothing," she whispered. "We will be trapped in here, easy prey if your enemies find us. You just said your Qwakaiva is weakened still. Let me go. I have to do something to protect you."

"Protect me?" His hand caressed her cheek. "Ah, my fierce one, we *will* do *something*. If you are willing—and can trust me—we just might survive this night."

Qwadalah covered his hand with hers. "Of course I trust you. But what else can we do but fight them?"

He showed her the sharp tips of his canines. "We will do the unexpected, that which is our only chance." To her surprise, he rose and scooped a handful of earth from the floor into her wooden bowl. Mixing the earth into a smooth paste with her blood, he showed her how to trace magical symbols upon his face and body with the paint.

Somewhere in the night outside a heavy foot came down on a branch with a loud crack, sending shivers of dread down her spine. Then, before she could raise an objection, he untied the belt from around her waist and eased the cloth from between her legs.

<<Cover me with your magic, my Red Blossom, my bright woman of power. Drown me in the musky scent of you,>> he said into her mind. Then he brought her hand to his lips, licking the last traces of red from her fingers one by one. <<Let me savour the rich taste of you, my Sweet, mm, yes. I am your Star Swimmer; that is what you may call me, your Star Swimmer. I will sing to you of love, my sweet one, and we will forget about the monsters stalking us in the night.>>

Outside a loud snuffling, then more footsteps crunched by the fire pit. Qwadalah shuddered, then, mastering her fear, she dipped her hand into the bowl and painted more magical symbols across his legs and belly. Placing his hands on either side of her hips, he raised her then gently lowered her onto the shaft of his now erect male organ.

More sniffing and another footfall came down hard in the trees behind the hut. He uttered a soft moan, a new urgency to his movements as he thrust his hips upward.

<<Swallow me up, my pretty human, yes, oh yes. Let your power flow over me. Suck my essence up inside you with my seed, so there is nothing left of me in this world for an enemy to find.>>

The part of my awareness that was separate from her and still Tasimu recognized the glowing trails of magic upon his flesh she had created. Those symbols I knew from Grandfather's teachings. They were the magical signs a Qwakaihi used to ward off evil, or to confuse and deflect an enemy's power.

I knew enough about the ways of men and women, even at my age, to anticipate what was coming. Suddenly frightened by the intensity of what I was experiencing, I wanted to break the contact and return my spirit to my sleeping body, but I couldn't. I was ensnared in a magical trap of my own making, as Mother added her Qwakaiva to mine, in order to relive this time with her lover.

The old people used to say, *"Be careful what you wish for."* And now, the joke was on me. I had conjured this; I had been determined to know—everything, and now to my shame I did.

All through the grey twilight of the summer night, the enemy prowled about the hut, but the alien monsters were confused and never attacked. Throughout that terrible, and yet wondrous night, my mother and the seal man who called himself Star Swimmer camouflaged themselves with her woman's Qwakaiva and made love. With the heat of the sun, the enemy phantasms left off their fruitless search. Still entangled in each other's embrace, the exhausted couple slept.

Star Swimmer allowed Mother to sleep till the sun heated the hut uncomfortably, then he opened the door flap. "Wake up, my sweet. We have to pack your things and leave while we still can."

Qwadalah sat up rubbing her eyes. "Leave this place? Why"

His lips touched her mouth, then his teeth nibbled playfully at her lower lip. "By twilight we have to be somewhere on higher ground, somewhere away from the lakeshore and its concealing mists. Then my enemies can't follow us."

"But—"

"No, there's no time for arguing. You'll have to go back to your village. I need to be gone from your world."

Gone? Her heart trembled at the thought. After what they had shared, how could she bear to let him leave her? No, it was impossible, too cruel to imagine.

Qwadalah allowed him to raise her to her feet, but resisted going further. "You can't go yet. You said last night that you aren't strong enough to leave. If it isn't safe for us here, then come back to my village. My mother will welcome you into our home as my husband. Stay here with me. You will be safe."

He picked up a skin bag and began randomly stuffing things into it. "Go back to your home? No, that is the last thing I will do. I will not draw those who track me into your people's unprotected midst."

She folded her arms across her chest, stubbornly refusing to help him. "I know you said before that you didn't want to tell me about your enemies, because you wanted to protect me. Well, that seems a poor excuse now. I want to know—in fact, I feel I have a right to know after what has happened."

He sighed and straightened to face her. "Yes, I agree, you have earned that right. Though I fear for your safety should they find me with you. Come. Let's sit by the fire and eat something. I will tell you what I can." Reluctantly she followed him out into the sunlight...

Their hasty meal finished, he tossed the last of the fish bones into the flames, and began. "Have your elders spoken to you about the mirroring of the worlds?"

She shook her head.

"You can ask your father when you return home. For now, I will say only that what happens in your world is mirrored in other realities—other worlds.

"All creation is linked. So, just as your homeland has been invaded by an enemy wanting to destroy your way of life, other worlds too have been invaded. What happens to one happens to the many. Oh, maybe not right away—the time lines between worlds aren't the same, but events have a strange way of repeating themselves from one reality to the next."

"Are you telling me that if the enemy in this other world wins control, the Chamuqwani will do the same in my land?"

"It is possible, yes. The changes, the destruction has already begun, My Blossom, hasn't it? Even in your own short life time, you must surely have been aware of that?"

Yes, she had. There was no need for her to speak; her expression told him her answer. He nodded and continued, "That is why Co'yeh and all the seal warriors fight so fiercely. We battle for the survival of your world as well as others—never forget that, my dear one." He kissed her hand, his lips a feathery touch upon her skin.

"Now, no more talk. We must go." He rose and entered the hut.

Clicking her teeth with exasperation, she followed him inside. "Your wounds aren't healed. How will you manage if you leave now?"

Dropping the now-filled bag, he came to her and took her in his arms. "I will manage, my sweet, because once again you are going to help me," he said, and kissed her.

She sniffed and rubbed at her eyes. "How?"

"By going back to your home, getting your father the Qwakaihi and bringing him to me in our new hiding place."

"My father won't help you! His power comes from the Otter. He hates Lake Seals; he thinks all of Co'yeh's kin are fish stealers and thieves."

Star Swimmer laughed, giving her and enigmatic smile. "I think under the circumstances, he will be overjoyed to aid me."

Each evening when they stopped for the night and made love, Qwadalah prayed their being together would never end, but in her heart she knew it must. Though it was the wrong time of her woman's cycle to conceive, she desperately wanted something of him to remain with her. So she focused her will on making her body comply with her wish. And by the time they neared the village she was sure she carried me, his son, tucked safely away in the warm darkness of her womb.

When they neared the village, Qwadalah hid her lover in the willow scrub along Hot Springs Creek and walked downstream looking for her father.

When she returned with him some time later, Grandfather's mouth thinned to a hard line as he recognized the violet eyes and brindle hair of a seal warrior waiting for them. And his temper flared even hotter, when his daughter put her arm around the waist of the creature and looked up at him with adoring eyes.

"What are you doing here, Soul Stealer?"

"Father, please, things aren't like you hear in the old stories. He hasn't tried to steal my soul. I found him on the lakeshore wounded by monsters from another world. He needs your help to elude them."

Grandfather snorted, unconvinced. A low rumble began in Star Swimmer's throat, quickly suppressed. Mastering his anger, he said, "I mean no harm to you and your kin, but I'm still too weak to leave on my own. I need your help, Otter's Qwakaihi."

His anger cooling somewhat, Grandfather said, "I will help you, if only to have you gone before you cause more trouble. What do you want from me?"

"I need you to help me open a portal," Star Swimmer said. "After that, with your further help, we will pass through into another reality—another time. If you follow my directions, you will have no trouble finding your way back home once I am safe."

Face still grim, Grandfather agreed. "When do you want to make this portal?"

The seal man looked up to the sky, checking the angle of the sun. "Come to the place where the creek runs into the lake just at twilight. I'll show you how to make the portal. We'll go at that time."

"All right. Come, Daughter, we're going back to the village now. Your Shillsham retreat is over."

"No." Qwadalah cried. Putting an arm about her lover, she faced her father defiantly. "I want to stay. I want to help."

Star Swimmer shook his head. Slipping out of her grasp, he took her hands in his. "No, my dear, your father is right. You must go back to your village."

"I know that, but let me stay with you now; let me help. I want to go with you into that other world for a time. You can use my Qwakaiva to help you heal—"

"No!" both men said in unison.

"But you said my woman's power was strong—I saved you before. I can—"

He laughed, deep in his throat and hugged her to him. "Oh, yes, your woman's power is strong, but it isn't invincible. You couldn't survive where I must go."

She leaned against him, drinking in the pungent scent of male sweat and fish that always clung to him. "Please, take me with you.

"No, mydear, I'm sorry."

Once more she hugged him, looking up into his violet eyes, willing him to accept her soul-gift. "I know you don't want to, but you do need what only I can give you right now. As I told you before, I want to help you—I freely give myself to you. Take what you need of my Qwakaiva to make you strong. For the sake of both our worlds, you must survive."

He let out a long sigh, and then acquiesced. "All right. I don't like it, but you are right; I do need your Qwakaiva."

"So, in spite of your lying protests, you will be true to your foul nature and accept my ignorant, foolish daughter's soul-gift after all." The bitterness in Grandfather's voice startled them.

They'd forgotten he was still there listening.

"You are quick to judge me, Otter's Qwakaihi, but I will be gentle and take only what I need to ensure I survive. And, remember in the months to come, I am not the only one who has stolen something."

The seal man refused to say more, answering Grandfather's glare with an infuriating, enigmatic smile that showed his canines.

Qwadalah stepped away from her lover and, hands on hips, glared at her father. "He is no thief. I am a woman grown now, and I make my gift to him of my own free will. And I will not come away with you. I will spend this last afternoon with my lover. Don't begrudge me the little time I have left to love him."

Grandfather studied her, and then dropped his eyes in surrender. "The damage has already been done. There is no point in arguing with you further, my girl. Like the rest of the women in your lineage, you are too stubborn for your own good. I will get my sacred bundle. The sooner he is gone the better for you and all of us."

For one last golden afternoon the lovers lay together in the sun while Grandfather prepared for the ceremony. When he returned he came with Grandmother and two of the old clan mothers. Over my mother's loud and tearful protests, she was led away.

Then, in the greyness that falls between day and night, in a place claimed by both land and water, the seal man formed the portal with my mother's life force and Grandfather's Qwakaiva. Linked by cords of luminescent silver light, they passed into another world—with me tagging along.

What I saw in that other reality, my child's mind lacked the true words to describe. It was a world of high stone buildings, where the air stung the eyes and burned the throat. We walked down paths of stone with bright lights of many colours all about us.

Around us screamed deafening noise—coming from everywhere at once. Pounding music blared from open doorways, wheeled carts made of shiny metals honked and rumbled as they moved along stone paved trails with no horse or dogs to pull them. Vacant-eyed people of many skin tones in odd clothing passed us without seeing us.

The black slime of despair clung to the walls of the buildings. The scent of rage, sharp, stinging, lanced out of shadowed alleys filled with angry voices in an unknown tongue.

Coming at last to a place of tall trees, grass, and water spraying up from a large stone pool, Star Swimmer halted. "I will go on alone from here. Sever your link with me, the way is safe. If you retrace your path quickly, before the luminescence fades, you will return to your world without mishap."

Grandfather hesitated, then asked, "What is this terrible place?"

The seal man smiled, but there was no mirth in his display of teeth. "Because this is the time and place where those who track me have gained nearly absolute dominion, they won't, I hope, think to look for me here."

Grandfather studied the lights and rumbling carts on the stone path behind them. "Will you be safe here? I've no wish to leave you weakened in such a dangerous place if you need my help."

The seal barked an ironic laugh. "Your generosity is noted, Man of the Otter." Then he grimaced. "And you are right about the many dangers of this place, but they will not trouble me. I will stay only long enough to regain my strength, then I too will leave."

"But where will you hide while you wait to renew yourself? If your enemies are so powerful—"

"Have no fear for me. I have an ally here. I have summoned him already. You must go now. He is coming." Star Swimmer took Grandfather's hand in parting. "Thank you. I know it wasn't easy to help one such as me, but you must leave now or be trapped here."

Just before Grandfather turned away, I saw the shadowed form of a man under the trees. As my dream conjuring fragmented, I had the disturbing sensation the one Star Swimmer hurried to meet, was me.

Chapter Seven

B oth ashamed and secretly proud of my daring, I woke the next morning exhausted. The sky was grey and leaden, matching the mood of my family. We were all still feeling the aftermath of last night's quarrel. Grandmother remained in the shelter, refusing to talk to anyone. Aunt Tuulah ate hurriedly then took Seicu and stalked off to visit other relatives.

There were dark circles under Mother's eyes as she moved stiffly about her morning chores. I wondered if she remembered sharing in my dream conjuring. Had my ruthless desire to know caused her pain?

Grandfather too looked as if he had had a restless night. He watched me eat my oat-mush with a single-minded intensity that made the hair on the back of my neck bristle in alarm. But he never said a word to me. I suspected he had guessed that I had abused my Gift in some way, and he was waiting for me to come and talk to him about it. I considered blubbering out my confession and begging both his and Mother's forgiveness, but I couldn't gather enough courage to do it.

A part of me was still angry that they'd hidden knowledge that I felt I had a right to know. And for that reason alone, I wasn't truly sorry for what I had done.

As Chumco had promised, I had uncovered what they'd kept from me, and now it lay like a heavy weight upon my heart.

"Tasimu, are you ill?"

Startled, I straightened up, blinking. "No, Amima."

Not sure she believed me; she touched my forehead to check for fever. Finding nothing to concern her she went back to drinking her tea.

After breakfast, Ko sauntered off to his mother's shelter and Grandfather left soon after. Then Mother went to visit with Shilshigua and Grandmother returned to the shelter for a nap. That left Samiqwas and me listlessly sitting by a dying fire with nothing to do.

I was considering rolling in my blanket for a nap, too, when Samiqwas poked me in the ribs. Startled, I opened my mouth to call him a bad name, then I saw Slylum and Matoqwa motioning for us to join them.

I scrambled to my feet. Samiqwas grinned and took off after our friends. "Be back later, Ami," I called as I hurried after the older boys.

"Where are we going?" Samiqwas was saying to Matoqwa as I caught up to them.

Matoqwa shrugged. "Who cares? Anywhere away from my mother's nagging will be fine with me."

Restless and board, we wandered among the shelters of people we knew from home, joking and challenging each other to feats of strength. But when Cohasi tripped over a sleeping child who sat up crying, a woman shook her fist at us and told us to go away. Chastened, we apologized and moved on.

"You could have gotten everyone in trouble, clumsy moose," I said to Cohasi. "Watch where you put your feet from now on."

Cohasi's face darkened and he balled a fist. "You're the one that better watch it, Little Rock Squirrel. You're the one who pushed me."

"Yeah, Little Rock Squirrel," Matoqwa echoed.

"Did not. You're just clumsy."

"So, now what?" Slylum said.

His face still red with anger, Cohasi growled, "Let's find some Convert boys and have some fun."

Matoqwa grinned and cracked his knuckles. "Sounds good to me."

Tigali shook his head. "No, too risky. The elders wouldn't like it."

"The elders wouldn't be mad if the convert boys started fighting us first. We'd be just defending ourselves, right?"

"Maybe.Let's go to the gate instead and see if we can go out to pick berries or fish," Tigali suggested.

"Great idea. I want to get some fresh air more than I want to fight Convert brats," Samiqwas said.

"If they let us out we could rummage through the midden behind the fort," Slylum added.

"Also a good idea," Matoqwa said. "Those lazy Chamuqwani in the town probably throw out lots of neat things."

When we arrived at the gate, four soldiers were smoking and lounging on the platform above it. The two dark-skinned ones I recognized from the steamboat, but the other two men's dirty uniforms had a different identification badge on their shoulders. They were probably from the nearby fort. One was a short man with greasy yellow hair; the older man, the one in charge, had no hair on the top of his head, but a mass of curly grey and black covering his chin.

When we approached, they glared down and asked us what we wanted. Slylum held up a roll of nettle twine and a rusty nail made into a fish hook. "Hey Sold'jah, I hungry," he said in the Chamuqwani language. "You let us out. We go fishing. Maybe bring one for you, eh?"

The older man in charge shook his head. "You brats get out o' here."

"Nice fat one," Samiqwas wheedled. "You like? I good fishmans."

The yellow-haired one seemed to be considering my cousin's offer, but one of Commander Mu'Dar's men growled, "No get out o' here!"

"You got candy, maybe?" I whined, deciding to join in the bantering. "I very, very hungry. No like lumpy mush."

Samiqwas made the praise call for my quick wits, then he started to dance in a circle chanting and waving his hands. "Can-dy, can-dy." Eyes alight with mischief, all my friends followed him.

We were making quite a noise, attracting the attention of many onlookers. Sensing excitement, other boys and girls hurried over to join the fun. Finally the one in charge had had enough.

"Quiet!" he roared. "You brats go back to your shelters right now."

"If you no got candy, maybe you got smoke, eh?" Matoqwa called out boldly. "If we no can go fish, we want smoke."

Cohasi made a loud praise call for his older brother and began chanting and dancing, but before many could take it up the soldier shouted, "No fishing! No candy! No smoking mix! Damn you all, get out of here or we'll put you in our jail. You brats want that, eh?"

We didn't, so we left laughing and punching each other on the arms.

At that point Cohasi repeated his suggestion to walk among the Converts' shelters. This time no one counselled against the plan. I trailed along with them, because I could think of nothing better to do.

Samiqwas noticed my brooding and needled me, "What's a matter, Little Rock Squirrel, are you sad because you didn't get candy??"

His teasing got everyone laughing. My face grew hot and I took a swing at him. I missed, which made them only laugh the harder.

Humiliated beyond reason, I stepped close and in a voice too low for the others to hear, I said, "Don't call me that baby name again or I'll make you sorry."

"Oh yeah, Little Rock Squirrel?" he said loud enough for the others to hear. He raised his fist. "What are you going to do, hit me?"

Before he could throw his punch I smiled in a mean way. "Have you forgotten what you heard last night? Go ahead and hit me—if you dare."

I wasn't really angry, but it wouldn't hurt, I reasoned, to let him worry for a while. He'd heard the talk last night; he knew I had other ways than brute force to get back at people who bothered me. He knew he'd better have a care—

What was I thinking? How could I even consider abusing my gifts for my own petty vengeance—and against my cousin—my best friend! My success with the dreaming the night before was making me a little drunk with the power of possibilities. I was horrified and ashamed of my bad thoughts.

His skin turned the colour of bleached rawhide. "I-I'm sorry—I'd never—I'm sorry!"

Not understanding what we'd said to one another, Cohasi jeered, "What's a matter, Little Rock Squirrel, afraid to come with us?"

Suddenly I felt the breath choke in my throat. I couldn't just wander around this camp with the rest of the boys anymore. I needed to talk to someone who could understand what I was experiencing; I needed to find Grandfather.

"Do what you want—you're all dog farts! I'm going back to our shelter." I yelled.

"Run back to your Mother, Little Rock Squirrel," Matoqwa taunted. "She may need you to sew up a hole in your uncle's shirt."

Cohasi doubled over laughing and the others followed.

Hands trembling, stomach churning, I turned my back and fled.

Chapter Eight

When I arrived out of breath at our shelter, no one was there but my sleeping grandmother. I hung around digging furrows with a twig in the dirt, hoping Grandfather would return. When he didn't, I left to search for him.

"He's gone to the priest's tent with the elders to talk about conditions in the stockade," an old aunty said. I thanked her and left.

Feeling resentful and a little desperate, I wandered aimlessly through the stockade, the bad feelings and the fear swelling like a bloated corpse inside me. I was alone—different—no one cared about me—and my family were all too busy with their own concerns to notice or help me. It wasn't fair! Muttering to myself I wasn't paying attention and bumped into someone carrying an armload of firewood. The woman let out a startled cry, dropping much of her load on the ground.

Am I doomed to do everything wrong today? "I'm sorry—I wasn't watching where I was going," I stammered. I picked up the wood, and offered, "Can I help?"

This stranger was a pretty young Qwani'ya woman. She had a round belly, full breasts, and a kindly smile. "Thank you." She straightened, rubbing her back. Giving me another warm smile, she led the way to her family's shelter.

When I finished stacking her wood and turned to go, she stood by her fire with a tin cup and battered pot in hand. "Thank you again." Setting the pot at the edge of the fire, she held out the steaming cup to me. "It'll be so nice when my own children are old enough to help with chores." She patted her belly. "This one is my first, so I'll have to wait a few years yet. Please sit." She waved me to a place by the hearth.

"My Uncle Chumco will be back soon. He's a great Qwakaihi and I'm sure he would enjoy meeting such a nice boy as you."

154

Chumco! My stomach lurched. *What have you done, foolish boy! Grandfather is going to be furious with you.* "Thank you for offering tea, but I should go, my mother—"

"Please. I've already poured it." She proffered the cup again. "It would be a shame to waste it. Surely you aren't needed so soon?"

It's only tea. Don't be rude. Drink It, then go. Feeling suddenly daring, I crouched by her fire and took the cup. Its resinous heat felt good on my dry throat. "Thank you."

As I sipped my tea, an older woman with pox scars on her face and a boy about three on her hip nodded as they passed into their shelter. A man, who might have been the younger one's husband, trailed a hand lovingly across her back and poured himself tea from the pot. He drank it in several quick gulps, and then left again. A shy girl of about my own age peeped out from the shelter to study me when she thought I couldn't see her.

"I can tell by your accent that you must be from Big Ice Lake," the young woman said. "I've never travelled so far up the river, but I've heard from my uncle that it's beautiful."

"It is," I agreed.

"Won't you tell me about it?"

"What would you like to know?" I drank more tea and felt the knot of unease in my gut untangle. Chumco's relatives seemed no different than other Qwani'ya families. And It eased my heart to talk about my home.

When the young woman rose and excused herself, I was surprised to see Chumco crouching and drinking his own cup of tea just to the left of me. He pointed with his lips to the empty cup still in my hand. "Come inside the shelter so we can talk in private."

My surprise must have shown on my face, because he laughed softly and motioned once more for me to set down the cup. "You wanted to talk to me, didn't you?"

I put down the cup before I dropped it. I wasn't consciously aware of calling him, but I certainly had been searching for *someone.*

Well, why not? I put down the cup and followed him.

To my surprise, the shelter's dark interior was empty. I hadn't noticed the people leaving. Chumco built up the tiny fire, then sat cross-legged on a rush mat, motioning me to join him. I sat and looked down at my hands nervously twisting a fold of my dirty shirt in my lap.

When I stole a glance at him, Chumco was watching me with a slightly unfocused gaze. I knew that look meant he was seeing me with his Spirit-Sight. It made me nervous.

At last, he said, "Last night's conjuring only one of your special lineage could have attempted. Were you successful?"

Startled, my head snapped up and I stared him in the eye. "Didn't you see? Surely I didn't imagine everything."

He shook his head. "No you didn't imagine seeing me. Your dream was real, a true gift of power. But it was your Qwakaiva and yours alone that insured the success of your conjuring."

Recalling Mother's intimate dream about her lover, I felt my face heat. "Yes. I learned what I wanted." *Maybe more than I wanted to know.*

"Start from the beginning and tell me."

And, so I did—everything. I told him about the argument between my female relatives, and what I had discovered about my conception.

"Wounded and dying the seal warrior who was my father fled from another world to the lakeshore near our home. Alone on her moon blood retreat, Mother found him and nursed him.

"Star Swimmer was still weak, so they risked all and came to Grandfather for help. He was angry, but agreed. Mother wanted to go with her lover, but that wasn't possible. Together the seal man and Grandfather created a portal and the seal escaped."

Chumco nodded gravely. "You did well. Your conjuring confirms much that I'd already suspected. Kunai has favoured you. Be grateful that such a wise and powerful benefactor has agreed to be your life-long Spirit Companion."

Any Spirit emerging from the depths of the lake to claim a human for its Spirit Companion would be more curse than blessing....

Taking a deep breath, I said in a halting voice, "Is Kunai's favour truly a blessing? Grandfather doesn't think so. And," I had to finish, "this morning I threatened Samiqwas with my Qwakaiva when he used my baby-name in front of our friends. He was afraid of me. Am I turning into a malicer because of my father's Qwakaiva and Kunai's protection? Will I hurt people whenever I'm angry?"

"Neither having your father's inheritance, nor having Kunai's regard will turn you into a malicer." He chuckled and shook his head. "What a crazy notion."

"People say—"

"Only the ignorant speak such nonsense."

"But—"

His expression stern, he held up a hand to stop me. "Your family and friends should learn to treat you with respect. You were right to be angry with your cousin, but you wouldn't have hurt him. Your sense of honour protected you from giving power to that evil—as I'm sure it always will. Your concern is commendable, but I have seen your Spirit. You're a good person, so be easy in your heart."

"What if—"

He dismissed my fears with a wave of his hand. "These insecurities will pass. The power you've inherited is like learning to hook a fish, shoot a bow, or any other skill. As you practice and learn to trust in your Qwakaiva and the Benefactor who guides you, your thoughts and feelings will sort themselves out. You'll know in your heart what is right for you to do with your Gift, and what isn't."

"But I may have hurt my mother with my meddling—"

"As for your mother, I don't believe you caused her any harm. You may have induced her to relive her time with her lover, but I suspect she allows herself to fall into that temptation quite often on her own. The argument with her mother probably helped trigger the memories the vision showed you."

He laughed and ran a hand through my hair. "Don't look so sad, young one. Untrained as you are, you still had the Qwakaiva to overcome your fear and insert yourself into her dream and moved with her throughout the events of that wondrous time. That shows the great potential of your lineage, so be content."

his eyes unfocused again, thinking. As if half to himself, he finally said, "The last part of your account is the most interesting of all. How you were able to follow your grandfather and the seal into that other world is—most intriguing."

I shivered recalling my last impression that it had been me my father hurried to meet in that unknown world. Whose dream had I been following then? Had my mind made that part up in its search for a conclusion? I didn't think so, but how could that unknown figure have been me?

When I voiced my doubts to Chumco, he shook his head. "No, I don't think you made it up. And before you ask, impatient one, no, I can't explain it either." He fell silent again, considering, then he said, "All I can say at this point is that like your father, you may have inherited the ability to move through space and time with more than your dreaming-body."

I felt my mouth drop open at that revelation. "I'm not saying it is true, mind—and you may never be able to master such skills, being half human, but perhaps your father will someday help you in this."

My father. I felt my heart pounding in my chest. Grandfather hated the seal; he would never help me, but Chumco— "Can you call him for me so I can ask him? There are so many things I want—need to tell him." Knowing more about my elusive father made my longing for him all the stronger. So far from Big Ice Lake, was I doomed never to see him again? My heart pounded within my chest.

He shook his head. "No, I can't do that for you. And don't look so disappointed. I haven't a link to him, but you do. I can teach you how to summon him yourself—in time. I'll make you my apprentice. Would you like that, eh? I could begin teaching you while we wait, and we can continue your lessons as we travel south. Are you interested? Are you willing to assist me in return?"

Make me his apprentice? Had I actually found someone who would—and could teach me? Then the icy water of reality dashed my growing excitement. "I'd like you to teach me, but my grandfather wouldn't permit it," I said. "He hates my father, I think. He doesn't want me to learn about him or his power."

"And yet, the Otter's Qwakaihi himself can't teach you. Isn't that so?"

I nodded reluctantly, my mind recalling all the times Grandfather had tried—and failed.

As if echoing my last thought, Chumco said, "Your grandfather is a wise and good man. I respect him, but I also think it's unfair of him to deny his gifted grandson the opportunity to learn how to use what the Unseen Ones have bequeathed, because of a personal grudge against his daughter's chosen mate."

I had to agree. I had a right to know and learn about my heritage. "You said a moment ago that you wanted my help in exchange for the teaching. What did you mean? What service can I possibly do for someone as powerful as you?"

Chumco visibly relaxed and smiled. "Do you remember in your dream if the seal man spoke of the 'mirroring of the worlds' and his war with those unnatural creatures who seek our destruction?"

I thought about it for a moment, and then nodded. "I didn't understand much of what he told Mother, something about many worlds being linked, and what happened in one would be mirrored in the others."

"Yes, that's right. Oh the time lines aren't always the same, but the wickedness and devastation that succeeds in one, will be felt in the others. Your father is a warrior who battles evil in all its guises—as am I. Would you like to join us?"

I smiled eagerly. If I agreed to his terms, I would be—helping my father—and maybe saving everyone. "Oh yes, I want this more than anything. What must I do for you?"

He caressed my cheek with a possessive gesture. "Well, as to that, I must swim into the Great Kunai's cave to seek the answer. What I do know for certain is that your deed will benefit us all, my brave little warrior."

Dismissing thoughts of payment, I agreed to become his apprentice and sat in front of him as he bade me. To my surprise, Chumco untied the thong around my braid, and began combing out my long dark hair with a finely carved wooden comb. As he worked, he sang a low chant under his breath. I closed my eyes, leaning into the pleasure of his gentle hands. The song brought back memories of my babyhood, Mother sitting me on her lap, untangling my hair with a brush made of poplar twigs. I smiled, feeling relaxed and safe for the first time since the steamboat came north that summer.

"You like this, hmm? That's right—relax and don't be afraid, my beautiful little seal. You are safe with me now. In time I will teach you many wonderful things."

When my hair ran in a smooth shiny river down my back, he cut off and gathered small clumps of the longest strands, weaving them together into a thin, four-ply braid.

Startled out of my trance-like lethargy, I sat up, suddenly nervous again. Ever since my babyhood I'd been warned about people who practice harmful magic using someone's hair in their conjuring.

"Why did you do that?"

He ignored my question while he worked with his prize. Then he held out the braid again to show me. It was now woven together to form a circle. He smiled at my surprise, placed the loop over his two hands and stretched them apart. "Why did I do this? I needed some part of you to aid me with our secret communications."

When I stared in confusion he left the braided loop to hang on one arm, rose, and rummaged in a leather sack propped against the shelter's wall.

He returned a few moments later with a finely woven loop made of leather, plant fibres, and grey hair. Sitting in front of me, he handed me the string. "This one is now yours. That string is made from fibres of powerful plant medicines, and the rawhide is from my guardian-animal, the lynx." He pointed to a coil of grey wound about the ends of the cord to hold it together. "The hair is mine and will help you form a link to me when you have need."

Not harmful conjuring, then. Still puzzled, I took it and automatically looped it over my hands as if I was going to make a string figure to amuse Seicu.

"Yes, that's right. I see you already have guessed my meaning."

I looked down at my hands and felt my face heat. "Not really, I just couldn't think of anything else to do with such a loop, but make the string figures like running dog and the raven's nest—the ones every child knows."

"Ah, but that is exactly what we're going to do with our strings, my little seal. We're going to focus our Qwakaiva on the loop, twine our fingers in special patterns through the string, and create the symbols of power that will teach you." He chuckled at my expression and held up the loop he'd made of my hair.

"Don't you see? I may not speak to you often in person, that's true, but by creating symbols in the loop made from your hair, I can open a communication between us. I'll see you in the centre of the pattern, and you'll hear my voice in your mind or see me in your dreams."

He tangled his hand through the loop, twisting it expertly into a simple pattern of intermeshed diamonds. "This one is called the Seer's Pool. It is how we will communicate." Then he dissolved that one and created another, more complicated pattern. "And then, there is this one. Let me show you one of its uses."

Chumco pulled on one of the pattern's cords. I took a ragged breath and looked into his face, my heart pounding in my ears.

He let go the cord and the pleasurable sensation died. "Did you like that, my little seal?" Seeing my expression, he laughed softly. "Yes, I believe you did. Such a simple thing, a woven cord, a child's toy—who would suspect its many wonders, hmm? There is no barrier between us now, and if you're careful, your grandfather will be none the wiser."

I dropped my eyes to the loop I held, experimentally draping it over my hand in the familiar pattern known as the Aseutl's Teeth. I wanted a moment to gather my wits, and that pattern was one of the easiest I knew. "Will I be able to speak to you with the aid of this string—or another person—like my father?"

"Me, yes. But as to your father? Perhaps. If you concentrate on the tasks I'll give you, and your Spirit-Gift is strong, then you may be able to communicate with him. But don't expect too much at first. That skill will take time to master. It isn't easy to pass into the timeless world where the magical peoples dwell."

My face must have shown my disappointment, because he patted my arm. "Be patient, young one. You can't learn it all in one afternoon."

Be patient? A lump of unbearable sadness rose in my throat and I swallowed hard. "But, Elder, soon we'll be gone from our homeland. I may never be able to talk to him—tell him—I-I have to do it soon."

Chumco shook his head. "Our leaving can't be helped. But always remember, as your skill increases, you'll be able to pass through the barriers of place and time within the Dream. You *will* find him."

"But how can you be so sure," I cried, feeling a little frantic.

"Trust me—you will. Now pay attention. Our time together grows short." He brought my focus back to the cord looped about my hands. "More important than a talk with your father right now, is how you and I will communicate.

For the rest of that afternoon I sat by the Qwakaihi's side, learning the figure of the Seer's Pool and practicing how to focus my Qwakaiva into the patterns I created. People came and went from the shelter, but they were only a blur in my awareness. All my attention was focused on mastering this new skill.

I thought of my cousin, and in the Seer's Pool I watched him and Matoqwa throw mud balls at a group of Convert boys. I brought up an image of Mother's face, and saw her picking berries with Aunt Tuulah on the hill outside the fort, while the black soldier and his men guarded them. My heart sang for joy of it. I was learning—yes, my new teacher said so.

Chapter Nine

Since that first afternoon with Chumco, I'd made a point each day of finding a quiet spot to make innocently—so I hoped others assumed—string figures for my private amusement. More and more I longed for Chumco's comforting presence in my mind, but he was stern with me and wouldn't always answer my insistent pleas.

Once, when my pestering became too much, he sent a searing burst of pain through our link that left me shuddering and gulping for air. In the next moment, he soothed me again, but the lesson was taken to heart. In future I would be more respectful.

I comforted myself with the knowledge that being a great Qwakaihi, like Grandfather, Chumco was busy. He had little time for an untrained boy. Though cautious during the day, I often sensed him coming to me in my dreams. I had no conscious memory of what we said or did, but on the morning after such an encounter, I felt listless and drained of energy.

Suddenly a fiery pain stung my forehead and Chumco's loop slipped from my hands. Thinking it was a bug of some kind I slapped at my face without looking round. The next time I felt the sting I was quicker. When I pulled my hand away from my neck, a small round mud ball rested in my palm.

Muttering a Chamuqwani curse, I sat up looking around for my adversary. All was quiet near our shelter; no one in the surrounding camps seemed to be paying me the slightest attention. My ears straining for any hint of movement, I felt around in the dirt by my knee and loosened a pebble from the soil.

Hearing a rustling off to my left behind our shelter, I threw my rock just as Samiqwas lifted his head and aimed his blow-reed. He laughed and we both slapped at our bodies as the missiles struck. "Why did you do that?"

"To get your attention," He smiled, but when I scowled, not wanting to joke with him, he came a little closer. "What's wrong with you these days, Tas?"

"Nothing's wrong with me. I don't know what you're talking about." I turned my back.

"Ever since the rapids you've been—different. And lately, like a love-sick girl, you disappear to play with your cord—" he pointed with his lips to the loop still dangling off my arm. "You don't want to go with me and our friends, and you don't even speak unless asked a direct question. Everyone is worried; don't lie to me. Are you sick? Or in love—who is she?"

"No, there's no girl! And I'm not sick—I just want you to leave me alone." Fear goading my anger, I aimed a punch at his head. He laughed and sat down beside me.

"Don't be cross with me, please. You know I was only teasing." Suddenly shy, Samiqwas dropped his eyes, tracing patterns in the dirt with his blow-reed. "Tas, just because I know now that your father was a seal man doesn't change anything ...You're still my relative—my friend. Is that why you're so ...?" he broke off, words failing him, a flush colouring his face.

I took in a deep breath and let it out slowly. Deep down, perhaps there was a seed of truth in his words. I did worry how people would behave if they knew I was a Siyatli. But my real reason was my apprenticeship.

But Samiqwas's concern was a warning I needed to heed.Refusing to answer his question, I asked one of my own. "What did you want?"

Going against custom, he rudely stared at me, hoping I would say more, but I met and held his gaze and at last he dropped his eyes. Instead he pointed with his chin to the soldiers pacing along the platform above the outer wall.

"See that soldier with the big red nose?" Puzzled, I nodded, he smiled. "I bet he's recently won at their gambling games."

"So?" I snapped up his bait. "How do you know that?"

His smile widened, showing lots of teeth. "Easy. See how he's laughing and joking with the others? He's very proud of himself. He must have won—and a big pile, too."

"Who cares?"

All serious, Samiqwas clicked his tongue in reproof. "What, can't you find it in your heart to wish him well? Rejoice for him—-be happy."

"Why should I be happy for that Chamuqwani? He has a warm bed, good food and games to amuse himself while I'm cold and hungry," I grumbled.

He clicked his tongue in sympathy, looking sad. "Poor, poor, Little Rock Squirrel, so very, very hungry. Do you think if we go to the gate and ask him he will give us candy to ease the pain in your belly? Won't that be nice, eh?"

He was baiting me, hoping to make me mad. I laughed instead, slapped him on the back and stood. I put away my loop, resigned. "Let's find our friends and try."

THE RAINS HELD OFF for the most part, but the season was turning. On our guarded forays outside the stockade to gather wood and wild foods, we could see the willows and aspens along the creeks changing from green to gold. The days dragged on, and still we remained in the stockade while the soldiers and Lord Hiram's agents argued over which of the troops were going with us, how many supplies to send, and the route we should take through the mountains.

When I woke in the night to people coughing and the Converts chanting, I prayed the agents and soldiers would hurry and make up their minds, before the bad Plague-Spirits found one of my relatives.

Traditional and Convert alike, all were growing anxious to leave. Many didn't want to go to the new land, but the thought of trying to survive the winter in the stockade was unthinkable. Tempers were short. Mothers snapped at children, husbands and wives argued, and sometimes a shouting match between two or more men ignited into a fistfight without warning.

That's how both Ko and my uncle Tli ended up in chains again and spent several days in the soldier's jail. It shames me now to admit it, but their prolonged stay was due in part to me.

Aunt Tuulah suspected her husband was drinking waskyja, but no one could figure out where or how he was getting it. The couple fought constantly and always about the same things—the dark-skinned soldier's interest in Aunt Tuulah—and Ko's spending his days at his brother's shelter instead of his own.

Gagayii's encampment was always noisy; many men gathered there, not just Ko. To pass the time, the men resorted to the Bone Game and other forms of gambling. It seemed harmless enough, because no one had anything much to lose. But sometimes when the priest was gone, off-duty soldiers joined the games.

"What does a ragged Qwani'ya man have that could possibly interest a Chamuqwani soldier?" Grandmother muttered loud enough for her daughters to hear. "They have no furs to trade, no fish, no meat, nothing, why would the soldiers bother visiting Gagayii's shelter? They aren't doing it because they like Ko and his brother. That's too fanciful to believe."

The next afternoon When Aunt Tuulah took Seicu to play with some cousins, Ko saw his chance and went off as usual. Not long after he left, Samiqwas ran back to tell Grandmother that the same off-duty soldiers were heading over to Gagayii's wife's shelter.

"Go find your Uncle Tli, my boy," Grandmother said. "Tell him it's important he come to see me right away."

"What are you planning?" Mother asked. "The trouble's between Tuulah and her man aren't Tli's worry. Shilshigua's family won't like Tli getting involved."

Grandmother folded her arms across her chest and glared. "I don't care what the woman's family likes or dislikes. Tli still has obligations to his mother-clan."

"I don't think this type of 'obligation' is what our ancestors had in mind when they gave us that teaching. Maybe Tuulah should just go over there herself," Mother said.

"Maybe she should just give the man's things back to his mother and be done with it—but she won't—and we both know that, too, my girl."

Mother let out a long suffering sigh and added a bit of spruce needles to the embers of the morning fire. "I wish you'd let them settle their own quarrels in their own way."

"And I wish you had more respect for your elders, instead of trying to tell me what to do." Grandmother turned to go in the shelter and saw Samiqwas standing as if frozen to the spot. "What are you waiting for? Go get your uncle."

Samiqwas jumped as if stung by a bee and raced off. Not long afterwards he returned with a worried and grumbling Uncle Tli. "What is it, Mother? My nephew says it's important."

"It *is* important. Ko has gone to his brother's wife's shelter again."

Tli snorted and folded his arms across his chest. "That's nothing new—hardly a reason to drag me away from my own family."

"We're your family too, or have you forgotten that? Don't you care about your sister's happiness and the wellbeing of your nephew and niece?"

Tli glanced at Samiqwas standing with downcast eyes by the fire and sighed. "I do care, and you don't have to always be reminding me about my obligations. What do you want me to do about Ko?"

A ghost of a self-satisfied smile curved the corners of Grandmother's lips. "I want you to go over there and find out what's *really* going on."

Tli laughed. "I don't have to barge in where I'm not wanted to know that. They're gambling."

"Ah, but why are Chamuqwani soldiers gambling with them, eh? Tell me that, my wise and all-knowing son, tell me that?"

"Soldiers?"

"It's true, Uncle," I said. "Samiqwas just came and told us he saw them heading to that encampment."

Tli fixed his stare on Samiqwas, who reluctantly nodded. "And it's not the first time," Grandmother continued. "Every time the priest and the elders are busy elsewhere they come."

Uncle Tli accepted a cup of spruce needle tea and drank it slowly as he thought about his answer. When he'd finished he set down the cup and rose. "All right, I'll go. Your news is troubling enough to need investigating."

"Be careful," Mother called after him.

He grunted a reply and without looking at us walked off in the direction of Gagayii's wife's shelter.

Not wanting to be left in camp with the women while something exciting was brewing, I said, "Ami, let Samiqwas and me follow him, so we can bring you news quickly."

"You boys are staying right here—out of harm's way." Mother said. "Tli will tell us when he finds out what's going on."

Ignoring her, I begged, "But, Ami, Uncle may not come back right away. First he'll want to go check on his wife and baby—and once he's at her shelter, Shilshigua or her mother might want him to stay with them. It could be tomorrow before he gets time to come tell you—please!"

Grandmother thought about it for a moment, then waved us off in a shooing gesture. We left quickly before she changed her mind.

Giving Tli time to make it to Gagayii's and join the game, Samiqwas and I crept close to a ripped spot in the shelter's cover to watch and listen.

All the men were sitting in a circle, taking turns shaking a leather cup containing little square rocks with painted dots on their sides. The soldiers had stacks of small strips of paper laid out beside them with some Chamuqwani writing on them. When one of the Qwani'ya men won the throw with the rocks, he received a mug of waskyja, poured out from a clay jug. When one of the soldiers won, the loser made his mark on a strip of the Chamuqwani paper the soldier held out to him.

At first Ko wasn't happy to see Tli crouching in the shelter behind the players, but when Tli made no outcry and only continued to watch the game, he finally lost interest in him, and went back to playing.

As the afternoon wore on, many of the men were getting very drunk. Ko and Gagayii were drinking, but they were also losing more than winning. They seemed almost sober in comparison.

"I think the soldiers are cheating," Samiqwas whispered, "but from out here I can't tell how they're managing it."

I nodded. "There's some kind of cheating going on, true enough. Whenever a Qwani'ya man gets angry at how much he's losing and threatens to quit, he always wins the next throw and a cup of waskyja, which keeps him playing and quiet for a while longer."

Samiqwas frowned, worried. "What should we do?"

I shrugged and turned back to watch. "There's nothing we *can* do. It's up to Uncle now."

At last Tli grew tired of just watching the game. Deciding to play a round for himself, he took a place among the players. Grandmother hadn't said anything about him playing. The sharp scent of danger stung my nose; maybe

Mother had been right. I wanted to warn Uncle Tli, but he was sitting across the circle from where Samiqwas and I hid. I didn't dare draw attention to myself by calling out to him.

When it was Uncle's turn, a Chamuqwani with a long scar across one cheek smiled and held out the leather cup to him. Tli took it and shook the cup, then tossed the rocks down on the blanket. He won, and the soldier poured out a large amount of the amber liquid into another cup and handed it to him. Tli took the cup, drank and made a face at the taste. The soldier laughed, urging him to drink more.

Tli occasionally had a drink of the Chamuqwani fiery liquor with Jombonni or some of the other men at the trading post, but he rarely got drunk. He took another drink, draining the cup and handed it back.

"Want to play again, me bucky?" the soldier asked.

"Depends. What else you got to trade besides waskyja?"

Startled, the scarred soldier glanced at his companions, and then he asked, "What else you want?"

Tli thought about it for a moment, then pointed to a long, black-handled knife in a sheath at the man's hip. The soldier laughed. "Nah, we can't play for my knife—Commander's orders. You buckies aren't 'pose 'ta have weapons."

Tli smiled when this was translated for him by one of the men from downriver who spoke the Chamuqwani language better. "All right, we will play for the stack of papers there."

To my surprise, when the soldier heard that, he became angry. Tli sat quietly, just staring at him as if he was stupid and didn't understand much. I'd seen that look before when Uncle was doing some of his most cunning trading. He was up to something, but I couldn't figure out what.

When the man quieted, Tli asked—all innocent, "Is only piece paper, eh? I can use to make fire. Why you no want trade?"

"Because I don't. Now, do you want to play or not? You're holding up the game."

Still not willing to be rushed, Uncle held onto the cup and the little rocks. He turned to the mixed-parentage man who'd been translating. "What's written on these pieces of paper? What do I truly forfeit when I make my mark on one of them?"

The man shrugged. "Nothing much. The piece of paper says that when we get to the Tribal Preserve you will give this Chamuqwani some of the treaty money owing to you and your wife."

"Me and my wife, eh? Not my sister's or my mother's portion?"

The man shook his head. "It isn't the Chamuqwani custom. For them, the man rules his home not his wife or his mother."

Gagayii belched and slapped Tli on the back. "It's a good system, eh, brother of my brother? In this new land there'll be no more bossy women to tell us what to do. A Chamuqwani man can even beat his wife and no one will care." Gagayii turned to the mixed-blood. "Isn't that true, Cousin?"

The man nodded sagely and took a drink of his own waskyja. "Yes, it's true. No more bossy women. The Chamuqwani god says so."

"Are you zaunks going to stop jabbering and play or what?" the scarred soldier growled.

"I'll play," Tli said. "If I win you give me that pouch." Tli pointed to a fine leather pouch that probably contained smoking mix hanging on the soldier's belt.

"All right. But to play for such a big prize we need some new dice." He reached out for the cup. Tli handed it over. The soldier took out the old set of rocks and put in another set that looked the same. As he handed them back, he said, "If you win I give you this fancy pouch here." He removed the pouch from his belt and laid it on the blanket. "And if I win, you put your mark on ten of these papers." He laid the stack of papers beside the pouch.

Tli shook his head and held up three fingers. The soldier laughed. They bargained for a time, finally settling on five. Over the soldier's protest, Tli picked up the cup and tipped the dice out onto his hand. He held them up one by one before tossing them back into the cup. When he finished, he smiled, displaying his teeth. "Dice no good. I want play with other ones."

The soldier's face grew red, and he gripped the handle of his knife. "Are you accusing me of cheating?"

"Why you so angry? I just like other rocks. Are you cheating?"

"No! of course not. You shut up or I'll—"

"Kill me?" Tli held up his empty hands for all to see. Then in Chamuqwani, he said, "Would kill unarmed man? Commander Mu'Dar or yellow-haired headman no like that, maybe. How you explain to priest what you do in here, eh?"

Tli turned to the men around him and resumed talking in our language. "Brothers, can't you see what these soldiers are doing? They are stealing from you. For a few drinks of *waskyja* you are selling away your children's birthright. Is that what you want?"

"What are you talking about, brother-in-law of my brother?" Gagayii shouted. "We play for only some of the Chamuqwani*waskyja*. If we lose we mark their paper; it is nothing."

"Get out," Ko cried. "You're spoiling everything!"

His voice dripping with contempt, Tli said, "It's nothing? Only paper? And what will you do in this new land when you hear your daughter cry, how will you sleep at night knowing you traded away the paper needed for food to feed your children? Will you care? Or will you just find another bottle, get drunk and forget about them?"

"I'll hunt to feed them, of course—you stupid meddler. You needn't worry about my family," Ko shouted, his face now also red as a berry.

Tli looked at the soldiers and then at Ko, his expression pitying. "And what are you going to do if there's no game to hunt, or the soldiers won't give us weapons to hunt with?"

"Did my wife send you here to spy on me?" Ko demanded. "No one asked you to come here—get out."

"You pitiful piece of dog shit, I knew it was a mistake when my sister married you. But you've a sweet way when you want something, don't you? What did you like more, my sister or the good trapping territory that came with the match?"

Ko and Gagayii got to their feet, Tli rose too. They squared off glaring at each other, crimson sparks shooting from their Spirit-Fires. I glanced at Samiqwas, his face was ashen, his eyes wide with fear. I wished Grandmother hadn't interfered, someone was going to get hurt—maybe killed. Probably Ko or Tli.

Soon everyone in the shelter was taking sides and yelling. To my surprise, the soldiers seemed as frightened as we were. Maybe not everyone guarding us was a part of their thievery.

"Now, Boys, settle down. Everybody have a drink on us. Make peace and then we'll get back to the game." The scar-faced soldier shouted. I doubt if anyone heard him over the din.

I didn't see who threw the first punch, but the next thing I knew, Ko and Tli were rolling around on the ground pummelling each other. Most of the men, being half drunk, became angry and confused by the yelling. Many other fights broke out. The shelter rocked dangerously, threatening to tip over. Scar-face and his friends cursed, trying to snatch up their waskyja and papers without getting their hands stepped on.

Adding to the uproar, Ko's mother and some of the nearby women in her lineage were screaming at the men to stop fighting and get out of their encampment. No longer trying to hide, Samiqwas and I rushed to the shelter's opening to look in. I heard a shout from up on the wall and looked up. There were more soldiers running along the walkway, heading for the stairs by the gate.

"The soldiers are coming," I shouted. Tli glanced round, and Gagayii hit him hard in the stomach. He doubled over, disappearing in the brawling mass of men.

Then we saw one of the soldiers inside cutting a slit in the shelter's back wall and forgot about my uncle. "They're getting away. We have to stop them!" Samiqwas shouted.

The first man through the hole I hit with a heavy piece of firewood, knocking him backwards into the fray. As Scar-face climbed through another cut a little further away, my cousin leapt onto his back, pounding him with his fists and shouting for someone to come help. Dropping his jug of waskyja, the soldier whirled round and round cursing, trying to dislodge him.

In the confusion that followed, I snatched up as many of the fallen papers as I could gather before a soldier saw me and aimed a kick in my direction. By that time, the soldiers from the wall had arrived, the black soldier who watched my aunt among them. I shouted for Samiqwas to let Scar-face go. My cousin jumped away. And as I'd hoped, before Scar-face could go anywhere, two of the soldiers grabbed him.

"Take your hands off me," he roared.

"You weren't on duty," one of the newcomers growled. "What you doing here?"

"When I heard all the noise I come down to help, and some zaunk brats attacked me."

"Here to help," another scoffed. "Not likely."

"Bugger your mother! I was."

I thought they were going to haul him away in chains like they were doing to the rest of the brawlers, but after more shouting his comrades believed him and let him go.

Fists balled at my side, I watched helplessly as Ko, Uncle Tli, and the rest of the gamblers were marched out of the gate. Ko's face was bloody, his expression sullen. Tli's eyes when he turned in my direction had the bitter, haunted look in them I'd seen on the steamboat, when he'd been kept for so long in chains. They were going to someplace bad, I could feel it. Standing beside me, Samiqwas was breathing heavily. When I stole a quick glance at his face, I saw tears glittering in the corners of his eyes.

After the gate closed behind our relatives, we slunk back to our shelter to make our report. Grandfather had returned, looking stern. Grandmother motioned with her chin for us to follow her into our tiny shelter. Once we were all crowded inside and away from curious onlookers, she demanded, "Tell us what's happened."

Between us, Samiqwas and I managed to stammer out an account of the afternoon's events. By the time we'd finished Grandmother's face was dark with anger and my aunt had buried her face in her hands sobbing. When Mother pulled her into her embrace Tuulah began to cry all the harder.

Grandfather let out a long sigh and rose to his feet. "I'll talk to Tsanqwati; we'll find out what they plan to do to our men. They shouldn't be punished for these soldiers' trickery."

Grandmother snorted but kept her opinions about the soldiers' justice to herself. When he was gone, she listened to her daughter cry for a time, then snapped, "Stop that."

Startled, the sisters looked up.

"I warned you about that man a long time ago, Tuulah, but you refused to listen. Now I give you one choice. You get up now and pack his things and return them to his mother's lodge. If you want to pack your own and go live in the Chamuqwani fashion, that's up to you, but I won't have that man in my household any longer."

"No!" Mother cried. "Can't you see how upset she is? Surely this isn't the time—"

"It is precisely the time. Tuulah, make up your mind."

Undaunted, Mother said, "Such a big decision can wait a while, 'til everyone has calmed down. Think of the children. They love their father."

Her attention drawn to them, Grandmother glanced at the trembling Samiqwas, and Seicu, sucking her thumb and looking frightened. Her eyes softened for a moment, then her mouth thinned into its hard line again. "Better to have no father, than a father like that one."

Mother gaped, then her eyes flashed in anger. "That was a very cruel thing to say—"

"Don't talk to me like that, Qwadalah," Grandmother said. "I am still your mother; show some respect—"

"I will when you deserve it!"

I had rarely seen Mother like this, and I trembled to see her so.

"Stop it, both of you," Aunt Tuulah said. She opened the door flap and crawled outside.

"Where are you going?" Mother called after her.

"To pack Ko's belongings. Mother is right. I should have done this a long time ago."

"Tuulah, wait—think. We'll need a strong young man to take care of us when we get to the new place. We're no more than women, old people, and children without him. The Chamuqwani won't listen to us—or care for us. We need a hunter in our lodge."

Standing in the doorway Tuulah put her hands on her broad hips and glared. "Then maybe it's time you find a husband of your own. You're right; we *will* need a strong hunter, but why is it always my responsibility to find a man to provide for us? Always refusing suitors, grieving for your lost seal man. Maybe I would have returned Ko's things to his mother a long time ago if you hadn't been so selfish." Without waiting for a reply, Tuulah turned her back on her startled sister and walked away.

Staring at the closing door flap, Mother's face flushed. She opened and closed her mouth several times, but no words came out.

"Never mind her harsh words. They mean nothing," Grandmother said. "Da'wabin, Tli, and your father will take care of us in this new land if we need men to hunt and protect us."

Mother gave her a pitying look and followed her sister out of the shelter. "I doubt if it'll be quite that simple."

Chapter Ten

Grandmother wasn't the only mother-in-law displeased with her daughter's choice of a husband that day. Not long after the news of the arrests got around, Tli's wife and some of his in-laws showed up at our camp. Carrying her baby on her hip, Shilshigua looked unhappy and maybe a little frightened. The heavy features of her mother and aunties were flushed and angry.

"Meddling Old Cow Moose, my daughter's husband has been taken to the fort and it's all your fault," Shilshigua's mother raged.

"My fault?" Grandmother cried. "How dare you accuse me—it was the soldiers who—"

"It was you, Chattering Crow, that sent him spying and gambling in the first place. What's wrong with you?" one of her aunties cried.

"Tli is a good son, who has a responsibility to his own mother-lineage. I merely asked him for help his sister—"

"His sister should keep her own marital difficulties to herself. Tli's main responsibility is to my daughter and her baby."

They hadn't brought back Tli's things, but Shilshigua's mother had a lot more to say about Grandmother's selfishness and meddling in the shouting match that followed.

When it was over and the intruders were gone, I huddled by the fire pit with my blanket over my head, feeling miserable, my stomach twisted in knots. I wished I knew where Samiqwas had gone. I was worried about him. But he had taken off with his little sister on his shoulders at the first sign of trouble.

Her mouth set into a stubborn line, Grandmother stalked into our shelter and hung a blanket over the entrance so she wouldn't be disturbed. Mother glared at the shelter, but made no move to go after her. At last she sighed and threw some spruce twigs onto the dying fire, in hopes the smoke would clear away the bad feelings hovering about our campsite.

One look at Grandfather's face when he returned at mealtime told me his news wasn't good. As we scooped out handfuls of thick mush from the large tin can we were using as a cooking pot, he said in a voice drained of emotion. "The soldiers have whipped Tli and put him in jail with Ko and the others."

"Whipped him?" Mother gasped.

"The Chamuqwani are all devils," Grandmother muttered and lowered her head to continue eating.

"Why did they whip our men?" Mother asked.

"In this case, the men were drinking and fighting. They caused a disturbance. That's against ChamuqwaniLaw, and so they were punished."

"What about the soldiers who gave them the waskyja and tricked them?" Aunt Tuulah wanted to know. "Were they whipped and thrown into the jail, too?"

Grandfather shook his head, his expression grim. "No, they weren't."

"Why not?" Samiqwas cried. "They were there and brought the waskyja. Tasimu and I saw them!"

Grandfather sighed and rubbed a hand across his face. "We all know what you boys saw is true, but Scar-face and his friends tell a different story."

"They're lying," I said.

"Yes, I'm sure they are," Grandfather said. "But there is no proof to say otherwise."

"And just how does this commander at the fort explain the *waskyja*," Mother asked.

"The commander doesn't know, but he believes some of the women who have been allowed out to forage got a jug from one of the traders. She hid it in her clothing when the guards were distracted."

"That's stupid," Grandmother said. "What Qwani'ya woman would conspire to get her husband drunk?"

Grandfather turned up his palms in a helpless gesture. "True enough, but the men at the fort don't see it that way. No argument Intercessor Raymonel or the elders offered swayed their decision."

"How long must they remain in the bad place?" Tuulah asked.

"The fort's commander isn't saying."

"What does Commander Mu'Dar say?" Mother asked.

"Nothing. In this place it is the yellow-haired one with one ear cut off who is in charge. The ones who are lying about their part in the matter are his soldiers. He chooses to believe them, not us."

"And just what do you plan to do about all this?" Grandmother said, glaring at her husband. "Your own son is in that terrible jail."

"And who caused him to be there?" Mother said. "You have no one to blame but yourself. Stop glaring or expecting Father to work miracles."

"You keep a respectful tongue in your head, my girl, or I'll—"

"Enough!" Grandfather said and emphasized his command with a flick of his power. The women fell silent, staring. "These accusations and angry feelings have got to stop! It won't help our relatives if we fight amongst ourselves. No one is to blame, and everyone is to blame. We must be of one mind, working together to resolve this."

A little calmer, but still angry, Grandmother repeated her earlier question, "What do you and the headman plan to do?"

Grandfather rubbed a hand across his face. When he dropped his hand to his side, I could see how exhausted he truly was. "Nothing more now. They've locked us in and won't open the gate again tonight. Tomorrow is a new day. We'll meet once more with the soldiers, and we'll find a way to resolve this."

He stood and held out a hand to Grandmother. "Come, my dear one, let's go to bed." She rose without a word and followed him into the shelter. The rest of us went to our beds not long after the old people were settled. I lay by Fire, wrapped in my blanket, and stared into its amber depths. Now that the sun abandoned the sky for longer periods of time, the nights were once more dark—and growing colder.

The Spirit-Lights snaked across the darkness in twisting patterns of green and violet. At the edge of my awareness I could hear the droning hum of their singing. I took a deep breath and closed my eyes, allowing my spirit to follow them away into the sky.

In my dreams, Chumco found me swimming among the stars and snagged my spirit in a net of luminous fibre. I wanted to stay among the lights, but he forced me to come with him.

<<The stockade is in turmoil over the arrests and your family's part in the incident. Tell me what you know about this.>>

I told him about Ko's drinking and Grandmother sending Uncle Tli to spy on the gambling games and what I'd witnessed. <<Please save my uncle, Elder.>>

<<Why do you need my help, young warrior, when you already have the means in your power to release your relative?>>

<<Me? I don't understand. How can I help?>>

<<You'd know exactly what I mean, if you would allow yourself to be guided by your Qwakaiva, instead of feeling sorry for yourself and your family.>>

<<How can I rescue them? I'm no great Qwakaihi—like you!>>

I was afraid for my uncle, angry with the soldiers for lying, and worst of all, I was heart-broken because Chumco wouldn't help.

<<Be at peace, young one,>> he soothed. <<Calm your mind and the answers will come, you're a smart one—I know you are. Trust me.>>

Still ensnared in his net, I tested the strands of my confinement, feeling ashamed and restless. Chumco loved and trusted me; why couldn't I trust myself? So many people were counting on me. Why couldn't I calm my fears and solve the riddle?

He was silent for a long time, thinking. At last he said, <<This injustice is but another example of the enemy's power, another victory that will be mirrored in that other world where your father battles. Such a pity. I'll pray for his safety.>>

Even within the Dream I felt the icy hand of dread close about my heart. <<Isn't there anything we can do to help him?>>

<<We can help him best by defeating the enemy that threatens us in this world.>>

<<How? I want to stop the Chamuqwani.>>

He smiled. <<So young and yet you're so eager. Brave Boy, there might be a way, but it will be dangerous.>>

<<Tell me. I'm not afraid.>>

<<Very well, I'll tell you the idea that has just now come to me. Because of my reputation, I can't approach the priest or the soldiers as openly as your grandfather, but perhaps I can do something in secret to defeat our enemy. I'll pray for our Benefactor's help. If Kunai favours me, I'll make the charm. You'll be my messenger. Would you like that, little seal?>>

<<Yes, I'll do anything to help you and my father.>>

He released me from his net. <<Good. Then we shall see if we can snatch the victory from out the enemy's closing jaws.>>

I pressed him for details, but he refused to say more. <<When I'm ready, I'll call you to me, little warrior. At that time, we'll test your courage, and you can discharge some of your debt to me.>>

Over my protests, Chumco sent my Spirit back into my body, plunging me into deep and dreamless sleep.

Chapter Eleven

G randfather's opinion that the situation would be quickly resolved the
next day was too optimistic. The day passed with our relatives still in
the soldiers' jail, in spite of endless hours of pleading and talk between our
representatives and the men at the fort.

When word got out that Uncle Tli and Ko's fight was the cause of the
arrests, there was a lot of bad talk going round about our family. People gave
us black looks as they walked by. After one name-calling incident ended with
me and Samiqwas getting our noses bloodied, we sat around our cook fire
looking glum. Our female relatives also spent most of the day by our fire,
since they weren't welcome in the camps of our relatives and friends.

Just before the evening meal when there was still no word of the men's
fate, Samiqwas whispered to me as we came back from the privy, "Do you
think the dark-skinned soldier that's always watching Amima would help us
get Uncle and my father free?"

I stared, nearly tripping over my own feet. "I don't know. Maybe. Do you
want to ask him?" I glanced up at the platform surrounding the stockade. He
was up there with a few of his men. As if his attention had been hooked by
our words, he was staring down at our shelter. "I'll go with you, if you do."

Samiqwas shook his head, a flush heating his cheeks. "Not you. I need
Amima."

Leaving me standing with my mouth hanging open, Samiqwas crossed to
the fire and spoke to Aunt Tuulah in a low voice. To my surprise, she agreed.
They waited until they saw the black soldier approach the gate, then she
whispered for Mother to watch the mush and they headed in that direction.

I started to slink off after them, but Mother stopped me. "One boy
running off is enough. Someone needs to amuse Seicu while I cook."

"But, Amima, I need to tell him what I saw, too."

She pointed to the hearth. "Sit. You can tell your story later, if he believes them and can help us."

I sat, sulking, trying to ignore Seicu playing with a grass doll. When she grew bored and began to fuss, I pulled out my loop of string without thinking, and started making string figures to amuse her.

I made the figure called the Raven's Nest, and then Sled Dog Running and a few others I thought she might like. Then, without consciously being aware of what my hands were doing, I formed the pattern of The Seer's Pool. An image of Aunt Tuulah and Samiqwas talking to the black-skinned soldier formed in the centre diamond almost immediately.

In my mind I heard Samiqwas say, <<But I saw them! I was just outside the shelter, on my belly, looking under the cover. There were three soldiers inside, Scar-face, the one with the big belly and the one with black woolly hair on his face and one tooth missing. They had waskyja and a cup with small painted rocks in it. When a Qwani'ya man won with the rocks, they gave him waskyja from the jug they'd brought.>>

<<My son doesn't lie, Soldier Man. Can't you do something to get my brother out of jail?>> Aunt Tuulah said.

The soldier's full lips twitched into a ghost of a smile, but there was no mirth in his eyes. Aunt Tuulah folded her arms over her breasts and waited. He studied her for a long moment, then finally he asked <<Your brother? And what of your husband? I hear he is also in the jail at the fort. What of him? Can we keep him?>>

Tuulah flushed, then her mouth thinned into an impatient line, and she tossed her braids over her shoulder. <<I have no husband.>>

The soldier raised an eyebrow, and she added, <<I took his things back to his mother. I repeat; I have no husband. Now are you going to help us or not?>>

<<So, it is as easy as that among your people? A woman just makes up her mind and returns a man to his mother.>> He smiled, his eyes travelling over her body in the way I'd seen men and women do when they wanted to couple with someone. Tuulah recognized his look, too. She raised her fist as if to strike him.

All teasing forgotten, he sobered and put up a hand to stop her. <<Your people's ways are so different from my own; but I shouldn't tease you at such

a time.>> He glanced down at Samiqwas, who looked angry enough to kill at that moment himself. <<Be easy with me as well, young warrior. I believe your story. I don't trust those men. My Commander would never have men like that in his troop. They deserve a flogging or worse, but without proof, Commander Magoss is unlikely to believe us.>>

Tuulah threw up her hands in frustration. <<But surely there must be something we can do, Soldier Man, to convince the fort commander that his men lie!>>

<<Ma'leubwey.>>

<<What?>>

<<My name, Pretty Qwani'ya Woman, is Ma'leubwey. I give you permission to call me Sergeant Ma'leubwey instead of 'Soldier Man.' What shall I call you in return?>>

<<Don't change the subject. Will you help us or not?>>

He sighed and gave her his smile again. <<I too won't lie to you and promise to do what I can't. But I *will* promise to speak to my Commander tonight. I know him well enough to say that he will do what he can. This is the best I can offer you. I am sorry it isn't more.>>

Tuulah's shoulders sagged in defeat. <<I am sorry too. Thank you for being honest with me, at least..>>

As they turned to go, my aunt looked over her shoulder at him one last time. <<My name is Tuulah.>> She turned and walked quickly away.

It was only me who saw his smile—or so I thought.

"Soldier like Amima." Seicu said and giggled.

I choked and dropped my string, staring at my little cousin as icy chills ran down my backbone. I'd been so intent on my conjuring, I'd forgotten about Seicu, sitting in my lap. I'd grown too complacent—gotten careless—Chumco was going to be furious with me. I trembled at the thought of Grandfather discovering my lessons and forbidding my apprenticeship.

How much had she seen or heard while looking into the pool with me? Feigning nonchalance, I asked, "What soldier man?"

She pointed to the sagging loop on my hands. "Man in picture, silly Rock Squirrel."

I felt my cheeks heat, but fear choked back my angry reply. I smiled instead and bounced her on my lap. She giggled. "Why do you think he likes her? Did you hear him say so?"

Seicu shook her head. "I just see. What him say?"

"I don't know, either; I just saw the picture, too."

Well, that was a relief. It was disconcerting enough that she'd seen anything, but if she told people that she'd not only seen pictures in my patterns but heard them talk as well, that would be my doom. But everyone saw a picture in the string figures; that was how the patterns came by their names. If she talked about my pictures, people would believe I was playing a harmless game and think nothing of it.

"More, want see more now!"

"No, I am too tired." Her face puckered up as if she were going to cry. "And I won't ever make the pictures for you again if you cry, or tell anybody, understand?"

She sniffed, but nodded. To distract her, I took her hand and stood. "Come, let's go meet them, I think I see them coming back now."

Chapter Twelve

T he grey dawn mist hung low over the stockade when I sensed Chumco's presence in my dreaming mind. <<It's time, little warrior. If you still want to help me defeat our enemy, then rise from your blankets and meet me by the privy.>>

<<I'll come.>>

<<That's good. I'm pleased with you. Hurry, I'm waiting.>>

I revelled in the joy of his approval, and I felt a now familiar warmth settle in the core of my body. But all too soon it was gone. Still ensnared within my dream, I watched as my physical-self threw my blanket about my shoulders and headed for the privy.

All was quiet in the stockade, most people's awareness not yet surfacing from the Lake of Dreams. No one called a greeting as I wove my way between the shelters. For those who were awake, I was just someone roused from sleep with a too-full bladder.

Chumco met me by the privy's privacy wall as I finished relieving myself. As he brushed by, he pressed a small leather-wrapped object into my hand. <<Take that to the priest's big tent. Conceal it somewhere inside, in a place where the bag won't be discovered. Put it among his things, if you possibly can.>>

He closed my hand around the charm. <<Go now and don't be afraid. My Spirit will be with you and protect you from harm.>>

I asked no questions; I just walked away as he disappeared behind the wall. Moving like a wraith through the sleeping stockade, I was hardly aware of my bare feet touching the cold ground. On the walkway above, the sentries dozed at their posts. People snored and coughed. A baby cried somewhere up by the gate.

At the priest's tent the morning fire had already been lit. A few sleepy Converts sat nearby, waiting for a pot of tea to boil. My footsteps faltered. <<What should I do now?>>

<<Continue walking,>> Chumco said. <<When the people around the fire can no longer see you, turn toward the wall and approach the priest's tent from behind.>>

With my blanket over my head and partially covering my face, no one recognized me or paid me any attention. I continued until I could no longer see them, then stepped past a group of snoring men, and squeezed behind a lean-to near the wall.

Still keeping close to the logs, I crept through the next encampment. But in the one closest to the priest's, a young boy popped his head out from under his mother's blankets and stared right at me. The green eyes grew round in his pale yellow face. I froze, as still as a rabbit scented by the dogs.

He opened his mouth, and I thought he would give me away for certain, but in the next moment his mother pulled him back under her blankets without looking in my direction. I moved hurriedly away when I heard his loud suckling at her breast.

At the rear of the priest's tent, I threw off my blanket and got down on my belly to peek under the canvas wall. The gossip around the stockade claimed that the priest and his women slept together in there—even though they weren't married or related. His Converts defended Intercessor Raymonel by saying that the priest and the Qwani'ya man studying with him, named Praiser Jon, slept behind one partition and the Mercy Women slept behind the other.

Looking into the dim interior of the tent, I saw no one sleeping in either straw-stuffed mattress on my side of the partition. The colourless dark robe protruding from a basket standing at the end of one of the beds gave me no clue, either.

<<Go inside, before you are discovered.>>

Crawling to the nearest stake I wiggled it back and forth till I could pull it from the ground. I worked on another, glancing up at the lightening sky. I would have to hurry; many people would be awake soon. I pulled the stake free, then slithered inside and stood, looking around. Was I in the priest's sleeping chamber or that of his women? I couldn't tell.

My instructions were to hide the bundle in a place where it wouldn't be discovered—at least for a time. But where would be a safe place? Surely not in the lidded basket containing clothes, nor would hiding it in the chest of holy objects I discovered be safe. And not in the boxes of hard-cake stacked by the bed. All these places would be examined frequently during daily use. Where then?

I was considering searching the other sleeping chamber, when I heard someone come into the tent's outer room. Fear hovered at the edge of my consciousness, waiting to strike. But my Spirit was still safely ensnared within Chumco's trance. I ignored its warning, allowing it to flow away like water falling from a seal's oily fur.

I crouched behind the stacked pile of food boxes at the foot of one of the beds, hoping the person would leave soon. My eyes darted about the dim chamber, sensing the urgency of the one who guided me.

Then, I heard the voices of more people coming into the tent. To my dismay, it didn't sound like they were going back outside any time soon. Before long someone might return to this place to collect something needed.

<<What should I do?>>

Anger and maybe a hint of desperation coloured the mental voice when he urged, <<Master yourself. Keep looking.>>

I took a deep breath and allowed my unfocused eyes to play across the items in the dim enclosure. I would find that special place—I would be brave...

Then, my attention happened to fall upon a small rip in the mattress by my shoulder. I pried my trembling fingers into the hole ripping it wider. I withdrew the talisman from my shirt and stuffed it deep into the moss and straw ticking. When it was done, I crept to the place where I'd pulled up the stakes and slipped out.

A wave of relief washed over me as I retrieved my blanket and threw it about my head and shoulders.

<<You've done well, my young warrior. Your father will be proud. I will leave you now, but I'll reward you for this later. You would like that, hmm?>>

A smile curved my lips at the thought. I had completed my task and pleased him—and maybe my father when he heard of it. Now I need only return to my own bed and rest and receive the sweet reward of pleasurable sensations I was learning to enjoy under his tutelage.

Fearing the child and his mother might be awake and notice me if I retraced my steps through their camp, I decided to go in the opposite direction.

I was just easing behind the next shelter's wall when a rough hand grabbed my blanket from behind and jerked me backwards so I nearly fell. "I saw you sneaking around back there, Boy. You nasty little zaunk, what did you steal?" My head whipped backwards as the hard-faced older Mercy Woman spun me round to face her. She repeated her question, shaking me by the shoulders.

I saw her angry grey eyes widen as she recognized me. "You again? I should have known." She tightened her grip. "Confess, what did you steal?"

I tried to pull away without hurting her, but she held on like a wolverine. Her loud voice was drawing the attention of the people by the fire and onlookers from the surrounding campsites.

"I'm no thief!"

"No thief? Then why were you sneaking around here so early in the morning?"

Why was I here; what explanation would she believe? Without giving myself time to think, I blurted out the first thing that came into my mouth. "I wanted to find Intercessor Raymonel. I've something to show him before he leaves for the fort. That's why I'm here early."

"That's a lie and you know it. You're just trying to talk your way out of a beating like all you zaunk brats."

I had been taught to respect people older than me, but this bitter woman was beyond my tolerance. Putting some force behind my blow I pulled free of her grasp. "If you don't like Zaunks and think we are all thieves and bad, then why are you here among us? Why don't you go back to where you came from?"

My smart mouth earned me a hard slap across the face, but before she could do more damage, the priest hurried over to us with some of his followers trailing in his wake.

"Celibress Vonica, what are you doing?"

She hadn't been aware of his approach until he spoke. Looking as fierce as a cornered mountain cat, she whirled round to face him. "I caught this lying boy sneaking round. There are some pulled up stakes over there," She pointed to the back of the tent. "He says he came to show you something before you go to the fort, but of course he is lying. He came here to steal."

The priest and the people with him turned their attention on me. I should have cringed at the anger and, yes, even hatred I saw in some of the Converts' eyes, but I was so indignant by that time, there was no room in my heart for fear. I reached into a pouch at my waist and drew out some of the papers I'd taken from the soldiers during the fight in Gagayii's shelter. I held them out to him.

"The scar-faced soldiers and the others say they weren't in the stockade until after the fight started, but that isn't true. They were there—many times. Grandmother was worried and so she sent my uncle to see what her daughter's husband was doing each day. My brother-cousin and I followed him. We snuck around the back of the shelter and saw what happened inside.

"The soldiers brought the waskyja with them and these pieces of paper with Chamuqwani writing on them. When a man won at the gambling the soldiers gave him waskyja. When a man lost, the soldiers made him put his mark on these pieces of paper. I picked these up during the fight. I came here to show them to you, because maybe they are important."

Intercessor Raymonel took them from my outstretched hand. As he looked them over, his face reddened, but I didn't think he was angry with me. The Mercy Woman asked him something in Chamuqwani and she wasn't happy with his answer, because she gave me a sour look.

"Are the papers important?" I asked him hesitantly when he continued to ignore me and stare at them.

Startled, he looked up and nodded. "Yes." He tapped them against his other hand and turned to an older man standing by his side. "Jon, this is all the evidence we need to get those poor men released." Returning his attention to me, he asked, "Son, why didn't you bring these to me sooner?"

I hung my head in shame, wanting to cry. So it was as Chumco had told me. I'd had the power to free my uncle all along, but I hadn't been paying attention. Feeling sick at heart, I stammered, "I forgot about them—I wasn't sure what they were—I didn't know they were so important."

I had just learned a hard lesson. I *had* known they were important in some way, if not exactly how. But I had allowed my Qwakaiva and my reason to be clouded by my emotions, and my Uncle Tli had suffered for my negligence.

Uncle and the others were released later that morning. Grandfather went to Shilshigua's camp to treat his wounds. He reported back to us that Tli was all right, though bitter and angry for the injustice done to him.

Ko must have gotten the news of his divorce, because he never came round, so Grandmother was denied the pleasure of turning him away.

As for Scar-face and the other soldiers involved, they were flogged after the priest threatened to report the yellow-haired commander to the Father Emperor. But the soldiers were allowed to keep the pieces of paper they'd tricked the men into signing.

We had been cooped up in this terrible place for too long. It was getting colder. People were sick, and this further example of injustice only added fuel to the flames of our resentment.

Part Three
Chapter One

"You will be leaving in four days." Just inside the stockade gate Sergeant Ma'leubwey stood with the fort's interpreter on a cart, the people assembling around him. "In preparation for our journey, the women will be issued leather, wool cloth, and blankets, so they can make the necessary clothing and foot gear."

"Praise to Djoven the Mighty and the Chamuqwani commander for this generous gift," a Convert man shouted.

The sergeant cleared his throat, his eyes fixed on the treetops showing just above the stockade wall. "You misunderstand," he finally said, "the cost of these supplies will be subtracted from the treaty money owed you."

"As if we wanted their money—as if we wanted to leave our land!" Samiqwas grumbled in a low voice beside me.

"So, we are expected to pay for our own removal," Uncle Tli shouted angrily "How very kind of you, Chamuqwani."

The soldier's mouth hardened, staring straight ahead. "I have my orders. The supplies will be arriving soon. Each man must line up. You will be required to place your mark in the ledger book to receive your family's allotment."

Glaring at everyone, Tli folded his arms across his chest. "I'm not marking any Chamuqwani paper."

"Please," Shilshigua murmured. "Think of our baby instead of your pride for once."

Tli's eyes dropped to the baby tucked into a side sling on her mother's hip. She smiled and held out a tiny hand to him. For just a moment his expression softened, then his mouth thinned into its habitual bitter line. He sighed and gave Shilshigua a stiff nod.

"What about the sick ones among us?" a downriver man cried. "My old mother and my youngest son are too ill to walk these hard mountain trails. Please, let those of us with ailing relatives build winter shelters and stay here until spring."

Sergeant Ma'leubwey shook his head when the interpreter finished translating. "That won't be permitted. The sick will be carried on sleds or pony drags until we come to a place where there are paths wide enough for carts to carry them."

The sergeant also told us that Commander Mu'Dar and his soldiers had been chosen to take us through the mountains and down the big river canyon leading south to the Chamuqwani lands. "Better him and his soldiers than that fool at the fort," Grandmother muttered.

Sneaking a look to the walkway where the sergeant and his guards now stood, Aunt Tuulah grunted her agreement.

ON THE FOURTH DAY THE sun rose in a haze of chalky light. In the midst of a lot of cursing and shouting, we were formed into a column and marched from the stockade. Like a big disjointed snake-monster, the line twisted and curved over the rocky path, leading to the Copper Falls Portage. Along with the Qwani'ya people and the soldiers who were going, there were also many pack beasts loaded high with supplies. Several pony drags carrying the worst of the sick moved slowly just ahead of the rear guard.

A cold wind blew in off the lake, knifing through our clothing as we turned our faces southward and began to climb. Willow and aspen flamed golden along the first portion of the trail. As we neared the higher elevations, the scrub was replaced by taller spruce and firs.

I was surprised when I learned that Intercessor Raymonel, his mercy women, and the big tent were also coming with us. He and his converts walked in a tight column just behind the leading soldiers. The priest and his followers sang hymns of thanksgiving to their god for the new land. They made a great noise, but behind their show of enthusiasm, tears glistened in the eyes of many.

The rest of us straggled in disorganized groups in their wake. Walking by Mother's side with a blanket pack of our belongings on my shoulders, I breathed in the crisp morning air. We were leaving, never to see this beautiful land again. That terrible knowledge grieved my heart, but in spite of that I was also relieved at being free of the stockade. Adding to my turmoil, I was dimly aware of Chumco's black rage, churning in the depths of my consciousness. The intensity of his emotion frightened me. I suspected he wasn't aware of our link, and I didn't dare draw his attention to that fact, but it fuelled the disharmony of my Spirit.

My grandparents walked together, but Grandmother seemed barely aware of her husband and his steadying arm. She moved with her eyes focused straight ahead, her mouth set into a hard line. From time to time, Grandfather glanced at her as if worried by the muddy fog swirling through her Spirit-Fire. She ignored him, refusing to answer any of his questions.

Aunt Tuulah followed them, carrying more of our belongings on her strong back. Samiqwas held his sister's hand and lifted her onto his shoulders from time to time when there was a rough patch in the trail.

Throughout the morning I heard many people sobbing, men and women alike. Often a person would stop to touch a tree or sing a song of farewell to a mossy boulder.

Grieving with the rest, I leaned my face against a tall birch, its pealing papery bark rough under my cheek. Small tremors vibrated through the trunk from the feet of the people and animals passing by. The tree's consciousness was sluggish with the cold. Winter and the long sleep filled its thoughts.

<<Good bye,>> I whispered. <<I will miss you.>> A leaf detached and fell atop my head like a tear.

Then, a sharp blow on the back of my leg brought me to my knees. A soldier with a riding whip in one hand and his thunder-weapon in the other glared down at me. "Keep moving," he growled.

I cried out, looking up bewildered. "I only want say good bye," I tried to explain. He raised his whip once more. I staggered to my feet and hurried to catch up with my family.

As I resumed my place, I noticed other soldiers riding along the column, shouting curses and threatening us. They seemed intent on keeping us moving at all costs, and our frequent stops to say good bye infuriated them beyond reason.

Just ahead of my family, walked Matoqwa, Cohasi, his mother, and an old uncle. Tears running down his face, the old man had difficulty paying attention to his niece's whispered attempts to hurry him. The trail was walled about with a thick stand of spruce and fir in that spot, and he wanted to say good bye to each tree. There was a sizable gap opening up between the rest of the column and those of us who followed behind.

The gap was finally noticed and several men trotted back, waving their weapons and shouting. Unfortunately, the old man was grieving too loudly to pay attention. He refused to move, his arms hugging the coarse grey bark of a tall fir.

Enraged, the soldiers beat him till he fell upon the ground. Matoqwa rushed forward to help his uncle, a young soldier hit him in the face with the butt of his thunder-weapon, and he sprawled beside the old man. Cohasi would have rushed into the fray at that point and gotten bloodied as well, but his mother grabbed him and held on, screaming at both him and the soldiers. Grandfather and other nearby people yelled at the men to stop.

Before the situation worsened, Sergeant Ma'leubwey rode up cursing. He flung himself off his horse, and demanded, "What's going on here? Why did you stop?"

Everyone wanted to tell their story at once. He shouted for quiet and finally it was sorted out. "You must keep moving," Sergeant Ma'leubwey said. Then, catching sight of my aunt among the waiting people, he offered a further explanation, "My men aren't being deliberately cruel. We have a long way to go today. It would be very hard on the children and the old people if we are forced to make a cold night camp on the portage itself. So you must stop these delays and keep moving." Then, without looking back, he mounted his mule and hurried up the trail.

All day we climbed with the booming of the falls ringing in our ears. The way was steep and slippery in places from wind-blown spray. We continued on until nearly dark and at last made a rough camp in a small hollow just off the main trail.

Wind gusted through the trees, spilling droplets of moisture on the soldiers watering the horses and mules. Men cut saplings and hammered

them into the ground. Over them they tied large canvas tarpaulins to act as
temporary shelters. The women and children cooked the evening meal and
did camp chores, while our men were set to digging a shallow privy trench.

Most of the soldiers did no work and stood around with their weapons
drawn, watching everyone. We had been told that for each person who
escaped one of our elders would be killed. The women had agreed under this
threat to give assurance for everyone's good behaviour. Women and children
would do the camp chores, forage for food and not try to escape. But in spite
of our pledge they didn't trust our men; they weren't allowed out of camp to
hunt.

Our ways were so different from Chamuqwani ways. As the black soldier
had told us on the steamboat, it was inconceivable to them that a woman's
word could bind an entire family including her strong and angry men folk.

Women and children could forage for food, however. So, after seeing
to the comfort of my grandparents within one of the shelters, I joined
Samiqwas and the older boys in making simple rabbit snares from nettle
cordage and willow wands. We slipped past the soldiers and laid our snares
along the game trails up and down the creek, hoping for some fresh meat for
the evening meal.

Drawn to the sound of rough water, I walked upstream past the others
and found a tumbling little patch of rapids. In a sheltered pool several black
trout were swimming. By lying flat upon a fallen log and crawling slowly out
over the pool, I was able to reach my hand into the cool water and catch hold
of several fine, big fish. I flipped them to the bank before the others caught
on to my tricks and headed for the bottom out of my reach.

Returning to the bank I killed the fish to stop their suffering. I thanked
them for the gift of their lives, then I strung them on some nettle cord and
headed back to camp. Samiqwas, Matoqwa, and Cohasi met me with some
rabbits flung over their shoulders. When he saw my fish, Matoqwa gave me
a curious look. Remembering the Seal that was my father, I felt my face heat
and dropped my eyes.

He laughed. "Trust a Siyatli to find fish where none should be."

"They were swimming in a pool by the rapids," I stammered and pointed
back over my shoulder.

Cohasi cocked his head, giving me a quizzical look. "So. Why are you explaining? I like black trout. Want to trade two for a rabbit?"

I hesitated, and then detached two from my string. "Sure." The transaction completed, Samiqwas called for a race.

Before returning to my own fire, I shared my catch with others among the People. Giving in to a perverse impulse I offered a nice fat black trout to Sergeant Ma'leubwey, which surprised him. I wasn't sure how I felt about his obvious interest in my aunt, but he was a good man, and I reasoned that it didn't hurt to have a friend among these enemy soldiers.

When I proudly displayed the last of my catch to Mother, she smiled at me. Splitting both rabbit and fish open, she laced them between sticks and propped them by the fire to roast.

Heavy fog rolled in after sunset. Lit by the blurred yellow light from our fires, the silhouettes of our guards, looming unexpectedly out of the gloom, reminded me of disembodied demons. I shivered in my blanket and drew its folds closer around me.

But in spite of the fresh meat, our meal that night was a sombre affair. No one felt like talking. We were all exhausted. Someone, maybe Samiqwas, was coughing. Seicu was fretful, barely eating. Mother put an arm about my shoulder and drew me closer. She gave me an encouraging smile. Tiny droplets of moisture clung to her hair. I nestled up against her without shame, feeling her solid warmth, and drowsed.

That was the last night of comfort I had for a long time.

Chapter Two

On the third day after we crossed the portage the weather changed. The air when we woke was cold, tasting of snow. The soldiers hurried us onto the trail as early as possible. No one complained over much; we all knew the signs of a big storm coming.

When the snowfall began around midday, it was gentle and sporadic. Large soft flakes fell silent as feathers for a time, and then they would stop, leaving the trail clear ahead of us.

Pausing to catch his breath after a particularly steep climb, Grandfather looked up at the iron-grey clouds hovering just above the treetops. "I don't think we will be able to make it to a sheltered camping spot in time."

Grandmother lowered her blanket from her head and looked up. "We should turn back; make camp by the spring where we rested earlier."

The shrubs around us had been recently browsed by a herd of elk. Their musk hung heavy in the air. Grandfather shook his head, still studying the sky. "No, I don't think so. The spring is too high and exposed. It doesn't have enough firewood for so many people. Better for us to keep moving."

She barked a mirthless laugh. "Keep moving and die in the coming blizzard."

Giving me a thin-lipped smile, Grandfather sighed. Grandmother was already walking along the trail, her blanket once more covering her head. Picking up his bundle, he hurried to catch up with her.

The soldiers pushed us mercilessly as the day wore on. Now that we had crossed the portage around the great falls, we were descending through the mountains in a series of winding game trails that mostly paralleled the course of the Copper River.

As the day darkened into afternoon, the wind blew harder. Then, the clouds suddenly let go of their burden in a blinding shower of white.

As I trudged beside Mother and Samiqwas, my feet and hands grew more chilled at each step. Wind moaned through the branches of the trees, and frost demons laughed and threw stinging icy flakes in my face. Seicu was coughing and wanting to be carried. Samiqwas tried, but stumbled often, lagging behind. Over the wind I could hear her plaintive cries.

Finally Mother and Aunt Tuulah stopped beside the trail, waving other blanketed travelers to pass on by, while they waited for Samiqwas to catch up. "Go on; your Grandmother may need you," Mother said to me. "I'll stay and help my sister."

I glanced up the trail where the shadowed figures of the old people, Uncle Tli, and his family were disappearing into the gloom. Snowy sleet stung my face. I turned away. Samiqwas drew near, staggering through the drifts, Seicu clinging to his back under their shared blanket.

I wanted to hurry after the rest, but a tendril of warning stabbed at my heart, cautioning against it. "Uncle Tli is with them. I'll stay with you," I shouted over the wind.

She gave me a curious look, but wasted no energy on arguing. When Samiqwas reached us, Aunt Tuulah took her shivering daughter in her arms, while Mother divided up Aunty's pack between herself, Samiqwas, and me.

All that took some time, and when we resumed walking there was no one in sight. The light was fading; blowing snow quickly obscured the trail. Mother took the lead, her walking stick cutting deep furrows into the growing drifts. "We have to hurry," she called. "Stay close or we will lose one another."

Frost demons mocked her words with their laughter. Tiny pale beings with asymmetrical faces and hard green eyes, they danced atop skeletal branches drooping under icy coatings of white. <<Where are you going?>> they called to me, as I passed.

<<Come to us. Rest a while. We know you are tired. Feel our kisses upon your cheeks. Stay and soon you will be warm and safe with us. We will love you forever.>>

I raised my face into the wind and shook my fist. <<Go away. Leave me alone! Your words are lies, Go away!>>

They howled, throwing stinging ice crystals into my eyes, so I had to close them. I stumbled over a hidden tree root and nearly fell. They laughed louder and threw more missiles.

<<Nasty little human, we will teach you to be respectful.>>

<<Bad boy, we know your secrets. We know,>> one said.

<<So arrogant—bad, bad, but you can't hide what you are and what you've done, from us,>>another cried.

<<In your heart, you are no different than us. We know.>>

<<No! I'm not like you. I don't know what you are talking about—go away—leave me alone!>>

I quickened my pace. Something deep in my soul trembled. I wanted to outrun their terrible words. My heart wasn't evil. I didn't know—didn't want to know—what they were talking about. <<Go away—leave me alone!>>

The gloom deepened; my feet and hands were numb. I focused my eyes on the hunched form of Mother right in front of me. I concentrated on putting one foot in front of the other. Something deep in my Spirit trembled. I wanted to outrun their terrible words.

The storm closed in around us. The wind howled through the trees. I could see no one on the path ahead of us. Had we missed their sign and now were lost? I wanted to use my new skills and call upon Grandfather for help.

Back at the stockade, if he'd paid any attention to me at all, he would have seen with his Spirit-Sight what I could no longer hide. Engrossed in my secret studies with Chumco, I'd welcomed his indifference—thought it a blessing, in fact. I'd constantly worried that I might do something that would alert him to my apprenticeship with a man he had warned me against. And for that same reason, I feared calling upon him, even though I craved his comforting presence in my mind.

Well, if I was afraid of Grandfather discovering my secret, then I should contact my teacher. Chumco could be gentle and loving when I pleased him, but his mood had been so unpredictable of late that I hesitated. Ever since the morning I'd put his charm in the priest's tent, his interest in me had waned. On the few occasions when he did allow me to communicate with him, he was impatient to end the contact, promising me more time—later. But as the storm and the darkness closed in about us, I realized I had little choice. My relatives and I would die without guidance.

Chumco must have sensed the urgency in my summons, because he answered without hesitation. <<Your mother has missed the path,>> he told me when I had explained our situation.

<<The camp is to the south and west in the next sheltered hollow. Tell her you will lead and I will send a Fetch to guide you.>>

Forcing my numbed feet to go faster, I caught up to Mother and pulled on her arm. "Amima," I shouted. "We're going the wrong way. We'll miss where the People have camped if we continue this way."

She stared at me dully, snowflakes coating her hair and eyelashes. When she didn't answer I begged, "Please, the Unseen Ones have shown me the way."

Aunt Tuulah and Samiqwas had reached us by then. "What's wrong?" Tuulah said. "We have to keep moving. It will be dark soon."

"My son says the Spirits have told him that we're going the wrong way," Mother explained.

Cold and swaying with fatigue herself, Tuulah seemed to take a long time understanding her words. Finally she motioned for me to take the lead.

Feeling the weight of the responsibility placed on my shoulders, I stepped away from the women and turned in a circle with my eyes closed, reaching out with my Qwakaiva to touch the pulse of the land about us. Chumco had said the camp was south and west. When I felt a tug on my awareness I stopped and opened my eyes.

The camp was in that direction; I could feel it now. And as if to confirm my judgment, I saw the glowing form of a Spirit-Lynx slipping through the trees ahead of me.

"This way," I called and took off through the forest after the Fetch.

Heading south once more, we climbed up a steep slope, staying in the trees as much as possible. Under the sheltering branches of the firs, the snow hadn't had time to collect into deep drifts. The travelling was easier. Before we reached the top, the Fetch turned us westward and began an angling descent downward onto a new trail.

My mentor lending me strength, I felt neither the cold nor my fatigue, but behind me I sensed the women's exhaustion increasing. Their strength was nearly finished. Ahead of us the Fetch was moving swiftly along this new path. I could barely make out its glowing form in the deepening gloom.

The snow was nearly to my knees in places along this new trail, and without snowshoes the going was difficult. <<Wait,>> I called to it in desperation. <<We can't go so fast over this deep snow.>>

The Lynx turned, its glowing yellow eyes surveying us with a cold indifference. <<You have the Qwakaiva to float atop the snow. Leave them and come.>>

Leave Mother, my aunt, my cousins? They would die without me. <<No! I can't do that. They are my kin.>> Did I possess such power? I trembled in my soul, afraid to find out—afraid to be tempted by such a discovery.

The Lynx turned its back on me and walked down the trail, disappearing into the gloom. "Please hurry," I shouted over the wind.

I don't know how long we struggled through the storm. I had lost the Fetch, but now knew where the camp lay, so I continued to plod in that direction with head lowered against the wind. Unthinking, more than half frozen, I focused on putting one foot in front of the other and kept moving.

Somewhere in that nightmare of wind, snow, and biting cold, a dark form loomed out of the storm in front of me. I raised my eyes and saw it was a man leading a mule, heading up the trail towards us. As he reached us, I recognized Sergeant Ma'leubwey.

I stopped, the others coming up beside me. I heard Seicu whimpering, complaining of the cold. Aunt Tuulah pulled the blanket over her face, trying to soothe her. Over my aunt's feeble protests, Ma'leubwey took the child from her arms and climbed onto the mule. Reaching down a hand, he pulled Tuulah up behind him.

"The camp isn't far," he told the rest of us. "Walk behind the mule and the going will be easier. Stay close and you won't get lost."

The sergeant left us beside the first roaring fire we came to, once we reached shelter. Someone pushed a hot cup of spruce needle tea into my hand. I sipped it gratefully and stretched my feet towards the fire. Seicu cried as her feet thawed. I knew how she felt; my own limbs ached with such a burning pain that it left me gasping.

Now that my mind was awakening from its plodding stupor, I wondered how many more of my people would be lost in the storm. Surely we weren't the only ones gone astray. I couldn't see much in the darkness and blowing snow. But I heard the sounds of axes chopping down saplings to make shelters for people to get out of the storm. I shivered as melting snow from the fire's heat ran down my chest. Where was the rest of my family? Were my grandparents and Uncle Tli safe?

I must have dozed off, for the next thing I remembered was jerking awake when someone laid a hand on my shoulder. I looked up; Mother and a bearded soldier were standing above me. She held out her hand. "Come, we must get under shelter before the storm gets worse."

I rose slowly, glancing across the fire. Samiqwas and Aunt Tuulah were gone. An old man and woman I didn't know were squatting in their place. All covered in snow, these new arrivals were shivering and holding out their hands to the blaze.

Confused, I hesitated and looked up at Mother. "Where—"

The soldier made an impatient gesture, motioning us to hurry. "Come quickly now. They're all right," Mother reassured me.

The soldier brought us to a shelter of saplings and spruce boughs, piled shoulder high with snow for insulation. He pulled aside a blanket stiff with ice. I heard a stranger shout, "No room. Go away."

Another voice, a woman by the sound, called out a name I didn't recognize, then began crying when she realized we weren't the person she was looking for. The soldier yelled at the people to shut up and motioned us inside.

After we crawled through the low doorway, the blanket was closed quickly. People grumbled, shifting their positions to make room for us. Inside the air was dark and moist, clammy against the bare skin of my forehead. It was still cold, but warmer than being out in the storm. As I squeezed in between Mother and the sobbing stranger, I whispered, "Amima, where is our family?"

"Don't worry. They're well. There just wasn't enough room in one shelter for all of us. Try to sleep now. There's nothing more we can do till the storm is over."

Listening to the wind howl outside our little nest, I knew she was right. I tucked my feet up for warmth and leaned my head against her.

When we were settled, Mother called out a polite greeting to the unseen occupants of the shelter, giving our use-names and where we were from. In spite of the initial resentment to our arrival, the people answered her with courtesy. There were four others already in this shelter, two women who were not related, an old man who was related to one, and a small child who constantly coughed.

While the storm lasted I huddled next to Mother and tried to forget about my cramped and numbing limbs. The snow outside fell thick and heavy, as silent as a stalking lynx one moment, then slamming against the branches of the shelter with a stinging fury the next time the wind gusted. Frost demons danced and gibbered around the shelter, taunting me. I was afraid and dared not allow myself to sleep as my mother suggested, for fear my Spirit would wander away and never return to my body.

Sometime during that long night my teacher checked on me. He was glad I was safe, but he offered me little comfort. His touch was impersonal, nearly as cold as the storm outside. Power radiated from his Spirit-Fire, making me tremble with excitement. He had gathered the Qwakaiva of the storm about him to work some great enchantment. I begged him to let me help him, but he silenced my pleas with a stinging command that left me gasping.

<<Then will you let me share my Qwakaiva with you, so I can at least help in some small way?>>

<<There's no need for me to draw upon your power at this time. The storm will lend me all I need. Later you can help, my brave little seal. You'll need all your strength to survive this night.>>

And with that he was gone, leaving me with the mocking laughter of the frost demons ringing in my head. <<Bad boy, bad boy, come, lend *us* your Qwakaiva. We won't refuse you. Come, give us your Spirit's Power—dance with us, we will love you forever.>>

THE STORM CONTINUED on into the next day. I ate flat, dry hard-cake from Mother's pack and melted handfuls of snow in my mouth when thirsty. Mostly I dozed between Mother and the woman separated from her family.

Though desperately afraid for her husband and little girl, she was also sensible enough to know that there was no point in looking for them until the storm abated. I tried hard to ignore her quiet sobbing, all the same.

Mother soothed her as best she could. "Your family might be safe. The soldiers are pushing people into any dwelling that has room regardless of kinship. So don't give up hope."

I learned later from Mother that thanks to Sergeant Ma'leubwey, we were some of the lucky ones who knew where all our family members sheltered. The sergeant had collected Aunt Tuulah and her children and put them in with my grandparents—and Tli and his family too were safe.

As the light began to fade the next afternoon, the storm finally died. The ache of my full bladder nearly bending me in half, I stumbled from the snowy mound of our refuge. When I returned to the encampment, I wandered over to a cook fire where I found Mother and Aunt cutting up dry-fish and tossing it into a large tin can with oat-mush and snowmelt. My stomach rumbled at the thought of something warm to eat.

Around me in the camp I heard the joyous cries of reunion and the frantic calls of lost family members searching by each fire for some of their own relatives. Pausing to brush the last of the clinging snow from my garments, I glanced up into the night sky. My heart felt swollen with gratitude for our good fortune. I offered up my prayer of thanksgiving to the Unseen Ones for their blessing. We had been lucky—this time. Above me the green serpentine Spirit-Lights writhed across an indigo sky already dotted with the shining eyes of stars.

While the women brewed spruce tea and cooked, the soldiers came around counting people. A low wind rattled through the branches of the firs, its breath against my face promised a cold night to come. I prayed there would be no more lives lost.

When I first saw Grandmother she was so stiff from the cold that she could hardly walk. She leaned heavily on Grandfather's arm as he led her to the fire. When she was settled, she sipped her tea and studied me with penetrating black eyes.

Waiting until I began to squirm, wondering what I'd done to displease her, she finally said, "My eldest daughter tells me that you saved her and her children from being lost in the storm. Did you call upon your father again?"

Grandfather's head turned sharply in my direction, awaiting my answer. I shook my head and dropped my eyes, suddenly finding much to interest me in the collection of spruce needles at the bottom of my cup. The wind gusted up just then, but the cold chill that ran down my back wasn't of the wind's making.

Grandfather's curiosity was aroused. And Grandmother's eyes were still boring into me, demanding more than a shake of the head in answer. She wasn't going to let the matter drop, so I took a deep breath and looked her in the eye.

"No, Ami, I didn't call upon my father. As I told you before, he can't help me now."

"Then who did help you, if not your father, hmm?"

I needed to be very careful how I answered. Grandfather could detect my dissembling, if he were of a mind. Chumco had told me, and I truly believed, that Grandfather's hatred for my father was so strong that he would do all in his power to prevent me from gaining any form of knowledge that wasn't his to control.

"There were wandering ghosts in the storm ... I begged one of them to help me—and it did. To spite the frost demons, maybe, because they were tormenting me."

Grandmother seemed disappointed, but satisfied with my answer. Grandfather gave me a searching look, unconvinced. To my relief he let the matter drop. I took in a deep breath and let it out slowly. I resolved to avoid being alone with him for a time. I hated keeping secrets from him.

I loved him and I knew he loved me, too. He only wanted what he thought was best for me, but was what he wanted truly the best for me? I was growing older. I would be a man soon—I kept telling myself that when the worm of doubt nibbled at my resolve. I had a right to choose what was best for me, didn't I?

After we ate, Samiqwas and I helped Uncle set up a branch and blanket lean-to. A blazing fire in front would help heat the shelter's interior for the night. The weather was clear and cold. As the evening lengthened, the camp settled into an uneasy silence. I huddled with the rest of my family on a bed of spruce boughs and tried to sleep. We would have to be up before dawn. The soldiers wanted us to get an early start.

Sometime in the night I was roused from troubling dreams by the sound of a child crying. Opening my eyes I saw Aunt Tuulah sitting up with a blanket about her shoulders, rocking a whimpering Seicu. The little girl was mumbling something about bad ghosts calling her. Tuulah was trying to soothe her.

I suspected that others of the family had been awakened by Seicu's outcry, but like me, no one was stirring out of the warmth of their blankets to help comfort her.

Or so I thought, then I saw Grandfather step into the firelight carrying an armload of branches. He put several thick limbs onto the blaze, but instead of returning to his bed, he sat down by the fire and stared into the night. Seicu was settling, yet he remained alert. Curious more than frightened now, I slipped from under my blanket and crawled from the shelter.

The air outside the lean-to was bitter cold, the night pulsating with Qwakaiva. Once away from the other sleepers, I could sense its unnatural power. Was this what had disturbed my cousin? Maybe. Like me, Seicu was sensitive to the Spirits. Questing for answers, I allowed a tendril of my spirit to slip from my body and go exploring.

Surrounding the entire camp were unknown powers that seemed to be born of the dark and the cold itself. Such Qwakaiva didn't frighten me, but I was certainly intrigued. Grandfather was too near for me to venture far, or stay long out of my body, but if I could find a quiet place...

Hoping to discover more, I rubbed at my eyes as if just waking, and headed for some nearby trees to relieve myself. I hadn't gone but a few steps, when Grandfather's low voice stopped me. "Unless you truly can't wait until morning, Grandson, I'd prefer that you don't break the protective circle I've just laid about us."

I froze. Stupid boy, how had I missed the glowing radiance nearly under my feet? Slowly I turned back to face him. "I can wait, Ati. What's wrong?"

"Good. It would be better if you didn't break the circle. Evil stalks this camp tonight, and I want you to stay safe."

Evil? I felt a chill rattle my bones and raise the hair at the nape of my neck. I hadn't sensed anything evil. There were no frost demons about—nothing harmful that I could detect. I turned back to the night peering into the darkness, trying to see what had disturbed him.

Focusing my Spirit-Sight, at first I saw only the golden shimmer of his shield. "Ati, I don't see anything—"

"Look in the shadows under the trees, Grandson."

Focussing my Gift, I sensed more than saw the grey wraiths under the firs. Then, I caught glimpses of distorted faces and slim, pale spectres, flowing purposely through the shadows. "Ah, I see them now. What are they, Grandfather? Have you seen their kind before?"

"I won't give them a name, lest I invoke their interest. And yes, I have seen their kind. But only once before and that was long ago."

"Was what you remember about them evil?"

"Yes."

"Has someone called them to come here?"

"That would be a logical assumption, Grandson, wouldn't it?"

Shocked, I blurted, "But who would do that?"

"I don't know yet, because there is more than one powerful mind conjuring Qwakaiva to battle this night."

"Warring forces of Qwakaiva?" Grandfather's words confused me. "How could that be?" Determined to know more, I focused my Spirit-Sight once more upon the wraiths moving through the camp.

Then, an invisible force sensed my meddling and lashed out with a bolt of directed malice. Before I could draw away, it came hurtling out of the darkness and exploded against Grandfather's shield in a cascade of blue fire.

I'd been spared the full force of the blow, yet it contained enough evil intent to have me clutch my unprotected stomach. A low buzzing whined inside my head. I cried out and staggered backward. Before I could fall, Grandfather's arm was around my shoulder, steadying me.

I saw the next one coming, and braced myself. Grandfather held up the Otter's talisman and chanted words of power. The barrier held firm, the evil dissipating harmlessly. As he helped me back to the fire, I heard the sounds of singing and someone chanting a loud prayer to the Thunderer.

Recalling Chumco's insistence that the priest was evil in spite of his seeming kindness, I shivered. "Ati, what is happening? Are the priest and his converts trying to kill us?"

He laughed softly. "No, I don't think so. I doubt if Intercessor Raymonel's Qwakaiva is that strong. Nor do I believe he would abuse his power in that way—"

"But, Ati, there is more going on over there than just singing and prayers. Someone among the Converts is malicing; I can feel—"

"Yes, there is malicing, but whether it is being consciously guided in our direction is another matter."

He must have seen the inner turmoil mirrored on my face, because he sighed and then added, "There are a lot of frightened people among us, Grandson, be they Convert, breed men, or keepers of the old ways. Some are trained, some are not, but anyone with strong Qwakaiva who speaks words of cursing with intent, whether he calls it prayer or not, is practicing malicing."

Worried by his sombre tone, I glanced around the sleeping camp once more. "If that's so, then we have to warn—"

"Those among us who keep the old traditions already know. As for the others, what could I say to them that wouldn't make things worse? Haven't you heard the priest say there is no such thing? They call it 'heathen superstition,' right?"

"But shouldn't we do something to protect the good people in this camp anyway?"

"Yes, those of us with the Gift do the best we can to protect everyone—though often in secret. No more talk now. Go back to bed."

Visions of heroic deeds bumping about in my head, I offered, "Grandfather, don't send me away like a baby. I'm not Seicu. I too have a Gift. Let me help you protect us."

He gave me a lopsided smile, but shook his head. "Someday perhaps, but tonight I can manage. Go to sleep. You are untrained. There is little you could do to aid me."

Once again my lack of training was being thrown back into my face by a skilled Qwakaihi. And whose fault was it that I *wasn't* trained? Not mine, I thought resentfully. His rejection stung and so I allowed my smart mouth to lead me into danger.

"I helped you well enough at the rapids. But if I am so *untrained*, then take what you need of my Qwakaiva to ensure our safety. At least in that way I can help."

The moment those words left my mouth I feared I had made a terrible mistake. When he needed power for his conjuring, I allowed my mentor to take some of my Soul's Essence, my Qwakaiva. In the way of those bonded to Kunai, I offered my Qwakaiva in exchange for his teachings. But such exchanges of power had never been the way of those claiming Qwa'osi as their Spirit-Benefactor.

Judging by his withering glare, I was sure he guessed Chumco and I were now bonded, but his next words surprised me—though they hurt nonetheless. "I am no soul-stealing seal man, taking what isn't mine—even when it is foolishly offered by an ignorant boy. Go back to bed. Now!"

Angry and resentful, tears stinging my eyes, I went to my blankets, but didn't sleep. My Spirit was excited by the danger present in the darkness. Why did everyone continue treating me like a baby?

Wasn't it me who helped save us from the Water Spirits in the rapids who wanted us to drown and join them? And wasn't it me who rescued my mother, aunt, and cousins from the Storm Demons who hid the trail from us and tried to kill us?

Samiqwas couldn't have done any of that—even if he was a year older than I was and considered nearly a man. Maybe Grandfather would change his mind and need my help after all. I comforted my wounded pride with that thought and after a while drifted back into my dreams.

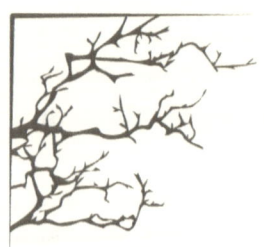

Chapter Three

Next morning the cold seeping through my blankets and ragged clothing finally woke me. I sat up, rubbing the sleep from my eyes. The camp was alive with activity, women packing bedding, soldiers tending the mules and horses, children hauling water from the nearby creek. Where people and animals hadn't churned the ground to brown, slippery goo, the drifted snow had a blinding intensity.

When I stepped behind a bush to relieve myself, I heard water dripping from tree branches deeper in the forest's gloom. A warm breeze caressed my face. It was early in the season for the snows to remain on the ground more than a few days.

The soldiers pressed us to hurry, allowing time only for a meal of their hard-cakes and tea, before urging us onto the trail. We had to leave these exposed lands behind. If real winter caught us in the high mountains, many more would die than the few lost in the blizzard.

During that day, and those that followed, I fell into a mind-numbing lethargy in which I had energy only to lift one foot after the other. Keeping my eyes closed to mere slits against the glare, I tried not to slip in the icy mud, praying I wouldn't fall down the bank into the growling river below us.

The weather grew warmer the further south we travelled, but there were still frequent autumn storms. The only difference was that instead of snow we had mud and bone-chilling rain to torment us. And the days were growing shorter, slowing our progress as well.

When it became clear to everyone that Aunt Tuulah had indeed divorced her husband, she began to receive the attentions of other unmarried men—including Sergeant Ma'leubwey. The sergeant rode alongside my aunt as often as he dared. When none of his superior officers were about, he would even take a turn at carrying Seicu to give my aunt a rest.

It was during such a time that I overheard him telling Tuulah how worried Commander Mu'Dar and his officers were. "With the growing number of sick ones among your people, plus the bad weather, all of this is slowing our progress much more than we expected."

Grandmother openly scowled her disapproval the moment the soldier joined us. Overhearing them, she complained, "It's a little late to worry now, isn't it? Your commander should have left us alone to winter in our homes—and protected us from those miners—instead of thinking only of the yellow rocks. Then none of this would be happening, would it?"

The sergeant had been carrying Seicu, Tuulah walking at his stirrup. Looking into my aunt's eyes he had ignored the rest of us after his initial greeting. I watched his mouth harden as he translated her words in his mind.

"My commander, like the rest of us, is one of the Father Emperor's soldiers. It isn't the duty of a soldier to question when he is given an order from a man carrying the Emperor's seal."

"So you obey without question or complaint, no matter how unjust the order, hmm?"

Aunt Tuulah shot her an exasperated look. "Mother, please."

"I speak only the truth, and this man knows it."

Tuulah stared at her mother's rigid back for a time, then sighed and held out her hands for her daughter. "Here, give her to me now. I'm rested. I can carry her. You had better go before someone comes looking for you."

"I only do what is my duty—"

"I know. Mother is cold and hungry. Pay no attention to her."

Ma'leubwey leaned from the saddle to place the blanketed Seicu in her mother's arms. Seicu whimpered, calling out his name. Ma'leubwey said something soothing to her in his own language and brushed damp hair off her forehead. Tuulah fastened her daughter in the side-sling and balanced her upon a hip, then resumed walking. Ma'leubwey straightened. Without looking at any of us, he said, "I'll check back later. If the doctor has any medicine left, I'll bring some for her when I come back."

"That would be good. Thank you."

After he was out of hearing, Grandmother stopped on the trail and turned to Tuulah. "Must both my daughters show their wilfulness by choosing unsuitable mates for their beds? That soldier is enemy. You had a good husband. Why do you bother with that Chamuqwani, Tuulah?"

Tuulah flushed, opening and closing her mouth several times before she could speak. When she finally found her voice, the words came out in an angry rush. "Wasn't it you who always told me I made a bad mistake in choosing Ko for the father of my children? And wasn't it you who recently told me that either Ko left, or I would be cast out, too?"

"Yes, I said those words, but that was before you began making such a fool of yourself in front of everyone. I would rather have a drunk for a son-in-law than that soldier. Have you no ears to hear what people are saying about you—about our family?"

"I don't care about what people say—"

"You should care—"

"Well, I don't. I'm not doing anything wrong."

"If you don't care for yourself, think about your children!"

Mother stepped between them. "Stop it!"

"Be quiet. I'm just stating the truth."

"I don't want to marry anybody," Tuulah cried. "So why are we arguing?"

"If you don't want Ko back under your blanket, there are plenty of good Qwani'ya men in this column from which to choose a new husband. You have no need to encourage that soldier."

My aunt didn't answer. Seicu began coughing, demanding her total attention. When the little girl dropped back into a fitful doze, Grandmother repeated her last remark. Tuulah said in a voice so filled with despair that I feared she too was becoming ill, "Leave me alone, Mother. I have no strength to argue with you. I'm not encouraging anyone. I've no time for suitors—of any kind. I only want to take care of my children."

"Mothers and sisters, husbands and wives, we all are saying cruel and bitter words to one another," Mother cried, wiping a hand across her eyes. "So many deaths—sickness—and what about our hurt and lonely children? Are all our Qwani'ya people going insane?"

She might have said more, but Grandfather interjected his calming presence at that point, drawing Grandmother away.

Grandmother was right about one thing, however, our family was going to need an experienced man to hunt and care for us in this new land. Ko's absence left a gaping hole in our lives, which even I could sense, now that I focused my attention on the problem.

Yes, Ko had his faults, periodic bouts of excess drinking being foremost among them. But he wasn't a violent or cruel man. He had been a part of mine and Samiqwas's lives from the beginning, taking my cousin fishing and hunting, and teaching both of us the nameless, simple things shared only between boys and men. Samiqwas was hurting, and our female relatives' arguing only made him feel worse.

We had been stopped for some time; people behind us had come up and stayed to listen. A sizeable gap was opening up between us and the rest of the column. As I began walking again, I glanced behind me. Samiqwas walked stiff-backed, facing straight ahead, acting as if he had heard nothing, but the colours of grief, fear, and yes anger writhed within his Spirit-Fire

Too exhausted to do more than eat, sleep, and walk, I hadn't felt much like talking and had accepted Samiqwas's long silences as a normal part of our harsh journey. Now I wasn't so sure he was right in his mind. Though Ko's family was never far from ours, Ko made no attempt to speak to us, or come to our fire of an evening to see his children.

Hearing Samiqwas coughing, I dropped back to walk beside him. "You sound like a seal out on the lake. I thought it was me who had a seal for a relative, not you," I said, hoping to make him smile.

He wiped his nose on his sleeve and stared, at first not comprehending my attempt at a joke. Finally his mouth curved into a faint smile. "But I do have a seal for a relative," he teased in return. "You."

We shared a laugh and I knew he felt a bit better.

Chapter Four

As the days passed while we made our slow progress down the Copper River canyon, I grew to hate the taste of the soldiers' rock-hard cakes. The cakes were filling when held in the mouth and softened by spit, but they were as tasteless as chalk, leaving the body craving something more substantial. But the soldiers kept us moving with few rest breaks during the day; there was no time to set snares or forage for more satisfying and nourishing food.

Commander Mu'Dar and his men ate no different than the rest of us, I can't fault them for adding to our suffering on that account, and yet we weren't used to such fare and more sickened because of it.

Mother and I were fortunate in maintaining our health. We suffered only the constant hunger and fatigue plaguing Qwani'ya and soldier alike. But Seicu's cough worsened, and that had everyone worried.

"Stupid soldiers! Don't they realize that people need better food to eat?" Aunt Tuulah complained as she hoisted her feverish daughter onto her hip.

"Father, isn't there anything you can do for her?" Mother begged as she settled her blanket pack onto her shoulders.

Grandfather looked up from scooping dirt over the fire we'd made to boil tea at our rest break. "I'll look for healing herbs along the path as we travel this afternoon," he said.

Grandfather seemed helpless against a sickness that caused coughing so severe it brought upon bloody vomiting. If a person's Qwakaiva wasn't strong enough to defeat the disease on his own, the sickness progressed to a fever and diarrhoea that left the person too weak to travel without help. Death usually occurred soon after that. And with Seicu and Samiqwas coughing, the fear of death in our family haunted all of our thoughts.

"What are you looking for? Maybe I can help." I said.

"To be honest, Grandson, I'm not sure." He brushed a hand across his haggard face and picked up his own pack. "This sickness is so powerful—the soldiers give me no time to search—and it's so late in the season, I don't know what plant I need to find. I just pray to all the Green Ones for their help. Hopefully one will speak to me if it has the Qwakaiva I need."

Most everyone had a touch of the coughing sickness—including many of the soldiers. But as Grandmother pointed out, "The soldiers may be getting sick, but none of them are dying like our Qwani'ya people are."

Other relatives whispered that there was a darker reason for the sickness and misfortune stalking the column. "Fires that flare up without warning, burning anyone close, pack beasts going lame overnight, strange accidents, unexplained injuries, what else could it be but a malicer's sorcery?" an old aunty confided to us one evening.

"No one's immune," Tuulah agreed, "The soldiers, too, are having their share of misfortune."

The aunty nodded solemnly. "Even if they say they don't believe in such things they can still be harmed."

Malicious sorcery, I tormented myself by day, worrying about my family's safety. At night, though I was so exhausted from carrying my heavy pack I could hardly keep my eyes open long enough to finish my portion of the evening meal I slept badly. My dreams were haunted by scenes of blood and killing.

I often woke to people coughing, tearful cries of mourning, the sounds of chanting and malice being conjured in the shadows. Nearly too afraid to breathe for fear the stalking evil spectres would notice me, I would lie shivering in my blanket unable to sleep. Then, I'd sense Grandfather's Qwakaiva enveloping me. His whispered song in my mind would banish my terror and I would be lulled at last into sleep.

Like Grandfather, the priest was tireless in his efforts to aid the sick. He would care for both Traditional and Convert alike. I grew to admire him and believed he wasn't aware of the conjuring being done in the name of his god. That was one of the reasons his injury was so upsetting to me.

Grandfather and I were visiting the soldiers' camp when the tragedy occurred. We'd come to see if Supply Master would give us grease to make a salve for Grandmother's swollen joints. While Grandfather talked, I happened to look around and saw Intercessor Raymonel in conversation with Commander Mu'Dar and a few of his officers. Sergeant Ma'leubwey was also among them.

I was surprised and a little curious to see the priest without his usual entourage of Converts. I moved a little away from Grandfather, hoping to learn what had brought him alone to the soldiers. Their expressions were sombre, but I couldn't hear what the men were saying. Between us were several soldiers talking and joking while they groomed the horses and mules.

Further across the clearing, off-duty soldiers sat about small fires cooking their own measures of the evening's rations. They were talking to one another—sometimes loudly—thus adding to the distraction. It was growing dark, but still light enough to see quite clearly; nothing was out of the ordinary—and yet ...

I was edging a little closer, when Grandfather called me. "Supply Master has no fat he'll give us. We'd better return to our fire."

We were nearly at the edge of the soldiers' clearing, when some unexplained premonition caused me to stop and turn. Intercessor Raymonel had just finished his conversation and had started walking back to his own tent. But instead of taking the long way round, as we had, he cut straight across the area where the soldiers were working.

Suddenly one of the mules broke away from the man grooming it and charged the priest. Lost in thought, the priest didn't notice his danger until someone shouted. By that time the crazed animal was nearly on top of him.

He flung up his arm to protect his face. The mule let out a loud bray as if terrified by something only it could see. Then, it reared. One hoof struck his upraised arm while the other slammed into his chest, knocking him to the ground. Shocked into immobility, no one stopped the beast as it disappeared into the brush.

In the next instant, pandemonium broke loose. Men shouted and other mules began kicking and braying wildly. Coming to my senses at last, I saw Grandfather running back across the clearing, heedless of his own safety. When I caught up to him, panting like a sled dog, he was kneeling beside the fallen man.

The young priest lay in a crumpled heap, groaning with pain. Removing the blanket from about his shoulders, Grandfather laid it on the ground and gently eased the man onto it, straightening his limbs.

The priest cried out as the old man touched his arm, jerking it away. Grandfather retrieved the arm and eased it down at his side. With skilled movements the Otter's Qwakaihi next allowed his hands to travel over the priest's body checking for other injuries, all the while keeping up a low-voiced conversation with his patient.

The air about us tingled with power. I stared down at the priest wondering if he could sense how Grandfather was helping him. I decided after watching for a time that he probably couldn't. Maybe it was the pain that dulled his awareness or maybe it was as Grandmother claimed, and all Chamuqwani were too wilful and ignorant to see what was all about them.

There was mud on the priest's face and a growing stain of red on his blue robe. I noticed he had lost the amulet of his god's power. The silver thunderbolt was gone from around his neck. It was odd that it should have fallen off, I remember thinking. I knew the priest would want it, so I began searching the ground around him, hoping to find it for him.

I finally spied it half-buried in a pile of fresh dung, the chain broken, the pendant twisted nearly beyond recognition. I wiped it off on some dead leaves and tried to mould it back into its former shape.

To my surprise the metal wasn't soft and malleable as I had assumed. The pendant was made of hard silver and wouldn't yield to my efforts to bend it. I stared at the twisted remains. Could a mule stepping on this have distorted its shape so violently? Maybe, but I wasn't convinced of it. Some great power had done this, and it made me afraid just to think about it.

Unsure whether to return the pendant or drop it back in the mud, I walked over to Grandfather, still holding it in my hand. Though obviously in pain, the priest seemed lucid. With my Spirit-Sight I saw the flare of Grandfather's Qwakaiva as he helped his patient. I was very proud at that moment. Grandfather seemed so knowledgeable and self-assured. I hoped someday when I had completed my lessons with Chumco, I would be a great Qwakaihi just like Grandfather.

"How bad is he hurt?"

Sergeant Ma'leubwey, Commander Mu'Dar, and two other soldiers were standing over us. It had been the sergeant who had spoken to us in our language, acting as translator.

"He has two cracked ribs and some bad bruising on his abdomen, which may mean he bleeds inside," Grandfather said without looking up.

"I've made a mess of myself haven't I, Commander?" Intercessor Raymonel said, speaking in Chamuqwani directly to the officer. "Stupid of me to be so careless around animals, wasn't it?" He tried to laugh, but the sound ended in a groan.

Grandfather laid a hand on his forehead, brushing back the priest's hair, checking for head injuries. "Lie still, Intercessor, while I finish my exam. You aren't to blame for what just happened. The mule was—"

"Bespelled, possessed?" he grimaced, finishing the thought. "Don't look so startled; I've heard the talk. But I can't believe in such primitive foolishness. I was merely careless—"

"I don't believe in such nonsense, either, but you are not to blame for this accident, Intercessor," Commander Mu'Dar said. "The Elder is right about that, at least. It's my soldier's fault, and he'll be whipped for his carelessness."

"No, please. There's no need—"

Cutting in on their conversation, Grandfather said, "This isn't important now. We need to bring him to a safe place where his injuries can be treated."

Commander Mu'Dar shouted an order and men were sent to bring a litter of canvas and poles to carry the priest away. In the distance I could hear many people shouting the news of the accident and I felt a knot of unease tangle in my gut. I glanced at Grandfather's face and caught his eye. He nodded slightly as if reading my mind. Yes, there was going to be more trouble over this; he feared it too.

The men had arrived by then with their litter of poles. He turned from me to caution the sergeant. "Tell them to be careful when they lift him. His arm is broken, too. He will need—"

"Don't touch him, you devil's spawn!" a woman shrieked. "Get away from the Holy Intercessor."

Racing towards us across the muddy ground came the older Mercy Woman. Wild-eyed and tangle-haired, the woman had lost her veil somewhere during her flight. Her face bleached white with anger, she shouted something else I didn't catch and held up the lightning-bolt pendant about her neck. The pack of grim-faced Converts trotting at her heels were furious as well. They glared at Grandfather and me as if this was our fault.

Breathing hard as she reached us, the Mercy Woman still had enough breath to spit out her bile. "Commander, keep that malicer away."

Commander Mu'Dar's dark features moulded themselves into a stony mask. "Nonsense, Celibress. You're merely distraught. The Intercessor was struck down by a runaway mule. The Elder here was merely trying to help."

"Help, bah! He is an evil sorcerer. I tell you—"

"Celibress Vomica, please," the weak voice of the priest said, silencing the shouting combatants. "I'm all right. And you know as well as I do that there's no such thing as sorcery. Help me up."

"Have a care," Grandfather said. "Take the litter. Your injuries are serious. Your ribs, there may be bleeding—"

The commander motioned for his men to bring the litter and place the protesting man upon it. "Go rest, Intercessor. I'll send the regiment's doctor to set the arm and have a look at your injuries."

As we turned to go, I suddenly remembered the pendant I still held. In the confusion, I quickly handed it to the sergeant. He seemed puzzled at first by what I'd given him, then his eyes widened as he recognized what it was.

"I found it in the mud," I murmured, then raced after Grandfather.

The old man was silent as we walked back to our fire. Intercessor Raymonel's injuries were no accident. When I'd held the pendant, I'd felt such hatred behind the intent to cause harm, it made me shudder with fear for all of us. Unable to keep silent any longer, I quickened my pace and took his hand. "Ati, I'm frightened—you felt it, didn't you?"

He sighed and squeezed my hand. "Yes, I felt the conjuring, unfortunately not soon enough to deflect it."

"Does someone truly want to kill the priest?"

"It would seem so."

"But why—who would want to do such a thing?"

"I don't know, but I intend to find out."

I would have liked to ask him more, but by then we had reached our camp, and the women were bursting with their own questions.

Chapter Five

Next morning the priest's injuries were the talk of the entire column. Everyone had an opinion as to what had actually happened. The converts no longer sang as they marched. Tension grew among the various factions of the Qwani'ya people. Accusations of sorcery were hurled back and forth by both Convert and Traditional alike. Everyone was afraid, never knowing who would be struck down next. Fights were a common occurrence each evening. The soldiers had their hands full keeping the peace.

In spite of his injuries, Intercessor Raymonel tried at first to go on with his usual routine of preaching and caring for the sick, but his wounds refused to heal. He developed a fever, which worsened as the days went on. Many begged him to rest and look after his own health, but he ignored them. Finally Commander Mu'Dar ordered him to be confined to a pony-drag litter for the march each day.

Within his blankets, he looked like a big baby in its cradleboard. Though I had no intention of converting to his religion I was sorry to see him so weak. Speaking low enough so no one else could hear, I asked Grandfather, "If his god is as 'mighty' as he and the Converts claim, how could something so bad have happened to him?"

"That's a good question, but one I can't answer."

"Is he going to die?"

Grandfather glanced at the loudly chanting Converts, and a frown creased his brow. "I have no way of telling that, Grandson. Only the Unseen Ones know a man's fate." He unfocused his eyes and I knew he was studying the priest with his Spirit-Sight. Turning away at last he seemed troubled by what he'd observed.

Whatever he read in my expression, he tousled my hair and added, "He is a young man. Surely he and his god have the power to defeat this sorcery, so don't worry about him. What will be, will be."

The priest's eyes were red-rimmed; his pale face was nearly as white as the snow on the high peaks. "How could anyone survive and look like that?" I blurted without thinking. "See, already he looks like a wraith. Surely death must hover near."

Grandfather chuckled and smiled to reassure me. "Death hovers near all of us, Grandson, I have told you that many times before. But in this case you are forgetting that much of the paleness you see is due to his Chamuqwani colouring, not the illness. But he is very weak and wouldn't be confined to the litter if his condition wasn't serious."

I focused my own Spirit-Sight on the sick man, but I was too inexperienced to detect what he'd discovered. "Can you help him?"

He shook his head. "I don't know, but there is such a wall of mistrust grown up between us that I doubt if the Converts, or the priest himself, would accept my help—even if I offered."

Grandfather rubbed a hand across his face and it suddenly occurred to me that he was an old man. This long journey and the needs of our Qwani'ya people were taking their toll on his strength. His powerful hunter's body was growing gaunt and bent with the burden of age and worry he carried.

Swallowing down my fear that he too might die, I placed my hand in his once more. He looked down at me, his smile forced. "Don't trouble yourself, my dear one, all will be well."

Would it? I wasn't so sure.

THAT NIGHT WE CAMPED in a sheltered hollow by a stand of aspens, their golden leaves aflame in the dying light. While the women made a fire and brought out rations for the evening meal, Samiqwas and I collected leather buckets from Supply Master and hurried to the creek for water. The evening was clear for once, the sky bright with stars and a silver crescent moon.

I raced Samiqwas to keep warm. Dead leaves crackled under my feet. Grey clouds of breath puffing away from my mouth, I pushed myself, hoping to leave the worries of my relatives behind. We filled our buckets quickly. But after several days of mist and rain, the night was so beautiful; I had no wish to return so soon to the encampment.

Lowering my head I placed my hands with fingers spread atop my head, snorted, and then challenged my cousin to a mock battle. I was a deer, a young buck deer, with a rack of new-grown horns atop my head, kicking up my hooves, glad to be alive. Samiqwas sat down his own bucket and joined in my play,

An older girl shouted at us to stop fooling around. Others needed the buckets to bring water to their families. Still grinning and stomping, we picked up the buckets and headed back to our fire. It had been fun to play like we used to—even for such a short time.

When we came near the encampment, I saw Ko and several Qwani'ya men I didn't know digging the privy trench. A bored soldier with his thunder-weapon held in the crook of one arm stood nearby supervising the work. Ko tossed a shovel of dirt out of the hole, then stopped to wipe sweat from his forehead. In the dim light I couldn't see his face, but his shrunken Spirit-Fire displayed his fatigue.

Samiqwas had seen his father, too, but he gave no sign of it. He would have walked on by the men without a second look, but I stopped him. "Those men look thirsty. Bring them a drink."

When he hesitated, I said, "I'll hurry on with my water so the women can begin the mush. I'll tell them the soldier made you bring him and his men water if you are worried about Grandmother finding out that you were talking to your father."

Samiqwas blinked rapidly a few times then nodded and walked towards his father, who was still watching us.

When I got back to the fire Mother took the bucket and poured its contents into the big tin can we used as a pot and set it atop stones within the fire. Aunt Tuulah glanced up from rocking a fretful Seicu.

"Where is my son?"

I sat beside her and held out my hands for the little girl. "I can take her. Samiqwas will be along soon. He is doing an errand for the soldiers."

A couple elders were visiting; Grandmother was occupied and not paying attention to my news. Tuulah accepted my explanation without comment, handed Seicu to me, and rose.

With the women's low-voiced talk in the back of my mind, I focused my attention on my sick little cousin. She seemed to have lost more weight since last I'd held her. Nestled in my arms, Seicu felt as light as wild goose down, and as hot as a rock heated in the fire. Her breath was a phlegmy wheeze, and her eyes were glassy and unnaturally bright. When she coughed, her whole body shook, leaving her gasping and breathless.

The night about us was so filled with life, the waxing moon, the twisting fires of the Spirit-Lights, the distant howl of a wolf, the scent of rutting elk on the wind, so much life, so much beauty. My heart felt as if it would burst from my chest and shatter on the ground. I wanted to suck up all the Qwakaiva of the night and pour it all into her tiny, feverish body.

"Hello, Little Bird, how is my baby feeling tonight?"

"I not baby."

"No, no, you're right. You aren't a baby. I'm the baby, right?"

"Little Rock Squirrel."

I forced myself to smile through my tears. "That's right; I'm your Little Rock Squirrel. Want to play with me?"

There was another bout of coughing, a long hesitation, then she whispered, "Yes."

"Shall we play hunter and sled doggy, or maybe fish in the net?"

She laughed weakly. "Silly Rock Squirrel. I too tired. Want see pictures."

"Pictures? I don't understand. Let's play another game."

"You know," she insisted. "Want magic pictures with the string."

"No, I can't make the pictures now. Maybe later."

"I want see pictures in string. Now." Seicu's last pronouncement had been quite loud and very clear. She'd promised not to tell—but she was so ill. It took a moment for my refusal to penetrate her fevered brain, but when she understood, she screwed up her face as if she was going to cry.

I glanced up to see if anyone was watching. When it appeared that no one was, I let out the breath I hadn't realized I'd been holding.

"All right, I'll make the pictures. Don't cry," I whispered.

"Yes. Show me."

Arranging the folds of my blanket as best I could to hide what I was doing, I drew out my string and held it out between us. Then I laced it through my fingers to form the diamond patterns of The Seer's Pool. "What picture do you want, hmm?"

"I want go home."

Home...

My heart gave a lurch; that would be an easy request to fulfill. My own Spirit longed to return to those happy times as well. With little effort, my mind formed a picture of our village in the centre diamond. I saw once more the long green lake tucked among the ice-capped peaks of the Aseutl's Teeth Mountains. Seicu and I walked along the shore, eating long sticks of striped candy from the trading post and tossing flat stones into the water to watch them hop. She giggled at the antics of an otter sliding down a muddy patch of bank at Hot Springs Creek, and laughed when his mate stole his fish and they played a game of tag.

"What are you and Seicu laughing about, Tas?" Samiqwas asked as he sat down next to me. Startled, my hands jerked, the string figure falling slack and slipping off my fingers.

As I looked up, I gazed directly into Grandfather's face. Hastily I looked away. *Oh, Ancestors protect me!*

I swallowed hard and answered my cousin with a forced note of cheerfulness. "I was just amusing Seicu by making string figures while we waited for you to come play with us."

Now that the pictures had disappeared, Seicu wasn't happy. Her cough returning, she was ready to have a tantrum. Quickly drawing her attention to her brother, I bounced her up and down on my knee. "Look, Seicu, Brother is back and wants to play with us."

"Make pictures for brother, too, Little Rock Squirrel."

Hastily I bent over her and whispered, "Shh. You promised, remember?"

"Want—"

"No, I can't. Brother doesn't have the right kind of Qwakaiva to see them. The pictures are only for you and me. Now be still."

I was saved further explanations when Mother announced that the mush was done, and Aunt Tuulah came to take Seicu.

I sat between Samiqwas and Grandfather, trying to act like nothing was wrong, but each mouthful of the gluey mass I swallowed lay like a rock in my protesting stomach. He said never a word to me, only sat calmly eating his mush, but I felt his presence looming over me.

By the time I finished, my gut was twisted in knots. I excused myself and headed for the privy, feeling as if all that I had eaten would force its way up again. I had to get away from the fire, out of Grandfather's sight.

In the shadows, I leaned my brow against the smooth bark of an aspen and tried to compose myself. Chumco had warned me and I'd disobeyed him. But surely making pictures to cheer up my sick cousin wasn't a bad thing? Why was it so terrible if Grandfather learned of my apprenticeship? He wasn't a petty man. Surely he would be happy if I'd found another Qwakaihi with gifts similar to my own who could teach me. I hated keeping secrets from him. But Chumco had sworn to stop teaching me if I told anyone—and I desperately wanted to learn all I could from him.

The one brief contact I had had with my father filled me with such a longing to know him. I wanted—no, needed him to love me and share a part of his life with me. Chumco said he would show me how to communicate with him. I need only be patient, obey and lend him my strength whenever he required my help for his own conjuring.

All these disturbing thoughts were bumping around in my head, making it hurt. I was tired and it was getting cold standing out here without my blanket. I needed to sleep. Pushing myself off the tree, I headed back to my family's campfire.

Wrapped up in my own childish fears, I'd failed to sense the mounting tension in the encampment that night. Hearing the strident tones of Celibress Vomica's voice among the angry people coming my way, I hung back waiting for them to pass. To my horror, they seemed to be heading towards my family's hearth.

Chapter Six

K eeping to the shadows, I raced ahead to give my family a warning. Aunt Tuulah and her children were already in their blankets in the lean-to, when I ran up. Only the old people and Mother still sat around the embers of the fire.

"Ati, the priest's mean woman is coming," I gasped, "and the people with her are angry."

Grandmother gave me a sharp look, her black eyes boring into my skull. "Angry? Why would they be coming here, foolish boy?"

My teeth chattering, I shook my head. "I don't know."

"Perhaps they want your help, Father," Mother suggested.

We could all hear them now, praying to their god to protect them, as they purged the camp of evil.

"No, my dear, " Grandfather said quietly. "I don't think so."

Handing me my bedding, Mother said, "Tasimu, go lie down in the lean-to. This doesn't concern you."

I needed no further urging. I slipped into the shelter and lay down, pulling the blankets over me. Once settled I peered out from under a fold of the covering. I was shivering.

"What's going on," Samiqwas whispered from the darkness. Both he and Aunt Tuulah were awake now, lying stiff and silent in their blankets.

"I don't know. Some angry Converts are coming," I whispered.

Grandfather stood and added more sticks to the dying fire, as the group stopped just inside its light. Giving no indication that anything was amiss, he turned to face them. "Welcome, friends, will you be seated by our fire and have some tea? It will take but a moment to reheat."

Celibress Vomica held up Djoven's amulet like a shield. "Devil, evil sorcerer, I want none of your poisonous brew."

"Then, why are you here?" Grandmother said, rising to stand beside her husband. "It grows late and we need our rest."

"We have come to tell you, Malicer," said a mixed-blood, brandishing a heavy stick of firewood like a club, "that we know of your evil. If Intercessor Raymonel dies because of your foul conjuring, I swear, by Mighty Djoven, you'll die, too." The rest of the angry Converts chorused an agreement to back up his threat.

The noisy group had attracted the attention of others who weren't asleep. The crowd surrounding our fire was growing.

Aunt Tuulah tucked the blanket she'd been sharing with Seicu tightly around her daughter and stood. In a low voice that only Samiqwas and I heard, she said, "When no one is looking, one of you boys sneak out and go find the sergeant or some other soldier that can speak our language. Tell him to come before there is bad trouble."

"I'll go, Amima," Samiqwas said.

"Good. But don't let anyone see you." Then without a backward glance, she walked out to join her parents and sister.

"... My father would never harm anyone!" As fierce as a mountain cat, Mother faced the Mercy Woman with eyes blazing. "Who has been looking after the priest and caring for his wounds—you? How dare you accuse my father of anything!"

Trembling with indignation, Mother pointed, and said, "Look at her hands; they are filthy. Does she ever wash them before she goes among the sick? Everyone knows that dirt can conceal a sickness. Did you people give up your good sense when you converted?"

"You foul-tongued liar, don't you dare talk about a holy Mercy Woman like that," a woman wearing a headscarf shouted. "One more word and I'll come over there and give you the sound beating you deserve."

"Beating, is it?" Grandmother said. "Since when does a Qwani'ya person try to beat another into respect? That is the Chamuqwani way, and a foul practice at that. Have you no shame?"

Grandmother's words seemed to embarrass some of the people. Many dropped their eyes under the onslaught of my female relatives' ire.

Into the stunned silence that followed, Grandfather said, "As many among the People will tell you, I am a Man of Power, a Qwakaihi. I'll not deny it." His voice grew harsh as if barely controlling a deeply felt emotion. "But what I will also tell you, and swear it, by the blood of my ancestors—and Qwa'osi the Otter from whom I claim my power, I have never—and will never—use my Qwakaiva to harm anyone."

"So you say, Malicer," someone in the shadows cried, "but I saw you and that nasty boy by the Intercessor when he was attacked. I say it is you who sent the devil to harm him. And again this afternoon, I saw you staring at his fevered body, mumbling your wicked death chants. We saw. We know. You can't escape our punishment!"

"I repeat. I've done no conjuring to harm anyone."

"Then how do you explain this," Celibress Vomica said. Holding out her hand to the firelight, she unwrapped a piece of cloth and displayed a tiny leather object. "Praiser Jon found this tucked into a slit in the Intercessor's mattress. He explained the symbols' meaning to me."

She held it out towards Grandfather. "Come closer. Take a good look, then tell me it isn't a charm to work great evil."

"I've no need to examine it closer. I can sense its malice from here. You're correct about its purpose, but you're wrong about who made it. I neither made the charm nor placed it within the priest's bed."

Until that moment, I'd nearly forgotten about the talisman. But I recognized the leather bag all too well. Chumco had given it to me and directed me to place it within the priest's tent while we were still back at the stockade. He'd never explained what was actually inside the charm. I knew only that by delivering it I was helping him, and also my father's struggle, against our common enemy.

No! It was impossible. The charm couldn't be what they claimed! My teacher was a great Qwakaihi, a warrior against evil! He would never—did I really know that? What if I *had* caused the priest's misfortune—and maybe others' sickness and injuries as well? What had I really done when I put that charm in the priest's tent? And now, these crazy people had come here to hurt Grandfather—blaming him—but it was me they really wanted.

Me!

I trembled like an aspen leaf in the wind. I wasn't a bad boy; I wasn't evil. They were lying about the charm—they had to be! Chumco could explain everything. But no matter the truth about the bag, I couldn't let my Grandfather be blamed for something that I had done. I had to confess, before someone was hurt. Teeth chattering from fear, not the cold, I put aside my blankets and crawled from the lean-to.

"L-leave Grandfather alone. He d-didn't do anything bad. I—"

"—Celibress Vomica, what is the meaning of this?"

The voice of the unknown speaker from the shadows hadn't been loud, but something in its timbre captured everyone's attention.

The Mercy Woman gasped and turned to face the man dressed in a dirty blue robe who staggered into the firelight, supporting himself with a sturdy walking stick.

"Intercessor Raymonel! You should be resting."

The priest swayed, leaning heavily on his stick. When one of his followers offered to help him, he waved the man away with the arm tucked into its sling. The gesture made him grimace, but he gritted his teeth against the pain, refusing to cry out.

"Maybe I should be abed." He glanced around taking in Grandfather's calm expression, the defiant postures of the women standing shoulder to shoulder with the old man, and the Converts' angry faces. "But so should all you good people. We have a long day's march ahead of us tomorrow. We all need our rest. Go back to your shelters now and get some sleep."

"But, Intercessor, we've found the evil one who has cursed you and so many others," someone shouted. "We're here to make him pay for his crimes, so he won't cause any more sickness among us."

There was murmured agreement to that statement. The priest held up his hand for silence. "Curses and evil sorcery?" Intercessor Raymonel shook his head as if he was very disappointed with them. "That's superstitious nonsense. I've told you many times before, Djoven the Mighty One will protect us. You must set aside your primitive ways and have faith in His justice."

"Show him the charm found in his mattress, Mercy," someone cried.

"Charm? Let me see this so-called evil charm then," the priest said, holding out his good hand for it. Reluctantly, Celibress Vomica showed him the leather pouch she was holding. To gasps of horror he picked it up and examined it. After taking a long look he turned to Grandfather, and asked,

"This pouch, should I assume that it was designed to make the ignorant believe it has power to do harm?"

"To do harm is its purpose, yes."

"But my father didn't make such a thing," Mother said angrily. "He would never use his Qwakaiva in such a terrible way."

"I agree, daughter," the priest said and tossed the bag into the flames.

Mother stiffened, then her eyes opened wide, as the bag burst into blue flame. She stared like the rest of us at the incinerating charm.

"Now, let there be an end to this foolishness," the priest said into the awed silence. "Go back to your beds and leave these good people alone."

"But, you were injured, and now you're ill. Someone among these devil worshipers, has caused—"

Raising his voice to drown out the rest of the Mercy Woman's words, he said, "Whether I am ill or in good health is up to Djoven. Celibress, I am very disappointed in you—all of you. I have given myself and my life into His keeping. I am His devoted servant and no idiotic jabbering of spells and witchery will harm me; I truly believe that." He fixed his followers with an angry stare. "Where is your faith, your acceptance of His will? All the time I've been among you haven't you learned anything? Celibress, how could you encourage this violence?"

Seicu coughed several times, then began to cry for her mother.

Her voice catching on a sob, Tuulah said, "If my father had the power over this sickness that you people claim, do you think he would harm those in his own family?" She headed for the lean-to. "My daughter is very ill. Go away. Your noise has awakened her."

"I'm sorry for that. I will pray for her."

Suddenly drained of energy, the priest stumbled and would have fallen if a burly Convert hadn't steadied him.

"You heard the Intercessor," a stern voice said. Commander Mu'Dar stepped into the light, a cluster of armed men fanning out around him. "Go to your fires and your beds. Any more disturbances like this one, and you will be punished severely."

"There will be no more trouble, Commander," Intercessor Raymonel assured him. "Isn't that right, Celibress? Praiser Jon?"

"Yes, Intercessor."

Chapter Seven

Within the realm of Dreams, Chumco's Spirit-Body had as much substance as did his physical one. I smelled the scents of smoky leather, tree resin, and lynx musk that always clung to him. Laying my face against the smooth skin of his chest, I allowed his ghostly arms to enfold me and hug me close. I welcomed his caresses back then, but the passing years have taught me the error of my childish assumptions. Chumco's touch wasn't the father's caress I craved. His purpose, I later believed, was to bind me all the tighter to him, forging my chains with desire as well as magical instruction.

But during the time of our journey, I knew nothing of that. I loved him—a part of me still does. And, I think in his way, he returned my affection.

Desire satiated, I lay content in his arms. His lips were a feathery caress upon my hair as he spoke, <<Tell me what has happened.>>

I knew without asking what he meant. And so I told him about the Converts, the Mercy Woman's accusations, and how Intercessor Raymonel had stopped them from doing us harm.

<<The Converts found the bag you gave me to put in the priest's tent. They said it was meant to do evil. Grandfather agreed with them. Is that true? Am I bad for putting it there?>>

Chumco sighed and stroked my hair to calm me. <<Sometimes, my little seal, I despair of you learning anything. Good, evil, haven't I told you countless times, that such concepts vary with a difference of perception? What may appear good and noble when seen from within the backwater pool in which we swim today, may turn out to be something entirely different when viewed from an eddy further down the river of time. There are no absolutes in the universe, only ambiguities.>>

An echo of the frost demons' mocking laughter tormenting me, I pressed, <<Did you know what the charm would do before I placed it among his things?>>

<<Not exactly, I knew only that the power placed in the bag by our Spirit's Companion Kunai would teach a lesson. How the lesson was taught was unimportant to me.>>

<<But what type of lesson was so significant that people must die to learn it?>>

His voice hardening, he spat, <<The lesson is to teach you, and those deluded Qwani'ya converts who have forsaken their ancestors, that Chamuqwani power isn't as great as the priest and those other chattering gulls, the Father Emperor's men, would have you believe. We have power, too. If you remember nothing else of what I teach you in the years to come, remember that. The Chamuqwani aren't omnipotent or invincible. You can fight against them and win.>>

<<But—>>

<<No more talk. I've allowed you to question my actions enough for one night. Can't you hear the Spirit-Lights singing to you? Let us dance with them, and renew our strength.>> Giving me no time to protest, Chumco pulled my Spirit from my sleeping body and we were away.

Shape-shifting into the Spirit form that gave me power, I soared high on leathery wings, my tail whipping out like a banner behind me. Gliding on the Spirit-Lights' fiery currents, I swooped and dived, my mentor laughing at my antics. Opening my mouth wide, I drank in their Qwakaiva, my belly growing round and tight with my gluttony.

I danced and sang to them of my joy, until passing by a luminous cloud, a shadowy being darted out of concealment and flung a net of glowing fibres over me. I shrieked and clawed frantically at the net, but the strands only tightened about me.

I heard a voice exhorting me to stop, but my terror made the voice unrecognizable. <<Free me,>> I roared. <<I will burn you with Qwakaiva, if you don't!>>

Matching my words with action, I opened my mouth to spew out the fire already rising from my belly, but I never got the chance. My captor had anticipated my plan. As soon as my mouth was open, he stuffed rotting lake weed down my throat until I choked.

<<Calm yourself, Grandson. I don't want to hurt you. Resume your true shape, so you can listen to me in a human fashion.>>

Keeping a tight hold on the mouth of his net, Grandfather's winged body hovered above me in a ball of golden light.

When I lay naked and gagging in human form at the bottom of his net, he said, <<I should've guessed the truth before now, but like a fool, I allowed my bitterness towards your father to blind me to what's been happening right under my nose. But that's not important now. Your apprenticeship is over, and I'm taking you back with me.>>

<<No! I don't want to go—>>

<<I'm giving you no choice. You're still a child in my care. You have no idea of the dangers Chumco placed in your path when he tricked you into helping him.>>

<<Not true; he didn't trick me—and he wouldn't harm me. I won't go with you—and I'm not a child. Mentor, help!>> I clawed and kicked at my luminous prison, but to no avail.

<<You speak of blindness,>> a cool voice said, <<but perhaps you've been blinded in other ways than your opinion of his father. Your grandson isn't the child you perceive him to be. He is a young warrior, and he can make his own decisions in matters of power.>>

My heart swelling with pride and relief, I ceased my struggles and looked up. Chumco in the radiant body of a winged Aseutl, floated lazily in the sky above us. He grinned, displaying his fangs and flexed his claws, threatening.

<<You'd better release my student now and return to your sleeping body—before someone gets hurt.>>

<<It's my grandson who is being hurt, Chumco. And I won't let him be tutored in your corrupted ways.>>

Chumco flew a little closer, his tail lashing the air like a mountain cat before it strikes. Still showing his fangs in a draconian smile, he said, <<Don't be too sure of that. I won't give him up easily. He's mine.>>

Grandfather ignored his threats and my struggles, continuing to keep a tight hold on the mouth of the net.<<Yours? You have no right to use my grandson in your power-hungry schemes.>>

<<<<I seek no power for my own aggrandizement—no more than you do yourself. Are you such a fool that you haven't realized that we are at war with these foreigners? They have come to claim our bodies, minds, and spirits, and they will stop at nothing, including corrupting life itself, to achieve their ends. Maybe you haven't seen the future, as I have. I tell you, our end is coming. Do you want our people, our way of life, to be destroyed?>>

<<Whatever the future may bring to us, if you use an innocent child in your schemes, then you are no different than those you claim to fight.>>

<<Innocent child?>> Chumco shook his head in mock reproof, the blue scales of his long neck glittering. <<I think this *innocent* child, as you call him, understands better than you—man of power though you claim to be. Tasimu is a warrior, as is his father, and as am I.>>

His voice hardening with emotion, Grandfather said, <<I understand well enough. You would use him, placing him in danger, or drain him to death if it suited your plans.>>

<<Not willingly. He is a very talented student. But if the need arose, yes. He is a warrior and knows the risks. In any combat there are bound to be casualties.>>

<<Casualties.>> Grandfather focused his attention on me, making me squirm. <<Hear what he's saying? Can't you see his evil now? Are you willing to sacrifice not only a portion of your Qwakaiva, but perhaps your very life for this man?>>

In truth, Chumco had spoken to me very little of risk and sacrifice. He had given me what I thought was love, teaching me both pleasure and obedience. But more binding than such misguided affection was our mutual affinity for Kunai's power.

Grandfather loved me, thought he knew what was best for me, but he could never teach me as Chumco could. The Great Aseutl, companion of my Spirit, swam in dark currents, where those bonded to Qwa'osi the Otter could never survive. I was my father the seal man's son, and as Chumco repeatedly told me, Kunai, Master of Enigma, was the wellspring of my Qwakaiva.

<<I see no evil in him, Grandfather. My teacher is right. I am a warrior. I would willingly give my life to help my people, if that is required of me someday.>>

<<You see? Are those the words of a child? He has no need of your protection any longer. Release him and be gone.>>

Ignoring Chumco, Grandfather gave me a pitying look. <<Ah but, Grandson, does Chumco truly see our future? I know his Spirit's Companion is named Master of Enigma, but what does that truly mean? Think, my dear one, *Enigma*. Like any greedy dragon, Kunai hoards his secrets. Can he be trusted to reveal all that is his to know—even to one who has his favour? Are Chumco's schemes worth your life if he's wrong?>>

<<I'm not wrong. Have you looked into the future? Have you seen the destruction that will befall our people if the pattern is allowed to continue as it is now unfolding? Blackened forests, dead and starving animals, the waters and air of our home fouled and stinking? Do you want this to happen? The Chamuqwani will make it so, if we don't stop them. The lives of our entire People may depend on what we do. What does the life of any one of us matter when we are playing for such high stakes?>>

<<I repeat; we can't afford to win if it means becoming like the enemies we fight.>>

<<And we can't afford to lose by being timid as you suggest. Enough talk. Let the young warrior choose for himself. It is his life and Qwakaiva after all. Now that he has been awakened to his Gift, he has that right.>>

Did I have that right? My Spirit trembled with the prospect of making such an important decision. This whole argument was so confusing. When I had agreed to become Chumco's student and help him, I'd wanted only to learn, so I could speak to my father and get to know him. I hadn't wanted to cause harm to anyone. But if we were at war as Chumco claimed—and Grandfather didn't disagree—then it was my duty to …

Oh, I wished they both would go away and just leave me alone—how I wished my father was beside me to help me know what to do!

<<Grandson, there is one more thing you must know before you make your decision.>>

Startled, I looked up. <<What?>>

<<If you choose to continue your apprenticeship with this man, you will have to leave the family and go to live with him.>>

Leave Mother, Samiqwas, Grandmother—and everybody? A tightness coming into my throat, I felt my vision blur. <<But why?>>

<<That is how these things are usually done, if you didn't know. And in this case I would insist on it. His ways are too different from mine.>>

Chumco must have seen my horrified expression. <<That won't be such a bad thing, my little seal. You would have to leave your family in a few years when you marry. And by coming to my household you will get the training you desire that much sooner—think on that.>>

Turning to Grandfather, he added. <<This is a very good idea. And to satisfy wagging tongues, I can even offer a marriage to explain his move. I have a niece with a daughter of a suitable age. Tasimu's Qwakaiva need be the only groom-portion exchanged. I will see to it.>>

<<Is this what you truly want to do, Grandson? If so, I will tell your mother and grandmother to make the necessary arrangements.>>

Marriage? A few moments before, I was happy, dancing with the Spirit-Lights, determined to continue my studies. Now, however, I wasn't sure what I wanted. Everything was happening so fast.

Suddenly a vision of Seicu's feverish eyes and stick-thin body, cradled in her mother's ragged blankets flashed before my inner eye. Then my Qwakaiva gave me the vision of her coming death. Choking on a sob, I buried my face in my hands.

<<What's wrong, Grandson?>>

Snarling, Chumco blew out a breath of flame Grandfather barely dodged. <<See what you have done with your threats of leaving? There is no need for him to come to my family's hearth until he is older. It is only your stubborn pride that would have it so.>>

With another breath of flame Chumco banished the net from around me. I was free now to go where I wished, but I ran to neither man. Instead I backed away, wishing only to run, but forcing myself to stand and face them.

I felt suddenly like a rabbit trapped between two hungry sled dogs. They both loved me, thought they knew what was best for me, but beneath their concern for my welfare I suspected lurked a darker purpose. Each seemed willing to tear me apart if it meant getting what he wanted.

<<Come to me, my little seal. Tell me what's wrong.>>

Chumco's voice had been filled with worry and tenderness, which made my question all the harder to ask. I was sure he truly loved me.

But it wasn't enough.

<<Tell me one thing before I decide. Did the charmed bag I helped put in the priest's tent also make my cousin ill? Am I the cause of her suffering and death?>>

Finally Chumco spoke in a voice tender with compassion. <<It's impossible to know that, young warrior. The seeds of my conjuring drifted like cattail down on the wind. The spell was meant to harm the priest and cause disorder among the Converts, but it had no particular focus other than that. We're making a hard journey, and your sister-cousin is young. Her ailment may have no greater cause than that.>>

<<Grandfather?>>

Grandfather had no further words of wisdom to offer. He shook his head. <<I honestly don't know. I've done all in my power to protect my family. It maybe as Chumco claims. She is young, and the ghosts of our ancestors have always called to her. Perhaps her Spirit feels it's her time to go to them. But whatever the cause of her illness, you aren't to blame. Don't trouble yourself on that account.>>

I laughed, hearing the rising note of hysteria in my voice. <<So much power, so much wisdom, and neither of you can give me a straight answer. Am I to blame or not?>>

<<Kunai's Gift of foretelling is stronger than those of my own Spirit's Companion. Have you had a vision?>>

<<Yes. And I'm to blame for her death.>>

<<The Chamuqwani are to blame,>> Chumco said angrily. <<They have forced us from our homes. Haven't I told you that often enough? We are at war ...>>

<<Yes, you have. War ...>>

Suddenly I realized I was more the child of my grandfather's lineage than I had ever imagined. Throughout the years of my childhood, his wisdom and quiet strength had always been there like a guiding beacon to show me the way. I could fight no combat where the innocent might be harmed by my actions. And with this revelation I knew that I had to make a great sacrifice.

I couldn't go with Chumco, not for the love of my father or for the sake of the magic my mentor could teach me. Losing Chumco as my teacher filled my heart with fear, my untrained gift snarling like a wolf caught in a trap at the thought. And yet I couldn't abandon my family and go with him.

My vision blurring with a bottomless sadness, I turned to Chumco. <<I love you, but my choice is to give back your token—I'm sorry.>>

Chumco laughed bitterly. <<I'm sorry, too. I have misjudged you. Of all whom I have taught, you are the one I had hoped would inherit my power.>> His voice was taunting when he continued. <<Such a gentle little ptarmigan, how noble, you don't want to hurt anyone. And the priest is such a good man—as are the rest of those carrion birds. They are all good people, hmm?>> He laughed again at my expression.

<<Ah, my little seal, someday when the priests take you to their special prison for children, you'll look back and regret your cowardice this night. Then you'll remember my offer and weep. You will wish you could swim against the currents of time to change your mind. But by then you will be alone and nearly powerless against Chamuqwani malice, with no one to blame but yourself—remember that, you have been warned—>>

<<Stop, you're only trying to frighten him,>> Grandfather shouted.

<<I'm not trying to *frighten* him or to sway him to what I desire—as you've done. I am merely predicting his fate.>>

<<Don't listen; he can't truly know your future.>>

<<I hope he remembers that when your treachery nearly destroys him.>> Chumco spat.

<<*My* treachery? You're talking nonsense.>>

<<We shall see.>>

<<He has made his choice, Chumco, leave us.>>

Chumco glanced at me for confirmation. I stared unblinking, unable to verify or deny Grandfather's claim. <<So be it.>> Then with an anguished roar, Chumco pumped his leathery wings and vanished into the swirling patterns of the Spirit-Lights.

My own cry of hurt and despair echoing through the night, I resisted Grandfather's efforts to comfort me and fled from him into the void of dreamless sleep.

Chapter Eight

The clear sky next morning gave me no pleasure. I awoke fatigued, my body aching, my heart heavy with grief. When I remained curled in my blanket long after the rest of the family was up, Mother came over and anxiously felt my forehead.

Too bad for me. I wasn't physically sick.

At her insistence I rose, made up my travelling pack, and then went to squat by the cook fire. I sipped at my spruce needle tea and poked at the bowl of mush Aunt Tuulah handed me. I stared into the flames, wishing I was going to die—like Seicu. My Qwakaiva writhed within me. Half-taught, half-alive, how could I face the empty years to come? I was nothing, a dried husk. Maybe the frost demons were right; I was bad. Maybe I should join them.

Startled out of my reverie by a sharp jab in the ribs, I looked up. Samiqwas grinned at me. "Hurry up and finish. I'm hungry."

I handed over my nearly full bowl to him. I'd forgotten that with only three bowls and four birch-bark cups between us, we needed to take turns.

"Here, you finish it. I'm not hungry."

Samiqwas stared at me as if I had just grown antlers on top of my head. "Not hungry?" He coughed and took a quick swallow of the cooling tea I had also given him. "Tas, are you getting sick, too?"

I laughed. I wanted to feel sick. I wanted to feel something—anything but the emptiness engulfing me. "No I'm not. I'm just not hungry—leave me alone."

From her place across the fire Grandmother handed her cup to Tuulah. With a voice unusually gentle, she asked, "What's wrong, my dear one?"

The last thing I wanted at that moment was Grandmother focusing her attention on me, no matter how kindly intended. I didn't want anyone wondering why I was in such a foul mood. Swallowing my irritation, I took a deep breath, and answered meekly, "I'm just tired, Ami, nothing more."

Neither Grandmother nor Mother seemed convinced, but I was saved the need for a further explanation. Grandfather had returned.

When I recognized who was coming, I dropped my eyes to the stones encircling the fire. I felt the tug of his power in my mind, but I refused to meet his eye. After what had happened between us, I was determined to deny him the satisfaction of seeing my pain.

When at last I gave in and looked up, he stood in front of me, holding the loop of string Chumco had made from my hair in one hand. Without saying a word, he held out his other hand. I knew without him asking, what he wanted. I reached into the pouch at my waist and handed him the loop Chumco had given me.

Grandfather took both loops and tossed them onto the dying cook fire. I watched the flames devour my last link with the man and the knowledge that I craved. I heard the women's whispered questions, but I was beyond caring what he said to them. Tears were blurring my vision, running silently down my cheeks, and I was powerless to wipe them away or stop them

Sometime later Grandfather sat down beside me. I sensed his nearness, but he made no attempt to touch me. He sat watching me cry, waiting for me to acknowledge him. When the flood of my grief had slowed to a trickle, he at last spoke.

"I know this has been hard for you. You are hurting now, but you did the right thing, Tasimu."

When I made no answer, he sighed. "It's true that I've no love for the seal Man who sired you, but what I know of him I have to respect—however much I hate to admit it. Kunai's kin, be they related to Co'yeh the Seal or other changeable creatures, some are more human in their perceptions of the world than others.

"Your father's Qwakaiva was nothing like that of your former teacher, I am sure of that. I don't think he would have wanted you to study with a man whose Qwakaiva is so—dark. Not all who share your affinity are like Chumco. When you are older and can better judge these things, you will find another mentor. One who is more suitable."

"Suitable to whom—you?" I laughed, my voice catching on a sob. "You know, Grandfather, you and Kunai's Qwakaihi are more alike than you would care to admit."

He seemed annoyed by the comparison, making me smile. "How so?"

I choked down bubbles of hysterical laughter. "How so? Both you and Chumco tell me I will please my father when I do what *you* want, that's how."

"You're hurting and can't see the sense of my words now, but I promise you this pain won't last. You'll find a better teacher someday." A ghost of a smile curved his lips. "That's *my prediction* for your future."

Thinking of the pain I'd endured to master Kunai's crystal gift, I barked a laugh. "That easy, hmm?" I shook my head sadly and rose to get my pack. It was time to go. The soldiers were shouting for the People to line up for the day's march.

"Oh, Grandfather," I told him as I turned away. "In some ways you are as naive as you think me to be. Always swimming with the Otter warrior in the lighter waters of sunlight and simplicity, it must be a joy to be one of Qwa'osi's favoured. You know nothing of the convoluted pathways and suffering that one bonded to Kunai must endure to prove worthy of an Aseutl's regard—you know nothing."

CHUMCO AND MANY OF his family members vanished from the column some time during the march that day. I doubt if Commander Mu'Dar and his men even noticed their leaving, but my Spirit knew, adding to my misery.

As well as I knew my own name, I knew they were returning north. With Chumco's power to aid them, they would survive in spite of the Chamuqwani. I could have been going home, too, if I had chosen otherwise. Had my teacher only stayed with the column as long as he had because of me? I would never know for certain.

Chapter Nine

I remember very little of the country through which we walked for several days after Chumco left. I put one foot in front of another, trudging through the mud, willing myself not to think, not to dwell upon my loss. Cold winter winds at my back, I ignored the drizzling rain falling from the iron-grey clouds overhead. The bleakness of most days was in its way comforting, matching my mood.

Samiqwas traveled beside me whenever the trail widened enough to permit it. But after several refusals of conversation, he remained silent and just walked. I was unable to tell him how much I needed his company, but I think he knew.

Perhaps respecting my wish not to be near him, Grandfather chose to walk with other relatives, taking Grandmother along with him. Seicu's blanketed form straddled her mother's hip, tucked into a sling strapped across Aunt's back, head lolling on Tuulah's shoulder. Mother walked beside Tuulah, the two sisters speaking softly, so as to not disturb the little girl.

From time to time Seicu's harsh coughing jarred me out of my misery. My fault. No matter what Chumco or Grandfather said. Seicu and many others were paying a high price for my knowledge. Ignorance of Chumco's purpose—if it had been ignorance—was no excuse.

And though I cursed myself for my wickedness, my hunger to learn was still so intense that I could barely hold back my tears. Conflicting emotions were tearing me apart. I hated myself for helping spread the illness, and yet I wasn't sorry for my decision to accept tutelage from Kunai's Qwakaihi, not sorry at all. And may the ancestors have mercy, I would do it once again if given the chance.

After a late morning rest break on one of those endless days, I saw Ko waiting beside the trail up ahead. Samiqwas must have seen his father about the same time, because a wide smile suddenly illuminated his face, and he quickened his pace. Not wanting to be left alone I hastened to keep up with him.

Wiping a drool of saliva from her daughter's cheek, Tuulah's head jerked up as Samiqwas hailed his father. Ko waved to his son and stepped out of the firs to walk beside his former wife.

Tuulah's expression soured as she recognized him. "What do you think you're doing?"

"Walking." He grinned hesitantly, "Same as you. I thought maybe—"

Tuulah quickened her pace. "I don't need any help."

"Tuulah, please, let me—"

"Go back to your mother—and your bottle. Leave us alone."

Ko swore a Chamuqwani curse as he hurried to catch up with her. "Woman, what bottle? I've drunk nothing but water for a long time now—"

"So you say, but do I believe it?"

"You should—"

"Why? When there is opportunity again, you will drink—we both know it."

Samiqwas's strangled cry of protest made her look down at his stricken face. "What's wrong with you?"

"Amima, please."

Ko cursed again and put a heavy hand on her shoulder, forcing her to stop and look at him. His big-nosed face was flushed with emotion. "Stop, you're hurting our children with this talk. There's enough anger and sadness among the Qwani'ya people. Don't make the disharmony of the world worse."

Tuulah seemed startled by his reminder of such a basic Qwani'ya teaching. She glanced down at Samiqwas's pleading expression, and her expression softened. Ko saw the look and he continued in a rush. "I don't care if you want that Chamuqwani soldier under your blankets—that's your right—I won't stop you. Make a fool of yourself over the man if you want."

"Fool? You're the fool, drinking and letting Chamuqwani trick you, then fighting with my brother and landing in jail—" Tuulah's voice rose with indignation. "After all that, you have the nerve to call *me* a fool?"

Ko held up a hand as if to ward off a blow. "I'm sorry—a bad choice of words. But don't change the subject. This isn't about you and me alone.

Whatever is between us, don't think for a moment that I've forgotten about my son and daughter, just because you gave my things back to my mother.

"Tuulah—I love them. I miss them—and they me. I want to see them, and help you care for them. Can't you find it in your heart to let me do that? Will that soldier be there to hunt for you and the old people in this new place? I don't think so. He'll follow his leader somewhere else as soon as we arrive there. He'll forget about you—and all of us."

Hearing her father's voice, Seicu roused from her fevered doze, and began coughing and crying. "Appi carry. Want Appi!" Raising her thin arms she held them out to him.

"Hello, my sweet baby." Ko's face suddenly contorted as if he were trying very hard to hold back tears. He glanced at Tuulah, eyes pleading. She hesitated, then lifted Seicu from the sling and handed her over.

Ko took his daughter carefully and cradled her in his arms. He brushed a hand across the little girl's forehead to push back her damp hair and spoke in a soothing voice till her coughing subsided, and she settled once more into a fitful sleep.

They walked along in silence for a time. At last, he said, "Why didn't you come tell me how sick she was?"

Tuulah snorted. "Why didn't you come ask, if you were so interested in your children's welfare?"

His voice low and gentle, Ko said, "Tuulah, my heart, please don't be angry. I wanted to come, but I—I wasn't sure if you or your mother would allow it."

The rock-strewn trail narrowed just ahead, tall spruce crowding the slope on either side of the path. Ko hung back to allow her to proceed him. When the trail widened so they could once again walk abreast, he said, "I wanted to, but yes I will admit it, I was afraid to come."

She stared at him, incredulous. "You, afraid? Why?"

He laughed softly and smiled. "You are a formidable woman—like your mother. Hasn't anyone ever told you that? Yes, I was afraid ..."

I heard no more after that. Mother placed a hand on my shoulder, forcing me to drop back. "Let them have their privacy," she murmured. I looked from my cousin's beaming face, to his parents talking in low voices as they walked together, and I nodded.

Then I heard the clop, clop of a horse's hooves and turned to see Sergeant Ma'leubwey riding down the column toward us. I watched his welcoming smile fade, as he saw Ko and Aunt Tuulah talking. His expression blank, he rode on past us without stopping. Mother turned her head to watch him pass, and sighed. "Poor Man. I believe he truly cares for my sister."

"Does Ko walking with Aunty today mean that he will be coming back to live with us, Amima? Samiqwas will be happy if he does."

"I don't know. It's too soon to tell. Right now Seicu's illness has brought them to an understanding. For that to become permanent, many things would have to change."

"You mean Ko would have to stop drinking waskyja."

She made a face but nodded. "There are other considerations as well. No one person is at fault when a marriage sours."

"You mean Grandmother would have to let him return. But she said she wanted Ko to come back."

Mother laughed softly and reached across to tousle my hair. "Your grandmother's approval would certainly help matters, but most important of all, Tuulah has to *want* him back—and she may not."

Then I understood. "Sergeant Ma'leubwey? But surely Aunty would choose a Qwani'ya man, father of her children, over a foreigner?"

"The Sergeant's ways are strange to us, but he's a good man, too—don't forget."

She laughed as if at a private joke. Then, her eyes unfocussed, as if remembering another time, another man, her voice softened. "There's no way of telling what will sway a woman's heart when all is said and done, now, is there?"

Recalling how I'd abused my gift to probe her dreams, I saw again a man with violet eyes and long brindle hair tangled in a passionate embrace with her, and flushed. "No. I guess not."

The sound of my voice seemed to pull her out of her reverie. She turned to me and smiled. Then she startled me by saying, "Enough talk about what doesn't concern us. Tell me instead what has happened to you."

Her question was so unexpected that it hit me like a cup of icy water thrown into my face. I thought about not answering her, or making up some frivolous tale to explain what she had witnessed when Grandfather severed my link with Chumco, but after further consideration I decided to tell her the truth.

With the emptiness welling up once more, I realized I didn't want to keep my feelings all stuffed inside any longer. It hurt too much, and if anyone could understand my longing for the Qwakaiva, and the father who had gifted it to me, it would be her.

So I told her—all of it.

After I finished we walked along in silence. The roar of a nearby creek, tumbling down from the crags above would have made talk impossible, anyway. The rain had stopped, and a watery autumn sun came out from behind the clouds. It painted the yellow aspens and dark firs with a golden hue that reflected off each glistening raindrop. The air was damp, smelling of tree resin and rotting leaves.

In a nearby tree a raven cawed and took to the air at our approach. I felt strangely at peace. Telling her seemed to have unburdened me of a heavy weight.

When we rounded a bend and left the noisy creek behind, Mother finally spoke. "Father is right, you know, Tas, you aren't to blame for what is happening to Seicu or anyone of the People. Perhaps you are too young to understand, but Father, and yes, I too, must take some of the blame for what has befallen us."

I gaped, tripping over a root in the trail. "You? Grandfather? How can you say such a thing? Grandfather warned me to stay away from Chumco—and you had nothing to do with any of this—"

"Ah, but I did in a way. You were growing up and you needed to know about your father. I knew that in my heart, but still I kept silent. I wanted to keep you forever young, never old enough to ask painful questions, never old enough to leave me—alone. With my selfishness, I fear I have done you a great wrong."

"No, Amima, that isn't true—and I will never leave you—I promise."

She laughed and tousled my hair again. "Of course you will someday—when you marry—and I would have it no other way." She laughed again at my expression, and added to reassure me. "But your marriage day isn't for a few years yet, so let us enjoy our time together while we can, hmm?"

To please her I agreed, but I was still uneasy in my heart with her talk of leaving. I'd told her of Chumco's marriage offer for me. Our parting would have already occurred, if I had chosen differently.

We walked in companionable silence for a long time before she spoke again. "I sense that you have been comforted somewhat by our talk, but there is still a disharmony in your spirit." She nodded as if I had spoken my agreement, then continued. "The cause, as I understand it, centres about your wish to learn more about your Qwakaiva. Isn't that true?"

This time I did nod, my throat too constricted to speak. I had never guessed she was such a perceptive woman.

"I can't give you the father you crave, no matter how much I wish it were so, but I can share with you what little I can. I will answer any questions you wish to ask me about him, and I will give you this."

Mother paused on the trail and removed a braided cord from her neck and handed it to me. The cord was threaded with a stone containing a natural hole through its centre. I'd seen this talisman since my earliest babyhood; she'd never removed it before that moment, to my knowledge.

Like the string Chumco had given me when he taught me to make the magical patterns, this cord was made from plant fibre and two colours of hair. My heart pounding, I glanced up and met her eyes. She nodded, affirming my unvoiced question.

"He found that special rock for me and I wove the cord to carry it, from my own hair, and some of his, left in my comb. This is all I have of him. But now, I give it to you."

"But—"

She put the cord over my head and patted my arm to reassure me. "It is all right, my son. It's time I left the past behind. In this foreign land I'll make a new life for myself. I would have burned this or thrown it into the Socanna River to find its way back to him, but something held me back. Now I know why. I was to give it to you."

I opened my mouth several times to reply, but I couldn't push the words past the lump swelling in my throat. I heard the sound of people talking. They were coming up behind us; we had lingered too long in one spot. Mother touched my shoulder and I moved with her, my mind still in turmoil.

My heart was overflowing, but my gratitude was tinged also with despair. I knew how much this token meant to her, and how hard it must be to let it go. I wanted it desperately, but why, oh why, hadn't she given it to me sooner. With Chumco's teaching to guide me, and with such a powerful talisman to aid me, I could have reached out to my father, told him of our plight, asked for his help, told him how I needed—loved him.

"Tas, what's wrong, don't you want my gift?"

I blinked tears from my eyes and kept walking. I wanted to blame her for waiting, but she hadn't known about my studies.

She heard me out when I tried to explain, then said, "I'm sorry I didn't give the talisman to you earlier when you confronted me that day before the soldiers came to our village. And later ... I thought you had forgotten about him again. But, Tas, you speak as if there is no hope of you ever getting to know him or learn more of the magic, and that, my dear one, isn't necessarily true."

I stared as if she had sprouted flowers from her fingertips. "How can that be? Grandfather isn't about to let me study with another bonded to Kunai. And, when I am a man, in this new place, we will be too far from Big Ice Lake. There will be no magic there, and no one left with Kunai's favour to teach me."

She laughed softly, waving to Aunt Tuulah who had stopped in the trail ahead to wait for us. "True, I'm no Qwakaihi, but I do understand a little of how the Spirit-Power works. Father has taken away what he felt was an unsuitable tutor, but he can't take from you the knowledge that has already been imparted to you."

If that were indeed true, then the cord made with my parents' hair was powerful. Someday I might have the strength to use it to contact my father on my own.

"And remember this as well, my dear one. Water is all about us no matter where we go. Even in the driest land, there is water under the ground. And Kunai and his kindred can always swim the black rivers under the earth. No matter where you are, Kunai's magic can help you and your father travel the hidden rivers to find one another."

Chapter Ten

That evening when the column halted for the night, Ko, still carrying Seicu, followed us to our campsite. Grandmother was startled to see him, but greeted him politely, and then she offered him a place at our hearth. Ko seemed flustered by her welcome, but after a quick glance at Aunt Tuulah to see if she would take offence, he accepted the old woman's invitation. Excusing himself, he went to his mother's fire to explain his absence.

I followed Samiqwas to the creek for water. I returned to our fire without stopping to trade good-natured insults with Matoqwa and some of our friends. Seeing me, Grandmother asked me to bring firewood, so I rose without a protest and went back to the creek.

After collecting an armload of branches from under the firs, I squatted on my heels by the fire to wait for the mush to finish cooking. I had no wish to talk to anyone or go off with Samiqwas and Matoqwa to set rabbit snares—even though they'd come back specially to get me.

"Maybe tomorrow," I said. "I'm too tired tonight."

Samiqwas made a rude noise, then trotted off with the others. I thought Grandmother was going to order me to go with him, but instead she pointed with her lips to my –sister-cousin. Seicu was fussing, wanting her father, but Ko hadn't returned from his mother's encampment. Aunt Tuulah was hard pressed to calm her, while still trying to help with the evening's chores.

The little girl felt as warm as cakes fresh off the griddle stone when I took her from her mother's arms. I smoothed the damp hair from her forehead and plastered a cheerful smile onto my face. "Hello, baby-girl, how are you tonight?"

Seicu's eyes brightened with indignation, her breath a phlegmy rumble in her chest. "I not baby."

I could feel the corners of my mouth wanting to smile. I had to work hard to control myself. "I'm sorry. I forgot." I straightened her blanket and fitted it securely about her head and shoulders to keep the cool evening air from chilling her. Seicu coughed and I held a rag to her mouth. It came away spotted with blood.

An owl hooted in the surrounding forest. It wouldn't be long. I could sense the ghosts hovering in the shadows to carry her Spirit back over the mountains to our true home by Big Ice Lake. I planted a kiss on her cheek and hugged her, knowing I was going to miss her.

At that moment I would have willingly renounced my Gift. I had no desire to possess a power that tormented me with such terrible knowledge of the future. "What would you like to play with me while your mother fixes your meal, hmm?"

"No want mush—icky. Want Appi hold me."

"I know; he'll be back soon, but for now let's you and me play."

"Yes, you show me pictures."

Show her pictures—pictures in the patterns of a string loop empowered with Qwakaiva. I took in a deep breath, wanting to cry, forcing myself to put aside self-pity and think only of my sick cousin. "I will try to make the pictures for you, my Little Bird, but I've lost my special string. I may not be able to do the magic with my new one. But I will try—just for you."

"Grandfather is watching you," Seicu said.

Startled, I looked up. She was right. His blanket about his shoulders, he squatted across the fire from us, sipping a cup of hot tea. "So he is. It will be all right; he knows our secret now. I will make the pictures if I can."

I wasn't sure I could, by any means. I prayed Mother was right about my lessons. To please my little cousin I would have done anything that night. Giving Grandfather what I hoped was a defiant look, I drew off Mother's cord from around my neck and laid it across my palms. Seeming to have a will of their own, my fingers pulled upon the cord until they had formed the pattern of the Seer's Pool.

As the power of the conjuring built, my Qwakaiva responded in kind. A knot I hadn't been consciously aware of untangled itself in my gut. I could do it; my Qwakaiva wasn't lost to me! "Where shall we travel within the pool, Little One? What do you want to see?"

"Want to go home."

Home. Yes, I should have expected that. We all wanted to go home. And so, I took her. Flying north on the wings of the magic, away from the sickness and heartache of this brutal march south into a future that I refused to know. Back to the Big Ice Lake we went, and a past where there was joy and love.

In truth I needed the distraction and comfort as much as Seicu. Reluctantly I dissolved the pattern when Aunt Tuulah came to feed her daughter and put her to bed.

As soon as I had eaten and done my chores, I collected my blankets and crawled into the lean-to. I lay like a caterpillar in its cocoon, listening to the sounds of people settling for the night. I tried to sleep, but the knowledge of Death's messenger hovering nearby, kept me wakeful. In truth, no one in our family slept much. Seicu's fever rose as the night progressed. Ko held her wrapped in blankets by the fire while Aunt Tuulah brewed cup after cup of a tea made from willow bark and pine gum that Grandfather had collected the afternoon before.

Palm slapping rhythmically against his thigh, taking the place of the drum he no longer owned, Grandfather's low-voiced chant begged Qwa'osi for the power to heal her. I wished him well with his effort. I added my own prayers to his, but with little hope of success. The cold chill of certainty formed like ice around my heart.

There was no way back for Seicu now.

The ghosts had always been jealous of her leaving them for the living world—we all knew that—had known it from her earliest babyhood. And now they had followed the little girl through the cold mountains to take her home.

Throwing my blanket over my shoulders against the chill, I gave up any pretence of sleep and rose to gather more wood for the fire. When I returned, I saw that the rest of the family had arisen to join the death watch.

Aunt Tuulah had given up offering Seicu tea. She sat cradling her daughter, singing a lullaby. Ko sat beside them his blanketed arm thrown over one of Tuulah's shoulders, holding both of them. Samiqwas huddled next to his father, his face a rigid mask, trying to hold back tears.

I stacked the dry branches near the fire and went to crouch next to Mother. Grandmother looked up, nodding her thanks for the wood. No one spoke much. I drank tea when it was offered me, but mostly I leaned against Mother and stared numbly into the shifting patterns in the flames.

I wished there was something more I could do besides wait. I wished there was something I could say to change things. But there wasn't.

Towards dawn, Seicu's breathing grew laboured. One by one we each came forward to take her hand and say our farewells. As I crouched in front of my aunt and took Seicu's thin hand in mine, she opened her eyes.

"Little Rock Squirrel."

"Yes, I am your little rock squirrel," I whispered and kissed her hand. "Safe journey, my Little Bird."

She looked at something over my shoulder and smiled. I turned my head and saw the impatient spectre, its dark wings unfurled. "Farewell, Little Bird." I squeezed her hand and rose so that Samiqwas could take my place. There wasn't much time.

Grandfather had stopped chanting and sat holding Grandmother's hand. His expression remained calm, but I was sure he had seen the skull-headed Owl, too. Grandmother cradled a forgotten cup of tea in her lap, her posture rigid. Her eyes dry, she stared at nothing.

As I took my place once more beside Mother, the death rattle began deep in Seicu's throat, and then she breathed no more.

Tuulah moaned, the sound welling up from the depths of her being. She hugged her daughter tight, sobbing and rocking. Ko cried out, throwing his arms about them both, whispering words of comfort, but she angrily pushed him away. He made no complaint, but I saw the bleakness in his eyes.

Mastering his emotions he leaned over to touch his son on the shoulder. Samiqwas was curled in a ball upon the cold ground, his head and face covered by his blanket. I could hear his uncontrollable sobbing coming from within its woollen folds. At his father's touch, he pulled down the blanket's corner. Ko's voice was low but firm.

"Get up, my son. I need your help. It grows light. There's much to do before the day's march. Let us see if one of the soldiers will give us a pick and shovel. They won't want us to stay behind, and they won't wait for us to bury your sister."

Grandmother and Aunt Tuulah were keening, joined now by other relatives from nearby campsites. My vision blurred and I turned away. I could feel the tears running down my cheeks and made no effort to stop them. It was right to mourn for a lost loved one, so the old people always said, but why did it have to hurt so much?

Mother touched my arm and spoke my name. "Tasimu, we'll need water to wash the body. Take the big tin can there by the fire and go to the creek." When I returned, Mother placed it over the flames to heat.

Tuulah made a strangled protest and clutched her daughter tighter. Grandmother crouched before her, holding out her arms. "You must give her to me now, my girl, it's time."

Tuulah shook her head, but Grandmother was persistent. Both Grandfather and Mother added their encouragement and at last, she gave her daughter's body into the old woman's care. With Mother's help, Grandmother laid the little girl on a blanket and together the two women began singing their prayers for the dead, as they washed and prepared the body for burial.

Relieved of her daughter, Aunt Tuulah sobbing hysterically, collapsed into Grandfather's arms. Murmuring soft endearments to her as if she was once more a child, he sat rocking her.

With the light, soldiers roused the camp to get ready for the march. It didn't take long for the news to spread that there had been another death during the night. Aunty Qwatsitsa came over with cooked food for those who could eat. Other relatives kept showing up to pay their respects and offer a hand with whatever needed doing.

When I saw I was no longer needed, I whispered to Mother that I was going to find Samiqwas. She nodded for me to go ahead. I found him with several of our men in a stand of young birches near the creek. He was helping his father dig the grave. To my surprise Sergeant Ma'leubwey and a few of his soldiers were also there, helping some of our relatives gather stones to place upon the mound as a marker.

Seicu was a little girl and even with such flinty winter ground, it didn't take long to make the hole. When all was ready, Ko leaned on the shovel looking exhausted. Uncle Tli tapped me on the shoulder and sent me back to our fire to tell the women.

When I returned, Seicu's body had been cleaned and shrouded in the ragged blanket in which she'd been carried throughout her illness. A few feathers, pretty stones, and other special charms had been laid beside the shroud as final gifts from friends and relatives.

When Grandmother saw me she rose to her feet. Still holding Tuulah's hand, Grandfather rose and stepped to the shroud. "Would you like me to carry her?"

Tuulah shook her head and picked up her daughter. With the old people on either side, she led the procession to the gravesite. I fell in beside Mother as Aunty Qwatsitsa raised her voice in a high-pitched keen.

The people stopped by the grave, forming a circle around Aunt Tuulah's family and my grandparents. I stared at that dark hole dug into this land that wasn't our home, my heart numb with grief. I didn't want my last sight of her to be a blanketed bundle lowered into that cold lonely ground. Instead I focused on pleasant memories, Seicu coming home with Esuuli from picking raspberries, her mouth and chin stained with juice. Then I saw her atop her brother's shoulders as we walked to the trading post for candy. I recalled Samiqwas and me on his bed, tickling Seicu until she screamed with laughter. They were all images to treasure in my heart.

The gathering fell silent as Grandfather raised his arms to the sky and sang the prayers to aid a Spirit upon its journey. I closed my eyes, feeling the tingle of power in the world about us, summoned by his Qwakaiva. The Unseen Ones dwelling in that land stroked my face with a feathery touch cold as ice. Among the birches a raven cawed, then took to the air, heading north. "Good bye, sweet baby, I will miss you," I whispered as I followed the raven's flight.

<<I not baby,>> a faint voice said, and the wind ruffled my hair.

In spite of my tears, I felt my lips curve into a smile. <<I know. I forgot again.>>

When it was over, Grandmother put an arm about her daughter's shoulders and led her back to our fire to collect our belongings. It was full day by that time. The soldiers were shouting for the People to get on the march.

As we were leaving the gravesite, I happened to look back and saw the Qwani'ya man studying to be a priest they called Praiser Jon and a few of the Converts, standing among the mourners. I touched Grandfather's arm to draw his attention to them.

"Yes, I saw them earlier."

Recalling the hateful words spoken by those people not long before, I couldn't keep the bitterness from my voice when I asked, "What are they doing here? What do they want now?"

Grandfather shook his head, giving me a reproachful look. Then he headed in their direction. Not thinking he would mind, I trailed along in his wake. Stopping in front of Praiser Jon, Grandfather spoke a greeting, then waited to see what he wanted.

Jon cleared his throat a couple times before he could bring the words out. "We came this morning to offer our condolences on behalf of both Intercessor Raymonel and ourselves. It's hard to lose such a young child."

Grandfather nodded, his expression solemn. "It's difficult. Your sympathy and your prayers are welcomed. How is the Intercessor?"

Jon rubbed a hand across his tired face. "Not so good."

"I'm sorry to hear that. I will pray for him."

Jon made a face at that, but voiced no objection. Unspoken words fluttered between the staring men like ptarmigans disturbed by a lynx, but neither seemed able to voice them. At last a soldier shouting for them to hurry up broke the silence.

As Jon turned to go, he said, "I'm sorry for what happened the other night. I've been told there was another Qwakaihi among us, one whose reputation is—well, it is of no importance now, because he has left us. I believe he was the one. You won't be bothered again."

Part Four
Chapter One

N ot long after we buried my cousin, the land through which we walked changed. Gone were the snow-capped peaks and fast water of the high country. The river slowed and widened, its green depths an enigma. The mountains shrank in size, becoming thickly wooded hills. Spruce and fir gave way to aspen, willow, and other leafless giants unknown to me.

Marching ever southward we trudged through this unfriendly forest, the trees' gaunt trunks seeming to close in about the column at every turn. The wind moaned through skeletal branches, whispering, <<Go back. You aren't welcome here. You don't belong to us.>>

As the land flattened, it became real for all of us, Traditional and Qwani'ya Convert alike, just how far the Chamuqwani were taking us from our homes. Oh, we'd been told that this Native Preserve was in a far place, but our minds hadn't comprehended the truth. Always there'd been a shard of hope that someday, when the enemy wasn't so vigilant, we could escape and return north. But now that last dream was gone.

On the morning we left the Copper River and headed westward through the hills, Aunt Tuulah snuck away from the column. No one had suspected what she planned. Tuulah had been quiet and withdrawn since Seicu's death, but that was to be expected; we all felt Seicu's loss. But for Tuulah the death had a deeper significance. She had been deprived of both the descendants of her mother-lineage. That fragmented her soul in ways no one suspected.

She told Mother later that unable to face a life in this new land without her daughters beside her, she'd wanted to return north, to lay herself across Seicu's grave and end her own life.

On the morning she left, she told the family she was going to walk with Ko and his mother. Tuulah had barely spoken to Ko since the funeral, but his mother was one to be pitied, having birthed only male children. She had no daughter to care for her. She was ill, and Sand's wife had her hands full with her own children, so no one thought this announcement odd.

It was only when Ko and Samiqwas came at the noon break, looking for her, that we realized that something was wrong.

"Isn't she with your mother?" Grandmother asked.

Ko shook his head. "No, my son and I have been walking with my mother all morning. She can no longer carry her pack. She is growing weaker. I came to see if Tuulah would ..." His voice trailed off as he realized what Grandmother had just said.

Voicing the question that was on all our minds, Samiqwas said, "Then where is Amima?" He looked from one bewildered face to another, seeking an answer. Finding none, I could see the sharp spikes of fear sparkling in his spirit fire.

Finally Grandfather said, "We don't know, Grandson." He stood up. "But perhaps I should ask some of our relatives if they have seen her. Would you like to come with me?"

Samiqwas nodded, still looking worried. As they walked away, Ko said, "I will ask around, too," and headed in the opposite direction.

After the men were gone, Grandmother let out a heavy sigh and rubbed a hand across her face. Speaking to no one, she sat by the fire, staring at nothing. I glanced at Mother, hoping for reassurance, but saw the same worry in her eyes.

No one came back with news, and then the soldiers shouted for the people to pack up and get back on the trail. Mother laid a hand on my arm, and asked in a low voice, "Tas, can you find her?"

I blinked. Uncertain what she meant. With an impatient gesture, she motioned to the cord around my neck, and repeated her request. "I don't know," I stammered.

I thought we had been speaking low enough not to be overheard, but Grandmother had keen ears. "What are you saying, Daughter, what can Tas do to find her?"

Mother straightened, and then explained. "I asked my son if he could use his Qwakaiva to find my sister."

"And can you, boy?"

There was such a tone of urgency in Grandmother's request that I nervously licked my lips. They were counting on me, but could I? Mother patted my arm reassuring me, urging me to try. "I don't know, Ami." I took a deep breath. "But I will try."

Taking the cord from around my neck, I placed it over my hands and formed the Seer's Pool. I took in several deep breaths, trying to swallow my fear and ignore my staring relatives.

It took a while, but at last the image of my aunt did form in the central diamond. She was walking in the thick forest we had passed through that morning, heading north. Probing the sending a little deeper, once her image had stabilized, I sensed both her determination and her bottomless despair.

Suddenly I knew that she was going back to Seicu's grave to die. I cried out, the cord slipping from my hands.

"What is it, Grandson," Grandmother snapped. "What's wrong?"

I looked up, still shuddering, horrified by what I had been shown. Ko, Grandfather and Samiqwas had returned, and they too were staring at me.

"Has something happened to Amima? Has she been injured?" Samiqwas's voice quavered as he asked his question. My heart went out to him; how could I tell him, hurt him even more? I took a deep breath to centre myself before answering. "She is all right—not injured. She is walking north."

"Heading home?" Grandfather asked. Had he been expecting it?

I shook my head, and said in a voice barely above a whisper, "Back to Seicu—to die."

He nodded as if that too was no surprise to him.

When I glanced around, I saw the surprise and horror reflected on the faces that looked back at me. No one spoke, no one questioned my pronouncement, all seemed to trust in my Qwakaiva—even Grandfather. They all seemed to have faith in one blessed with Kunai's Gift of knowing such things.

Finally it was Ko who broke the silence with a Chamuqwani curse. "Foolish woman, what is she thinking? I have to go—have to bring her back." Before any of us could stop him, he raced off.

Grandfather muttered something under his breath and rose, too. "He is going about this the wrong way. If he tries to go after her in his present state, the soldiers will stop him—maybe hurt or kill him. Samiqwas, run after your father. Tell him to wait for me—"

As soon as the words left Grandfather's mouth, Samiqwas was up and racing after Ko. I would have followed him, but Mother grabbed my arm, holding me back.

"Never mind Ko for the moment. Go find Sergeant Ma'leubwey. Tell him what's happened. If Ko's temper gets the better of him, he will only end up in shackles again and be of no use to anyone. But the sergeant can help. He will not let my sister do this terrible thing. He will go back to find her."

What Mother said made sense, so instead of following Grandfather and my cousin, I ran through the soldier's campsite, looking for the sergeant.

I found him sitting around the fire with some of his men, just finishing up his meal. When I stammered out what had happened, he rose immediately. A few of his men trailing in his wake, he headed for the picket lines and the path north.

As Grandfather had predicted, Ko hadn't waited for him, or tried to explain to the sentry the urgency of his need to go back—or that he wasn't trying to escape. So, when he was stopped by two soldiers who didn't speak our language, he tried to fight his way past them, and he was beaten for it.

When the sergeant and his men arrived, Ko was lying on the ground. Grandfather crouched beside him, trying to explain to the soldiers, while at the same time stop the bleeding of a long cut on Ko's arm. Samiqwas looked angry enough to fight both soldiers single-handed, but as yet had done nothing but shout at the soldiers to stop hurting his father. One of the men had raised his weapon in a threatening gesture, but dropped it to his side at the sergeant's shouted order.

With Ma'leubwey there to translate, the matter was quickly sorted out. But Ko had punched one of the soldiers before he was knocked down, and the punishment for such an offence was a whipping and several days' march in chains.

Ko was led away cursing after Grandfather bound his wound with a temporary bandage cut from his blanket.

When he was gone, Grandfather rubbed a hand across his face and turned sad eyes to Sergeant Ma'leubwey. "My daughter lengthens the distance between us with each passing moment. What will you do?"

Ma'leubwey sighed, looking troubled. I could tell by the chaotic colours of his spirit fire that he was afraid for my aunt. He wanted to go after Tuulah, but his duty was here with the column. It was a hard choice for one who had given his allegiance to such an inhuman and uncaring monster as the Chamuqwani Emperor's Army.

Hoping perhaps to ease the sergeant's decision, Grandfather said, "If you will allow it, I will go back for her. My daughter is unwell; grief has driven her mind out of harmony. I give you my word that I will return with her and not try to escape."

Ma'leubwey sighed and shook his head. "I can't allow that, Elder, even though I'm sure you wouldn't try to escape." He shook his head again and swore. "No, it is impossible. I have my orders."

One of his men spoke up at that point, and there was a low-voiced conversation between them in rapid Chamuqwani. I never learned what the man said to him, because the sergeant ordered us to grab our packs and begin the afternoon's march.

Not long afterwards I saw him riding at a fast trot down our back-trail. His men must have agreed to cover for him while he looked for my aunt. I prayed that his Captain wouldn't punish him too severely for his kindness.

Chapter Two

That afternoon dragged on endlessly. Samiqwas refused to stay with us and stalked off to walk with his father. Heedless of the guards' threats, he trudged doggedly behind Ko and a few others who were in chains for breaking the soldiers' rules. I would have liked to follow him, but Grandmother forbade it.

"One boy running off to bait the bear is enough. You will walk with your family and stay out of trouble for once." I wasn't happy with her pronouncement, but I reluctantly had to agree.

By design, we chose to walk near the end of the column. I looked back frequently, but there was no sign of the sergeant or my aunt during the march that day.

We camped that night in a grassy ravine near a murky pool of water. As soon as camp was set up, Captain Mu'Dar listened to the charges brought against Ko, and then one of his men administered the punishment. Ko was given five lashes of the whip for striking the soldier. He also had to march in chains for the next three days.

Samiqwas told us the disheartening news, then begged to be allowed to remain by his father. He would be needed to help out with chores at his paternal relatives' camp, so Ko could rest. Grandmother reluctantly agreed. With a whispered word to me to bring him news of his mother when we heard, he raced off to Ko's mother's hearth.

The four remaining members of our family made a simple camp that night. No one felt like eating lumpy mush, so Mother used the tin can to boil up tea, then passed around pieces of hard-cake to soften in the hot liquid.

By dark there was still no sign of the sergeant or my aunt. We were sitting about the fire feeling miserable, when Grandfather spoke to me. "Grandson, those who are bonded to the otter warrior, as I am, haven't the Gift for seeing, as do those whom Kunai favours. Will you try your conjuring again, and see if you can tell us what has happened?"

By the expression he tried to hide, I guessed that admission of powerlessness, and plea for my help, cost him. But knowing that gave me little pleasure. I was worried, too.

"I can try, Ati," I said as I slipped the cord from my neck, "But I don't know if I can. I'm not sure if distance plays a part in what I can see." And then, I couldn't help pushing in the barb, "I am only half trained, you know."

His expression remained blank as he nodded. "Do the best you can. We will understand if nothing comes of it."

And so, with all their eyes focused upon me, I slipped the cord over my hands once more that day, and formed the Seer's Pool. I concentrated my Qwakaiva on the darkness in the central diamond and was rewarded with an image of Aunt Tuulah and Ma'leubwey, riding atop a tired horse, heading for the camp.

Qwakaiva crackled and whirled in the air about me. Blood pounding in my head, I released the enchantment and took in a deep breath of satisfaction. I had done it! Twice in one day—this proved beyond doubt that I hadn't lost my power.

Still smiling to myself, I turned to my family. "He has found her. They are riding down the trail towards our camp."

Grandmother breathed a sigh of relief and allowed herself a faint smile. "Foolish girl, does she think she is the only one who has ever lost a child? She should have more sense—and I plan to tell her so."

Mother made an exasperated noise in her throat. But I understood Grandmother's bluster. Hoping perhaps to distract the women from starting an argument, Grandfather asked me, "How long before they get here?"

"I don't know, Ati. The trail they rode was very dim. I couldn't recognize any land marks we might have passed earlier today. It may be soon. The sergeant wouldn't want to be gone any longer than necessary, lest his captain learn of his absence."

I had been guessing, but later when I saw the bloody stripes branded across the man's back, I realized the love he must have for Aunt Tuulah. He had made a great personal sacrifice to ensure her safety.

After giving my relatives my news, I begged permission to find Samiqwas and Ko to tell them as well. Grandfather nodded and I hurried off, before someone changed their minds.

I found both in Ko's mother's shelter. Ko lay on a blanket stripped to the waist, the old woman plastering his back with mud. Samiqwas was squatting by his father and seemed relieved by the news. Ko and his mother weren't so pleased. Oh, they were glad that my aunt had been found, they just weren't happy about who had found her.

Ko's mother scowled and told her son to get dressed. "You will never win her back now, my son. It's time you faced the truth and let me find you another wife. That woman has shamed you and all of us, so let the soldier have her. There are plenty of fine Qwani'ya women needing a good husband; no need to waste your time sniffing after that one."

His mother might have said more, but Ko happened to glance at his son's stricken face and told her they would discuss it later. I was startled by the woman's comments as well, but I couldn't help but notice how much she had sounded like Grandmother when she spoke of Ko. It felt odd to think of people talking about my aunty in such a bad way.

Suddenly I remembered Chumco speaking of how good and evil were only questions of perspective. The truth of his words made me shiver. At that moment I felt incredibly lonely. In spite of all that had happened, and all I knew about Kunai's Qwakaihi, I still missed him. I missed him with a deep ache that nearly shattered my heart at times.

Ko's mother sent us boys back to our own hearth at that point, so we heard no more of their discussion. Once away from their fire, however, Samiqwas baulked at returning directly back to our camp. He wanted to sneak past the sentries, so we could wait further down the path. He wanted to see his mother as soon as she arrived.

When I hesitated, he challenged, "You afraid of getting caught, Tas? Are you afraid of getting a beating like Appi?"

Well, yes, that *was* a sobering thought. But on the other hand, I had no wish to hurry back to our fire with such excitement afoot. "No, of course not. I'm not afraid of the soldiers and their whip. And I'll hit you if you say that again. I'll go with you."

He grinned and started for the edge of the camp circle. I grabbed his shoulder to slow him. "Wait a moment. If you run off without thinking, like your father, we really will risk a whipping."

He drew back his free hand to strike me, but I hurried on. "Just listen for a moment, before you punch me. I'm not saying we shouldn't try it, I'm just saying that in order to safely sneak out of camp, we need to split up. Once past the firelight, we can meet down the path where the sentries can't see us."

Samiqwas thought about it for a moment, then nodded his agreement. "You're right. Two boys sneaking about the animals will be easier to pick out than one. I'll go round by way of the picket lines and you go the other way. We will meet on the path where it bends back into the trees. No one should be able to spot us that far out."

Samiqwas left me, and I took a moment to centre my spirit, before I headed in the opposite direction. I hid in the shadows near the privy trench and when no one was about, I stole into the willows to make a wide circle around the encampment.

The night was clear, a deep indigo paling to green near the western horizon. Stars winked above me, but this far south, no Spirit-Lights snaked across the sky to aid me in my conjuring. Breathing deeply I reached out to gather the power of this new land, praying my Qwakaiva would answer and conceal me from unfriendly eyes.

I got past the guards all right, but I misjudged how far I'd travelled through the trees before I turned east towards the path. When I at last found my way back to it, I was much farther along the trail than I'd planned. The camp noise was far too distant. Samiqwas would be waiting impatiently for me to join him nearer to camp.

I was about to hurry back, when I heard the sound of a lone horse coming towards me from the other direction. Not wishing to be discovered, I eased back into the shadows.

It wasn't long before Sergeant Ma'leubwey and my aunt came riding the horse past where I crouched among the bushes. I breathed a sigh of relief when I saw them. I planned to wait till they passed me, then follow them back to camp, picking up Samiqwas along the way. But my plan had to be changed. As they passed me, I heard Aunt Tuulah tell him to stop the horse so she could get off.

Ma'leubwey reined in the animal. "What's wrong? We aren't to the encampment yet. Why do you want to walk now?"

Tuulah slipped off the horse as soon as it slowed, before giving him an answer. "A prisoner should not be seen riding behind her captor. Your captain won't approve."

Ma'leubwey uttered a curse and dismounted to walk beside her. Tuulah ignored him and kept on walking. He caught up to her in two easy strides and spun her roughly to face him. "All afternoon you refuse to talk, and now these are the first words you say to me? What is a matter with you, crazy woman? The God alone knows why I bothered—"

"So leave me alone. I never asked—never wanted you, or anyone to bother—"

"I don't care what you wanted, *I wanted*, and I'm not going to let you throw away your life, die for no reason."

"Damn you, I have a reason," Tuulah's voice rose to a near shriek. "Let go of me! What I do is none of your affair."

When he only firmed up his grip on her arm, Tuulah let out an anguished cry and struck him hard with the fist of her free hand. Ma'leubwey cursed and made a grab for her, allowing the horse's reins to slip through his fingers. The horse shied and trotted off down the track, stopping not far away to browse on the shrubs by the trail.

The sergeant was a tall man and well-muscled, but in spite of his natural advantages, I could tell even in the darkness that my enraged aunty was putting up quite a resistance. I stood frozen, fearing he might hurt her. I couldn't decide whether to try to intervene, or run back to the camp for help.

Then as suddenly as their struggle began, it ended. Aunt Tuulah collapsed against him sobbing, and he gathered her into his embrace. Murmuring soft endearments he leaned his cheek against her bowed head and held her while she cried.

When she quieted enough to hear him, he said, "O my fierce little mountain cat, haven't you figured out by now that I could never just walk away and let you die? If I were to do that, I would die, too."

"Ma'leubwey, you don't understand. Both my daughters lost to me, my mother-line has ended. I am nothing—a dead woman without my daughters beside me."

"Don't be ridiculous. You aren't an old hag; you can have more children—" At that point his words were cut off by a loud slap. He cursed and I heard the sounds of them tussling again.

When he had pinned her arms, Tuulah cried angrily, "Let me go! You don't understand—and why should you, coming from a people who care only for their male children. Girl children to you mean nothing, but to me, my daughters meant *everything*. And now they are gone!"

"Hush, hush, you know nothing of my people. You call us all Chamuqwani, but the peoples who make up the empire are not all the same—with the same customs and beliefs. And you are wrong. I cared very much about the baby daughter I lost to a fever when she was no older than your little girl."

"You did? I-I didn't know." Tuulah sniffed back her tears and raised her face to look into his. I doubt even standing so close she could have seen much of his expression in the darkness, but it probably didn't matter, because at that point, he kissed her.

I was creeping further into the trees when his next words halted me again.

"My darling, you aren't the only one who has buried loved ones. Before I joined the army, I lost a wife and three children to the spotted fever. I hurt so bad; I wanted to die, too, but after more rational thought on the matter, I decided not to bring the shame of a suicide upon my family. I stayed my hand."

Tuulah sniffed and asked in a soft voice, "What did you do instead?"

He chuckled and kissed her. "A similar remedy to what I now offer you."

"You're talking in riddles," she said impatiently. "No, don't try to kiss me, explain. What did you do?"

"I joined the Emperor's army and took myself as far away from my home and family as I could. It was a bitter medicine, cutting myself off from all I had known, suffering the hard life and discipline of a soldier, but in time the wound closed and the hurting eased."

Tuulah laughed. "I doubt if your captain would allow me to join your company as a new recruit. That is hardly a solution for me."

He joined her in her laughter. Still holding her around the waist, he walked to where his horse cropped the dry grass along the path. "True enough, my captain wouldn't allow you to enlist—nor would I want him to—even though you would make a fierce warrior. No I had something else in mind that would have a similar result."

"What?"

"My enlistment is over soon. I am tired of soldiering. Marry me. Let me take you home with me, to my land and my mother. She will like you."

Tuulah stopped abruptly, causing the sergeant to pull on the horse's reins. It let out a snort of protest. "Take me home to your mother?" Tuulah began to laugh.

"What's so funny about that?"

"You are serious, aren't you?"

"Of course I am." Dropping his arm from around her waist he gathered up the horse's reins and stalked ahead of her down the path.

Tuulah stifled her laughter and hurried to catch up to him. "Ma'leubwey, wait. I'm sorry; I meant no insult. You startled me that's all. I never dreamed—I had no idea you were serious. You really want to marry me?"

Still annoyed with her, he snapped, "I said so, didn't I?"

"Yes, you did."

They walked along in silence for some time before he broke the impasse by asking, "And will you accept my offer?"

She hesitated, then said, "I don't know yet."

"Take some time and think about it then." I saw his white teeth gleam in the starlight as he smiled at her. "You might surprise yourself and like my island home. It is very far away. There's no snow there, however. It's always warm there, but there are mountains and trees and fast-running streams that flow down to the big ocean."

He had used a word in his own language unknown to her, so she asked, "What is an *o'see'an*?"

"Hah! You don't know what is an ocean? Well, I guess maybe you wouldn't. It is like a big, big, big lake, only the water is salty not fresh to the taste."

"You are teasing me."

"No, I swear it's true. Come with me and you'll see for yourself ..."

We were nearing the camp now, so I allowed them to get further ahead. Samiqwas hailed them as they rounded the next bend, but even then I didn't join them. My heart was troubled by what I'd overheard. Aunt Tuulah hadn't said she would marry the soldier, but then again she hadn't refused him either.

Poor Samiqwas. What would it be like to lose a mother—especially now, after Seicu's death? Or would the soldier want to take my cousin with him, too? My heart gave a lurch at the thought of losing my best friend along with everything else that had happened.

Should I tell him what I had overheard? It would certainly cause him some worry if I did. And it might all be for nothing if Aunt refused to leave the family and go with the soldier. I might be upsetting everyone for nothing, if I repeated what I had learned from my spying, so best to keep quiet, I reasoned. Becoming an adult was a far more complicated affair than I had led myself to believe.

When I at last crept back to our fire, Aunt Tuulah was sobbing in Grandmother's arms, and the rest of the family looked angry enough to spit fire. Squatting down beside Samiqwas, I asked in a low voice, "What happened?"

"What happened? Where were you? I waited—"

"Never mind that—I got lost. What's happened?"

"The soldiers were waiting for Sergeant Ma'leubwey when he returned with Amima. They put the shackles on him, then took him away and whipped him."

Chapter Three

A few more days of walking and the thick forests gave way to the cleared lands of Chamuqwani settlements and farms. Once we arrived in more populated country, the soldiers became strict with us. Rule breaking brought severe punishments. We had to keep together during the day's march, and no one—not even children—were allowed to hunt or forage, for fear of angering the Chamuqwani living there.

At night we slept in buildings made to house animals, or set up camp in a farmer's unused field. No one was permitted to stray past the outer limits of the encampment. Sentries were vigilant. But in spite of the risks, and the warnings of our elders, we boys were hungry. We tested these adult-imposed limits constantly.

These daring night-time forays became a test of Qwani'ya prowess. It was an intoxicating challenge, to defy the enemy and sneak into an unsuspecting farmyard, to scavenge what we could for ourselves and our starving relatives.

As we passed from the trees, the path widened to become *Road*, a new word to me, and a wonder to behold. *Road* seemed to stretch out endlessly before us. It was so wide several people, horses, or wheeled boxes pulled by horses, could move or pass one another without mishap, while travelling upon it.

Each day we passed snowy fields fenced in by long ribbons of thin iron wires that snagged in clothing and flesh if a passer-by came too near. Beyond these barriers squatted wood and stone buildings with tall sloping roofs.

The Chamuqwani cabins I had grown accustomed to seeing in northern settlements were also square, not round like our own dwellings. My people thought such buildings unnatural, because Spirits of both blessing and disharmony could become trapped in their corners. But at least, in their outer colouring, northern cabins blended in with the life around them. They weren't such a shock to the eye as these southern houses.

Here the people made no attempt to harmonize with the land. These dwellings flaunted their discord, in vivid reds, blues, and bright yellows that hurt the eye. They proclaimed the Chamuqwani conquest over the land—land stolen, I later learned, from other tribal peoples.

When we were marched past these unnatural dwellings, people stopped their work to come out and stare at us. Seeing the wonder and bewilderment in many a blue eye that chanced to meet mine, I would pass the time wondering what they thought when they looked at us, tramping through their well-ordered lives. Ragged and dirty, gaunt of face and limb from sickness and starvation, did we invoke fear, pity, or just indifference? What would I feel if I were in their place?

In truth I saw a range of emotions when I gazed upon the inhabitants of this new land with my Gift. The people we encountered often seemed as bewildered as we did ourselves. Others, however, especially when we were herded through their villages, lined up on the side of Road to curse us, calling us "dirty zaunk" and other cruel things. I looked at the whirling colours in their spirit fires, as their reddened faces spat out their venom, and I felt a deep sadness enveloping me.

Weighed down by the force of their emotions, I had to struggle to put one foot in front of the other or I'd be engulfed in their madness. These Chamuqwani didn't know us. They had never seen us before; why did they hate us so much?

But to be fair, not all the Chamuqwani people we met along Road were mean; in truth, many saw our plight and were moved to pity us. Some even offered us food and other little kindnesses along the way. I recall one incident of generosity offered to us by a farmer and his family that helped me balance the hurt and anger that was festering inside my heart.

We had stopped to make camp in a field where a grain crop had recently been harvested. We were far enough south that, even though winter had caught up to us, there was only a light dusting of white covering the stubble in the field.

After walking past the open gate, I hurried to the wagon where Grandmother had been riding to offer her my help.

Not long after we arrived to walk upon Road, Captain Mu'Dar had set a rider ahead to the nearest army post. The soldier was ordered to give news of our coming, so the lord's men could send more food and other supplies. Much to our relief, he was also ordered to bring back wagons to carry the sick, young children, and old people too weak to keep up with the column.

Instead of continuing on into the field, that evening the wagons stopped in the farmyard. I couldn't help slowing my pace to gawk. The house where the people lived was large, built of both stone and flattened pieces of wood. It had also been painted a bright red with white trim around each window and door. There must have been steps inside to go from one level to another, because I saw many windows at different heights, going up to a high, peaked roof.

Clustered about the outskirts of the farmyard were several buildings, both large and small, that—I'd been told earlier—Chamuqwani farmers used to house their animals, or as warehouses for tools and extra food. Behind these I saw fenced squares of ground. Over the top rails of the fences long-eared mules and the spotted fat beasts called Milk-Cai watched the excitement.

As I peered from behind a corner of the wagon while I waited for Grandmother's turn to climb down, I saw Captain Mu'Dar and a few of his officers standing near the long porch of the big house. They were talking to two men, a fat man with a long grey beard, and a younger, taller man with similar heavy features, who was probably his son.

There was also a black dog in the farmyard that had been tied up to a tree at the first sight of our arrival. To my disgust, the beast was barking like a crazy thing, so I couldn't hear what the men were saying. No one looked angry, so I hoped everything was all right. I was too tired to walk further that night. But if this Chamuqwani changed his mind after seeing us—as had happened before—the soldiers would make us move on.

Some brown and white birds with red feathers atop their heads strutted about, pecking at the ground and getting in everyone's way. I knew by that time that these silly birds were called Chicken. The Chamuqwani in those parts were too lazy to hunt, so they kept such foolish birds for their meat and eggs.

While watching the birds, I happened to catch Samiqwas's eye. He gave me the barest of nods and mouthed the word, "Later."

I'm sure my eyes widened at his boldness. Some of the soldiers were wise to our tricks by that time. We'd almost been caught during our last raid. I glanced at the talking soldiers, took a deep breath, and just as silently nodded my agreement. My stomach rumbled at the thought of anything other than hard-cake and oat-mush to eat.

I was desperate enough to go along with my cousin's proposal, but the Spirits blessed us, and we were saved the temptation of breaking the rules, for that night at least.

When I glanced around once more, a young woman with a girl of about three or four clinging to her skirt, was heading towards us. In my half-starved condition, she seemed incredibly fat and healthy, but in truth, she wasn't overly heavy, only nicely rounded, as the women in my own family had once been.

She was a pretty woman, for a Chamuqwani I supposed, fox-haired and pink-cheeked. She wore a long brown skirt, with a clean white apron over it. Around her shoulders was a heavy woollen shawl. She also carried something in a cloth-wrapped bundle in one hand.

As she approached nearer she must have smelled the pungent odours of wood smoke, grime, and sour sweat that always clung to us, because she wrinkled up her nose and slowed her pace. She hesitated as if uncertain if whatever she had in mind was such a good idea after all. Then she strengthened her resolve and continued towards us.

Shilshigua had been riding in the same wagon with Grandmother. Hollow-eyed and thin as a winter aspen branch, she handed down the tiny bundle that was their failing daughter to Uncle Tli. At his call, I rushed over to help Shilshigua climb from the wagon.

Tli looked no better than his starving wife. Over the course of our march he had grown almost skeletal. His patched tunic and leather breeches sagged upon his gaunt frame. I secretly agreed with Grandmother when she claimed that he must be giving most of his food ration to his wife and child.

The baby let out a forlorn wail, as she left the warmth of her mother's arms. At that sound, the young farm woman forgot about our bad smell, and alien appearance. Without hesitation now, she walked forward and held out her wrapped bundle to Shilshigua.

"For you and the baby," she said slowly in Chamuqwani.

I don't know if Shilshigua understood her, but a look passed from one young mother to the other. An understanding grew between the two women in that moment. Shilshigua took the bundle and mumbled her thanks in our language.

There was no need for an explanation of what lay under the cloth. The rich smells of cooked meat and baked bread were a fragrance that couldn't be masked by the smells of sweat and animal dung surrounding us in the farmyard.

As the little family headed out into the field, I caught a glimpse of Tli's face and was startled by the naked anger I saw reflected there. Like me, he must have seen the pity in the woman's eyes. But unlike his wife who blessed her for her generosity, Tli was shamed by her gift, and hated her for it. I understood his rage, while at the same time I wasn't above whining for handouts along the march if I thought I could benefit by it.

Turning back to the woman, I saw her attention had been captured by some of the younger children, who were crowding about her, hoping for more treats. Frightened by all the dirty newcomers crowding round, her own daughter began to cry. Looking flustered, she picked up the child and would have gone to her house, but by then her retreat had been cut off.

It wasn't long before the child's loud cries had attracted the attention of the talking men. At a word from the captain, one of his officers detached himself from the group and stalked over to rescue mother and child. Brandishing his riding whip, he shouted, "Get away from here, you little vermin or I'll skin you alive. Get, I say, get!"

The little ones scattered, before he could make good on his threat. Grandmother muttered something angry under her breath about the man's parentage, as I helped her down from the wagon.

Very stiff after sitting in the wagon all day, Grandmother was unsteady on her feet. She needed a strong young shoulder to lean on while she made her way to our family's shelter. Samiqwas was taller and stronger than I, so it was decided that he would take her the rest of the way.

I should have been right behind them, but the sudden touch of my Qwakaiva halted me. The Power wanted me to stay by the wagon a while longer. Something good would come of it, if I did. Even without that prompting I might have remained; I was curious to see more of the farm woman's reaction to the soldier's threats.

As I'd suspected, she wasn't any happier about the soldier's rude behaviour than Grandmother. While Grandmother had learned, through bitter experience, to keep her opinions mostly to herself, this Chamuqwani had not—and she told the man exactly what she thought of him.

"They are only children—and starving at that. How can you be so cruel?"

"Sorry, missus, if I upset you, but I have my orders. And you don't know these zaunk brats like I do. They will pester you to death or steal anything that isn't nailed down if you encourage them. Your men-folk better keep a close watch—"

"Don't call them zaunks. And maybe if you and your captain took care of these people better—fed them properly—they wouldn't have to steal, now would they?"

I didn't understand most of what she said after that, but the man's face turned red as a berry as she continued. When she quieted, the soldier stammered another apology and hastily retreated back across the yard.

After he'd gone, she put down her still sniffling child and glanced around the busy farmyard, the uncertainty coming once more into her grey-green eyes. It was then that she spied me leaning against the wagon. Her face still flushed from her argument, she beckoned me to her.

Suddenly uneasy, I thought about running away, but another nudge of the Power made me decide against it. There was no reason to fear her. I hadn't stolen anything as the soldier claimed—yet.

The little girl peeked out from her concealment behind her mother. She wrinkled up her nose at me and stuck out her tongue. Unlike her mother, the child was brown-haired and dark-eyed, just a little older than Seicu would have been.

If she'd lived.

Qwakaiva crackled in the air between us. Pain knifed through my chest and I sucked in a long slow breath as I centred my spirit once more. This girl wasn't my little cousin. This girl was healthy, loved and protected, not lying in a cold grave back along the river trail like Seicu. To hide the resentment I feared the mother might see on my face, I dropped my eyes and waited.

Speaking slowly and loudly, so I might understand, she said, "Boy, you come with me." I nodded and followed her.

Picking up the child, she balanced her on her hip, then headed for the big house. Still keeping an eye on me, the little girl stuck her thumb in her mouth and leaned her head on her mother's shoulder.

Chapter Four

We walked around the corner and took a short path screened by tall berry bushes. I could no longer see the soldiers and my heart eased its pounding. From back here I could also see a well-used trail heading into the field where the encampment lay. Whatever the woman wanted, I would be glad to take this path rather than risk being spotted by the soldiers in a place where I had no business.

At the back of the house, she put her daughter down and opened the door. Through the opening I saw a large room with a long table standing in the centre of the floor. Along the far wall stood the biggest woodstove I'd ever seen. Though I could see several pots boiling away atop it, the stove looked as clean and shiny as if it had just come from a trader's store.

Also in the room was an older woman, her greying hair tucked up under a white headscarf. Her hands covered in flour, she looked up as the door opened. White dough lay in a mound on the table in front of her. Two boys of about my own age were sitting at the far end of the same table, drinking tall glasses of something white.

My stomach growled loudly at the good smells of frying meat, onions and baking bread wafting out of the room. She must have heard my gut, for the woman turned back and smiled, making me flush with embarrassment.

"Wait here," she said and closed the door behind her.

I could hear her talking inside, but no one returned to open the door again for a long time. In the farmyard on the other side of the hedge, horses stamped, and the men caring for them joked and talked. One of the cai beasts let out a sad moo that was answered by others of its kind.

Around me were the sounds and bustle of many people going about the evening's tasks, but in this place I was alone except for an old man who was digging roots in the dried-up garden nearby. He had looked up as I passed by with the farm woman, then went back to his work. I worried that he might not like me hanging around, but he said nothing about my being there, so I ignored him.

After the old man filled his pail and left, I glanced once more at the closed door, and then I hesitantly sat on the back step to wait.

"There you are," Samiqwas called out. I looked up and saw him easing quietly around the little hut where the chickens were kept. Coming over to me, he folded his arms across his chest, and asked, "What are you doing here?"

I shrugged and pointed with my chin to the closed door behind me. "The farm woman told me to wait here—so I am."

"If the soldiers see you, there will be trouble."

I shrugged and stayed where I was. He grinned and sat down beside me.

"There are some nice fat birds in that little hut over there," he said to the air.

I grinned, and without looking in his direction I asked, "Mm, and do you have a plan for getting some of them out without the soldiers or the farmers catching us?"

"Um—maybe. Tigali and Matoqwa think we can—"

I made a rude noise cutting him off. "I want no part of a hunt Matoqwa has helped plan."

"You aren't being fair, Tas, it wasn't his fault about the dog last time."

"And what about the dog *this time*? That ugly black mutt will yap its head off if it catches our scent anywhere near this place after dark—listen to it even now."

Samiqwas gave me a cunning smile, so like Uncle Tli when he planned some good trading. "I am listening. And, I am also watching. No one is paying the noisy beast a bit of attention. Nor are they likely to pay attention later, because the beast is stupid and barks at everything—all the time."

He had a point and I told him so, but knowing that didn't make me feel any easier in my mind about the coming raid.

"And besides," he added with another sly smile. "Fat black dog probably tastes as good as chicken. So if he gives us any trouble ..."

I quickly put a hand over my mouth to stifle my laughter. Then I glanced around to see if anyone had heard us. Soldiers were talking in the big red building where animals were kept. If they came out and saw us, there would be trouble—big trouble ...

Maybe the farm woman had forgotten me and we should go back to the encampment. I opened my mouth to suggest that, when the door opened. With the two boys I'd seen at the table behind her, the young woman came out, each of them carrying sacks and wrapped parcels of food. Samiqwas grunted and I saw his eyes widen in the light streaming from the house.

She was startled to see him waiting with me, but she smiled and pointed to the things she and the boys were laying out on the porch.

"For you, all this." She had the boys open the sacks to show us as she named their contents in her language. "These are carrots, these beets and those potatoes, and here are apples—you will like them best, I think—they are very good. And lastly, here are some eggs and flour for your mother."

Frowning, she glanced at Samiqwas, then she handed me a covered basket still warm from the kitchen. I could smell the fried meat, mushrooms and other good things inside the cloth covering.

"I guess there's enough in there for two hungry boys, so sit down right here and eat the nice supper I fixed for you special."

I hadn't understood everything she said, but I knew what she expected. I glanced at Samiqwas, and he made a slight shake of the head. The good smells were driving us both crazy. We wanted nothing more than to pounce on this bounty, but we could not. There were too many hungry relatives back in the encampment for us to be selfish. We weren't babies, and we fancied ourselves young warriors. We would wait, and take only a share.

Misunderstanding our hesitation, the uncertainty I'd seen earlier came back into her eyes. "What's wrong? I know you are hungry. Why don't you boys eat?"

One of the farm boys made a rude comment to the other about stupid zaunks not knowing what good food was, and maybe they should cook us up some cow shit instead.

The woman scolded them, but it didn't matter to me. The words had been spoken, and the Aseutl of anger inside my soul snarled at the insult. Once again, I felt the fiery currents of my Qwakaiva rouse.

Our tormentors were stocky muscular brats, probably used to hard labour, well-fed and outweighing both Samiqwas and me. I cared little about the odds arrayed against us. If they wanted to fight; I was ready. I glared, wishing at that moment that I could speak Chamuqwani perfectly, so I could insult them back in kind.

Samiqwas knew enough of the boy's language to know when we were being insulted, too. Shifting his position so only the boys could see, he made the rude gesture that the soldiers often used. The smaller, and probably the younger of the two, let his eyes grow wide. Samiqwas grinned and cracked his knuckles like Matoqwa did before a fight.

Suddenly netting some good sense, I pushed back the anger and laid a hand on my cousin's shoulder. If we got into a fight, the soldiers would come. They would punish us to be sure, but more importantly, we would forfeit all this food our family and sick relatives needed. "Remember the People," I whispered.

When I was certain he understood me, I turned to the woman, and in my best Chamuqwani tried to explain. "Is good food." I lifted the cloth, sniffed appreciatively and smiled. "Me want eat. But no can." I shook my head to emphasize my point.

"We bring," I pointed with my chin to the encampment taking shape in the nearby field. "Mama hungry, Grandma hungry, little cousins, Uncle and Aunty hungry. We take, we share." And then, in spite of my stink and my rags, I said, "Is Qwani'ya way."

She must have heard the pride in my voice, because she studied me in a new way, for a long moment. Finally she nodded solemnly. "Yes, Boy, you are right. It is a very good way. This world would be a better place, if more thought the same as you. Take the meal and the rest of the food back to your family and be welcome to it."

As she turned to go back inside, I stopped her. "You want I make wood for you?"

She seemed puzzled by my broken Chamuqwani, so I pointed to the wood pile and mimed chopping wood for her. I saw the tears pool in her eyes, and it made me proud to have bested her. She hadn't expected me to offer payment for her charity.

"Thank you, but there is no need." She pointed at the two boys, who definitely didn't look happy at receiving her attention again. "The boys can get what I need. You had better go now, before the food in the basket grows cold and your families begin to worry about you."

We needed no further urging. Under the angry gaze of the farm boys, Samiqwas and I divided up the sacks between us. I stuffed the still warm basket under my tunic and then we were off down the little path I'd noticed before, back to the encampment.

"I think we should cancel the hunt tonight," I said, when we were tramping through the dry grass of the field where no one could hear us.

"That may be a good idea, because she might give us more in the morning—I saw her face when you spoke of the Qwani'ya. She was impressed with you."

I could feel my face heat, but I was secretly grateful for his praise. To cover my embarrassment, I made a rude noise and kept walking. "What do I care what she thinks."

The trail we were following twisted about to come near a little creek, almost hidden behind a few willow and aspen. He laughed. "Maybe we can still have a hunt. There might be some rabbits or wild birds in the brush by the trees."

He pointed with his lips to the ribbon of trees snaking around the edge of the field. "No one should complain if we hunt there. And there is plenty in these sacks to feast on anyway if we can't get past the sentries—"

Our speculations were cut short at that moment, by the sound of boys shouting. From where we stood, the commotion was shielded by the aspens, but it seemed to be coming from down by the creek. I recognized Matoqwa's battle cry and that of Cohasi and Slylum, answering him through the din.

Samiqwas and I looked at one another, then without a word spoken between us, we hid our plunder in the nearby thicket, and raced to join the battle. We neither knew nor cared who Matoqwa and our friends were fighting. We'd heard the call and were on our way to join the fray. As we crashed through the brush, making no attempt to be quiet, Samiqwas and I let out several loud whoops of our own, to let our friends know it was us, and not more enemy coming up behind.

Expecting to see some Convert boys attacking our little war band with stones and mud balls, I was startled to see several Convert boys crouching down among our friends when we burst out of the trees. They were all engaged in lobbing missiles at a group of Chamuqwani boys on the other side of the creek. Farther back in the trees on our side, some girls stood with tin buckets in their hands, adding their own chorus of praise calls to the din, whenever one of our warriors hit his target.

It was obvious to me what must have happened. Boys and girls from the encampment had been sent for water at the creek, and some boys from the farm on the other side took exception to our invading what they considered *their* territory.

It had happened before, but what was surprising about this combat, was that Traditional and Convert alike fought together. Always before the Convert children had tried to distance themselves from our brushes with the enemy. Or, even worse, they waited till we had run off the Chamuqwani children, then attacked us as well.

At the arrival of more reinforcements for our side, the boys across the creek had had enough, and they hastily retreated. Emboldened by this show of weakness, our friends with Tigali in the lead, broke from cover to pursue them down our side of the creek, shouting rude words in both Chamuqwani and our own language.

One Chamuqwani, smaller and slower than the others, fell behind the retreating pack. A well-aimed stone hit him square in the back and he fell. At his cries for help, one of the larger boys turned back. His rescuer was tall with hair yellow as straw. He was nearly man-grown and when he saw the younger boy on the ground, his face purpled with rage. Shouting curses at us, he brandished a thick stick like a club and raced through the shallow water. Coming out on our side of the creek, he knocked Matoqwa to the ground.

I was the nearest to Matoqwa, but still too far away to give warning of the blow. The rest of our war band was occupied in chasing the others; no one but me had seen the larger boy's attack.

Matoqwa had been taken totally by surprise, too. He hadn't had time to defend himself, before he was struck down from behind. As he tried to get to his feet, the yellow-haired boy knocked him down again. Fury contorted his features as he raised the club for another blow.

This attack had gone far beyond a war game to stave off boredom. This farm boy was ready to kill. Qwakaiva sizzled down my arms; my hands grew suddenly warm. I tasted my own rage, and without hesitation, I threw the rock in my hand with all the strength of my arm and the Spirit-Power I'd summoned.

The stone I'd thrown wasn't overly large, but my aim was true. It hit the Chamuqwani right between the eyes. He staggered backwards, dropping his stick. Blood welled up where the rock struck and poured over his nose and eyes.

My blow seemed to knock some sense back into him as well. He was outnumbered and wounded. He shook his head and wiped some of the blood from his face onto his sleeve.

"You go or I hit you again," I shouted.

He snarled and raised his stick. I grinned and showed him the rock in my other hand. Whatever he saw in my face made him hesitate. Then he heard the smaller boy calling to him. He threw down his weapon. Daring me to throw, he turned his back on me, and waded back across the creek.

I shouted my own curses at his retreating back, but I let him go without risking the throw. If I'd hit him, the incident might have provoked a real war, drawing back the others to continue the battle. And with everyone's temper high, someone might have gotten seriously hurt.

And, if I'd missed—which could have happened as easily as not—he would have turned round to taunt me. That kind of humiliation would have been unbearable.

By that time Matoqwa had regained his feet and stood watching the two disappear behind a small rise in the land. When they were gone, he turned to me and grinned. "It's a good thing for me that your cousin has finally taught you how to throw straight, Siyatli Boy."

I grinned back, pleased. Matoqwa and I would never have an easy friendship, but he had been right when he told me back in the stockade that all us Qwani'ya boys needed to stick together. Remembering that as we went to find the others, I asked, "I was surprised to see those Convert brats fighting alongside us."

He snorted. He was rubbing his shoulder and I could tell it must hurt him. "It was the other way round, cousin. The farm boys started the trouble by attacking the Convert boys first. The Chamuqwani were calling them 'zaunk,' just like they do the rest of us. It was a laugh, watching those Converts trying to explain, in their best Chamuqwani, that they were different from us—and stop trying to hit them—they were good followers of the Chamuqwani god."

"Maybe they will stop bothering us now that we saved their skinny backsides."

"Don't count on it," Samiqwas muttered.

By this time we had been joined by several of our friends eager to know what had just happened. As we were trading war stories and joking around, the girls called out, wanting to know if it was safe. We lingered by the creek grinning and displaying our battle wounds for them to admire, while they filled their pails.

"So, since we are all here, let's talk about our plans for tonight," Cohasi suggested.

Samiqwas and I looked at each other and shared a grin. "There's no need to raid the farmyard tonight. My cousin and I have already done so," he said.

Ignoring the good-natured taunts made at our expense, we led them back to the cache of food we'd hidden before we joined the fight. Everyone's eyes widened when they saw our plunder.

Our little war band shared the nice supper the farm woman had prepared for me, and then we sauntered back to camp to divide the rest of the booty. Our relatives and friends greeted us like great hunters when we arrived with our sacks of food.

We never did make a hunt in that place. Captain Mu'Dar bought several cai that were too old to give milk from the fat farmer and his neighbours. We stayed on that farm for two days feasting and regaining our strength for the march yet to come.

And the farm woman was right. The apples were wonderful. I had never tasted anything so sweet and good before.

Chapter Five

As we travelled deeper into this country of rolling grasslands and farms, we saw more and more Chamuqwani settlements. Most were much larger than villages in the north. The soldiers called these places *Town*. I found them noisy and frightening as did the rest of my family. In Town the people lived all crowded together in big and small houses.

The paths between the buildings down which the soldiers marched us, stank of rotting garbage and animal dung. Smoke stung our eyes and the breath burned in our chests. It was terrible there.

"Is this what our kindred sold our land for?" I heard a man from Broken Shell Mound Village say to Uncle Tli. "They promise us a better life if we leave our beautiful home and become like them. How is living in noise and filth in a village as crowded as a rock squirrel's warren an improvement over what we had?" Tli let out a bitter laugh. Then they passed on, and I heard no more.

Each day we continued further south and west out of the mountains. Though skeletal and weak, Intercessor Raymonel tried to continue with his work among us. Many feared for his life if he went with us to the Preserve. That was why Captain Mu'Dar insisted that as soon as we came to a settlement containing a temple to their god, he must remain there to regain his health.

He journeyed with us longer than the captain wished, however. There wasn't a place suitable, until we reached the town where we too stopped walking. From that point we would travel to our new home on something called *Train*.

This big Town sprawled in a smoky valley by a wide muddy river. Here there was also a massive temple to Djoven the Mighty. Next to the temple was a long low building where many priests and some nuns lived. It had been arranged that Intercessor Raymonel would stay at the priests' house. The two

Mercy Women he had brought with him to the north would also stay behind to care for him.

The rest of us were allowed to rest in the shelter of its courtyard, while the priest said his goodbyes. The temple's inhabitants offered us a simple meal of bread and dried fruit while we waited.

As I sat down on a cold stone bench to rest and eat my portion, I happened to look up. Fearsome monsters had been carved into the walls above the massive temple doors. They gave me quite a scare, until I realized they were but stone.

Gnawing on a slice of the sweet dried fruit, I studied their brutish faces and skeletal clawed hands. Qwakaiva pounding in my skull, I found myself unable to look them in the eye. Instead I dropped my eyes to the courtyard, scanning the human faces of my exhausted relatives.

The monsters were only carvings of stone, weren't they? Or could these town priests, with the help of their fearsome god, transform them into living beings with their alien Qwakaiva. If they chose, could they send them in pursuit of their enemies?

I shuddered. I'd been sent a warning. The God and his minions would have their revenge on me someday. There would be a reckoning for what I'd done to one of their own.

On our journey I had received many unwelcome revelations about the Chamuqwani. After seeing this big town, for the first time I had some idea how vast the land was over which the Chamuqwani Emperor held dominion. So many people, so much power, I doubted if even Chumco understood the true nature of the enemy trying to destroy us.

Looking once more at the stone monsters perched upon the temple wall, I despaired, believing that even with all the power of the Great Aseutl to defend us; we could never defeat the Empire.

There were many tearful goodbyes and prayers offered up to listening gods, by both Convert and Traditional alike, as the temple healers took intercessor Raymonel away. He promised to meet us on the Preserve as soon as he regained his health.

Still feeling uneasy from the Spirit-Sending, I had no tears to offer him. He looked to me wraith-thin and as pale as any ghost. Perhaps Chumco's conjuring might claim him in spite of all his followers' efforts on his behalf.

Was I sorry for the part I'd played in his misfortune? When I looked inside my heart for an answer, I could find none. I was too tired, too hungry, and there had already been too many deaths. What did it matter if there was one more?

Standing beside Grandfather as the priest was taken away, I decided to voice a portion of my thoughts on the matter. "Grandfather, I wonder if he will recover. He is so weak and pale. It's going to take many prayers to heal him if he does survive."

There must have been something in the tone of my voice that gave offence, because Grandfather scowled at me with disapproval. "Tas, you and all of us should add our prayers to those of his followers."

I thought he was referring to my putting Chumco's talisman among the priest's things. Suddenly I felt the bite of ghostly claws scarring my back and shivered. There was nothing, of course; the monsters were still frozen upon the walls when I glanced up. My momentary cowardice acting like a goad, I answered just as sharply, "Why should I pray for *him*? Why should I care?"

Before answering, Grandfather rubbed a hand across his face. I saw the muddy colours of fatigue in his Spirit Fire, and I suddenly realized with so many depending on him among the People, he couldn't afford to falter, but so far from Big Ice Lake and the source of Qwa'osi the Otter's power, his Qwakaiva was failing. He hid it well, but I could see it, now that I'd focused my inner-eye upon him.

My relationship with Grandfather since Chumco's leaving had been difficult. A part of me agreed with what he had forced upon me, when he made me choose between my studies and my family. But that didn't mean that I wasn't angry with him for it. In spite of my mixed feelings, this was a frightening revelation. My strong, kind, and always caring grandfather, someone who had always been there to offer me his love and guidance, might not survive this journey either.

Grandfather sighed as if it were a great effort to be patient and answer me. "You are becoming an angry person, Grandson. Someone I barely know any more. I would ask you to have a care. When a soul carries so much hate, it is easy prey for evil ghosts, seeking a living host in our world."

I had no words to answer him. For what the enemy had done to me—to all of us, I knew anger and hatred snarled inside me like a caged beast. I knew, but I neither could, nor wanted to control it.

He seemed to sense my unspoken reply and only sighed. "To answer your question about Intercessor Raymonel, you should pray for him, Grandson. By losing him, we have lost someone who genuinely cared about our welfare. He was a Chamuqwani who was willing to speak on our behalf to powerful men of the Empire, Chamuqwani who have the means to help, or make bad trouble for us.

"With him gone, there is no one to speak for us but some of the breed men studying to be priests. And I seriously doubt if they have the Qwakaiva—even if they invoke their god to help them—to make those powerful men listen to them."

Yes, I could see that, he need say no more. To such men, someone like Praiser Jon or Headman Tsanqwati from home, were only zaunks—like the rest of us.

THE SOLDIERS BEDDED us down that night in a large stone warehouse by the river. We were closed into its dark emptiness and guards posted at its big doors. The rest of the captain's men were given leave to drink *waskyja* in the drinking houses that lined the streets by the river.

Like everyone else, I spent a miserable night in that place. Dampness flowing off the water seeped through the stone walls of the warehouse, sucking the heat from my body and chilling my soul. On the road outside our shelter, drunken men shouted and fought, their cries punctuated at times by women's high-pitched laughter.

And most disturbing of all were the hoots and rumbles of machines. All night long these known and unknown noises assaulted my ears, making it impossible to sleep. I dreaded what the dawn would bring.

Next day we were going to take a ride on Train. We were told there was nothing to fear—Train was no different than travelling on the steamboat.

Train was only another big machine. The difference was only that it travelled across the land rather than water.

I didn't find that explanation comforting. Anxious and miserable, I sat awake in the darkness, listening to the chug and rumble of its wheels, rolling along its metal pathway

At dawn the big doors opened, letting in the pale grey light of a misty winter morning. I had been curled up beside Mother and my grandparents. Samiqwas and Aunt Tuulah, we assumed, had spent the night with Ko and his mother.

Since leaving the mountains Ko and Tuulah's marital relations had changed as often as the weather. One moment they talked together like sensible people, then later they growled at one another like feuding mountain cats.

I think it was the confusion, plus the crowding and the darkness in the warehouse that led no one to suspect that Tuulah had not joined us in our confinement. It was only as we were led from the warehouse and marched to the place where Train waited, that we noticed that she was missing.

"Where is my daughter," Grandmother asked as Ko and Samiqwas took their places in line behind us, to receive a morning ration of water and hard-cake.

Puzzled, Ko looked at his son, then shook his head. "We have not seen her since yesterday. Isn't she with you?"

"Where's Amima?" Samiqwas glanced from one concerned adult face to the other. The fear spikes flared in his spirit fire.

"I thought she was getting over our daughter's death. I thought ..." Ko's voice trailed off before speaking what we all feared.

The river was so close. In the confusion of being herded into the warehouse last night, had she managed to elude the guards and slip away to kill herself at last?

No, that didn't feel right. I didn't know what was going on, but I knew that Aunt Tuulah wasn't lying dead at the bottom of that cold muddy river. My Qwakaiva assured me of that.

"I will walk up and down the column and look for her," Grandfather said.

Grandmother laid a hand on his arm. "The soldiers have warned us to stay put. You might get hurt if you anger them now." Grandmother focused her black eyes on me. "Maybe there is another way to find out what has happened."

I took a deep breath as all their eyes focused on me. It was one thing to make the conjuring in the privacy of our camp along the trail; it was a far different matter to draw attention to myself in the middle of this bustling confusion. Before she could ask me, I heard myself say, "Aunty is all right. I don't know exactly what has happened, but I sense that she is well and we will see her soon."

Ko frowned and would have liked to ask for more details, but at that moment the column began to move. He hurried to rejoin Gagayii's family and his mother.

Samiqwas fell into step with me, rather than follow his father. "Are you sure Amima is all right, Tas?"

Tuulah wasn't dead if that was what he meant. Whether she was right in her mind, her spirit in harmony that was another matter entirely. When I focused the power of my Gift upon her, I sensed the turmoil of her emotions, but I didn't tell my cousin that. I feared he would know what she had done soon enough.

Instead I plastered what I hoped was a reassuring smile on my face, and said, "She isn't dead, Cousin. You will see her soon."

Samiqwas smiled back, but I saw the worry in his eyes.

"I know you aren't telling me all you know. Please tell me."

I pretended like I hadn't heard him and kept moving.

When we arrived at the place where Train lived, I was surprised to learn that Train was nothing more than a long string of boxes on wheels. The first of the boxes was made of metal and had a steam engine inside it, similar to what I had seen on the paddle-wheeler back home. Behind this was another box filled with wood to feed the fire that made the steam. Black smoke puffed from Train's tall stack, and the monster chuffed and rumbled like a living thing.

There were many different wagons being pulled by Train. Some had windows and seats inside. I could see the faces of people staring out as we walked past them. Farther back were wagons with no windows where animals and other supplies were carried.

We were marched to some of those rough dirty wagons. Still smelling of their former inhabitants, we were ordered to climb inside and make ourselves as comfortable as we could in the musty straw.

As we waited our turn to be loaded, tension grew. My family kept glancing back at me with worried looks. They had trusted me, but where was Tuulah? I shook my head. I didn't know. I had been so sure, my Qwakaiva—

Suddenly Mother cried out, "Amima, look!"

Standing just in front of Samiqwas and me, she pointed to a Chamuqwani man and woman heading down the platform towards us. They were peering into the faces of each group of people they passed, as if searching for someone.

Ko had left his mother to ask for news, and was standing with us when Mother drew our attention to the couple. He must have recognized them too, because his face flushed as dark as a thundercloud. Then I recognized them as well.

Coming towards us down the line of waiting people, was Sergeant Ma'leubwey with a strange woman clinging to his arm. The sergeant had discarded his ragged uniform and was dressed in a broad-brimmed hat, black coat and trousers like a Chamuqwani farmer or trader.

Though gaunt, the woman beside him was resplendent in a pleated green skirt, white blouse, and brown woollen cloak. She wore soft leather boots on her feet, and her hair was braided and pinned atop her head in the Chamuqwani fashion.

"Oh, Tuulah, sister, what have you done?" Mother breathed.

When Tuulah saw us, her steps faltered, but the sergeant kept hold of her arm and continued walking towards us.

Stopping in front of Grandmother, Tuulah licked her lips, then said in a husky voice, "Hello, Amima."

Grandmother's eyes travelled from Tuulah's new boots, to the clean and scented braids atop her daughter's head. I could sense all the questions souring in the old woman's gut, but also knew she was too proud to voice them.

Mother too was staring at the changed woman before us, and at last she broke the silence by asking, "Tuulah, what does this mean? What have you done?"

Tuulah glanced from her sister to the sergeant waiting calmly beside her. She opened her mouth a few times before she could get the words to come out, but when they came they were like a bees' nest dropped in our laps.

"I am not going with you to theTribal Preserve. Ma'leubwey and I have married in the Chamuqwani fashion. His time in the army has ended. He and I will go back to his home to make a new life together. I came only to say good bye."

Finding her voice at last, Grandmother snapped, "You cannot. I forbid it!"

Tuulah sighed. "I know this is hard for you, Amima, but I have made up my mind; I am going. You can't forbid me. It is my life."

Falling silent, the two women continued to glare at one another. Sergeant Ma'leubwey glanced from one to the other. Hoping to placate Grandmother and the rest of us, he said to no one in particular, "Surely you have been aware of my feelings for your daughter for some time now. There is no need to worry; I will take good care of her. I promise you that."

Grandmother's eyes blazed as she turned on him. "If you want to take care of my daughter so much, then be a proper son-in-law and come with us to this new place."

"No, Mother, he can't do that—Chamuqwani laws won't allow it. The Preserve is only for our people. And besides, I don't want him to live there, even if he could. I want to make a new life for myself away from—I am going with him, and that is that."

"And what of our son, Tuulah, did you think of him when you were planning this 'new life' with this black Chamuqwani?" Ko snarled "What of him, hmm?"

Looking as hurt and bewildered as if someone had hit him with a rock right between the eyes, Samiqwas stood rigid as a fir tree, his hands clenched into fists at his sides.

Tuulah detached herself from Ma'leubwey and took a few steps towards him. Samiqwas stared down at the muddy platform, refusing to acknowledge her. With a sob catching in her throat, Tuulah held out her hands to him, her eyes pleading. "Oh, my son, I'm so sorry. Please try to understand. Soon you will be grown and married, and then—I would have nothing—I'd be all alone—please, forgive me."

Ma'leubwey spoke then, adding his entreaties to hers. "You are a fine young warrior. I would be honoured to call you my son. I offer you a place in my home as well, should you wish to come with us."

"No, he will not," Ko said. He stepped forward and in defiance of Qwani'ya custom, he put an arm around Samiqwas's shoulders, hugging him close. Samiqwas remained rigid, but did step a little closer to his father. "He remains here with the rest of his family and his people.

"Tuulah, if you are determined to leave us, you will go alone. You will not take my son. Under Chamuqwani law, he is mine. I say no."

Ma'leubwey sighed. "That is your right. So be it then."

"No!" Tuulah cried. "He is mine and you can't stop me from taking him if he wants to go with us."

Ko let out a bitter laugh and folded his arms across his chest. "I can, and I will, because it is the law. We are not in our homeland any longer—you have no claim here."

"Ko is right," Grandmother said, unexpectedly adding her own opinion to the argument. "You have chosen to leave the People and live like a Chamuqwani—then go live like one. Your clan rights are forfeit. I have only one daughter now, and her name is Qwadalah."

Horrified, Mother cried, "No, Mother, you can't mean it!"

"Stop it all of you," Samiqwas shouted. "Why don't you ask me what I want? Instead, you argue over me like hungry sled dogs."

In the silence that followed, Grandfather asked, "What do you want to do, Grandson? This new place I suspect won't be an easy place to live. Would you like to go with your mother? I think we can all agree that we want what is best for you, my dear one, no matter what is law, or clan rights. Your heart's wellbeing is what's most important."

Grandfather's words had acted as a healing balm to everyone. I glanced at my cousin, hoping he would meet my eye, so I could offer him my love and my strength. I couldn't imagine life without him by my side, but if he wanted to go ...

Samiqwas refused to meet anyone's eye. Returning his attention to the muddy ground, he looked like he wanted to cry.

Lifting his head at last, he stared directly into his mother's eye. "I will stay with my People. They will need me."

"You are a brave young warrior," Ma'leubwey said. "I respect your decision."

At that point Train blew its loud whistle. Everyone jumped. Soldiers shouted for the stragglers to hurry.

The sergeant bowed to Samiqwas in the Chamuqwani fashion of showing respect, then took Tuulah's arm once more. "Come, you knew this parting would not be easy, but we must go." He pointed to the handful of soldiers waiting impatiently for him to finish. The platform about us was nearly empty. "They too must go, my dear."

Mother rushed forward to hug her sister. Grandfather and I came forward as well to wish the couple good fortune. Grandmother pulled her blanket over her head and refused to acknowledge anyone.

Tuulah looked at her son with tears in her eyes, but he too turned away. Taking his father's hand, he climbed through the open wagon door at our backs.

The rest of us followed, Grandfather helping my stumbling Grandmother, Mother and I right behind them. The soldiers hopped aboard and closed the big door, sealing us in our box for the journey. As it closed, I saw Tuulah lean against Ma'leubwey and bury her tear-stained face against his chest.

I had barely enough time to find myself a place in the straw, before Train gave a violent lurch and our wheeled box began to roll forward, picking up speed as we headed out of Town.

Through a crack in the wooden wall I could see the land flying past as we travelled ever westward. Exhausted I lay down in the straw with my blanket about me and tried to relax. I craved the oblivion that awaited me in sleep. Three days, the soldiers said. Then we would reach the Kamloopeno Basin where our new home awaited us.

I was afraid, but like my cousin, I would be strong. The People would need me and my Spirit-Gift. As I hovered at the threshold of sleep the words to an ancient prayer came into my mind.

I spoke them with all the power of my Qwakaiva. "Unseen Ones, Great Mystery, give me strength so that I may help my People to live."

The End

A TRIBAL HISTORY OF Long Ago, Rushton Archives: Conclusion of first interview with subject 297

TASIMU'S STORY IS CONTINUED in Book Two, *When Memory Dies*

Words in the Qwani'Ya Language:

Qwani'Ya Tsa'adi, or Fish People, what the Indigenous people living by Big Ice Lake call themselves

Qwa'osi the Otter Warrior, a guardian spirit protector of the Qwani'Ya

Co'yeh the Lake Seal, the Otter's rival, a spirit with both light and dark aspects

Qwakaiva, a difficult word to translate in its full meaning, similar to what we might refer to as magic, chi, life force or medicine

Qwakaihi, a shaman, someone gifted with great power and uses the gift for the good of others

Aseutl, a snake-like dragon figure some say lives at the bottom of Big Ice Lake

Kunai, a magical being of great power, and benefactor of Tasimu

Wannigua, a little demonic spirit that often teases or taunts people

Shillsham Ceremony, the ritual period of isolation that all Qwani'Ya girls must do to prepare for womanhood

Chamuqwani, a term the Indigenous people use to refer to the Imperial invaders of their land

Unfamiliar Terms in the Chamuqwani Language

Zaunk, a degrading term used by soldiers and settlers from the empire to express their contempt for all Indigenous peoples they discovered during their conquest

Bucki, a derogatory term for an Indigenous man or boy

Cloocha or Cloocha-whore a demeaning term for an Indigenous woman or girl

Don't miss out!

Visit the website below and you can sign up to receive emails whenever Celu Amberstone publishes a new book. There's no charge and no obligation.

https://books2read.com/r/B-A-YGQM-QXTSB

BOOKS 2 READ

Connecting independent readers to independent writers.

Also by Celu Amberstone

Rituals
Blessings of the Blood: A Book of Menstrual Lore and Rituals for Women
Deepening the Power: Community Ritual and Sacred Theatre

Tales of Tasimu
Taste of Memory
When Memory Dies
Abandoning Memory

Tales of the Kashallans
The Dream-Chosen
The Hunted Kashallan
The Outlawed Bond
Uncertain Refuge
Prey of the Umwira
Blood Magic's Snare
Kashallan Alliance
Treacherous Campaign

Standalone
Refugees and Other Stories

About the Author

Celu is of mixed Cherokee and Scots-Irish ancestry. Celu Amberstone was one of the few young people in her family to take an interest in learning Traditional Native crafts and medicine ways. This interest made several of the older members of her family very happy while annoying others.

Legally blind since birth, she has defied her limitations and spent much of her life avoiding cities. Moving to Canada after falling in love with a Métis-Cree man from Manitoba, she has lived in the rain forests of the west coast, a tepee in the desert and a small village in Canada's arctic. Along the way she also managed to acquire a BA in cultural anthropology and an MA in health education. Celu loves telling stories and reading. She lives in Victoria British Columbia near her grown children and grandchildren.

About the Publisher

Kashallan Press is an independent publisher releasing books by author Celu Amberstone. Among her books are critically-acclaimed works now re-released by Kashallan Press, and new works showcasing her talents in writing both fiction and non-fiction.

www.ingramcontent.com/pod-product-compliance
Lightning Source LLC
Chambersburg PA
CBHW031204020726
47499CB00002B/482